ISBN 978-1-330-46051-1
PIBN 10065426

1 MONTH OF
FREE
READING

at

www.ForgottenBooks.com

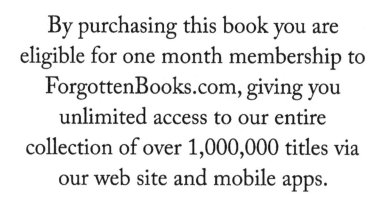

By purchasing this book you are eligible for one month membership to ForgottenBooks.com, giving you unlimited access to our entire collection of over 1,000,000 titles via our web site and mobile apps.

To claim your free month visit: www.forgottenbooks.com/free65426

English
Français
Deutsche
Italiano
Español
Português

www.forgottenbooks.com

Mythology Photography **Fiction**
Fishing Christianity **Art** Cooking
Essays Buddhism Freemasonry
Medicine **Biology** Music **Ancient
Egypt** Evolution Carpentry Physics
Dance Geology **Mathematics** Fitness
Shakespeare **Folklore** Yoga Marketing
Confidence Immortality Biographies
Poetry **Psychology** Witchcraft
Electronics Chemistry History **Law**
Accounting **Philosophy** Anthropology
Alchemy Drama Quantum Mechanics
Atheism Sexual Health **Ancient History**
Entrepreneurship Languages Sport
Paleontology Needlework Islam
Metaphysics Investment Archaeology
Parenting Statistics Criminology
Motivational

THE SAGA LIBRARY

EDITED BY

WILLIAM MORRIS

AND

EIRÍKR MAGNÚSSON

Vol. IV

HEIMSKRINGLA

Vol. II

THE STORIES OF THE KINGS OF NORWAY

CALLED THE ROUND WORLD

(HEIMSKRINGLA)

BY SNORRI STURLUSON

DONE INTO ENGLISH
OUT OF THE ICELANDIC

BY

WILLIAM MORRIS

AND

EIRÍKR MAGNÚSSON

VOL. II

LONDON
BERNARD QUARITCH, 15 PICCADILLY
1894

WICK PRESS:—CHARLES WHITTINGHAM AND CO.
TOOKS COURT, CHANCERY LANE, LONDON.

CONTENTS.

THE STORY OF OLAF THE HOLY, THE SON OF HARALD.

THE STORY OF OLAF THE HOLY, THE SON OF HARALD.

CHAPTER I. THE BRINGING UP OF OLAF THE HOLY, SON OF HARALD.

OLAF, the son of Harald of Grenland, was brought up with his stepfather, Sigurd Sow, and his mother, Asta. Rani the Wide-faring was with Asta, and he gave fostering to King Olaf Haraldson. Olaf was early a well-thewed man, goodly to look at, of middle height, and wise and deft of speech he was at an early age. Sigurd Sow was a great husbandman, and kept his folk hard at work; and himself fared often to look after acres and meadows, or live stock, or to the smithing, or wheresoever his men were busy at other things.

CHAPTER II. OF OLAF AND KING SIGURD SOW.

ON a time it befell that King Sigurd would ride away from his house, and no man was home at the stead; so he bade Olaf, his stepson, to saddle him a horse. Olaf went to the goat-house, and took there the biggest buck-goat and led it home, and laid thereon the saddle of the king, and then went and told him he had harnessed him the nag. Then went King Sigurd thither, and saw what Olaf had done. Then said he: "'Tis clear enow that thou art minded to wash thine hands of all my bidding. Belike thy mother deemeth it seemly that I have no biddings to thee that are not to thy mind; and it is easily seen that we are not like in temper, for thou art of mickle higher mettle than I."

Olaf answered little, and went away laughing.

CHAPTER III. OF THE PROWESS OF KING OLAF.

OLAF HARALDSON, as he grew up, was a man of scarce high middle stature, but very thick-set, and stark of thew; light red of hair, broad-faced, bright and ruddy of countenance, of eyes wondrous good, fair-eyed and swift-eyed, so that it was awful to look him in the face if he were wroth. Olaf was a man of mickle skill in many matters; he knew well the craft of the bow, and of all men was the best in shooting of hand-shot: a good swimmer, deft and skilful in all smith's work, his own no less than other men's. He was called Olaf the Thick. He was bold of speech and clear-spoken, early fulfilled of all ripeness, both as to pith and wisdom; beloved was he of all his kindred and acquaintance; masterful in games, and would be at the head of all others, as was but due because of his dignity and birth.

CHAPTER IV.   THE BEGINNING OF THE WARS OF KING OLAF.

OLAF, son of Harald, was twelve winters old when he stepped on board a warship for the first time.   Asta, his mother, got Rani, who was called King's fosterer, to be leader of the host, and to be with Olaf in his faring, whereas Rani had often been on viking before. When Olaf took over host and ships, the host gave him the name of king, as the wont was; for such war-kings as became vikings bore forthwith the name of a king, if they were king-born, although they had no lands to rule over.   Rani sat at the tiller, and therefore some men say that Olaf was but a thole-man, yet he was king over the host notwithstanding.

They made east along the land, and first unto Denmark. So says Ottar the Swart when he sang about King Olaf:

> King fight-strong !   Yet a youngling
> The steed of the blood of meadows
> Didst thou thrust out toward Denmark;
> Thou, to dear valour wonted !
> Most gainful was thy going.
> O King! now art thou mighty
> Through such-like prowess.   Learned I
> Clear of thy fare from Northland.

But when it was harvest, he sailed east round the Swede-realm, and then fell to harry and burn the land; for he deemed he had to requite the Swedes with full enmity for taking the life of his

father Harald. Ottar the Swart says in plain
words that he went then east out of Denmark :

> Land-ward ! ye thrust with oar-blades
> The brave ships into the East-salt,
> And bore the shields of lime-tree
> Down from the land a-shipboard.
> Ye used your sail, and shipped ye
> Your rudder, the sea-caster,
> Whiles rent your oars the many,
> Much-rowed, great seas beneath you.

> Feeder of swans of fight-ale,
> To folk was fear abounding
> Because of thy faring : sithence
> Thou wastedst Sweden's nesses.

CHAPTER V. THE FIRST BATTLE.

THAT autumn Olaf fought the first battle
at Sotisker, which is within the skerries
of Sweden ; there he fought with vikings,
and he is named Soti who was their captain, and
Olaf had much less company but bigger ships.
He laid his ships between some sea-rocks, and for
the vikings it was unhandy to lay them aboard.
They (Olaf and his folk) brought grappling hooks
aboard the ships that lay nighest to them, and
drew them in, and then cleared them. The vikings
made off, and had lost a great host of men.
Skald Sigvat tells of this fight in the song in which
he told the tale of the fights of King Olaf:

> The long sea-log was bearing
> The young king's-kindred seaward,
> And so it was that all folk
> Sithence the king's wrath dreaded.

But he of men the noblest
The first time wolf's foot reddened
At Soti's-skerry east there.
Of many a thing I mind me.

CHAPTER VI. WARFARE IN SWEDEN.

KING OLAF next went on east by Sweden, and put into the Low, and harried on either land.   He went all the way up to Sigtun, and lay off ancient Sigtun.   So say the Swedes, that there be still there the stone-heaps which Olaf let be made under his gangway ends. But when autumn set in Olaf Haraldson got to know that Olaf the Swede-king drew together a great host, and also that he had done chains athwart Stocksound, and set guard thereover. But the Swede-king was of mind that King Olaf would there bide the frosts, and he held Olaf's host of little worth, for he had but a small company. So King Olaf went out to Stocksound, and might not get through there, for a castle was on the west side of the sound and an host of men on the south.   But when they heard that the Swede-king was gone aboard ship, and had a great host and a multitude of ships, King Olaf let dig a dyke through Agni's-thwaite into the sea.   At this time great rains prevailed.

Now from all Sweden every running water falls into the Low, and out to sea there is one oyce from the Low, so narrow that many rivers be wider.   But when great rains or snow-thaws prevail, the waters fall with such a rush that through Stocksound the water runs in a force, and the

Low goes so much upon the lands that wide-about be floods. Now when the dyke got to the sea, then leapt out the water and the stream. Then King Olaf let take inboard all the rudders of his ships, and hoist all sails top-mast high. And there was a high wind at will blowing. They steered with the oars, and the ships went apace out over the shoal, and came all whole into the sea.

Then the Swedes went to see Olaf the Swede-king, and told him that by then Olaf the Thick had got him away out into the sea. So the Swede-king rated soundly those who should have watched that Olaf gat not away.

That is now called King's Sound, and there is no passing with big ships there save when the waters swell to their utmost. But some men will have it that the Swedes got aware whenas Olaf and his folk had dug the dyke through the thwaite, and the water rushed through ; and withal, that the Swedes went thither with an host of men, being minded to balk Olaf from passing through ; but as the water dug out either side, then fell in the banks, and with them the people, and a multitude of men was lost there. But the Swedes gainsay this, and reckon it vain that any men were lost there.

King Olaf sailed in autumn for Gotland, and arrayed him for harrying there. But there the Gotlanders had a gathering, and sent men to the king, and bade him tribute for the land. To this the king agreed, and took tribute of the land, and sat there the winter through. So says Ottar the Swart:

Thou wonnest, O warrior-wager,
Tribute from folk of Gotland,
And durst not men against thee
With brand to ward their island.
So ran the Isle-syslings' war-host;
I heard that the wolf-kind's hunger
Thawed east-away.   That youngling
Calls many lesser-hearted.

CHAPTER VII. THE SECOND BATTLE.

HERE tells the tale that King Olaf went in springtide east to Isle-sysla and harried; he made a land-raid there, and the Isle-syslings came down and held battle with him.   There King Olaf had the victory, drove the rout, and harried and wasted the land.   So it is said, that first when King Olaf and his came into Isle-sysla, the bonders offered him pay, and when the pay came down, he went to meet them with an host all-weaponed, and then things went otherwise than the bonders were minded; for they came down with no pay at all, but with war-weapons rather, and gave the king battle, as was said before. So says Skald Sigvat:

Again it was that Olaf
Went to wage second point-thing
Down in the ravaged Isle-land;
Nor hidden was the treason.
All-wielder! there the yeomen,
Who ran, to their feet were owing
The ransom for dear life's sake:
For wounds afield few waited.

CHAPTER VIII. THE THIRD FIGHT.

SO thence he sailed back to Finland and harried there, and made land-raids, but all the folk fled into the woods and emptied the dwelling-places of all chattels. The king fared far up into the land and through certain woods. There they came upon some dale-dwellings, where the countrysides are called Herdales. They got but few chattels and no men. Then the day wore, and the king turned back to his ships. But as they came into the wood, an host thronged on them from every side, and shot at them, and set on hard and fast. The king bade his men shield themselves, and smite again as occasion served ; but that was unhandy, for the Finns let the wood ward them. But or ever the king came out of the wood, he lost a many men and many got wounded, and so reached his ships in the evening. The Finns made in the night wild weather and storm at sea with their sorcery. But the king let weigh anchors and hoist sail, and so they beat through the night about the land. So that time as oftener the king's good luck prevailed against the wizardry of the Finns ; that night they got clear of Balagarth-side and thence out into the open sea. But the host of the Finns went along up on land as the king sailed outside. So says Sigvat :

> The third one of the steel-wreaths
> Of the king's son waxèd hard now,
> When was the Finn-folk's meeting
> In the stark raid on Herdales.

The sea-waves there were smiting
The galleys of the Vikings
In the Low where Balagarth-side
Lay neath the bows of the surf-skates.

CHAPTER IX. THE FOURTH BATTLE, IN SOUTHWICK.

THEN King Olaf sailed to Denmark and there happened on Thorkel the High, the brother of Earl Sigvaldi, and Thorkel betook himself to journeying with him, for he was already arrayed to fare out to the wars. So they sailed south along Jutland-side, and to where it was called Southwick, and there won many viking ships. But vikings who lay out ever, and ruled over a great host, let them be called kings, though they had no lands to rule over. Here King Olaf gave battle, and a great fight befell, and King Olaf got the victory and much wealth. So says Sigvat :

The king once more, as folk say,
Wielded uprise of Gunn's song
The fourth time : I have heard how
The warrior-wight won glory;
There whereas peace unlittle
Was cleft betwixt the king's hosts,
Down there in slender Southwick,
Well known unto the Dane-folk.

CHAPTER X. THE FIFTH BATTLE, OFF FRIESLAND.

THEN King Olaf sailed south to Friesland, and lay off Kinnlim-side in heavy weather. So the king went aland with his host, but the folk of the land rode down to meet them, and fought with them. So says Sigvat the Skald:

> O Cower of evil-doers!
> The fifth of fights thou wonnest,
> Helm-grim. The bows tholed tempest
> By high Kinnlima-side then,
> Whereas rode down the war-host
> Against the lord-king's galleys;
> But stately strode the king's host
> 'Gainst the warriors in the battle.

CHAPTER XI. THE DEATH OF SVEIN TWIBEARD.

THEN sailed King Olaf west to England. This was the tidings there, that Svein Twibeard the Dane-king was that time in England with the Dane-host, and had then sat there for a while and harried the land of King Æthelred. At that time the Danes had gone wide over England, and things had come to such a pass that King Æthelred had fled from the land and fared south into Valland. The same autumn that King Olaf came to England it betid there that King Svein, the son of Harald, died suddenly anight in his bed; and it is the say of Englishmen that Edmund the Holy did slay him after the manner in which the holy Mercury slew Julian the Apostate. Now when King Æthelred learned these tidings in Flanders, he turned straightway back to England; and when he came back into the land, he sent word to all men who would take fee hereto, to wit, for conquering the land with him. Then drifted to him a great multitude of folk; and withal thither came to his aid King Olaf with a great following of Northmen.

Now first they made for London and went up the Thames with the host of the ships, but the Danes held the city. On the other side of the river there is a great cheaping-town called Southwark; there the Danes had great arrayal: they had dug great dykes, on the inner side whereof they had built a wall of wood and turf and stone, and therewithin they had a great host. King Æthelred let make a hard onset, but the Danes warded them, and King Æthelred might do nought against them. A bridge was there across the river, betwixt the city and Southwark, so broad that waggons might be driven past each other thereover. On the bridge were made strongholds, both castles and bulwarks looking down stream, so high that they reached a man above his waist; but under the bridge were pales stuck into the bottom of the river. And when an onset was made the host stood on the bridge all along it and warded it. King Æthelred was mickle mind-sick, how he was to win the bridge. He called together for a parley all the captains of the host, seeking counsel of them how they should bring the bridge down. Then King Olaf said he would risk laying his men on to it, if other captains were willing to set on also. At this meeting it was settled that they should lay their host up under the bridge. Then each one set about arraying his men and ships.

CHAPTER XII. THE SIXTH BATTLE.

KING OLAF had great flake-hurdles made of willow-twigs and green wood, and let sheds of wicker-work be taken to pieces, and all these he let lay over his ships, so widely that they went right out-board. Thereunder he let set staves so thick together and so high that it was both handy to fight from under, and it was full stout enough against stones if they were cast down thereon. Now, when the host was arrayed they fell on a-rowing up the river ; and when they came near to the bridge, there was cast down on them both shot and stones so great that nought might hold, neither helms nor shields; and the ships themselves were wondrous broken thereby, and many withal backed out. But King Olaf and the host of the Northmen rowed right up under the bridge and lashed cables round the pales that upheld the bridge, and then they fell to their oars and rowed all the ships down stream as hard as they might. The pales dragged along the ground even until they were loosened under the bridge. But inasmuch as an host under weapons stood thickly arrayed on the bridge, there were on it both a many stones and many war-weapons, and the pales having broken from under it, the bridge broke down by reason thereof, and many of the folk fell into the river, but all the rest thereof fled from the bridge, some into the city, some into Southwark.

And after this they made an onset on Southwark, and won it.

And when the townsfolk saw that the river Thames was won, so that they might not hinder the ships from faring up into the land, they were afeard, and gave up the town and took King Æthelred in. So says Ottar the Swart:

> O battle-bold, the cunning
> Of Ygg's storm! Yet thou brakest
> Down London Bridge: it happed thee
> To win the land of snakes there.
> Hard shields be-craved had roar there;
> There too they sprang asunder,
> Hard iron-rings of the war-coats.
> Therewith the battle waxèd.

And still he sang this:

> Thou broughtst to land, and landedst,
> King Æthelred, O Landward,
> Strengthened by might! That folk-friend
> Such wise of thee availèd.
> Hard was the meeting soothly,
> When Edmund's son thou broughtest
> Back to his land made peaceful,
> Which erst that kin-stem rulèd.

Yet again thus saith Sigvat:

> True is it that the sixth fight
> Was whereas fell on Olaf
> At London Bridge: the swift king
> Bade Ygg's brunt to the English.
> There were the Welsh swords biting,
> Their dyke the Vikings warded.
> But some deal of the war-host
> Held booths in level Southwark.

CHAPTER XIII. THE SEVENTH BATTLE.

KING OLAF was with King Æthelred through the winter. Then they had a great fight on Ringmar Heath in Wolfkelsland. That dominion belonged then to Wolfkel Snilling; there the kings won the victory. So says Sigvat the Skald :

> Yet once again let Olaf
> Be held a seventh sword-thing.
> It was in Wolfkel's country,
> E'en as my song here sayeth.
> There stood the Ella's kindred
> The Ringmar Heath all over ;
> The host fell ; wrought the toil there
> The ward of Harald's heirship.

Yet again Ottar tells of this fight thus :

> O king, I heard that thy war-host
> Piled up a dead heap heavy
> Far from the ships, and reddened
> All Ringmar Heath in blood there.
> There thick and fast before thee
> In shield-roar land-folk louted,
> And many a band of English
> In flight fell ere the end was.

Then the land was yet wider laid under the sway of King Æthelred ; but the Thing-men and the Danes still held many burgs, and in many places the Danes yet held the land.

CHAPTER XIV.   BATTLES   THE EIGHTH AND NINTH.

KING OLAF was captain of the host when they held on to Canterbury, and fought there right on until they won the town, killing an host of folk there, and burning the town. So says Ottar the Swart:

> Thou wroughtest, king, great onset
> On the kings' kin; Canterbury
> The broad, upon a morning,
> O thou blithe king, thou tookest.
> Full fiercely o'er the dwellings
> Played fire and reek.   Fair kin's son,
> Thou winnedst the fight: there heard I
> Thou smotest down men's life-days.

Sigvat counts this the eighth fight of King Olaf:

> I wot that the battle's meter,
> Peril of Wends, here wrought him
> The eighth of stours.   The stark ward
> Of warfolk set on the work there.
> Port-Reeves might not ban Olaf
> Of their town of Canterbury;
> To the valiant of the Port-folk
> 'Twas many a thing brought sorrow.

Thereupon King Olaf had in hand the guarding of the land in England, and went with warships about off the coast and hove into Newmouth; there was before him an host of the Thing-men, and they had battle, and King Olaf won the victory. So says Sigvat the Skald:

> The young king all unlaggard
> Wrought red polls for the English.
> Brown blood came on the brands there,
> Once more in fight at Newmouth.

> There fell the host of Dane-folk,
> Where drave most spears on Olaf.
> Fight-wielder from the East-land,
> Now have I rymed nine battles.

Thereupon King Olaf fared wide about the land and took tribute from the folk, or else harried them. So says Ottar :

> O far-famed king, in nowise
> The folk of the kin of England
> Might aught prevail against thee,
> When scat thou tookst relentless.
> Unseldom were folk yielding
> Gold to their lief lord rightful.
> Whiles, heard I, things full precious
> Fared down unto the sea-strand.

There King Olaf tarried this time for three winters.

CHAPTER XV. THE TENTH BATTLE, IN RINGFIRTH.

BUT in the third spring King Æthelred died, and then his sons Edmund and Edward took kingdom. Then King Olaf went south over sea, and he fought withal in Ringfirth and won a castle on the Knolls wherein the vikings sat, and he broke down the castle. So says Sigvat the Skald :

> The tenth was all fulfillèd
> With the drift of the wall of battle
> In Ringfirth fair.   The war-host
> Held thither as the king bade.
> There let the king be broken
> The Knoll's high house of the vikings.
> Thereafter prayed they never
> For speeding such as that was.

CHAPTER XVI. BATTLE THE ELE-VENTH AND THE THIRTEENTH.

THEN King Olaf went with his host west to Grisla-pool, and fought there with vikings off William's-by, and there King Olaf won the victory.   As Sigvat says :

> Eleventh stour, O Olaf,
> Thou wroughtest where the lords fell
> In Grisla-pool.   O pine-stem !
> Young from that war-thing cam'st thou.
> Heard I that yon brisk battle,
> Fought off the town of the trusty
> Earl William, harmed the war-helms.
> The tale to tell is little.

Next thereafter he fought west in Fettlefirth, as says Sigvat :

> The fair-fame's follower reddened
> The wolf's tooth for the twelfth time
> In Fettlefirth : was fated
> Thereat life-ban of many.

Thence Olaf fared south right away to Seliu-pool and had a fight there ; and there he won the town called Gunvaldsburg, a great and an ancient one, and there he laid hands on the earl who ruled over the town and hight Geirfin.   Then King Olaf held parley with the men of the town, and he laid a fine upon it, and claimed in ransom for the earl twelve thousand gold shillings.   And the money he laid on the town was paid him.   So says Sigvat :

O bright lord of the Thrand-folk,
The thirteenth stour thou wroughtest
At Seliapool in Southlands,
Where slain was very fleeing :
Doughty the king let march in
To Gunvaldsburg the ancient ;
And on the earl lay hand there,
Who had to name e'en Geirfin.

CHAPTER XVII. FIGHT THE FOUR-TEENTH, AND KING OLAF'S DREAM.

AFTER that King Olaf went with his host west to Charles-water and harried there, and there had a battle. But while King Olaf lay in Charles-water and waited for fair wind, being minded to sail on to Norfisound and thence out into Jerusalem-world, he dreamt a noteworthy dream, that there came to him a man noble-looking and well-favoured, yet awful to behold, and spoke to him, bidding him give up his mind of faring out into far-off lands : " Fare back to the lands of thy birthright, for thou shalt be a king of Norway for time everlasting." He deemed the dream to betoken that he should be king over the land, and his kinsmen after him, for a long time.

CHAPTER XVIII. BATTLE THE FIF-TEENTH.

FROM this vision he turned back his ways and laid him against Peita-land (Poitou), and harried there, and burnt there the cheaping-stead called Warrand. So says Ottar:

O young king battle-merry,
Peita thou lett'st be wasted;
Thou triedst shields bestainèd
In Tuskaland, O lord king.

And still further Sigvat says thus :

The lord above the Mere-folk,
Reddener of mouths of metal,
When from the south he wended,
Made way along Loire-water.
Before those Niords of battle
Was Warrand burned.   So call they
A town far off the sea-board,
In dwelt-in Peita country.

CHAPTER XIX.   OF THE EARLS OF ROUEN:

KING OLAF had been a-warring west in Valland for two summers and one winter. At that time there had worn from the fall of Olaf Tryggvison thirteen winters.   That while earls had ruled over Norway: first Eric and Svein, the sons of Hakon, and afterwards the sons of Eric, Svein and Hakon ; and Hakon was the son of a sister of King Knut Sveinson.   In Valland that while were two earls, William and Robert, whose father was Richard, Earl of Rouen, and they ruled over Normandy.   Their sister was Queen Emma, whom Æthelred, King of the English, had had for wife.   Their sons were Edmund and Edward the Good, Edwy and Edgar. Richard, Earl of Rouen, was the son of Richard, the son of William Longspear ; he was the son of Rolf Wend-a-foot, the earl who won Normandy, who was the son of Rognvald the Mighty, Earl of

Mere, as is written afore. From Rolf Wend-a-foot are come the earls of Rouen, who long thereafter claimed kinship with lords in Norway, and set store thereby for a long while after, and were at all times the greatest friends of all Northmen, and all Northmen had peace-land in Normandy if they cared to take it.

In the autumn King Olaf came into Normandy and tarried there through the winter in Seine-water, and had there a land of peace.

CHAPTER XX. OF EINAR THAMBAR-SKELFIR.

AFTER the fall of King Olaf Tryggvison Earl Eric gave truce to Einar Thambar-skelfir, the son of Eindrid, the son of Styrkar. Einar went with the earl north into Norway, and it is said that Einar was of all men the strongest and best bowman in Norway, and the hardness of his shooting beyond all other men. He shot with a blunt shaft through an ox-hide raw-wet which hung on a pole ; he was skilled at snow-shoeing better than any other man, and was a man of the greatest prowess and valour; of great kin he was, and wealthy withal. Earls Eric and Svein gave to Einar their sister Bergliot, the daughter of Hakon ; she was a woman most high-mettled. Their son was called Eindrid. The earls gave to Einar great grants in Orkdale, and he became the mightiest and noblest man within the laws of Thrandheim, and the greatest stay and the dearest friend to the earls was he.

CHAPTER XXI. OF ERLING SKIALG-SON.

WHENAS Olaf Tryggvison ruled over Norway he gave his brother-in-law, Erling, half the land-dues along with him, and therewith a moiety of the king's revenues between Lidandisness and Sogn. King Olaf wedded another sister of his to Earl Rognvald, the son of Wolf, who for a long time ruled over West Gautland. Wolf, the father of Rognvald, was brother to Sigrid the Haughty, the mother of Olaf the Swede-king. Earl Eric was not well pleased at Erling's having so mickle dominion, and he took to himself all the king's revenues which King Olaf had made over to Erling. But Erling took, just as before, all land-dues throughout Rogaland, so that the dwellers of the land paid often twofold land-dues, for otherwise he wasted the dwelt-land. Of fines and forfeitures the earl gat but little, for bailiffs might not hold out long there, and even the earl himself went a-banquetting there only if he had a throng of men about him. So says Sigvat:

> The brother-in-law of Olaf
> (That trustiest son of Tryggvi),
> E'en Erling awed the earl's kin,
> As the king's own self availed not.
> The nimble lord of the yeomen
> Gave also unto Rognvald
> Another of his sisters:
> Life-luck unto Wolf's father.

Earl Eric did not venture upon fighting with

Erling, for this cause, that he had many and great kinsmen, a mighty man, and well-beloved. Moreover, he sat alway with many folk about him, even as if there were a king's court. Erling was oft a-warring in summertide, and gat wealth to himself thereby, whereas he kept up his wonted state and lordliness, although now he had lesser revenues and of less surety than in the days of King Olaf his brother-in-law. Erling was of all men the goodliest, the biggest and strongest, skilled at arms better than any man, and in all feats of prowess most like unto King Olaf Tryggvison ; he was a wise man and eager-minded in all things, and the greatest warrior withal. Whereof Sigvat telleth :

> None was there of the landed
> Of those that lacked of lordship,
> Who more of fights had fought in
> Than had the mighty Erling.
> The bounteous man was bearing
> His pith into the onset,
> First entering many a battle,
> And last for the most part leaving.

It has alway been the say of men that Erling was the noblest of all landed lords in Norway. These were the children of Erling and Astrid : Aslak, Skialg, Sigurd, Lodin, Thorir, and Ragnhild, whom Thorberg, son of Arni, had to wife.

Erling had ever about him ninety freed-men or more, and the wont there was, winter and summer, to have drinking by measure at day-meal board, but at night-meal board the drink was not measured. But at those times when the earls were anigh, he had about him two hundred men or more.

Never went he about with fewer men than a twenty-banked keel full manned. Erling had a large cutter of two-and-thirty banks, and large of hull at that ; in her he went a viking warfare, and to the folk-levy, and aboard her were two hundred men or more.

CHAPTER XXII. OF ERLING THE HERSIR.

ERLING had ever thirty thralls at home, besides other serving-folk ; to his thralls he allotted each day's work, which being done, he gave them leave and leisure, each one who wished, to work for himself in the dusk or at night ; he gave them acre-land wherein to sow corn for themselves, and to get them money by the increase thereof ; he set a price and ransom on each of them, and many redeemed themselves the first or the second year, but all in whom was any thrift redeemed themselves in three years. With that money Erling bought himself other thralls.

But as for his freed-men, some he set to herring fishing, some about other ingatherings, while some cleared woods, and in the clearings set up house ; all of them he made folk of some substance.

CHAPTER XXIII. OF EARL ERIC.

WHENAS Earl Eric had had sway over Norway for twelve winters, there came to him word from Knut the Dane-king, his brother-in-law, that Eric should go with

him on warfare to England with his host; for
Eric was much famed for his wars, in that he had
gained the day in two battles of those which had
been the most fiercely fought in the Northlands :
one wherein Earl Hakon and Eric fought the
Joms-vikings, the other wherein Eric fought with
Olaf Tryggvison.　As telleth Thord Kolbeinson :

> Praise have I whereas heard I
> How that the lord be-praisèd
> Sent word to the lord the helm-wont,
> The lord of lords be-landed,
> That without fail should Eric
> Yet once again betake him
> To dear and lovesome meeting.
> Well wot I the king's pleasure.

The earl would not lay the king's message
under his head ; he fared out of the land, but he
left behind Earl Hakon his son to heed the land,
and gave him into the hand of Einar Thambarskelfir, his brother-in-law, that he should be the
earl's counsellor in the ruling of the land, for he
was as yet not older than seventeen winters. Eric
came to England and met King Knut, and was
with him when he won London. Earl Eric fought
to the west of London, where he felled Wolfkel Snilling.　So saith Thord Kolbeinson :

> The gold-wise let join battle
> Unto the west of London,
> The well-praised grove of the sea-horse
> Held battle for the land's sake.
> There e'en it was that Wolfkel,
> All daring in the shield-rain,
> Gat sore strokes of the Thing-men,
> Where shook warfolk's blue edges.

Earl Eric was in England one winter, and had certain battles, but the next autumn he was minded to go on a pilgrimage to Rome; but therewith he died of a blood-letting there in England.

CHAPTER XXIV. THE SLAYING OF EDMUND.

KING KNUT had many battles in England with the sons of Æthelred, King of the English, and now one, now the other got the victory. He came to England the same summer wherein Æthelred died. Then Knut gat for wife Emma, the queen; and their children were Harald, Hordaknut, Gunnhild.

King Knut made such peace with King Edmund that each of them should have one-half of England. In the same month Eadric Streona slew King Edmund, whereupon King Knut drove out of England all the sons of King Æthelred. So says Sigvat:

> Knut slew therewith
> All sons together
> Of Æthelred,
> Or drove forth each one.

CHAPTER XXV. OF OLAF AND THE SONS OF ÆTHELRED.

THAT summer came the sons of Æthelred the King to Rouen in Valland to the brothers of their mother, whenas Olaf Haraldson came from his western viking-fare, and were all together that winter in Normandy, and made fellowship between them on such terms that King Olaf should have Northumberland if they should get for themselves England from the Danes. Then sent Olaf to England that autumn Rani his fosterfather to gather folk there, and the sons of Æthelred sent him with tokens to their friends and kinsmen, but Olaf handed to him much money to the end that he should lure folk to them. And so Rani abode in England through the winter, and got the faith and troth of many mighty men ; for to the folk of the land it was more to their will to have a home-born king; yet by then was the might of the Danes waxen so great that all the folk of the land were broken under their dominion.

CHAPTER XXVI. A BATTLE OF KING OLAF.

IN the spring they went from the west all together, King Olaf to wit and the sons of Æthelred, and came to England at the place called Youngford, and there went aland with their company, and made for the town. Therein were awaiting them many folk such as had promised them their aid. The town they took, and slew a many men.

But when the men of King Knut were aware thereof, they gathered together an host, and soon waxed so many that the sons of Æthelred had not strength against them, and saw that the best they might do was to get them gone and away west back to Rouen again. Then King Olaf sundered him from them, and would not go to Valland. He sailed north along England all the way to Northumberland, and hove-to in the haven which is called Wald, and fought there with the town's folk and chapmen, and got the victory there and much wealth.

CHAPTER XXVII. THE JOURNEY OF KING OLAF TO NORWAY.

KING OLAF left the longships behind there, but fitted out thence two roundships, and had then two hundred and sixty men all byrnied and well chosen. He sailed north into the main in harvest-tide, and had right heavy weather at sea, so that there was peril of life ; but whereas they had a doughty company and the good luck of the king they got safely through. So says Ottar :

> O Bounteous of the tempest
> Of corpse-fire, thou arrayedst toward
> Two westland keels.   In peril
> Oft thrustedst thou, kings' thoft-mate !
> Strong stream of sea-waves' welter
> The cheaping-ships had mangled,
> If at that while less worthy
> Had been the crew within board.

And again thus :

> Nought had ye fear of Ægir
> All o'er the wide sea faring ;
> No folk-lord found him ever
> Crew doughtier than your sea-lads.

O son of Harald, often
The craft was strained full sorely,
But the ship cast off the high seas,
Or e'er ye made mid Norway.

Here it is said that King Olaf came from the west
upon the midmost of Norway, and the island where
they landed is called Sele, and lies off Stad. Then
spake King Olaf that he was minded to think it
was a happy day on which they had landed at Sele
in Norway, and said it would be a good token
that so it had come to pass. Then they went
up on the island, and the king stepped with one
foot into mire, steadying him with the other knee.
Then spake he: "Lo, now I fell," says the king.
Then answers Rani : " Thou falledst not, king, but
settest thy feet fast in the land." The king laughed
thereat, and said: "So may it be, if God will."
Then they went down to the ships, and sailed
south to Wolfsounds. There they heard of Earl
Hakon, that he was south in Sogn, but was looked
for to come north so soon as a fair wind befell, and
but one ship he had.

CHAPTER XXVIII. EARL HAKON TAKEN IN SAUDUNGSOUND.

KING OLAF steered his ships inward out
of the high water-way when he came
south past Fjalir, and turned in to Sau-
dungsound and lay there ; each ship they laid near
either shore of the sound, and had between them a
thick cable. At that very hour rowed into the sound
Earl Hakon Ericson with a fully-manned cutter,

he and his men thinking that but two chapmen ships were in the sound; so into the sound they rowed forth between the ships. Now King Olaf and his men haul the cable up under mid-keel of the cutter, winding it with windlasses; and forthwith when the cutter was fast, it rose aft and sank forward, so that the sea fell in over the prow, filling the cutter, which presently turned over. King Olaf took there Earl Hakon swimming, and all such of his men as they might lay hand on; but some they slew, and othersome sank to the bottom. So says Ottar:

> Feeder of blood-seas' blue choughs,
> Fulfilled of wealth, thou tookest
> The brave-found Hakon's cutter,
> And them withal aboard it.
> Feeder of mew of Thrott's Thing,
> A youngling sought'st thou hither,
> Thy birth-lands rightly craving,
> Nor might the earl withstand it.

Earl Hakon was led on board the king's ship. He was the goodliest man that men had set eyes on; mickle hair he had and fair as silk, and a golden band done about his head. He took his seat in the fore-hold. Then said King Olaf: "No lie is it that is told of you kinsmen, how well-favoured ye are to look on; but gone now is the luck of you."

Then spake Hakon: "This is no ill-luck which we have fallen on. It has long been that now one, now the other is overcome. So has it fared betwixt my kinsmen and thine, that now one, now the other has come to his above. I am come but

a little way from the age of childhood.   Nor were
we now in a good way to defend ourselves : we
wotted not any unpeace at hand; maybe some
other time we shall come off better than now."

Then answers King Olaf : " Dost thou not misdoubt thee, earl, that now a thing hath befallen
thee whereby henceforth thou wilt never gain or
lose the day ? "

The earl says : " As at this time, thou, O king,
must be master."

Then says King Olaf : " What wilt thou do,
earl, that I let thee fare for this time whithersoever
thou willest whole and unscathed ? "

The earl asks what he biddeth him.

The king answers : " Nought else than that
thou fare from the land and give up thy dominion,
and swear oath to this, that thou wilt hold no
battle against me from henceforth."

The earl answered and gave out that so would
he do.   Now the earl winneth oath to King Olaf
that never henceforth shall he fight against him,
nor defend Norway with unpeace against King
Olaf, nor fall on him.   Then King Olaf gave life
to him and his men withal ; and the earl got back
the ship which he had had thither. So row men now
their ways thence. Hereof telleth Sigvat the Skald :

> The mighty king, the fame-fain,
> Quoth he had need be seeking
> A meeting with Earl Hakon
> In Saudungsound the ancient.
> The stern young lord there met he
> The earl, of earls the second,
> And born of highest kindred
> Of all men of the Dane-tongue.

CHAPTER XXIX. EARL HAKON'S JOURNEY FROM NORWAY.

THEREAFTER the earl gat him ready at his speediest to leave the land, and sailed west to England, where he fell in with King Knut, his mother's brother, and tells him how all had gone between him and King Olaf. King Knut gave him a wondrous good welcome; he set Hakon at his side within his court, and gave him great dominion in his realm; and so Earl Hakon tarried there a long while with Knut.

When Svein and Hakon ruled over Norway they made peace with Erling Skialgson with this covenant, that Aslak, the son of Erling, gat for wife Gunnhild, the daughter of Earl Svein; and they settled that father and son, Erling and Aslak, should have all those grants which Olaf Tryggvison had bestowed on Erling. So Erling became full friend of the earls, and hereto they bound themselves with oaths to each other.

CHAPTER XXX. ASTA MAKES READY.

KING OLAF the Thick now turns east away along the land, and had in many places motes with the bonders; and many became his liegemen, while some gainsaid it, such to wit as were kinsmen or friends of Earl Svein. Therefore King Olaf went with all speed east to Wick, and hove with his host into the bay, and beaches his ships, and then turns his ways up into the land. And when he came to Westfold,

many men greeted him well, of them who had
been acquaintance or friends of his father; and
there were a many of his kindred there about
the Fold.　In the harvest-tide he went upland to
King Sigurd his stepfather, and came there early
on a day.　But when King Olaf came near to the
homestead, certain serving-lads ran before to the
house and into the chamber.　Therewithin sat
Asta, the mother of King Olaf, and some women
with her.　Then the lads told her of King Olaf's
journey, and this withal, that his speedy coming was
to be looked for.　Asta stands up forthwith and
called upon carles and queans to dight the place at
their best; she let four women take the array of
the guest-chamber and adorn it speedily with
hangings and bankers; two men bore in haulm on
to the floor; two set up the trapeza and the great
bowl; two set out the boards and served up the
victual; two she sent away from the stead; two
bore in the ale; but all the rest, men and women
alike, went out into the garth.　Those sent away
went to King Sigurd where he was, and brought him
his robes of estate, and a horse with a forgilded
saddle and the bit beset with smalts, and all done
with gold.　Four men she sent away into all four
corners of the countryside, and bade to her all the
great people there for a banquet, whereas she was
making a welcome-ale for the coming of her son.
All other men who were there at home she bade
don the best raiments they had, and lent good
clothes to those who owned none such themselves.

CHAPTER XXXI. OF THE ARRAY OF KING SIGURD.

KING SIGURD SOW happened to be out in the fields when the messengers came to him and told him of these tidings, and of all the todo that Asta was at in the house at home. He had a-many men there, some of whom cut corn, some bound it, some carted it home, while othersome stacked it, or stored it into barns. But the king and two men with him would whiles be going into the acres, whiles there whereas the corn was being stored. Of his array it is told that he had on a blue kirtle, blue hose, and high shoes laced to the leg; a grey cape he had on, and a wide-brimmed grey hat, and an orle round the face; a staff in his hand, with a forgilded silver knop and a silvern ring therein. So is it told about King Sigurd's manner of mind, that he was a man of mickle business, and a great husband of his stock and store, and looked himself after his own household; no man of show was he, and rather few-spoken withal; he was the wisest of all men who were then in Norway, and wealthiest in chattels; peaceful withal was he, and nought griping. Asta, his wife, was openhanded and high-mettled. These were their children : Guthorm was the oldest, then Gunnhild, then Halfdan, then Ingirid, then Harald.

Now spoke the messengers : " Such words Asta bade us bear thee, as that she deemed she would set great store by thy now doing after the manner of a great man, and she prayed that thou shouldest rather take after the kindred of Harald Hairfair in thy courage, than after Rani Thin-neb, thy mother's father, or Earl Nereid the old, though men of mickle wisdom they were."

The king answers: "Great tidings do ye tell, and verily ye put them forth to me eagerly. Much has Asta erst made of such men, as it was less her duty so to do by them than now, and well I see that she hath still the same temper as aforetime; and with mickle eagerness she takes this matter in hand, if she will so lead her son out, as that it be done in as stately a fashion as now she leadeth him in. But so meseemeth, if this shall be so, they that pledge themselves to this cause will be giving due heed neither to their wealth nor their life. This man, King Olaf, is fighting against exceeding odds, and upon him and his redes lieth the wrath of the Dane-king and the Swede-king, if he hold on the way wherein he now is."

CHAPTER XXXII.   THE BANQUET.

NOW when the king had thus spoken, he sat down and let draw off his footgear, and did on his feet a pair of cordovan hose, whereto he bound gilded spurs; thereupon he cast off cape and kirtle, and arrayed himself in costly raiment, and over all a cloak of scarlet, and girt himself with a sword adorned, and set upon his head a forgilded helm, and then mounts his horse.

He sent workmen about into the countryside, and chose for himself thirty men in goodly raiment who rode home with him. But when they rode up into the garth before the house, then saw he where, on the other side of the garth, forth flew the banner of King Olaf, he himself following it, and an hundred men with him all well dight. All about between the houses withal stood men in array.

Straightway King Sigurd greeted his stepson King Olaf and his company from on horseback, and bade him in for a drinking with him; but Asta went up and kissed her son, and bade him tarry with her, saying that all was welcome to him that she might give him, both lands and folk. King Olaf thanked her well for her words. She took him by the hand and led him after her into the guest-chamber and up to the high-seat. King Sigurd got men to give heed to their garments and give corn to their horses, but he went to his high-seat, and with all bravery was that banquet done.

CHAPTER XXXIII. PARLEY BETWEEN KING OLAF AND KING SIGURD.

BUT when King Olaf had been there no long while, it befell one day that he called to him for talk and counsel King Sigurd, his stepfather, and Asta, his mother, and Rani, his fosterer. Then King Olaf took up the word: "So it is," says he, "as ye know, that I have come hither to this land after having been for a long while in the outlands. All this while I and my men have had for our maintenance but such as we have sought us in war; and in many places have we had to run the risk of body and soul therefor.

Many a man, as sackless as he were, hath had to
forfeit his wealth at our hand ; yea, some their life
into the bargain ; while outland men sit on the
wealth which erst my father owned, and his father,
and each after the other of our kinsmen, and
whereunto I am lawfully born.   Nor are they
content with this, but they have taken to them
moreover all that we kinsmen owned who are
come down from King Harald Hairfair in a
straight line; to some they allow a little thereof,
to othersome nothing at all.   Now shall that be
unlocked to you, which for a long while has abided
in my mind, to wit, that I am minded to claim my
father's heritage, and that I shall go see neither
the Dane-king nor the Swede-king, nor pray for
aught of it from them, although they have now for
a while called their own that·which was the
heritage left by Harald Hairfair.   Nay, sooth to
say, I am rather minded to seek mine heritage at
point and edge, and for that end to crave the avail
of all my kindred and friends, and of all such as
may be willing to turn them to me in this matter.
And in such wise am I minded to set afoot this
claim, that one of two things shall be : either that
I shall own and rule over all that dominion from
which they felled King Olaf Tryggvison, my
kinsman, or else, that I shall fall here on my own
kin-heritage.   Now I look for this from thee,
stepfather Sigurd, and from such other folk in the
land as are right-born to kingdom here, according
to the laws which Harald Hairfair set up, that ye
will not be lacking so much that ye will not rise up
to thrust away from you this shame of our kindred,

in such wise that ye will put forth all your might
to strengthen him who is willing to take the lead
in raising up our kindred. But whether or no thou
art willing to show manliness in this matter, yet
know I the mind of the commonalty, that all folk
would be fain to rid themselves of the thraldom
of outland lords so soon as they may have a man
to trust in.

"Now for this reason have I broached this matter
to none before thee, that I know thou art a wise
man and knowest well how to look to it, in what
way this enterprise should be set afoot at the out-
set, whether by privily talking it over to certain
people, or by setting it forth in open speech to all
folk. I have now somewhat reddened tooth on
them, in that I laid hands on Earl Hakon, who
now has fled out of the land and given over to me
with sworn oaths that part of the realm which
heretofore was his. Now I am minded to think
that I shall have an easier task on hand in dealing
with Earl Svein alone, than it would have been if
they had been both together in the warding of the
land."

Now King Sigurd answereth : " No little
matter abideth in thy mind, King Olaf. And
meseemeth, as I account it, this matter is rather
one of high mettle than of foresight, and, forsooth,
it is to be looked for, that long asunder is my
littlemindedness from the high heart which is
in thee ; for then, whenas thou wert but a little
way from thy childhood, thou wast already filled
with mastery and overbearing in all things whereas
thou mightest ; moreover, now thou art much

tried in battle and hast shaped thyself after the
fashions of outland chieftains.   Now, I wot well,
that when thou hast once made up thy mind to this,
it will be of no avail to let thee ; moreover, it is
but meet that matters of this kind should weigh
heavily in the mind of men who are somewhat of
champions, whenas the whole kindred of Harald
Hairfair and their kingdom falleth down.   But to
no pledges will I bind me until I know the mind
or the undertakings of other kings of the Uplands.
However, thou hast done well in that thou didst
make known to me this purpose before thou
spakest it out loud to the folk.   I will promise
thee my furtherance with kings and other lords,
and the rest of the folk of the land withal.   And
therewith, King Olaf, art thou welcome to my
wealth for thy furtherance.   But on this one
condition I will that we bear this before the
commonalty, that I see first how far it is likely
that there should be any furtherance thereof,
or any avail forthcoming for so great a matter.
For, make thy mind up to this, that thou hast
taken much on thine hands, if thou shalt deal
in masteries with Olaf the Swede-king, and with
Knut, who is now king both in England and
Denmark ; and with strong props must thine
affairs be stayed, if they are to prosper.   But not
unlike do I deem it, that thou wilt speed well
with folk-raising ; for the whole folk is fain of
new things.   So fared it erst, when King Olaf
Tryggvison came into the land ; for thereof all
folk were fain ; yet for no long while did he enjoy
his kingdom."

When the redes had gotten so far, Asta took up the word: "So is it with me, son, that I am fain of thee, and of this fainest, to wit of thy much might and pith ; to that end will I spare nought that I have to give. But there is but little of profitable counsel to be looked for whereas I am ; but this would I rather, if there were such a bargain to be made, to wit, that thou shouldst be over-king of Norway, though thou livedst no longer in the kingdom than did Olaf Tryggvison, rather than thou shouldst be no greater a king than Sigurd Sow and shouldst die of old age."

After these words they broke up the meeting.

There tarried Olaf a while with all his company, and King Sigurd entertained them at table one day with fish and milk, one day with flesh-meat and ale, turn and turn about.

CHAPTER XXXIV. CONCERNING THE KINGS OF THE UPLANDS.

AT this time there were many kings in the Uplands who ruled over folk-lands, and were mostly come of the kin of Harald Hairfair. Over Heathmark there ruled two brothers, Rœrek and Ring, and in Gudbrands-dale, Gudrod. In Raumrealm also was a king; and one king there was who had Thotn and Hatha-land ; in Valdres there ruled a king likewise.

Now King Sigurd Sow had a meeting with these folk-kings up in Hathaland, whereat was also Olaf Haraldson. Then Sigurd laid before the folk-kings, with whom he had bespoken the

meeting, the business of Olaf his stepson, and prayed
them for help, both as to men, counsel, and
alliance.   He told up how needful it was for
them to put from their hands the oppression
whereunder the Danes and Swedes had laid
them ; and said that now would be forthcoming
the man who would lead in this adventure.
Therewithal he told up many deeds of prowess
which King Olaf had done in his journeys and
warfare.   Then spoke King Rœrek: " True it is
that greatly has come down the might of King
Harald, since not one of his kinsmen is an over-
king in Norway.   Now the folk of this land have
tried it diversely.   King Hakon Athelstan's
fosterson was king here, and all folk liked it well.
But when the sons of Gunnhild ruled over the
land, all men wearied of their tyranny and wrong-
doing, so that men would liefer have outlandish
kings to rule over them, and be freer to do as
they would, seeing that the outlandish lords were
ever far away, and meddled but little with the
ways of men, so that they had of the land such scat
as they had settled for themselves.   But when
Harald the Dane-king and Earl Hakon fell out,
the Joms-vikings harried in Norway, and the
whole throng and multitude of the people betook
them to withstanding the vikings and thrust from
off them that unpeace. So folk egged Earl Hakon
on to hold the land in the Dane-king's despite,
and to ward it with point and edge.   But when
he deemed that he was fully come into dominion
through the furtherance of the people of the land,
he became so hard and so overbearing to the

land-folk that men tholed him not, and the Thrandheimers themselves slew him, and had into dominion Olaf Tryggvison, who was law-born to the kingdom, and in every way had the makings of a ruler in him. The whole throng of the land thrust in to have him for a king to rule them and to rear up anew the realm which Harald Hairfair had made his own. But when King Olaf deemed himself fully established in his dominion, no man was free before him to do his own will; and in overbearing fashion he went at us small kings, claiming for himself all the dues which King Harald had gathered in here, yea, and in some things going still further than he did. But so far from men being free to do as they would, no one might so much as have his way as to what god should be trowed. But since he was taken from the land, we have till now held to the friendship of the Dane-king, and in him have we had great avail in all things which we needed to crave for ourselves; self-freedom therewithal, and easy life in the land, and no overbearing. Now is this to be said as to my mind, that I am well content with things as they are; I wot not, though a kinsman of mine rule in the land, whether my right shall be bettered in aught thereby. And but I know it, I shall have no share in this adventure."

Then spake Ring his brother: "I shall uncover my mind. Methinks it is better, even though I have but the same lands and dominion, that a kinsman of mine should be king in Norway than outlandish lords; for then might our kindred be uplifted again here in the land. Now my mind forebodes me, as concerning this man, Olaf, that his fate and fetch will rule it whether he shall get the kingdom or not; but if he become over-king of all Norway, then, methinks, he will be deemed to be in better case who can tell up more matters for his friendship. As now he is in no way better off than any one of us; nay, so far worse, that we háve some land and dominion whereover to rule, but he has none at all; and we no less than he are rightly born to the kingdom. Now shall we make us men of such avail to him as to win him the highest dignity here in the land, and back him up with all our might. Why then should he not reward it us well, and remember it long for good, if he be of such great manhood as I think, and as all men say? Now shall we risk the venture to bind friendship with him, if I may have my will." Thereupon stood up one after the other and spoke; and the upshot was, that most were rather more willing to bind fellowship with King Olaf. He promised them his full friendship and right-booting, if he should be sole king over Norway. So this covenant they bind with sworn oaths.

CHAPTER XXXV. THE KING'S-NAME GIVEN TO OLAF.

THEREUPON the kings called together a Thing; and then Olaf set forth to the folk this counsel, and the title he has to the kingdom there; he craveth of the bonders that they take him for king over the land, and promiseth in return the ancient laws to them, and therewithal to ward the land against outland war-hosts and lords; to this end he spoke long and deftly, and gat good word for his speech. Then stood up the kings, one after the other, and all furthered this cause and errand before the folk. And at last it came to this, that Olaf was given the king's-name over all the land, and the land was doomed to him according to Upland law.

CHAPTER XXXVI. KING OLAF'S JOURNEY ABOUT THE UPLANDS.

THEN King Olaf set out on his journey, and let banquets be arrayed for him wherever there were kingly manors; and first he fared about Hathaland, and then sought north into Gudbrands-dales. Then matters went as King Sigurd had guessed, in that folk drew to him so mickle, that he deemed he was not in need of the half thereof, and had by then wellnigh three hundred men. By reason of this the banquets as settled beforehand served him not; for it had heretofore been the wont that kings fared about the Uplands with a following of sixty or seventy men, but never more than an hundred. So the king fared swiftly over the land, staying but one night in each place. But when he came north to the mountains, then dight he his ways and came north over the mountain, and fared on till he came down north from the mountains. King Olaf came down to Updale and tarried there for a night. Then he fared through Updalewood and came down in Middledale, where he craved for a Thing and summoned to him the bonders. Then spoke the king at the Thing, and craved that the bonders should take him for king, offering them in return right and law, even as Olaf Tryggvison had done. The bonders had no might to hold strife against the king, and so it ended, that the bonders took him for king and bound themselves thereto with sworn oaths. But they had before sent news down to Orkdale and also to Skaun, and let tell of the goings of King Olaf all that they wotted.

CHAPTER XXXVII. AN HOSTING IN THRANDHEIM.

EINAR THAMBARSKELFIR had a manor at Houseby in Skaun; but when came to him the news of the farings of King Olaf, he straightway let shear the war-arrow, sent it to all four quarters, and summoned thane and thrall with all weapons; and this went with the bidding, that they were to ward the land against King Olaf. The arrow-bidding went to Orkdale and even to Gauldale, and from all thereabout an host was drawn together.

CHAPTER XXXVIII. KING OLAF'S FARING TO THRANDHEIM.

KING OLAF fared with his host down to Orkdale, and fared all quietly and with peace. But when he came down to Griotar, he met there the gathering of the bonders, and they had more than seven hundred men. So King Olaf arrayed his company, for he deemed the bonders would be minded to fight. And when the bonders saw this, they fell to arraying them, but that went all the less smoothly whereas beforehand nothing had been settled, as to who should be captain over them. Now when King Olaf saw how unhandily matters went with the bonders, he sent to them Thorir, son of Gudbrand, and when he came, he said that King Olaf had no mind to fight them, and named twelve men who were the noblest of their flock, and bade them come to meet King Olaf. The bonders took that, and went forth over a certain edge-hill which was there, whereas stood the battle of the king. Then spake King Olaf: "Ye, bonders, have now done well, in that I have now the choice of speaking with you; for that will I tell you, concerning my errand hither to Thrandheim. And this in the beginning, that I wot ye have heard erst that I and Earl Hakon met last summer, and so ended our dealings, that he gave to me all the dominion which he had here in Thrandheim, which is, as ye wot, the Orkdale-folk, the Gauldale-folk, the Strind-folk, and the Isle-folk withal. And I have here the witnesses who were there, and saw the handsel between me and the earl, and heard the words and oaths, and all the covenant which the earl made with me. Now, I will bid you law and peace even according to that which King Olaf Tryggvison bade you before me."

He spoke long and bravely, and it came to this, at last, that he bade the bonders two choices, one

to come under his hand and to yield him obedience, and the other to have a battle with him
then and there. Thereupon the twelve bonders
went back to their band, and told them how they
had sped, and sought rede from all the company
as to which to take. Now although they wrangled
over this between themselves for a while, yet they
chose in the end to come under the king's hand;
and this was bound with oaths on the bonders'
behalf. Then the king arrayed his journey,
and the bonders made banquets of welcome for
him.

Thereafter the king journeyed down to the sea
and betook himself a-shipboard. He had a
twenty-benched longship from Gunnar of Gelmin;
another twenty-benched keel had he from Lodin
of Vigg; a third twenty-benched craft he had
from Angrar on the Ness, which homestead Earl
Hakon had owned, and the steward thereover
was he who is named Bard the White. The king
had besides some four or five cutters, and speedily
he fared and held in up the firth.

CHAPTER XXXIX. THE JOURNEY OF EARL SVEIN.

EARL SVEIN was then up Thrandheim
at Steinker, and let array there a Yule
feast; there was a cheaping-stead. Einar
Thambarskelfir heard that the men of Orkdale
had come under the hand of King Olaf, and so
sent to Earl Svein men with the news, who first
went down to Nidoyce and took there a rowing-

cutter which Einar owned.   Thereupon they sped
up the firth and came late on a day up to Steinker,
and bore these tidings to the earl all about the
journey of King Olaf.   The earl had a longship
which floated tilted before his homestead.   So
forthwith the same evening he let flit aboard his
loose money and the raiment of his men, and
drink and victuals, as much as the ship would
hold, and they rowed down firth straightway that
same night, and came at dawn of day to Skarn-
sound.   Thence they saw where King Olaf came
up the firth with his host, and so the earl turned
towards land inward of Maswick; a thick wood
was there, and they lay so close to the cliffs that
leaves and limbs reached out over the ship.   Then
they cut large trees and set them out-board
right down to the sea, and the ship might not be
seen because of the leafage, nor was it full daylight when the king rowed up past them.   The
weather was calm, and the king rowed up past
the island.   And when they were hidden out of
each other's sight, the earl rowed out into the
firth and all the way down to Frosta, where they
made land ; for there was the earl's dominion.

CHAPTER XL. THE COUNSEL OF EARL SVEIN AND EINAR.

EARL SVEIN sent men out into Gauldale
for Einar his brother-in-law; and when
Einar came to the earl, the earl told him
how all things had gone between him and King
Olaf, and this therewith, that he was minded to

gather an host together and go to meet King Olaf
and fight with him.   Einar answers thus : " Take
we our counsel heedfully, and let us keep spying
thereafter as to what King Olaf may be minded
for; let this alone be heard of us, that we are
keeping quiet; for then, if he heareth not of our
hosting, may be that he will sit down in quiet at
Steinker over Yule, whereas now there are all things
well arrayed.   But if he hear that we have on
hand an hosting, he will make out of the firth forthwith, and we shall have nothing of him."   So was it
done as Einar spoke, and the earl went a-feasting
among the bonders of Stiordale.

Now King Olaf, when he came to Steinker,
took all the goods for the banquet and had them
borne aboard his ships, and gat also ships of burden
therefor, and took with him all victuals and drink,
and gat him gone at his speediest and held out to
Nidoyce, where King Olaf Tryggvison had let set
a cheaping-stead and reared a king's-house ; but
before that there was only one house in Nidness,
as is writ afore.   But when King Eric became
ruler of the land he favoured Ladir, where his
father had had his chief abode, but he left un-
heeded the houses which King Olaf had let build
on the Nid ; and some were now tumbled down,
while othersome, though standing, were scarce
meet for dwelling in.   King Olaf steered his ships
up into the Nid ; and forthwith he let dight for
dwelling the houses yet standing, and rear those
up again which were fallen down, and had thereat
a throng of men ; and he let flit into the houses
both the drink and the victuals, being minded to

sit there Yule-tide over.   But when Earl Svein and Einar heard this, they laid their plan on their side.

CHAPTER XLI.   OF SIGVAT THE SKALD.

THORD SIGVALDI'S SKALD was the name of a man of Iceland; he had been for a long time with Earl Sigvaldi, and later with Thorkel the High, the brother of the earl, but after the fall of the earl, Thord turned chapman.   He happened on King Olaf when he was on his western viking-fare, and became his man and followed him ever after; and when these tidings befell he was with the king.   Sigvat was the son of Thord, and was fostered with Thorkel of Apewater.   But when he was wellnigh a full-grown man, he fared out from the land with certain chapmen; and the ship came to Thrandheim in the harvest-tide, and the shipmates took quarters in the countryside.   This same winter came King Olaf to Thrandheim, as hath been written e'en now. But when Sigvat heard that his father was there with the king, he went to the king, and met Thord his father, and abode there awhile.   Sigvat was early a good skald; he had made a song on King Olaf, and bade the king give ear to it; but the king said he would have no songs made on him, and says he knows not how to listen to songcraft. Then Sigvat answers:

> All-noble scather of mirk-blue
> Steed of the tilt, now hear me;

For well can I in song-craft,
And sure one skald thou mayst have,
Though wholly thou mayst thrust off
The praising of all other,
For thee, All-Wielder, surely
Shall I get good might of singing.

King Olaf gave to Sigvat for song-reward a
golden ring which weighed half a mark. Sigvat
became one of King Olaf's body-guard. Then he
sang :

O Battle-Niord, fain took I
Thy sword to me ; that would I,
Nor blamed the deed thereafter.
Yea, 'twas a thing praiseworthy.
O stem of the lair of the brother
Of the serpent, well we bargained :
A true house-carle thou gettest,
And I a right good master.

Earl Svein had let take half sailing-fees for the
Iceland ship, as had been the wont aforetime ; for
Earl Eric and Earl Hakon had one half of that
revenue just as of all others in Thrandheim. But
when King Olaf was come there, he appointed his
men to gather in half sailing-fees from Iceland
ships ; but those of this ship went to see the king,
and prayed Sigvat for his help, so he went before
the king and sang :

Prayer-wearing shall they call me,
The gladdeners of fight-vulture,
If now for the cloaks I pray me,
Erst sea's fire have we taken.
Waster of lair of mead-worm,
Half sailing-dues yet grant thou
To go back to the round-ship ;
'Tis I myself have craved it.

CHAPTER XLII. OF EARL SVEIN.

EARL SVEIN, he and Einar Thambarskelfir drew together a great host, and went out to Gauldale by the upland ways and make out for Nidoyce, having wellnigh twenty hundred men. King Olaf's men were out on Gaulridge keeping guard on horseback, and got to spy how the host went down Gauldale, and brought the king the news by midnight. So forthwith King Olaf stood up and let wake the host, and straightway they went aboardship and bore out all their raiment and weapons, and everything they might get away with, and thereupon rowed out of the river. Even at that nick of time came the host of the earl into the town, and they took all the Yule victuals and burnt all the houses. So King Olaf fared down the firth to Orkdale, and there went off from the ships, and so fared up through Orkdale right up to the mountains, and east over them to the Dales. It is told of this, to wit, that Earl Svein burnt the homestead of Nidoyce, in that lay which was made on Klæng, the son of Brusi :

All-wielder's half-made houses,
By the very Nid-side burnt they.
Deem I that fire the hall felled,
On the host the flame shot ashes.

CHAPTER XLIII. OF KING OLAF.

THEN King Olaf fared southward along the Gudbrands-dales, and from thence down to Heathmark. Through the heart of winter he went all about a-guesting, but when spring set in, he drew an host together and went down to the Wick; from Heathmark he had a large company which the kings gat for him. Thence fared many landed-men and rich bonders, and in that band was Ketil Kalf from Ringness. From Raumrealm, too, King Olaf had some folk: King Sigurd Sow, his stepfather, came and joined him with a large following.

So they made down for the sea and betook themselves aboardship and made ready from the inner Wick, and a fair host and a mickle had they. But when they had dight all their host, they made out for Tunsberg.

CHAPTER XLIV. OF EARL SVEIN'S HOST.

FORTHWITH after Yule Earl Svein gathered an host together all about Thrandheim, and biddeth the muster, and dighteth his ships. In those times there was in Norway a multitude of landed-men, and many of them were mighty men, and of so great kindred that they were sprung from the blood of kings or of earls by but a short tale of forefathers, and mighty wealthy they were withal. But all the trust of the kings or the earls that ruled over the land was in the landed-men ; for so it was, that in every folk-land the landed-men ruled over the throng of the bonders. Now Earl Svein was friendly with the landed-men, and therefore he sped well in the muster of his host. Einar Thambarskelfir, the brother-in-law of Earl Svein, was with him, and many other landed-men ; many, too, who in the winter before had sworn oaths of fealty to King Olaf, both landed-men and bonders. Now forthwith when they were ready they set off out of the firth and held south along the land, and drew together men out of every folk-land. But when they came south past Rogaland, then came to meet them Erling Skialgson, and had a great host, and with him were many landed-men. On they held with all the host east to Wick, and it was at the time when Lent was wearing that Earl Svein sought in to the Wick ; he brought his host past Grenmar and came to anchor off Nesiar.

CHAPTER XLV. OF KING OLAF'S HOST.

THEN King Olaf held with his host down the Wick, and but short way there was now between them, and each knew of the other on the Saturday before Palm Sunday. King Olaf was aboard the ship which was called Carl's-head, on the stem whereof was carven the head of a king, and that he himself had carved. That head was long sithence in Norway used on ships which chieftains steered.

CHAPTER XLVI.   KING OLAF'S TALK.

ON the Sunday morning, as soon as day dawned, King Olaf stood up and arrayed himself and went ashore, and let blow up for all the host to go ashore.   Then had he talk with the host, and tells all folk that he had learnt that there was but a short way between him and Earl Svein. " Now," said he, " shall we get ready, for there will be short while to abide till we meet. Let men now get their weapons, and let each one bedight him and his place whereunto he has already been marshalled, so that all men be all-dight when I let blow for departure; sithence row we in close array ; let none fare before the whole fleet fareth, and let none lag behind then, when I row out of the haven ; for we may not know whether we shall come upon the earl where he is lying now, or whether they be seeking to set on us.   But if we meet each other and a battle befall, let our men close up the ships, and be ready to lash them ; at first let us but ward us, and take we good heed of our weapons, lest we bear them on to the sea, or hurl them into the deep.   But when the battle is pitched, and the ships have been grappled, then make ye the brunt as hard as ever ye may, and let each one do at his manliest."

CHAPTER XLVII. BATTLE OFF NESIAR.

KING OLAF had on his ship an hundred men in ring-byrnies and Welsh helms. Most of his men had white shields with the holy cross laid thereon in gold, while some were drawn with red stone or blue ; a cross withal he had let draw in white on the brow of all helms. He had a white banner, and that was a worm. Then he let sing him the Hours, and thereafter he went aboard his ship, and bade men eat and drink somewhat.

Thereafter he let blow the war-blast, and they set off out of the harbour, rowing in search of the earl.

But when they came off the haven where the earl had lain, there was the earl's host under weapons, and was minded to row out of the harbour ; but when they saw the battle of the king they began to lash the ships together, and set up their banners, and made ready. But when King Olaf saw that, they fell to their oars, and the king laid aboard the ship of Earl Svein, and straightway the battle was joined. So says Sigvat the Skald :

> The king wrought men much onset
> Where he thrust into the battle
> On Svein amidst the haven.
> Red blood on Rodi's deer fell.
> Their valiant king held onwards,
> Relentless, where he wrought him
> The war-mote bold. There Svein's men
> Were binding ships together.

Here it is said that King Olaf went into battle,

but Svein lay before him in the harbour. Sigvat
the Skald was there in the battle; he wrought
forthwith the next summer that "lay" which is
called the Nesiar-ditties, and there he tells carefully of these tidings:

> I know how that craftsmaster
> Of point-frost let lay Carl's-head,
> All nigh unto the earl there,
> Unto the east of Agdir.

The fight was of the fiercest, and it was a long
while ere one looking over it might see which way
it would turn. Fell a many on either side, and a
multitude were wounded. So says Sigvat:

> No need to taunt Earl Svein then,
> Or Olaf battle-merry,
> For the breeze of the moon of battle,
> Or gale of the din of sword-edge.
> For each of that twain of warriors,
> They had full choice of hewing
> Where each on each fell. Never
> Came host to worser fight-stead.

The earl had the more numerous host, but the
king a chosen crew aboard his ship, that had
followed him in war, and was so bravely dight, as
is aforesaid, that every man had on a ring-byrny,
and thus they gat no wounds. So says Sigvat:

> Glad saw I the cold byrnies
> Over our shoulders falling,
> In the host of the king the noble:
> Hard there betid the sword-din.
> There was my black hair hidden
> By Welsh helm from the shaft-flight.
> Fight-fellow, then I knew us
> So dight in the host of battle.

CHAPTER XLVIII. THE FLIGHT OF EARL SVEIN.

BUT when folk began to fall on board Earl Svein's ship, and some were wounded, and the crew grew thinner along the gunwale, then King Olaf's men turned to boarding the earl's ship; so the banner was borne up aboard the ship which lay nearest to that of the earl, and the king himself followed the banner. So says Sigvat:

> The golden staff rushed on there
> Where we furtherers of the sark-din
> Of Gondul went 'neath banners
> With the glorious king on war-ship.
> Aboard that steed of tackle
> 'Twas nought as when a maid bears
> Mead to the king's wage-takers;
> 'Twas metal-greeting rather.

There was then a brisk brunt, and of Svein's men some fell thick and fast, but othersome sprang overboard. So says Sigvat:

> All wroth we rushed on swiftly
> Up on the ship: there heard we
> High crash of meeting weapons;
> Brands reddened shields to-cloven.
> There went the wounded bonders
> Out-board whereas we battled.
> Unfew swam corpses beach-ward,
> Ships bravely dight were taken.

And again this:

> The white shields we came bearing
> For us there folk did redden:

Easy it was to see it
How there we dealt the sword-voice.
The young king whom we followed,
Methinks the war-ship boarded.
Blood gulp gat the fowl of battle
There, where the swords were blunted.

Then the fall of men turned to the host of the
earl, and the king's men set upon the ship of the
earl, and were on the very point of boarding her.
But when the earl saw to how hopeless a pass
things were come, he called upon his forecastle-
men to cut the cables and let loose the ships, and
even so they did. Then the king's men caught
the beaks of the ships with grapnels, and thus
held them fast. Then the earl cried out that the
forecastle-men should hew off the beaks, and even
so they did. So says Sigvat:

'Twas Svein himself that fiercely
Bade hew off the black beaks there ;
Ere that thrust was he wellnigh
Into ill-hap full fashioned,
Whereas we wrought, and made there
Good cheer unto the raven.
For Ygg's black chough the host hewed
Corpses around the ships' prows.

Einar Thambarskelfir had laid his ship on the
other board of that of the earl, and his men threw
an anchor into the prow of the earl's ship, and thus
they all drifted together out into the firth ; and
after that the whole host of the earl took to flight,
and rowed out into the firth.

Bersi, the son of Skald-Torfa, was in the fore-
hold of Earl Svein's ship ; so when the ship
glided forth by the fleet, then speaketh King Olaf

on high when he knew Bersi, who was a man easily known, the goodliest to look on of all men, and wondrous well bedight of weapons and raiment: "Fare ye hail, Bersi!" "Hail to thee, king!" said he. So says Bersi in that song which he wrought, when he came into King Olaf's power, and sat in fetters:

> Thou badest this craftsmaster
> Of song-craft hail be faring,
> And such-like did I answer
> Unto the fight's swift driver.
> I loth of hindrance, bidder
> Of fire of the good ship's outland,
> Sold the same word of the high-born
> That I bought of the bole of byrny.

> I have seen Svein's mighty trouble,
> We two have fared together
> Where bright cold tongues of war-swords
> Were singing loud and swiftly.
> No man forsooth henceforward
> Shall I follow, none full surely
> That shall be nobler bidder
> Of the tempest of the wave-elk.

> O swayer of wound-serpent,
> I crawl not so before thee,
> (This year forsooth I tarry
> In Ati's skate no little.)
> That I, O wage-good captain
> Of war-hosts, should throw over
> Dear friends, or come to loathe them.
> Young knew I there thy foeman.

CHAPTER XLIX. EARL SVEIN'S FARING FROM THE LAND.

NOW fled ashore some of Earl Svein's men, but some gave themselves up to quarter. Then Earl Svein and his host rowed out into the firth, and laid their ships together, and the chiefs had parley together ; and the earl sought rede of the landed-men. Erling Skialgson counselled that they should sail to the North-country and get an host together, and once more fight with King Olaf. But inasmuch as they had lost much folk, most all of them urged the earl to leave the land and go meet the Swede-king, his brother-in-law, and strengthen himself thence with war-host; and that counsel urged Einar Thambarskelfir; whereas he deemed that as then they had no means wherewith to fight against King Olaf. Then sundered their host, the earl sailing south about the Fold, and Einar Thambarskelfir with him. Erling Skialgson, and many other landed-men besides, such as would not flee away from their birthright lands, went north to their homes, and that summer through Erling had a great company about him.

CHAPTER L. PARLEY BETWEEN KING OLAF AND KING SIGURD.

KING OLAF and his men got aware that Earl Svein had laid his ships together ; then King Sigurd egged on to fall on the earl and file the steel home. King Olaf says he

will first see what counsel the earl taketh up,
whether they keep the host together, or it sun-
dereth from him. Sigurd said he would belike
be having his way : "But this my mind forebodes me," says he, "that with thy temper and
masterfulness thou wilt but late make those big-
bucks trusty men, whereas they have erst been
wont to hold themselves big against their lords."
Now the onset came to nought, and soon they
saw how the earl's host sundered. Then King
Olaf let ransack the slain; and they lay there
certain nights, and shared the war-gettings. Then
Sigvat the Skald sang these staves :

Yea, this I deem moreover,
That many a murder-craftsman
Who fared from the North shall fail him
Of home-fare from that hard stour.
Full many a sound-sun's spender
From off the splice-knot's war-steed
Sank down unto the sea-ground.
At sea we met Svein soothly.

Now the fair Thrandheim maidens
This year shall never taunt us,
Though lesser was the king's host ;
Forsooth of brunt was somewhat.
That host the brides shall rather
Mock now, if one be mockèd,
Who beardling went in onset.
The skerries' field we reddened.

And still this :

The king's might waxeth, whereas
The Upland-men will further
This sender-forth of deck-steed ;
Svein, this hast thou found for thee !

Tried is it, that Heathmarkers
Must win more work than drinking
The ale of the fight-up-stirrer:
The flight of corpse-worms had they.

King Olaf gave good gifts to King Sigurd Sow
his stepfather at their parting, and to the other
chiefs withal who had given him help.   To Ketil
of Ringness he gave a keel of burden of fifteen
benches, and Ketil brought that ship up along
Raumelf all the way up into Miors.

CHAPTER LI. OF KING OLAF.

KING OLAF held spies over the farings
of the earl; but when he heard that the
earl was away from the land, then fared
he west along the Wick; drifted an host to him,
and he was taken for king at Things, and in this
wise he fared right on to Lidandisness.   Then he
heard that Erling Skialgson had a great gathering; so the king tarried no longer at North Agdir,
for he fell in with a brisk wind at will, and he fared
at his speediest north to Thrandheim, for there he
deemed was all the pith of the land, if he might
there bring the folk down under him while the
earl was away from the land.   But when King
Olaf came to Thrandheim, then was no uprising
against him there, and there he was taken to king;
and he set him down there in the harvest-tide at
Nidoyce, and there dight him winter-quarters. He
let house a king's garth, and reared Clement's
Church there whereas it now standeth.   He
marked out tofts for garths, and gave them to

goodmen and chapmen, or to any others he would, and who were minded to house. He sat there with many men about him, for he trusted the Thrandheimer's good faith but little, if so be the earl should come back to the land.

The Up-Thrandheimers were wyted most herein, whereas thence he gat no king's dues.

CHAPTER LII. EARL SVEIN AND OLAF THE SWEDE-KING TAKE COUN-SEL TOGETHER.

EARL SVEIN fared first to Sweden to Olaf the Swede-king his brother-in-law, and telleth him all about his dealings with Olaf the Thick, and sought counsel of the Swede-king as to what he shall take up. The king saith the earl had better be with him, if he will have that, and have there such dominion to sway over as he deemeth befitting; "or else," says he, "I shall hand over to thee host enow to seek the land from Olaf's hand." This the earl chose, for all his men egged him thereto, whereas many of them who were there with him had broad lands in Norway.

Now as they sat and counselled together over this matter, they came to accord to fare next winter by land, across Helsingland and Iamtland and thence down upon Thrandheim, for the earl trusted the Up-Thrandheimers best for steadfastness and help if he came there. But in the meanwhile they made up their mind first to go a-warring in the summer-tide into the East-ways to gather wealth.

CHAPTER LIII.   DEATH OF EARL SVEIN.

EARL SVEIN went with his host east into Garthrealm and harried there, and abode there through the summer; but when the autumn set in he turned, together with his host, to Sweden. Then gat he the sickness which brought him to bane. After the death of the earl, the company that had followed him went back to Sweden, while some turned to Helsingland and thence to Iamtland, making their way from east over the Keel to Thrandheim, where they told the tidings which had befallen in their journey. Then the tale about the death of Earl Svein was known for a truth.

CHAPTER LIV.   OF THE THRANDHEIMERS.

EINAR THAMBARSKELFIR, together with the company which had followed him, went in the winter to the Swede-king and was there holden in good cheer. Therewithal were many other folk who had followed the earl. The Swede-king took it mightily ill that Olaf the Thick had sat him down in his scat-land and driven away Earl Svein; for that cause the king vowed the heaviest lot on Olaf, as whenso he might bring it about; says he, that Olaf would not be so over-bold as to take under him the dominion which had been the earl's before, and all the men of the Swede-king were of one mind with him that so

would it be. But when the Thrandheimers heard
for a truth that Earl Svein was dead, and that he
was not to be looked for in Norway, then turned
all the commonalty to the obedience of King Olaf.
Then fared many men from Up-Thrandheim to
meet King Olaf and became his men, while othersome sent words and tokens that they were wish-
ful to serve him. That harvest therefore he went
into Up-Thrandheim and held Things with the
bonders, and in every folk-land he was taken to
king. Thereupon he went back out to Nidoyce,
and let thither be gathered all the king's dues and
made ready there for winter-quarters.

CHAPTER LV. THE KING'S GARTH HOUSED.

KING OLAF let house a king's garth at
Nidoyce. There was done a big court
hall with a door at either end, but the
high-seat of the king was in the midmost of the
hall. Up from him sat Grimkel, his court-bishop,
and next to him again other clerks of his; but down
from the king sat his counsellors. In the other
high-seat straight over against him sat his marshal,
Biorn the Thick, and then the guests. If men of
high degree came to King Olaf, they were well
seated. By litten fires should ale be drunk. He
appointed men to their services according as custom
was among kings. He had about him sixty body-
guards and thirty Guests, and assessed them wages
and gave them laws. Withal he had thirty house-
carles to work all needful service in the garth and

at whatso ingatherings were needful ; he had many
thralls withal.　In the garth also was a mickle
hall wherein slept the body-guard, and there was
withal a mickle chamber wherein the king held
his court councils.

CHAPTER LVI.　OF THE WONT OF KING OLAF.

IT was the wont of King Olaf to rise betimes in
the morning and dress and take a hand-bath,
and then to go to church to hear matins and
morning-tide, and then to go to council to appease
men, or to talk and tell whatso else he deemed
needful.　He summoned to him rich and unrich,
and all such as were accounted wisest.　Often let he
tell before him the laws which Hakon Athelstan's
fosterson had set forth in Thrandheim.　He framed
laws by the rede of the wisest men, and took out
or added whatever seemed good to him ; but the
canon right he framed by the counsel of Bishop
Grimkel and other clerks, and set his whole heart
on putting down heathendom and ancient wonts
wherein he deemed was Christ-scathe.　At last it
came to this, that the bonders yeasaid these laws
which the king set forth.　Even as says Sigvat :

> Dweller in loft of yoke-beast
> Of the wave, 'tis thou must fashion
> The land's-right standing steadfast
> Amidst the host of all men.

King Olaf was a man of good manners,
full mild, few-spoken, open-handed, but wealth-
grasping.

Then was with King Olaf Sigvat the Skald, as was writ afore, and othersome Iceland men. King Olaf asked after it carefully, how Christian faith was holden in Iceland, and deemed it lacked much of being well; for they told the king of the holding of the faith there, that it was allowed in law to eat horseflesh, and cast out children, even after the fashion of the heathen, and other things else, wherein was Christ-scathe. Withal they told the king of many of the great men that then were in Iceland. Skapti, the son of Thorod, then had the law-say in the land.

The manners of men wide in lands would he ask of such men as wotted clearest thereof, and led most his questioning towards the holding of Christ's faith in Orkney and in Shetland and in Faroe, and learnt that widely it fell far short of being well kept. Such talk would he oftenest have in his mouth, or discourse about law or the right of the land.

CHAPTER LVII. CONCERNING THE MESSENGERS OF OLAF THE SWEDE-KING; AND OF THE DEATH OF ASGAUT BAILIFF.

THAT same winter came from the east from Sweden messengers from Olaf the Swede-king, who had two brothers over them, to wit, Thorgaut Harelip and Asgaut Bailiff with four-and-twenty men. But when they came from the east over the Keel into Veradale, they summoned a Thing of the bonders and had parley with them, and claimed of them then and there

dues and scat on behalf of the Swede-king. But
the bonders took counsel together and were of one
consent that they would yield what the Swede-
king craved, if Olaf, King of Norway, should claim
no land-dues of them on his behalf; said they,
that they would not pay dues to both of them. So
the messengers left and made their way down
along the dales, and at every Thing holden they
got from the bonders the same answers, but no
money; thence they fared out to Skaun and had
a Thing there, and again craved the payment of
dues, but all fared the same way as before. Then
they went to Stioradale and craved Things there,
but the bonders would not so much as come
thither.

Now the messengers saw that their errand was
nought, so Thorgaut was minded to fare back
east. "Meseems," said Asgaut, "that we have
not yet sped the king's errand; I will fare to meet
King Olaf, since the bonders put their case to
him."

So he had his way, and they fared out to the
town, where they took harbour.

Next day they went to the king as he sat at
table, and greeted him, and said that they were
come with an errand of the Swede-king. The
king bade them come see him the next day. So
that next day, when the king had heard hours, he
went to his Thing-house and let call thither the
Swede-king's men, and bade them put forth their
errand.

Then spoke Thorgaut, telling first on what
errand they fared and were sent; and next how

the Up-Thrandheimers had answered. After that he bade the king settle what-like speed their errand thither should have.

The king says: "While earls bore sway here over the land, it was nought wondrous that the folk of the land should pay their dues to them, since they had a birthright title to the realm, rather than that they should lout before outland kings; it was more right, moreover, that the earls should give fealty and service to such kings as had rightly come to the realm here, than to outland princes, up-rising with unpeace against the rightful kings and cutting them away from the Land. But for Olaf the Swede-king, who claimeth Norway, I know not what title, in which there be truth, he hath thereto; but hereof we may mind us what man-scathe we have gotten at the hands of him and his friends."

Says Asgaut: "It is not to be wondered at that thou art called Olaf the Big, so bigly as thou answerest the message of such a lord; unclearly wottest thou, how heavy to bear shall be the wrath of the king, as they have come to know to their cost, who had more of pith than meseems thou wilt have. But if thou wilt masterfully hold the realm rather, thou wert better go meet him and become his man, and then we will pray along with thee that he be pleased to enfeof thee of this realm."

Then answereth the king, and took up the words in lowly wise: "Other rede have I for thee, Asgaut. Fare ye now back to your king, and tell him this, that early next spring I shall dight me east for the land-marches, where of old was the sundering of the realms of the King of Norway and of the

Swede-king; and then he may come thither if he will, so that we may frame peace together, on such terms that each of us rule over that realm to which we have birthright."

Then turned away the messengers and back to their harbour, and made ready for departing; but the king went to table. Thereafter the messengers went into the king's garth, but when the door-wards saw that, they told the king thereof, who bade them not let the messengers in : " I will not speak with them,' says he. So the messengers went their ways.

Then says Thorgaut that he is minded to turn back with his men, but Asgaut says that he has made up his mind to carry the king's business through. Then they parted, and Thorgaut took his way up to Strind, but Asgaut and his men, twelve in all, turned up to Gauldale and thence out to Orkdale, being minded to fare south to Mere, there to carry out the business of the Swede-king.

But when King Olaf was ware thereof, he sent the Guests after them : they happened on them at Stone, out on the Ness, laid hands on them, and put them in bonds and led them up to Gauledge, and there raised a gallows and hanged them where they might be seen out of the firth from the high sea-way. These tidings Thorgaut heard or ever he fared back from Thrandheim. Thereupon he went all the way until he fell in with the Swede-king, and tells him all that had betid in their journey. The king was full wroth when he heard this said, and there was no lack then of high words.

CHAPTER LVIII. PEACE MADE BE-TWEEN KING OLAF AND ERLING SKIALGSON.

NEXT spring King Olaf Haraldson bade out folk from Thrandheim, and dight him to fare east into the land. Then, also, Iceland ships got ready to leave Thrandheim. King Olaf sent word and tokens to Hialti Skeggison, bidding him come meet him; he sent word also to Skapti the Speaker-at-law, and to those other men who bore most rule in Iceland, that they should take out of the law that which to him seemed to war most against Christendom. And therewith he sent friendly words to all the people of the land together.

The king sailed south along the land and tarried somewhat in every folk-land, and held Things with the bonders. And at every Thing he let read out the Christian law and the ordinances thereunto appertaining. There and then he undid many evil wonts and heathendoms amongst the people; whereas the earls had holden well to ancient laws and the right of the land, but as to Christendom they let every one do as he would. At that time things had gone so far that in most places along the seaward countrysides men were christened, but Christian laws were unknown to most folk; but about the upper dale-land and fell-dwellings folk were yet widely all-heathen; for so soon as the people had their own way with it, that troth abode fastest in their memory which they had learned when they were bairns. But to those who would not shape them to the will of the king in the holding of Christendom, he threatened evil dealings, were they rich or unrich.

At every Law-Thing Olaf was taken for king over all the land, and then no man gainsaid him more.

When he lay in Kormtsound the word went between him and Erling Skialgson that they should make peace, and a meeting for peace was appointed in Whiting-isle. Now, as soon as they met, they spoke together themselves about the peace, and Erling deemed that there was somewhat to be found in the king's words other than what had been told him; for he spoke for this, that he would have all those grants which Olaf Tryggvison had given him, and after him the Earls Svein and Hakon likewise : " Then I shall become thy man, and be thy faithful friend," says he.

The king answers : " It seems to me, Erling, that it would be no worse for thee to take of me as great grants as thou didst take of Earl Eric, a man who had done to thee the greatest man-scathe ; but I shall make thee the noblest landed-man in the land, though I will bestow my grants of my own will, and will not let it be, that ye landed-men have a birthright to the heritage of my kindred, and that I must needs moreover buy your services for many times their worth."

Erling had no mind to pray the king in this matter, for he saw that the king was not to be led. He saw, withal, that he had two choices to hand : the one, to make no peace with the king, and take the risk how things would go, or else, to let the king have his own way; so this he chose, much though it was against his mind, and spake to the king: "That service which I give to thee of mine own will, shall be of most avail to thee." So then they dropped the matter. After that Erling's kinsmen and friends came forward, and prayed him to yield, and do with wit rather than mastery: "Thou wilt,' said they, "be ever the noblest of landed-men in Norway, both for thy prowess, and thy kindred, and thy wealth."

Erling found that this was wholesome rede, and that they did by goodwill who spoke thus. Thus he did then, and became the king's man on such terms as the king determined in the end; and so they parted, being at peace in words at least. So King Olaf went on his ways east along the land.

CHAPTER LIX. THE SLAYING OF EILIF THE GAUTLANDER.

STRAIGHTWAY when King Olaf came to the Wick and that was known, the Danes fared away, they who held bailif-ries there of the Dane-king, and sought to Denmark and would not abide King Olaf. But King Olaf went on up the Wick, holding Things with the bonders, and all the folk of the land came under him, and so he took to him-self all the king's dues there, and tarried about the Wick that summer through. From Tunsberg he held east over the Fold all the way east beyond

Swinesound. Then began the realm of the Swede-
king. Over those parts he had set for bailiffs, Eilif
the Gautlander over the northern lot, and Roi
Squint-eye over the eastern, all the way to the Elf.
He had his kindred on both sides of the Elf, and
great lands in Hising; he was a mighty man and
of plenteous wealth; Eilif also was a man of great
kin. Now, when King Olaf brought his host into
Ranrealm, he summoned the men of the land to a
Thing, and there came together to meet him those
men who dwelt about the islands there, or nigh
unto the sea. Now, when the Thing was set,
spake Biorn, the king's marshal, bidding the bonders
take to them King Olaf, even as had been done elsewhere in Norway. A man hight Bryniolf Camel,
a noble bonder, stood up and said : "We bonders
know what has been the rightest land-sundering
from of old between the King of Norway and the
Swede-king and the Dane-king, to wit, that the
Gaut-elf has ruled it from the Vener Lake to the
sea, but northward the Marklands have ruled it even
unto Eidshaw, and thence the Keel all the way
north to Finmark ; withal, that now one, now the
other, have overrun each other's lands. The Swedes
have ·long had dominion all the way to Swinesound ; yet, sooth to say, I wot that many men
are of will that they had liefer serve the King of
Norway; but men lack boldness in the matter,
seeing that we have the realm of the Swede-king
both to the east of us, to the south and inland of
us, all about, while it may be looked for that the
King of Norway will speedily depart north away
into the land, where there be broader country-

sides, and then have we no might to uphold strife against the Gautlanders. So it behoves the king to look to some wholesome rede for us, fain as we are to become his men."

Now when the Thing was over, Bryniolf was the guest of the king in the evening, and so also the next day, and many things they talked over together in privy wise. Thereupon fared the king east along the Wick, and when Eilif heard that the king was there, he let bear spying on his ways. Eilif had thirty men of his following, and was up in the dwelt-lands on the border of the Marklands, and had there a gathering of bonders.

Many bonders went to meet King Olaf, while others sent him words of friendship.

Then men went between King Olaf and Eilif, and the franklins prayed both, for a long time, to appoint a Thing betwixt them, and in one way or another settle peace. They said to Eilif that it was to be looked for of the king, that if folk did not shape them according to his word, they might look for exceeding hard dealings at his hands; and they said that Eilif should not lack folk. Then it was settled that they should come down and have a Thing with the bonders and the king. But then King Olaf sent Thorir the Long, the Guest-captain, and six of them, all told, to Bryniolf. They had byrnies under their kirtles, and hats over their helmets. The next day the bonders came thronging down with Eilif; Bryniolf was there then amongst his company, and Thorir in Bryniolf's following. The king laid his ship whereas was a certain cliff jutting into the sea; there he stepped

aland and sat down on the cliff together with his
host ; but above the cliff was a field whereon was
the gathering of the bonders, but Eilif's men stood
up in a shield-burg around him.

Biorn the Marshal spoke long and boldly on
behalf of the king.   But as he sat down, up stood
Eilif and began speaking, and in that nick of time
Thorir the Long stood up and drew his sword and
hewed Eilif on his neck, so that off went his head.
Then sprang to their feet the whole crowd of the
bonders, but the Gautlanders took to their heels
and ran off, and Thorir and his men slew some
amongst them.   But when the host halted, and
quieted down from the turmoil, the king stood up
and bade the bonders sit down ; and they did so,
and many things were spoken, but in the end the
bonders became the king's men and yeasaid him
allegiance.   But on his part he promised them in
return not to part from them thereupon, but to
tarry there until he˙ and Olaf the Swede-king
should have settled their troubles in one way or
another.   After this King Olaf laid under him all
the northernmost bailiwick, and went that summer
all the way east to the Elf, and got all the king's
dues along the sea-border and from the islands.
But when summer wore, he turned back north
towards the Wick and made up along Raum-elf.
In that water is a great force called Sarp, and
from the north by the force a ness goes into the
river.   There let King Olaf do a wall, right across
the ness, of stones and turf and wood, and let dig
a dyke on the outward thereof ; and here he reared
a mickle earthen burg, and within the burg he

set up a cheaping-stead, and a king's garth he housed there, and let make Marychurch; there also he let mark tofts for other garths, and got men to house the same . Through harvest he let flit thither such ingatherings as were needed for winter fare, and sat there through the winter with a great multitude of people, having appointed his own men to all bailiwicks there. ,He forbade all flitting of goods from the Wick up into Gautland, both herring and salt, which the Gautlanders might ill lack. The king had a great Yule-bidding, and bade to him many wealthy bonders from the countrysides.

CHAPTER LX.   OF EYVIND UROCHS-HORN.

THERE was a man hight Eyvind Urochs-horn, of East-Agdir kindred; he was a big man and of mighty kin, and went every summer a-warring, whiles West-over-sea, whiles into the East-ways, or south to Friesland. He had a twenty-benched cutter well-found. He had been at Nesiar and given aid to King Olaf, and when they parted there, King Olaf avowed him his friendship, and Eyvind, in return, pledged his aid to the king wheresoever he would crave it. This winter Eyvind was a Yule-guest of King Olaf, and took good gifts of him. There was also with the king at the time Bryniolf Camel, and he had for a Yule-gift from the king a gold-wrought sword and therewithal the manor called Vettland, the greatest of chief-steads.   Bryniolf sang a ditty about the gifts, whereof this is the ending :

> The famed lord he gave me
> Both brand and Yettland.

Then the king gave him the title of a landed-man, and the greatest friend of the king was Bryniolf ever after.

CHAPTER LXI.   THE SLAYING OF THRAND THE WHITE.

THAT winter Thrand the White went out of Thrandheim east into Iamtland to call in scat on behalf of King Olaf the Thick ; but when he had fetched in the scat, the men of the Swede-king came there and slew Thrand, him and them twelve together, and took the scat and brought it to the Swede-king.   That heard King Olaf, and it liked him ill.

CHAPTER LXII.   CHRISTENING OF THE WICK.

KING OLAF had bidden Christian law throughout the Wick even in the same fashion as north away in the land; and that sped well, whereas to the men of the Wick Christian wonts were known much better than to folk north away in the land, in that both winter and summer was much thronging of merchants there, both of Danish and Saxon ; the Wick-men, withal, were very busy in chaffering journeys to

England and Saxland, or to Flanders or to Denmark ; but some were out a-viking, and took up their winter-quarters in Christian lands.

CHAPTER LXIII. THE FALL OF ROI.

IN the spring King Olaf sent word for Eyvind to come to him, and they had a talk long in privity. Soon thereafter Eyvind got ready to fare a-viking. He sailed south along the Wick and lay-to in the Oak-isles west of Hising. There he heard that Roi Squint-eye had gone north to Ordost, and had drawn together folk there and land-dues on behalf of the King of Sweden, and was then to be looked for from the north. Then Eyvind rowed into Howesound, but Roi came even then rowing from the north, and in the very sound they met and fought. There fell Roi the White and nigh thirty men ; and Eyvind took to him all the wealth that Roi had had. So Eyvind went thence into the East-ways and was a-viking through the summer.

CHAPTER LXIV. THE FALL OF GUD-LEIK AND THORGAUT HARELIP.

THERE was a man hight Gudleik the Garthrealmer, of Agdir kindred, a mariner, and a mickle chapman ; wealthy withal, and one who went on chaffering journeys to sundry lands ; he would often go east into Garthrealm, and for that cause was called Gudleik the Garthrealmer. Now this spring Gudleik dighted his ship, being minded to go in the summer east to Garthrealm. King Olaf sent him word that he would see him. So when Gudleik came to him the king told him he wished to be in fellowship with him, and prayed him to buy him dear havings hard to get in the land. Gudleik said it should be as the king would. Then let the king pay him such wealth as it seemed him good, and Gudleik went into the East-ways in the summer.

They lay awhile off Gothland, and here it befell as oft, that they were not all of them too close of their words, and the islanders got wind of it that on board the ship was a chaffering fellow of Olaf the Thick. Gudleik went into the East-ways in the summer all the way to Holmgarth, and bought there the cloths full-choice which he was minded for the king for his robes of state, and therewith furs of great price and a glorious table service.

In harvest-tide, when Gudleik fared from the east, he fell in with contrary winds, and for a long time they lay beside Isle-land. Now Thorgaut Harelip had in the autumn espied Gudleik's journeyings, and he came here upon them with a longship and fought with them. They warded themselves long, but inasmuch as mickle were the odds, Gudleik fell, and many of his shipmates, and many were wounded. So Thorgaut took all their wealth to him, together with the treasures of King Olaf, and he and his shared among them equally all the prey. "But," he says, "the treasures shall the Swede-king have, for," says he, "they are some

deal of the scat which he hath to take of Norway."
So Thorgaut went east away to Sweden.

Now the tidings were speedily known : a little
after Eyvind Urochs-horn came to Isle-land, and
when he heard this he sailed away east after Thorgaut and his company, and they happened on each
other in the Swede-skerries and fought.   There fell
Thorgaut and the most part of his company, the
rest jumping overboard into the deep.   So Eyvind
took all the wealth they had taken from Gudleik,
and King Olaf's treasures withal.   Eyvind fared
back to Norway in the autumn, and brought his
treasures to King Olaf.   The king thanked him
well for his journey, and promised him his friendship once more.   At this time King Olaf had been
King of Norway for three years.

CHAPTER LXV.   THE MEETING OF KING OLAF AND EARL ROGNVALD.

THIS same summer King Olaf had out the
folk once more, and once more fared all
the way east as far as the Elf, and lay
there long through the summer.   Then passed
word-sending between King Olaf and Earl Rognvald and Ingibiorg, Tryggvi's daughter, the earl's
wife.   She furthered with all her might the helping of King Olaf, and was most headstrong in the
matter.   For two causes this went that way ; both
because there was mickle kinship betwixt her
and King Olaf, and moreover, because she might
not forget it of the Swede-king that he had been
at the fall of King Olaf Tryggvison her brother,

and for that sake she deemed she had a claim to the sway over Norway. Now by her pleadings the earl's mind was much turned towards friendship with King Olaf, and at last it came to this, that the earl and the king set a day between them and met at the Elf. There they talked over many things, and most chiefly about the dealings betwixt the Norway-king and the Swede-king; and both said, what indeed was true, that both to the Wick-men and to the Gautlanders the sheerest waste of their lands was in it, that there should not be peace of markets betwixt the lands. Now in the end they made truce and peace between themselves till the next summer; and at parting they gave gifts to each other and bespoke friendship between themselves.

CHAPTER LXVI. THE ILL-WILL OF THE SWEDE-KING TO KING OLAF HARALDSON.

THEN the king fared north into the Wick and had for himself all king's dues all the way to the Elf, and all the folk of the land had then come under him. King Olaf the Swede harboured so great ill-will against Olaf Haraldson that no man was to be so bold as to call him by his right name in the hearing of the king. They called him the Thick Man, and ever gave him hard words whenso he was spoken of.

CHAPTER LXVII. BEGINNING OF
THE PEACEMAKING STORY.

THE bonders of the Wick spoke among
themselves saying, that the only thing
to be done was that the kings should
make agreement and peace between them, and
deemed they were ill bestead if the kings should
be ever harrying each other; but this murmur
no one durst bear boldly before the king. Then
bade they Biorn the Marshal to flit this case
before the king, that he send men to meet the
Swede-king to bid him peace of his own hand.
This Biorn was loath to do and begged off; but
for the prayer of many of his friends he promised
at last to lay this matter before the king, but said
that his mind foreboded him that the king would
take it unmeetly that he should yield in aught at
all to the Swede-king.

This summer came from the west from Iceland
Hialti Skeggison at the behest of King Olaf, and
forthwith he fared to meet King Olaf, and the
king gave him a good welcome, bade Hialti abide
with him, and showed him to a seat beside Biorn
the Marshal; and thus the two became messmates,
and good fellowship grew up speedily betwixt them.

But on a time whenas King Olaf had parley
with his host and with bonders, and the affairs of
the land were talked over, Biorn the Marshal
spoke: "What art thou minded, king, as to that
unpeace which here is betwixt the Swede-king
and thee? Now each side has lost many men at
the hands of the other, but no settlement is there

now, any more than before, as to what of the
realm each shall have. Thou hast now sat here
in the Wick one winter and two summers, and left
at the back of thee all the land north away hence;
now men are growing weary of sitting here, they
who have lands and heirship in the north-country.
Now it is the will of landed-men and of others of
thine host, and of the bonders withal, that one road
or other this should be sheared out; and seeing that
now truce and peace is established with the Earl
of the Westgauts, who here are the nearest
neighbours, men deem that the best thing would
be, that thou send men to the Swede-king and
bid him peace of your own hand, and many of
them who are about the Swede-king would stand
up for that matter; for it is to the gain of both
sides, those, to wit, who dwell in the land both
here and there."

At Biorn's talk the folk made good cheer.
Then spake the king: "That rede, Biorn, which
thou hast here upborne, it is meetest that thou
shouldst have framed for thyself, and thou shalt fare
on this errand; thou shalt thrive by it, if it be well
areded; but if man's peril come therefrom, then
thou thyself hast too much hand therein; but
withal it is thy service to speak that before many,
which I will let speak."

Then the king stood up, and went to church,
and let sing high mass before him, and then went
to table.

Next day spake Hialti to Biorn: "Why art
thou unmerry, man? Art thou sick, or wroth with
any man?"

Biorn tells Hialti of the talk between him and the king, and says that this is a doomed man's errand.   Answers Hialti: "So it is to follow kings, that such men have mickle honour and are of more worship than other men, but oft come they withal into peril of life, and it behoves them to be well content with either lot. Mickle may can a king's good-luck; and much renown may be gotten in the journey if it turn out well."

Biorn said: "Thou makest light of the journey; mayhappen thou wilt fare with me, for the king said that I should have my fellows on the journey with me."   Says Hialti: "Fare will I soothly, if thou wilt; for hard to find meseems will be another seat-mate when we be sundered."

CHAPTER LXVIII.   THE JOURNEY OF BIORN THE MARSHAL.

A FEW days later, when Olaf the king was in council, came Biorn there, and they twelve together.   So he tells the king that they are boun to fare on their errand, and that their horses were standing saddled without. "Now will I wot," saith Biorn, "with what errand I shall fare, and what rede thou layest down for us."   Saith the king: "Ye shall bring these my words to the Swede-king, that I would set peace between our lands, according to the boundaries which Olaf Tryggvison had before me; and let that be bound by fast words, that neither of us overstep them.   But as to the loss of men, there is no need to speak thereof, if peace shall be, for the Swede-king may nowise boot us with fee for all that man-scathe which we have gotten of the Swedes." Then the king stood up, and went out with Biorn and his men, and took forth a well-wrought sword and a finger-ring, and handed it over to Biorn and said: " This sword I give to thee ; it was given to me last summer by Earl Rognvald. To him shall ye go, and bring him my word that he give thee his counsel and help, that thou mayest push through thine errand ; and I shall deem thou hast done well, if thou hearest the word of the Swede-king, whether he say yea or nay. But this ring thou shalt hand over to Earl Rognvald, and these tokens will he know."

Hialti went up to the king and bade him farewell : " And much do we need, king, that thou lay thy good luck on this journey." And he bade they might meet hale again. The king asked whither Hialti would fare. " With Biorn," says he. The king says : " It shall better this journey if thou fare with them, for thou hast often been approved a man of good luck. Know this for certain, that I shall lay my whole soul on it, if that may weigh aught, and I shall lay my luck to thine and to the luck of all you."

So Biorn and his folk rode their ways and came to the court of Earl Rognvald, and he was welcomed goodly thereat. Biorn was a renowned man and known to many by sight and by speech ; of all such, to wit, as had seen King Olaf; for at every Thing Biorn stood up and spoke out the king's errand. Ingibiorg, the earl's wife, went up to

Hialti and kissed him. She knew him; for she was with Olaf Tryggvison, her brother, when Hialti was with him, and she claimed kindred between the king and Vilborg, the wife of Hialti. There were two brothers, sons of Viking-Kari, a landed-man of Vors, Eric Bioda-skull, the father of Astrid, the mother of King Olaf Tryggvison, to wit, and Bodvar, father of Olof, who was the mother of Gizur the White, the father of Vilborg.

There were they now in good cheer. But on a day Biorn and Hialti went to have a talk with the earl, him and Ingibiorg, and then Biorn giveth out his errand and showeth the tokens to the earl. The earl answers: "What mishap has come to thee, Biorn, that the king willeth thy death? All the less it is well with thine errand, that I am minded to think that there will be no man who speaketh these words before the Swede-king, who will come away without paying the penalty. Over high-mettled a man is Olaf the Swede-king that he should suffer any to put forth talk before him which is against the mind of him."

Answers Biorn: "Naught has come to hand to me whereby King Olaf should be wroth with me, but many are his counsels both concerning himself and his men, wherein seemeth peril to whomso taketh them up, unto such, to wit, as are of little heart. But all his redes have hitherto taken a lucky turn, and even so, we hope, it will fare once more. Now, sooth to say, earl, I will go see the King of the Swedes, and not turn back till I have let him hearken all those words which King Olaf commanded me to bring to his ears, unless hell

ban it me, or fetters, so that I may not bring it to
pass. This will I do, whether thou give any heed
to the king's word-sending or not."

Then said Ingibiorg : " Swiftly I shall lay bare
my mind. My will, earl, is, that thou put thy
whole heart into furthering the message of Olaf,
Norway's king, so that this errand reach the ears
of the Swede-king, whatever wise he may answer
it. Though there lieth hereon the wrath of the
Swede-king, or the loss of all our dominion and
wealth, I would far rather risk this, than that it
be told that thou layedst under head the message
of King Olaf for fear of the Swede-king. Hereto,
by thy birth and strength of kindred, and all thy
dealings, thou mayest well be so free here in the
Swede-realm as to speak thy speech, that is
well beseeming, and which all men will deem
worth hearkening to, whether they who hearken
be many or few, mighty or unmighty, yea, though
the king himself should be a-hearkening."

The earl answers : " None may be blind as to
whither thou eggest me. Maybe thou shalt have
thy will in this, that I promise the king's men to go
with them, so that they may bring it about to flit
their errand before the Swede-king, whether the
king like it well or ill ; but my own counsel I mean
to follow as to how to go about the matter. For I
will not run after the headlong ways of Biorn or
of any other man in so mickle a matter of trouble.
Therefore I will that they tarry until such while
as meseemeth likeliest that some furtherance may
be of this errand."

Now when the earl had unlocked to them that

he would further them in this matter, and lay-to his might withal, then Biorn thanked him well and said he would follow his rede. And Biorn and his company tarried there with the earl a right long while.

CHAPTER LXIX. CONCERNING THE TALK BETWEEN BIORN AND INGI-BIORG, TRYGGVI'S DAUGHTER.

INGIBIORG was exceeding well with them. Biorn talked to her about his case, and deemed it ill that his journey should be tarried so long. And about this matter she and Hialti, yea, and all of them, would hold discourse. Then said Hialti: " I shall go to the king, if it be your will. I am not a man of Norway, and the Swedes will lay no wyte on me, and I have heard that about the Swede-king there are Icelanders who are well beholden there, and are of my acquaintance: the king's skalds, to wit, Gizur the Swart and Ottar the Swart. Then I shall pry into the matter what I may learn of the Swede-king, if this be so unlikely as it is now said out to be, or whether there be some other stuff in it; and I shall hit upon that for an errand which me-seemeth may fall thereto."

This Ingibiorg and Biorn deemed to be a device of the most wit, and they agreed thereto between them steadfastly. So Ingibiorg dighteth Hialti's faring, and got him two Gautland men, and bade them so much as that they should follow him, be his handy-men, and do service to his body, and go

his errands withal.   For spending-silver Ingibiorg
did over to him twenty marks weighed.   She sent
with him words and tokens to Ingigerd, the
daughter of King Olaf, begging her to give all
her mind to his affair in whatsoever he might find
it needful to crave her aid.   Straightway departed
Hialti, when he was ready.   But when he came to
King Olaf, he speedily happened on the skalds
Gizur and Ottar, who were all-fain of him, and
went with him forthwith before the king, and told
him that there was come a man, who was from the
same land as they, and was of the most worship
in that land, and they prayed the king to give him
good welcome there.   The king bade them take
Hialti and his fellow-travellers into their company.

Now when Hialti had tarried there a while, and
made himself known to men, he was held of much
worth by every man.   The skalds were often
before the king, for they were bold of speech, and
oft in the daytime they would sit before the high-
seat of the king in fellowship with Hialti, and in
all things they gave him the most worship.   Then,
withal, he became known to the king by word of
mouth, and the king was full of talk with him, and
asked him many things of Iceland.

CHAPTER LXX.   OF SIGVAT THE
SKALD.

THIS had happened before Biorn fared
from home, that he had asked Sigvat the
Skald to fare with him, who was then
with King Olaf; but men were not eager for this

journey. Between Biorn and Sigvat there was
good friendship.   He sang :

> Erst have I had good dealings
> With all the worthy marshals
> Of the war-bold king, e'en such as
> Before our lord's knee wend them.
> Oft hast thou earned me, Biorn,
> At the king's hands things goodly.
> O, fight-ice reddener, good yet
> For me thou mayst, for thou canst it.

And when they rode up through Gautland,
Sigvat sang these staves :

> Oft was I wet and merry,
> When shaved the heavy weather
> King Olaf's sail all wind-blown
> Out in the firths of Strind-land.
> The deeps' steed swept an-amble,
> Keels cut the lace of Listi,
> Whenas we let the cutters
> Sweep o'er the sound to leeward.

> Ships of the valiant Shielding
> By the isle we let float tilted,
> When summer was beginning,
> Off the good land and glorious.
> Comes autumn, when the horses
> Of Ekkil spurn the thorn's moor,
> Then must I take to riding.
> My diverse deeds now sing I.

But when they rode up through Gautland, late
one evening, then sang Sigvat :

> Now runneth steed an-hungered
> Long tracks to the hall in the glooming,
> The hoof the greensward rendeth,
> And little daylight have we ;

> O'er brooks my horse me beareth
> Far off the folk of Daneland;
> In the dyke the lad's horse stumbled;
> Now day and night are meeting.

Then rode they into the cheaping-stead at Skarar along the street, onward to the garth of the earl. He sang:

> The lovely dames shall look out,
> And maidens see the reek there,
> Whereas we ride right swiftly
> All through the town of Rognvald.
> Whip horse! so that the good wife,
> Heart-wise, may hear afar off,
> Within the house, our horses
> Running the hard trot garthwards.

CHAPTER LXXI. OF HIALTI SKEG-GISON, WHEN HE WAS IN SWEDEN.

ON a day Hialti, and the skalds with him, went before the king. Then Hialti took up the word: "So it is, king, even as is well known to thee, that I have come here to see thee, and have gone a long journey and a hard; but when I had come across the sea, and I heard of your highness, it seemed to me an unlearned journey, to fare back without having seen thee and all thy glory. Now this is a law that prevaileth between Iceland and Norway, that Iceland men, when they come to Norway, have to pay there land-dues; but when I came over the sea, took I the land-dues of all my shipmates. Now, knowing that it is most right, that to thee is all the power that is in Norway, I fared to find thee that I might pay thee the said land-dues."

Therewith he showed the king the silver, and poured into the lap of Gizur the Swart ten marks thereof.

The king said : " Few have brought us such things out of Norway this while past. And I will can thee thanks, Hialti, and my good-will, that thou hast been at the pains to bring the land-dues unto me, rather than to yield them to our un-friends ; yet will I that thou take this money of me, and my friendship therewith."

Hialti gave thanks to the king with many words. Thenceforth Hialti got himself into the greatest good-liking with the king, and was oft in talk with him.   The king deemed, as was sooth, that he was a wise man, and deft of word.

Now Hialti tells Gizur and Ottar that he is sent with tokens to the warding and friendship of Ingigerd, the king's daughter, and prays them to bring him to talk with her.   They said that there would but little pain go thereto, and on a certain day they go to her chamber, where she sat at the drink with many men.   She greeted the skalds well, for they were well known unto her.   Hialti bore to her the greeting of Ingibiorg, the earl's wife, and said that she had sent him thither for her ward and friendship, and he brought forth the tokens thereof.   The king's daughter took it well, and told him he was welcome to her friendship.   There they sat a long while of the day, and drank.   The king's daughter asked Hialti of many tidings, and bade him come thither oft to have talk with her.   This he did, and often he came there and had talk with the king's daughter, and so told her, under privy trust, of the journey of Biorn and his men, and asks what she thinks as to how the Swede-king will be likely to take that matter, that peace be set between both kings. The king's daughter answers and says, that she was minded to think there was no avail in seeking that the king should make peace with Olaf the Thick, and she said that the king was gotten so wroth with Olaf that he might not hear him named.

It fell one day, that Hialti sat before the king and talked with him, and the king was then right merry and very drunk. Then said Hialti to the king: " A very great glory of many kinds is to be beholden here, and now, what I often have heard told in tale has become a very sight to me : that no king in the North-lands is as noble as art thou. Full mickle grief it is that we should have so long to seek hither, and so perilous, first over a mickle main-sea, and then across Norway, unpeaceful for faring unto them who would seek hither in friendly wise. Or why do not men look to it, to bear words of peace betwixt thee and Olaf the Thick ? I heard it much talked about both in Norway and in West Gautland that all folk were fain if peace might be ; and this was told me for truth concerning the words of the King of Norway, that he would be glad to make peace with thee, and I wot that what brings it about is this, that he must needs see that he has far less might than ye have. Moreover, it was said, that he was minded to woo Ingigerd thy daughter, and such a bidding would be likeliest for a hale peace, and he is a man of the greatest mark, from what I heard truthful men tell of him."

Then answers the king: "Such things thou shalt not talk, Hialti; but I will not lay blame on thee for these words, for thou knowest not what thou hast to be ware of. Nowise shall that Thick Man be called king here in my court; and to lean on him is of far less avail than many folk give out; and even so wilt thou deem, if I tell thee that such alliance may be nought meet, whereas I am the tenth king at Upsala of them who have taken that kingdom one after the other, we having been kinsmen, and been sole kings over the Swede-realm, and over many other wide lands, and we have been all over-kings over other kings in the North-lands. But in Norway are but little dwellings, and far sundered, and there have been but kinglets. But Harald Hairfair was the greatest king in that land, and he had to do with kings of the folk-lands, and broke them down under him; yet he knew what was meet for him, and not to covet the realm of the Swede-king, and for that reason the Swede-kings let him sit in peace; and moreover this went thereto, that there was kinship betwixt them. But whenas Hakon Athelstan Fosterson was in Norway, he sat there in peace until he warred in Gautland and Denmark; and thereafter a flock was set up against him, and he was cut off from his lands. The sons of Gunnhild withal were cut off from life so soon as they became disobedient to the Dane-king. Then Harald Gormson laid Norway to his own realm and revenue, and yet we deemed King Harald Gormson as of lesser might than the

Upsala kings, inasmuch as Styrbiorn, our kinsman, cowed him, so that Harald became his man;
but Eric the Victorious, my father, strode over the
head of Styrbiorn, when they tried it out between
them.   But when Olaf Tryggvison came to Norway and called himself a king, we did not let that
avail him, for I and Svein the Dane-king fared
against him, and cut him off from life.   Now have I
gotten Norway to me, and with no less of might
than thou mightest now hear, and by no worse
title have I come by it than this, that I have fallen
on with war, and overcome the king that ruled it
erst.   Now thou mayst deem, wise man, that it
will be far from me to let that realm loose to the
Thick Man; and indeed it is a marvel that he
should not bear it in mind how hardly he got out
of the Low when we had penned him up there;
for I ween he had then something else in
his mind, should he escape alive, than to have
to strive oftener with us Swedes.   So, now, Hialti,
thou shalt not again have this talk in mouth before
me."

Hialti deemed that the outlook was nought
hopeful that the king would listen to any parley of
peace.   So he left off, and fell to other talk.

A while after, when Hialti was a-talking with
Ingigerd, the king's daughter, he told her of all
the converse between the king and himself.   She
said she looked for such answers from the king.
So Hialti bade her put in some word with the
king, saying that that would perchance avail most.
She said the king would not hearken to whatever
she might have to say: "Yet," says she, "I may

put it forth if thou wilt." Hialti said he would thank her for so doing

On a certain day Ingigerd, the king's daughter, was a-talking with King Olaf, her father, and when she found that her father was light of heart, she said: "What art thou minded about thy strife with Olaf the Thick? Many men are now bewailing that trouble; some say that they have lost wealth, othersome, kinsmen, and all, a land of peace at the hands of the Northmen; and as matters now are, it is for none of thy men to come into Norway. It was uncalled-for of thee to lay claim to the kingdom of Norway; a land poor and ill to traverse, and a folk untrusty; and men in the land would have any one for king rather than thee. Now, if I might have my way, thou shouldst let thy claim to Norway lie quiet, and break into the East-lands rather for that realm which has been swayed over by Swede-kings of old time, and which Styrbiorn our kinsman hath but late laid under him, and let Olaf the Thick have the heritage of his kindred and thou to make peace with him."

The king answered in wrath: "This is thy counsel, Ingigerd! that I let loose the sway of Norway, and give thee in marriage to Olaf the Thick! No!" says he, "something else first! Rather shall it be that this winter at the Upsala-Thing I shall lay it bare to all Swedes that all folk shall be out before the ice is off the waters, and I shall fare into Norway and waste that land with point and edge, and burn all up, and thus reward them their untrustiness."

And therewith was the king so wood wroth,

that not a word might be answered him.   So she
went away.

Hialti was keeping watch on her and went
straightway to see her, and asks how her errand
to the king had sped.   She said it had fared as
she doubted, that no words might be brought
before the king, and that he vowed threats in return
for them; and she bade Hialti never get on to
this matter before the king.

Ingigerd and Hialti, whenas they talked together, would often be speaking about Olaf the
Thick.   He told her often about him and his
ways, and praised him as he knew how, and that
was the truest to be told of him.   To such things
she took kindly.   And once again, as they were
talking together, Hialti said: "King's daughter,
shall I, with thy leave, say that before thee which
stirreth in my mind?"

"Speak thou," said she, "so that I hear it alone."
Then spoke Hialti: "How wouldst thou answer,
if Olaf, Norway's king, were to send men to thee
on the errand of wooing thee?"   She blushed
and answered unhastily, and quietly withal: "I
have not a steadfast mind as to my answers to
that; for I am minded to think, that with such
answers I shall have no need to deal.   But if Olaf
be a man so well endowed of all things as thou
tellest of him, I should not know how to wish for
my husband to be otherwise, if it be not so that
thou hast gilded him with praise in many ways."

Hialti said that he had given nothing out
about the king better than it was.

They talked about this privily very often.

Ingigerd bade Hialti beware of speaking of it before other folk; "for this cause, that the king will be wroth with thee if he know it of a truth."

Hialti tells these things to the skalds Gizur and Ottar, and they said that it was the happiest of redes, if it could be brought about. Ottar was bold of speech and fond of great lords, and speedily he was on this matter with the king's daughter, and told her the same like things as Hialti, concerning the king's manly prowess. And she and Hialti and they, all of them together, talked oft on the matter; and as they would at all times be talking of this, and Hialti had got to know for sure, what end his errand had come to, he sent away the Gautland men, who had followed him thither, and let them go back to the earl with letters, which Ingigerd the king's daughter and Hialti himself sent to the earl and Ingibiorg. Hialti also let them get wind of the matters he had broached to Ingigerd, and of her answers likewise. The messenger came back to the earl somewhat before Yule.

CHAPTER LXXII.   KING OLAF'S JOURNEY TO THE UPLANDS.

WHENAS King Olaf had sent Biorn and his men east into Gautland, he sent other men to the Uplands, on the errand of bidding guesting for him, for he was minded that winter to go a-guesting about the Uplands; for it had been the wont of the former kings to fare over the Uplands a-guesting every third winter. He started on the journey in the autumn

from Burg, going first up to Vingulmark; and went
about the journey in this way, that he took his
guesting inland in the neighbourhood of the woodland dwellings, and summoned to meet him all the
men of the countrysides, and those most chiefly
who dwelt farthest away from the main dwellings.
He ransacked men's ways of heeding Christ's
faith, and wherever he deemed they came short,
he taught them right manners; and if there were
any who would not leave off heathendom, he laid
such penalties upon them, that some he drove
away from the land, some he let maim of hand or
foot, or sting their eyes out; some he let hang or
hew down; and none did he let go unpunished who
would not serve God.   In this manner fared he
about all that folk-land; and he punished with even
hand mighty and unmighty.   He gave them clerks,
and placed them so thick about the country as he
deemed would do best.

In this wise fared he throughout that folk-land.
He had three hundred fighting-men when he went
up to Raumrealm.   He speedily found that the
further he made his way inland, the less was
Christian faith holden to.   But he dealt therewith
throughout in the same guise, and turned all the
folk to the right faith, and laid heavy penalties on
whomsoever would not hearken his words.

CHAPTER LXXIII. THE TREASON OF THE UPLAND KINGS.

NOW when the king who then ruled over Raumrealm heard this, he deemed that a great trouble was toward; for every day there came to him many men who bewailed them to him about these matters, some mighty, some unmighty. The king took that rede that he fared up into Heathmark to see King Rœrek, for that he was the wisest of those kings who then were there. Now when the kings fell to talk together, they agreed to send word north to the Dales to King Gudrod and to Hathaland withal, to the king that was there, bidding them to come to Heathmark to meet King Rœrek and him of Raumrealm. They laid not that journey under their head, and so these five kings met in Heathmark, at the place called Ringacre. The fifth of the kings was King Ring, the brother of King Rœrek.

Now the kings went into parley first by themselves, and he, who was come from Raumrealm, was the first to take up the word, telling the tale of the journey of King Olaf the Thick, and all the unpeace that he wrought, both in the taking of men's lives and in the maiming of men; some he drove out of the land, and seized the wealth of those who in aught gainsaid him; over the land, moreover, he went with an armed host, but not with the number of folk which was lawful. Furthermore, he says that he had fled thither before this unpeace, and that many other mighty men had fled away from their birthright lands out of Raumrealm. "Now, though this trouble be as yet nighest unto us, there will be little while to wait ere ye will have to sit under such things, and therefore it is better that we take counsel all together as to what rede we shall take up." Now when he had closed his harangue the other kings left the answering thereto to Rœrek. He said: " Now has that come to pass, which I misdoubted me would be, when we met at that Thing in Hathaland, and ye were, every man of you, most eager that we should heave up Olaf Haraldson over our heads; to wit, that to us he would be 'hard to take by horn' so soon as he had gotten the sole rule over the land. Now there are two choices to hand: one, that we all go and meet him and let him shear and shape all matters betwixt us and himself, and that I deem the best to take up; the other, to rise now up against him ere he has fared wider over the land. For though he have three or four hundred men, that makes no overwhelming odds, if we be all in one mind together; but most often it happens that, when there are many together, all of equal powers, it goes worse for them as to victory, than winning does for him who is a sole leader of his host; so therefore it is rather my counsel not to set on our fortune against Olaf Haraldson's."

Thereafter spake each of the kings what words seemed good to him; some letting, others urging, but no settlement of the matter was come to, for they showed, that to either case were drawbacks to be seen.

Then Gudrod the Dale-king took up the word,

and spake thus : " Marvellous to me is it, how greatly ye tangle your purpose in this matter, and how all-fearsome ye are of Olaf. We are here five kings together, not one of us worser of birth than Olaf. We it was who gave him strength to fight Earl Svein, and by our avail he hath gotten the land. But if he now begrudges each one of us the little dominion which we have had heretofore, and layeth on us torments and cowing, then can I this to say for myself, that I will have myself away from the king's thraldom, and I call that one amongst you no man, who is adread of this, to cut him off from life, if he fareth into our hands up hither in Heath-mark ; for this is to be told you, that never shall we stroke a free head so long as Olaf is alive."

Now after this egging-on they all turned to that counsel. Then spake Rœrek : " So meseemeth about this counsel of ours, that we must needs make our bond as strong as may be, lest any totter in good faith to the rest. Now ye are minded, when Olaf comes hither into Heathmark, to set upon him at some appointed meeting. Now, I will not trust you herein if some of you be then north-away in the Dales and others out away in Heathmark ; so I will, if this counsel is to abide steadfast amongst us, that we be together day and night until this rede be carried out."

This all the kings yeasaid, and so fared away all together. They let dight a banquet for them out at Ringacre, and there they drink in gild brother-hood ; but have spies away out in Raumrealm ;

other spies they let go out forthwith, one out
another in, so that they know day and night what
the tidings are about the journeys of King Olaf
or the number of his company.

King Olaf went guesting up along Raumrealm,
and did all in the samelike wise as is aforetold.
But when the entertainments fell short, for the
sake of his much company, he let the bonders
add fare to eke out the banquets in such places
where he deemed it needful to tarry, but in some
places he stayed a shorter while than had been
settled beforehand ; so his journey up to the Water
was quicker than had been appointed afore.

Now when the kings had gotten fast to the
counsel aforesaid, they sent out word, and summoned to them the landed-men and the bonders
of might from all those folk-lands ; and when they
came there, the kings had a meeting with them
alone and laid bare to them their counsel, and
settle an appointed day whenas that rede shall
be carried through.   They settle withal that each
of the kings shall have a company of three hundred
men.   So they send back the landed-men that
they may gather men together, and come meet
the kings at the place appointed.   This rede most
men liked well, and yet it fell here, as the saw
says, " Each hath a friend amidst unfriends."

CHAPTER LXXIV. MAIMING OF THE KINGS OF THE UPLANDERS.

AT this meeting was Ketil of Ringness. But when he came home in the evening, he ate night-meal, and thereafter he arrayed him and his house-carles, and went down to the Water and took the ship of burden which he owned and King Olaf had given him, and ran out the craft; but all the gear appertaining to it was there in the ship-house. That then they took and benched themselves for rowing, and pull off down along the Water. Ketil had forty men all well weaponed.

They came early in the day down to Waters-end, and thence fared Ketil with twenty men, and let the other twenty keep guard of the ship. King Olaf was then at Eid, in the uppermost part of Raumrealm, and Ketil came there whenas the king was coming back from matins, and he greeted Ketil well. Ketil says that he will talk with the king speedily; so they go aside to talk, the two of them. Then Ketil tells the king what rede the kings have on hand, and all the mind of them, that, to wit, whereof he wotted. Now when the king knew this, he calls men to him, and sends some into the countrysides bidding call in to him the nags; but some he sent to the Water to take row-boats, all they might get, and have them up to meet him; but he went to the church and let sing mass before him, and went thence forthwith to table. But when he had had his meat, he got ready at his speediest, and went north to the Water, and there

some ships came up and met him. So he himself
stepped aboard the ship of burden, and with him
as many men as the craft would hold, but every
one else took ship wheresoever he could get it.
In the evening they put out from the land; the
weather was calm, and they rowed up along the
Water, and now the king had with him nigh four
hundred men. Before dawn he was up by Ringacre, and the warders were ware of nought till the
folk were come up to the stead. Ketil and his
men knew well the chambers wherein the kings
were sleeping, and the king let take all those
chambers, and guarded them, so that no man
might get away. And thus they waited for light
of day. The kings had no means of warding themselves, and so were all laid hands on, and led
before the king. King Rœrek was an exceeding
wise man and hard of heart, and King Olaf deemed
him untrusty, even though he made somewhat of
a peace with him. He let blind Rœrek of both
eyes, and had him with him; but he let shear out
the tongue of Gudrod the Dale-king; but of Ring
and two others he took oath, that they should fare
away from Norway, nor ever come there again;
but of landed-men and bonders, who were proven
to be of this treason, some he drove out of
the land, some were maimed, but of some he
took peace. Of these things telleth Ottar the
Swart:

> The spoiler of brand of hawk's-field,
> Now hath he given in payment
> Unto the lords of the land here
> Things ugly for their treason.

Host-ranker, thou aforetime
Gavest the kings of Heathmark,
They who with guile beset thee,
A guerdon well befitting.

Fight-thronger, thou hast driven
The kings beyond the land-mark ;
Brand-reddener, now thy valour
Mightier than theirs is proven.
Lord king, each fled before thee,
As all men wot; and sithence
The word-reed didst thou hopple
Of him who sat most northward.

O'er all that land thou rulest
Which five kings held aforetime,
And thee the high God strengthens
With mickle gain, meseemeth.
Broad kin-lands east to Eid there
All under thee are lying :
No Gondul's-fires' be-thronger
O'er such land sat aforetime.

King Olaf then laid under him the dominion
which these five kings had had, and took hostages
of landed-men and bonders. He took guesting-
fees from the north, as far as the Dales, and wide
about Heathmark, and then turned back out to
Raumrealm, and thence west to Hathaland.

This winter died Sigurd Sow, his stepfather.
Then turned King Olaf to Ringrealm, and Asta,
his mother, arrayed a great banquet for him. And
now Olaf alone bore a king's name in Norway.

CHAPTER LXXV.   OF THE BROTHERS OF KING OLAF.

SO it is said, that while King Olaf was at the banquet with Asta, his mother, she led forth her children, and showed them to him.   The king set his brothers, on one knee Guthorm, and on the other Halfdan.   The king looked on the lads, and then knit his brows and looked wrathfully on them, and both of the lads drooped.   Then Asta bore to him her youngest son, who was hight Harald, who was then three winters old.   The king frowned on him, but he looked straight into his face.   Then the king caught at the hair of the lad and pulled it, and the lad laid hold of the king's beard and pulled in return.   Then said the king : " Revengeful wilt thou be later on, kinsman."

Next day the king was strolling abroad about the stead, and Asta, his mother, with him ; and they went to a certain tarn, and there were at play the lads, the sons of Asta, Guthorm and Halfdan. There were done big homesteads and great barns with many neat and sheep : this was their play, to wit.   A little way thence along the tarn-side, by a certain clay-creek, was Harald, and had wood shavings, and they floated by the land a-many. The king asked him what that meant.   He said they were his warships.   Then laughed the king and said : " Maybe, kinsman, that it may come about that thou shalt rule over ships."

Then the king called thither Halfdan and Guthorm.   And he asked Guthorm : " Whereof wouldst thou own the most, kinsman?" "Corn-fields," says he. The king said: "How wide wouldst thou have thine acres?" He answers: "That would I, that all this ness which goeth into the water were all-sown every summer." But ten steads stood there. The king answers: "Mickle corn might stand thereon."

Then the king asked Halfdan what it was that he would own most of. "Kine," saith he. The king says: "How many kine wouldst thou have?" Halfdan said: "So many that when they went to the water they should stand close to each other all round it." The king answered: "Big store will ye two have, therein taking after your fathers." Then the king asked Harald: "Of what willest thou to own the most?" He answers: "House-carles," says he. The king asked: "Now, how many wilt thou have?" "That would I, that they might eat up at one meal all the kine of Halfdan my brother." The king laughed and said to Asta: "Here, belike, thou art rearing a king, mother!" No more of their words are told of as at that time.

CHAPTER LXXVI. OF THE LAND-DEALING AND LAWS IN SWEDEN.

IN Sweden it was an ancient custom, while the land was heathen, that the chief blood-offering should be at Upsala in the month of Goi; then should be done blood-offering for peace and victory to their king. Thither folk should seek from the whole realm of Sweden, and there at the same time withal should be the Thing of all the Swedes. A market and a fair was there also, which lasted for a week. But when Sweden was christened, the Law-Thing and the market were holden there none the less. But now, when Sweden was all christened, and the kings forbore to sit at Upsala, the market was flitted, and held at Candlemas, and that has prevailed ever since, and now it is held for but three days. There is holden the Thing of the Swedes, and thither they seek from all parts of the land.

The Swede-realm lieth in many lots. One lot is West Gautland and Wermland and the Marks, and all that thereto appertaineth ; and such a wide dominion is that, that under the bishop, who is thereover there are eleven hundred churches. Another lot of the land is East Gautland, where there is another bishopric, and therewith goeth now Gothland and Isle-land, and altogether this is a still wider bishopric. In the Swede-folk itself one part is called Southmanland, which is one bishopric. Then there is the part hight West-manland or Fiadrundland, that is one bishopric. Then is that hight Tenthland, the third part of Swede-land. Then the fourth is called Eighth-land, then the fifth, Sealand, together with what thereto appertaineth, lying east away along the sea. Tenthland is the best and most nobly peopled of Sweden. Thither louteth all the realm. Upsala is there, with the king's-seat, and there is an archbishop's chair, and thereby is named the Wealth of Upsala. So call the Swedes the King's wealth, they call it Upsala-wealth. In each shire of the land is its own Law-Thing, and its own laws in many matters. Over every "law" is a lawman, who hath the most to say among the bonders, for that shall be law which he ruleth to declare. But if king, or earl, or bishops fare over the land and hold Thing with the bonders, then the lawman answereth on behalf of the bonders, and in such way they follow him all, that even men of the greatest power scarce dare to come to their Althing without the leave of the bonders and the lawman. But in all matters where the laws sunder, they must all yield to the Upsala-law, and all other lawmen shall be under-men of the lawman who is of Tenthland.

CHAPTER LXXVII. OF LAWMAN THORGNYR.

THERE was then in Tenthland a lawman hight Thorgnyr; his father is named Thorgnyr, son of Thorgnyr. These forefathers had been lawmen in Tenthland through the lives of many kings. Thorgnyr was then an old man. He had a great court about him, and he was called the wisest man within the realm of Sweden. He was a kinsman of Earl Rognvald and his fosterfather.

IV.

CHAPTER LXXVIII. MEETING OF EARL ROGNVALD AND INGIGERD, THE KING'S DAUGHTER, AT ULLER-ACRE.

NOW we have to take up the story where-as came to Earl Rognvald the men whom Ingigerd, the king's daughter, and Hialti had sent from the east. They laid their errands before Earl Rognvald and his wife Ingi-biorg, and said the king's daughter had often spoken to the Swede-king about peace between him and King Olaf the Thick, and that she was the greatest friend of King Olaf; but that the Swede-king waxed wroth whensoever she men-tioned Olaf, and that she deemed there was no hope of peace as matters stood. The earl told Biorn what he had heard from the east, and Biorn said still the same as before, that he was not minded to turn back till he had met the Swede-king, and says the earl hath promised him to go with him to meet the Swede-king. Now the winter weareth on, and forthwith after Yule the earl arrayeth his journey, taking with him sixty men, and in that journey was Biorn the Marshal and his faring-mates. The earl went east all the way to Sweden, and when he got further inland, he sent his men before him to Upsala and sent word to Ingigerd, the king's daughter, that she should fare out to Ulleracre to meet him, for there she had large manors. But when the words of the earl came to the king's daughter, she laid not the journey under her head, but got ready to go with

many men. Hialti betook himself to this journey
with her. But before he went away he went
before King Olaf and said: "Sit thou hailest
of all kings! and sooth it is to say that I have
never come, where I have seen such glory as
here with thee, and that word shall I ever hereafter bear about, wheresoever I may come. I
will pray this of thee, king, that thou be my
friend."

The king answers: "Why lettest thou on so
journey-proud? whither away then?" Hialti
answers: " I will ride with Ingigerd, thy daughter,
out to Ulleracre."

The king said: " Fare thee well, then; a wise
man thou art, and well-mannered art thou, and
knowest well how to be with noble lords."

Then went Hialti his ways. But Ingigerd, the
king's daughter, rode out to her manor of Ulleracre,
and had there a great feast arrayed for the earl.
Then the earl came there, and a good welcome he
had, and tarried there certain nights. He and the
king's daughter spoke of many things, and most
about the Kings of Sweden and Norway, and she
telleth the earl that she deemeth the outlook
toward peace but hopeless.

Then said the earl: " How wouldst thou, kins-
woman, take it, if Olaf, Norway's king, should woo
thee? To us it seemeth about the likeliest for
peace, if such affinity might be brought betwixt
the two kings; but I will not follow up that matter,
if I know that it thwarts thy will."

She answers: " My father will have the choice
on my behalf, but of all my other kinsfolk thou

art he whom I would most take for counsel in matters whereon I deem that much lieth. But how good a rede deemest thou this?"

The earl urged her much thereto, and told of many things to the fame of King Olaf, such as were right glorious. He told her carefully of all those haps as had of late befallen: how King Olaf in one morning had laid hands on five kings and taken from them all their kingship, and laid their lands and realms to his own dominion. Many things they spoke about this matter, and were well agreed on all things between them. The earl went away when he was ready, and Hialti went with him.

CHAPTER LXXIX. OF ROGNVALD AND LAWMAN THORGNYR.

ROGNVALD the earl came one day at eve to the manor of Thorgnyr the Lawman. Mickle was that stead and grand. Outside there were standing men who gave good welcome to the earl, and took into their charge their horses and baggage. The earl walked into the guest-chamber, and within it there was a great multitude of folk. In the high-seat there sat an aged man, and never had Biorn, he and his, seen so big a man. His beard was so long that it lay on his knees and was spread out all over his breast; a goodly man was he, and a noble-looking. The earl went up before him and greeted him. Thorgnyr welcomes him well, and bade him go to the seat wherein he was wont to sit. The earl sat down on the other side right over against Thorgnyr.

They tarried there for certain nights before the earl put forth his errand; then he prayed that he and Thorgnyr should go together to the council-chamber. So Biorn and his journey-mates went in thither with the earl. Then the earl took up the word, and told of that, how Olaf the Norway-king had sent his men east thither for the making of peace; long he spoke withal of this, what a trouble it was to the West-Gautlanders, that un-peace went thence against Norway; he told withal, how Olaf the Norway-king had sent men thither, and that now the king's messengers were come there, and that he had promised them to go with them to meet the Swede-king; and further he said that the Swede-king took the matter so heavily, that he set forth, that it should do for no man to further that business.

"Now so it is, fosterfather," says the earl, "that by myself I may not prevail in this matter; and for this cause have I sought to thee, that there whereas thou art, I look for wholesome counsel and furtherance."

Now when the earl came to the end of his talk, Thorgnyr was silent for a while; but when he took up the word he said: "Wondrously ye shift you herein: ye long to take lordly names, yet can ye no good rede and forethought, so soon as ye come into trouble. Why didst thou not forethink thee hereof before thou behightedst this journey, that thou hadst no might to speak against King Olaf? Forsooth I deem it nowise unworshipful to be amongst the tale of bonders, and be free of my words to speak that I will, though the king be by. Now I shall come to the Upsala-Thing and give thee there such backing that thou mayst speak there fearlessly in the face of the king whatever liketh thee."

The earl thanked him well for this promise, and he tarried on with Thorgnyr and rode with him to the Upsala-Thing. There was a great multitude assembled, and there was King Olaf with all his court.

CHAPTER LXXX.   OF THE THING OF UPSALA.

THE first day, when the Thing was set, King Olaf sat on a chair, and there was his body-guard around him. But on the other side of the Thing-stead there sat on one stool Earl Rognvald and Thorgnyr, and before them sat the body-guard of the earl and the company of Thorgnyr's house-carles; but behind the stool, and all about the place in a ring, stood the throng of the bonders; and some went on to bents and howes that they might hearken thence.

But when the king's business had been told, such to wit as it was the wont to speak out at Things, and that matter was ended, then Biorn the Marshal stood up beside the stool of the earl and spoke aloud: "King Olaf hath sent me hither on this errand, that he will bid peace to the King of Sweden, and such boundary therewith betwixt their lands as of ancient time hath been between Norway and Sweden."

He spake in a high voice, so that the King of Sweden heard him clearly. Now when the Swede-king first heard King Olaf named, he thought that the man would drive through some errand of his; but when he heard spoken of peace and the boundaries betwixt Sweden and Norway, then he wotted who must needs be at the bottom of the matter. So he sprang to his feet and called out aloud that that man should hold his peace, saying that such things would by no means do. So then Biorn sat down.

But when hearing was got, the earl stood up and spoke. He told of the message of Olaf the Thick and his bidding of peace to Olaf the Swede-king, and therewithal that the West-Gautlanders sent to King Olaf all words they might that he should make peace with the King of Norway. He told forth what trouble it was to West-Gautlanders that they must forego all those matters of Norway wherein was increase of the year, and on the other hand that they must sit in the way of their onsets and harrying, if Norway's king should gather an host and come with war upon them. The earl said further that King Olaf had sent thither men with the message that he was minded to woo Ingigerd, his daughter.

When the earl left off speaking stood up Olaf the Swede-king. He answers in heavy wise as to the peace, and laid on the earl heavy reproaches and great, whereas he had dared to make truce and peace with the Thick Man, and had made friends

with him.   He charged him with being a proven
traitor to him, and said it was meet that Rognvald
should be driven out of the realm, and that he got
all this from the egging-on of his wife, Ingibiorg :
it had been the unwisest of counsels which he had
taken up at the bidding of such a wife.   Long he
spoke and harshly, and turned his speech against
Olaf the Thick.   But when he sat down, there was
a hush at first for a while.

CHAPTER LXXXI. THE SPEECH OF THORGNYR THE LAWMAN.

THEN stood up Thorgnyr.   And when he
arose, all the bonders got to their feet
who had been sitting before ; and all
rushed forward who had been in other places, and
would listen to what Thorgnyr had to say.   So at
first there was a great din from the thronging and
the weapons.   But when there was a hearing
spake Thorgnyr :

"Another way goeth now the temper of the
kings of Sweden than the wont was aforetime.
Thorgnyr, my father's father, remembered Eric,
the Upsala king, the son of Emund, and told this
of him, that while he was in his lightest age, he had
out every summer a gathering, and fared to sundry
lands, and laid under him Finland and Kirialaland,
Estland and Kurland, and wide about the East-
lands ; and even yet may be seen those earth-burgs
and other great works which he made ; yet was he
not so haughty as not to give ear to men who had
due errands to talk over with him.   Thorgnyr, my

father, was with King Biorn for a long while : well
he knew his ways. Throughout the lifetime of
Biorn his realm stood with mickle might and
nought of waning ; and he, withal, was mild to his
friends.

"I myself may remember King Eric the Victorious, and was with him in many a war-faring.
The realm of the Swedes he eked, and warded it
hardily, and it was good for us to bring our matters
before him.

"But this king, who is now, lets no man be so
bold as to speak to him but that alone which he
is pleased to allow ; for this he striveth with all
his might, but letteth his scat-lands go from him
from lack of diligence and doughtiness. He
hankers after this, to hold the realm of Norway
under him, but no Swede-king has set his heart
upon this thing aforetime, and it worketh unrest to
many a man. Now that will we bonders, that
thou, King Olaf, make peace with Olaf the Thick,
Norway's king, and give him thy daughter Ingigerd. And if thou wilt win again for thyself those
realms in the East-ways which thy kinsmen and
forefathers have had there, then will all we follow
thee to that end. But if thou wilt not have that
which we set forth, then shall we make an onset
on thee and slay thee, and not suffer of thee any
unpeace or lawlessness. Even so did our forefathers of old time, who at the Muli-Thing steeped
five kings into one ditch, such as aforetime had
been fulfilled of pride towards them, even as thou to
us. Now, say speedily, which choice thou wilt take."

Therewith the throng of folk made forthwith

mickle clash of weapons and din. But the king
stood up and spake, and said that he will let all be
even as the bonders will it; says he, that even so
had done all Swedish kings heretofore, to let the
bonder's rule with them in all matters whereon
they had will to do. Thereat the murmur of the
bonders was stayed.

Then spoke together the heads of the people,
the king, the earl, and Thorgnyr, and made peace
and covenant at the hand of the Swede-king, even
according to the words which Norway's king had
already sent to that end. At this Thing it was settled
that Ingigerd, the daughter of King Olaf, should
be given in wedlock to King Olaf Haraldson.
The king gave her plighted troth into the hand
of the earl and handselled to him all his bidding
over this betrothal; and they parted there at the
Thing with matters thus ended. But when the
earl fared home, he and Ingigerd met, and spoke
together on the affair. She sent to King Olaf a
cloak of pall, much gold-embroidered, and silken
fillets.

So the earl went back to Gautland and Biorn
with him. Biorn tarried there a little while, and
then fared back to Norway together with his
journey-mates; and when he met King Olaf and
told him the end of his errand, even as it was, the
king thanked him well for his journey, and said, as
was true, that good luck had stood Biorn in stead,
whereas he had brought through his errand
amidst this unpeace.

CHAPTER LXXXII. OF THE TREASON OF KING RŒREK.

WHEN spring came, King Olaf went down to the sea and let dight his ships, and called out folk to him; and that spring he fared down the Wick all the way westward to Lidandisness, and thence he fared all the way north to Hordland. Then he sent word to the landed-men, and named all the mightiest men from the countrysides, and arrayed this journey at the stateliest, whereas he went to meet his troth-plight. The wedding-feast was to be in autumn, east on the Elf, by the boundary of the realms.

Now King Olaf had with him King Rœrek the blind. And when his hurts were healed up, King Olaf gave him two men to serve him, and let him sit in the high-seat beside himself, and kept him in drink and raiment, in no worse wise therein than he had aforetime kept himself. Rœrek was few-spoken, and answered in a manner stiff and short when people spoke to him. It was his wont to let his foot-swain lead him abroad a-days, and away from other men; then would he beat the boy, and when he ran away from him he would tell King Olaf that the boy would not serve him. Then King Olaf changed his serving-men for him, but all went as before, that no serving-man could hold it out with King Rœrek. Then King Olaf got for the following and guarding of King Rœrek one Svein, a kinsman of King Rœrek, who had been his man before. Still Rœrek held to his wont as to his cross-grained ways and lone walks.

But when he and Svein were alone together, Rœrek grew merry and full of talk ; he called to mind then many things that had happened aforetime, and such withal as had befallen in his lifedays, when he was king ; he would bring to memory his former life, and also who he was who had changed it, with his rule and his bliss, and made of him but a bedesman. "And yet this I deem my hardest lot of all," says he, " that thou, or any other kinsman of mine, in whom there were the makings of a man, should now be such outcasts of their stock as to take revenge for no shame at all of those done to our race."

Suchlike wailings oft had he uppermost.

But Svein answers and says that they had to deal with men mighty beyond measure, and they had as then but little might. Spake Rœrek : " Why should I live long amidst shame and crippling, but that it might perchance so befall that, blind as I am, I should overcome him who overcame me in my sleep. So may we happily slay Olaf the Thick, now that he feareth nothing for himself. I shall lay down rede thereto, nor would I spare my hands for the deed, if I could but use them ; the which, however, I may not do by reason of my blindness, and therefore thou shalt bear weapons on him ; and forthwith, when Olaf is slain, I know by the soothsaying that is in me, that the realm returneth under the sway of his unfriends. Now maybe that I shall be king, and then thou shalt be my earl."

And so his word prevailed that Svein said yea to carrying out this folly.

Now this was how the plot was laid. When the king got ready to go to evensong, Svein stood without in the porch, and had a drawn short-sword under his cloak. But when the king came out of the chamber, then was he speedier than Svein had looked for, and he saw the face of the king; then he paled, and waxed as wan as a corpse, and his hands fell down. The king noted fear on him, and said: "What now, Svein! art thou minded to bewray me?" Svein cast away the cloak from him, and the sword withal, and fell at the feet of the king, and said: "All in God's power, and in thine, king!" The king bade his men take Svein, and he was set in irons. Then the king let show Rœrek to a seat on the lower bench; but he gave peace to Svein, and he fared away out of the land. Then the king gave to Rœrek another chamber to sleep in than that wherein he slept himself; in that chamber many of the guard slept; he gat two men of the body-guard to tend on Rœrek night and day. These men had long been with King Olaf, and he had tried their trustiness unto him; though it be not told of that they were men of great kin.

Now King Rœrek did so, turn and turn about, that whiles he held his peace for many days, so that no man could get a word out of him, and whiles he was so merry and glad, that they deemed it good game of every word he said; but whiles again he said but little, and nought but ill. So was it withal, that whiles he would drink every man off his settle, and made all them good for naught who sat nearest to him; but oftenest he drank but little.   King Olaf gave him pocket-money in plenty; and oft would he do thus, that he would come to his chamber before going to bed, and let bear in sundry casks of mead, and gave to drink to all the lads of the sleeping-chamber; whereof was he well-beloved of them.

CHAPTER LXXXIII.   OF FINN THE LITTLE.

THERE was a man called Finn the Little, of Upland blood, but, as some would have it, a Finn of kindred; he was of all men the smallest and the swiftest of foot, so that no horse might overtake him running.   Of all men was he best skilled on snow-shoes and at the bow.   He had been a long while a serving-man of King Rœrek, and had oft gone such errands of his as were affairs of trust.   He knew the ways all about the Uplands, and all great men there he knew to talk to.   But when King Rœrek was taken captive, Finn threw himself in with their following, going mostly in company with the knaves and the serving-men; but whenever he might bring it about, he came to do service to King Rœrek, and many a time he got to talk to him; but the king would speak with him but for a short while at a stretch, as he desired not that their talk should be misdoubted.   But as the spring wore, and they fared down into the Wick, Finn vanished away from the host certain days, and then came back again and tarried a while. Thus fared he often, and therefore no heed was given to it, for there were many runagates with the host.

CHAPTER LXXXIV. SLAUGHTER OF KING OLAF'S BODY-GUARD.

KING OLAF came to Tunsberg before Easter, and tarried there a long while of spring. There came to the town at that time many ships of chapmen, both Saxons and Danes, and folk from the Eastern Wick, and from the North-country, so that there was a right mickle throng. The season was abundant and drinkings mickle. On an eve as it befell, King Rœrek was come to his chamber somewhat late, and had drunk much, and was then very merry. Then came thereto Finn the Little with a mead-cask full of spiced mead of the strongest. This the king let give to drink to all within, until each fell asleep in his seat. Then was Finn gone away, but light burned in the chamber. Then the king waked up the men who were wont to follow him, saying that he wanted to go into the yard. They had a lantern with them, for it was pitch-dark abroad. In the yard there was a large privy standing on posts, and one had to get up to the door by steps. Now while Rœrek and his men sat in the yard they heard how a man said, "Cut the devil down!" And then they heard a crash and a thump, as of something falling. King Rœrek said: "They will be full drunken who are thus dealing together; go ye thereto and part them." They bestirred them speedily and ran out; but

when they came forth unto the steps he was first
cut down who went last, yet both were slain.
There were come the men of King Rœrek, Sigurd
Scrip, who had been his banner-bearer, he and his,
fifteen together; and Finn the Little was there
also. They dragged the corpses up between the
houses, and took the king, and had him away with
them, and leapt into a cutter which they had there,
and rowed away.

Now Sigvat the Skald slept in the chamber of
King Olaf, and he stood up in the night and a
foot-swain with him, and went to the great privy;
but when they were coming back, and were going
down the steps, Sigvat slipped and fell on his
knee, and thrust down his hand, and it was wet
thereunder. "I deem," says he, "that the king
has gotten for many of us the tub-ship's foot to-
night," and laughed withal. But when they came
to the chamber, where light was burning, the foot-
swain asked: "Hast thou hurt thyself, or why art
thou all over blood?" He answered: "I am not
hurt, but this must betoken tidings." He then
called up Thord, son of Foli, the banner-bearer,
his bed-fellow, and they went out, and had a lantern
with them, and soon found the blood; then sought
they, and speedily found the corpses, and knew
who they were. They look out and saw that there
lay a big tree-butt, and therein great gashes, and
it was known sithence that this had been done by
way of a feint, in order to draw them out who
were slain.

Sigvat and his mates spake between them that
it was needful that the king should know these

tidings as speedily as might be. They sent the swain forthwith to the chamber wherein King Rœrek had been. There all men were asleep, but the king was away. The swain wakened them who were therewithin and told them the tidings; and men stood up and fared forthwith into the yard whereas the dead bodies were. Now though it was deemed needful that the king should know of these things as soon as might be, yet none durst waken him. Then said Sigvat to Thord: "Which wilt thou rather, bedfellow, wake the king or tell him the tidings?" Thord answers: "On no account do I dare to waken him, but I will tell him the tidings." Then spoke Sigvat: "Mickle is left of the night yet, and it may be, ere day dawns, that King Rœrek will have gotten him such a hiding-place that thereafter he be not easily found; but as yet they must have got but a short way off, for the bodies were yet warm. Never shall such a shame overtake us as not to let the king know of this treason. Go thou, Thord, up into the chamber and await me there."

Then went Sigvat to the church and called up the bell-ringer, and bade him ring for the souls of the king's guards, naming by name the men who had been slain. The bell-ringer did what he bade him; but the king was waked by the ringing, and sat up. He asked whether it was already time for matins. Thord answers: "It is a worse matter than that. Great tidings have befallen: King Rœrek has vanished away, and two of thy body-guard are slain."

Then asked the king after the haps there, and

Thord told him thereof such as he knew. Then stood the king up and let blow a gathering for the guard; and when the company gat together, the king named men for the faring out all ways from the town to seek Rœrek by sea and land.

Now Thorir the Long took a cutter and went with thirty men, and when daylight broke, they see two small cutters fare before them.

But when they saw each other, either side rowed at their mightiest. There was King Rœrek with a company of thirty men; and as they drew closer to each other, Rœrek and his men turned towards shore, and there they all leapt aland, saving the king, who sat down in the poop. He spake and bade them fare well and meet hale.

Then Thorir and his folk rowed into the shore, and therewith Finn the Little shot an arrow, which came on the midmost of Thorir, and gat him his bane; but Sigurd and his men all ran away into the wood.

The men of Thorir took his dead body and King Rœrek withal, and brought them down to Tunsberg.

King Olaf himself took in hand the guarding of King Rœrek, and he had him carefully watched, and paid great heed to his wiles, and got men to ward him day and night. King Rœrek was then of the merriest, and no man could find in him that he did not like all these things as well as might be.

CHAPTER LXXXV. OF KING RŒREK'S PLOTTING.

IT befell on Ascension day that King Olaf went to high mass. Thereat the bishop went in procession round the church leading the king; but when they came back into the church, the bishop led the king to his seat in the north side of the choir, and there sat hard by King Rœrek as he was wont; he had his cloak-hood over his face. But when King Olaf had sat down, King Rœrek laid his hand on his shoulder and felt him about, and said: "Precious raiment hast thou now, kinsman," says he. King Olaf answers: "Now is a great high-tide holden in memory of this, that Jesus Christ stied up to heaven from earth."

King Rœrek answers: "This I do not understand, so as it be fast in my mind, what ye tell of Christ; for much of what ye say seemeth to me somewhat past belief, yet many wonders have befallen of old."

But when the mass was uphoven, then King Olaf stood up and held his hands over his head and bowed towards the altar, and his cloak fell down off his shoulders. Then King Rœrek sprang to his feet swift and hard, and thrust at King Olaf a sax-knife which is called "rytning;" the thrust came on the cloak by the shoulders, but the king was bent down, so that the clothes were much sheared but the king was nought wounded. But when King Olaf found himself thus set on, he leapt forth on to the floor. King Rœrek thrust at him a second time with the sax and missed him, and said : " Fleest thou now, Thick Olaf, before me, the blind ? "

The king bade his men lay hands on him and lead him out of the church, and so it was done.

After these things King Olaf's men urged him to let slay King Rœrek; " For it is," said they, " the greatest trial of thy luck, king, to have him with thee, and to spare him, whatsoever outrage he taketh to ; for he watcheth thereover night and day, to take away thy life. But so soon as thou sendest him away from thee, we see not any man who may guard him that there be no likelihood of his getting away ; but if he get loose, he will forthwith have up an host and do many evil things."

The king answers : " It is rightly spoken, that many a man hath taken his death for less deeds than Rœrek's ; but I am loth to mar the victory which I won over the kings of the Uplanders, when I took those five in one morning, and got all their dominions, in such wise that I needed not be their banesman, whereas they were all my kinsmen. Yet now I scarce may see, whether Rœrek may or may not yet drive me into a corner to let slay him."

Now the cause why Rœrek had put his hand upon the shoulder of King Olaf was, that he would wot whether he was in byrny.

CHAPTER LXXXVI. THE JOURNEY OF KING RŒREK TO ICELAND.

THERE was a man named Thorarin, son of Nefiolf, a man of Iceland, and of North-land kin, not of high degree, but of all men the wisest and the sagest of word; outspoken in the face of lords; a great seafarer, and was long in the outlands. Thorarin was the most ill-favoured of men, and that mostly for the ill fashion of his limbs; his hands were big and un-shapely, and yet were his feet more unshapely by far.

Thorarin happened to be staying at Tunsberg, when those tidings befell which are aforesaid; he knew King Olaf to talk to.

Thorarin was then dighting a cheaping-ship of his own, being minded for Iceland in the summer. King Olaf had Thorarin for guest for some days, and talked over many things with him, and Thorarin slept in the king's chamber. Now one morning early the king lay awake, but the other men in the chamber were asleep; the sun was risen but little, but it was full daylight within. Then saw the king how Thorarin had stretched one of his feet out from under the bed-clothes; he looked on the foot awhile, till the men in the chamber awoke. Then spoke the king to Thorarin: "I have been now awake for awhile, and I have seen a sight by which I set a great store, and that is a man's foot so fashioned that none, methinks, shall be uglier here in this town."

And he bade other men look thereat whether it

seemed so to them; and all who looked said it was true that so it was.

Thorarin found what was being talked of, and answers: "There be few things so utterly odd, that no likelihood there be of meeting another such-like; and it is likeliest that even so it shall be now."

The king said: "None the less will I hold to it that a foot so ugly shall not be found, yea even though I have to lay a wager on it."

Spoke Thorarin: "I am ready to wager thee hereon, that I shall find an uglier foot in the town."

The king says: "Then shall he of us twain, who holdeth the truest, choose a boon of the other." "So it be," says Thorarin.

Then he stretched from under the clothes the other foot, and no whit fairer was that to look upon, and the little toe was off it, to boot. Then spoke Thorarin: "Look here now, king, here is another foot, and it is by so much the uglier than the other that here is one of the toes off. So I have won the wager."

The king answers: "This other foot is by so much the unfairer, that there are on that five frightful toes, but on this one but four; so it is mine to beg the boon of thee.' Thorarin said: "Worshipful is the Lord's word! What is the boon thou wilt take at my hands?"

He answereth: "This, that thou flit King Rœrek to Greenland, and bring him to Leif, the son of Eric." Thorarin answered: "Never have I been in Greenland." The king says: "For such a seafarer as thou art, it is now high time to fare to Greenland, if thou hast not come thither before."

At first Thorarin had but little to say as to this matter. But as the king held to his urging of the matter, Thorarin did not altogether thrust it away from him, but spake thus: "I shall let thee hear, king, the boon it was in my mind to bid of thee, if I had won the wager; this, to wit, that I would have bid thee of service in thy guard. Now if thou grant me that, then were I the more bound not to lay under my head that which thou willest crave of me." The king yeasaid this, and Thorarin became of his body-guard. Then Thorarin dight his ship, and when he was ready he took to him King Rœrek. But when they were parting, Thorarin and King Olaf, Thorarin spake: "Now it may so befall, king, as is not unlike, and often cometh to pass, that I may not carry out the Greenland journey, but may be carried on to Iceland or some other of lands; how then shall I part with this king in such wise as shall like thee?"

The king says: "If thou come to Iceland, then hand him over to Gudmund, son of Eyolf, or to Skapti the Speaker-at-law, or to some other of the chiefs, such as will take him, with my friendship, and the tokens thereof. But if thou shouldst be borne on to other lands, of such as be nigher hereto, see thou so to it, that thou wot surely that Rœrek come never again to Norway; but do thou this only if thou mayst do nothing else." Now when Thorarin was ready, and the wind

was fair, he sailed all along the outer way, without
the isles, and north beyond Lidandisness he put off
into the main sea.   He gat not a wind speedily,
but he was most heedful not to make land.   He
sailed south of Iceland, and had an inkling thereof,
and so west of the land into the Greenland main.
There he got great gales and heavy seas, and as
the summer was wearing he made Iceland in
Broadfirth.   Thorgils Arison was the first man of
worship there to come to them.   Thorarin telleth
him the message of King Olaf, the bidding of
friendship, and the tokens that went with the
taking of King Rœrek.   Thorgils took the
matter well, and bade King Rœrek come to him,
and for that winter he tarried with Thorgils
Arison.   But he was ill content there, and bade
Thorgils let bring him to Gudmund ; and he says
that he deemed he had heard that at Gudmund's
there was the greatest stateliness in Iceland, and
to him he had been sent.   Thorgils did as he
bade, and got men to bring him to Gudmund of
Madderwalls.   Gudmund gave Rœrek a good
welcome for the sake of the king's message, and
he was with Gudmund another winter.   Thereafter he was ill content there; so Gudmund got
him an abiding-place at a little stead hight Calf-
skin, where were but few serving-folk, and there
Rœrek dwelt the third winter ; and he would say
that, since the time he had left kingship, there
was the place was most to his mind, for there he
was held of all of the most worship.   But the
next summer Rœrek got the illness which brought
him to his bane.   So it is said, he is the only king

that rests in Iceland. Thorarin, son of Nefiolf, long sithence held him a-seafaring, but was whiles with King Olaf.

CHAPTER LXXXVII. BATTLE IN ULF-REKSFIRTH.

THE same summer that Thorarin fared with Rœrek to Iceland, Hialti Skeggi-son went out to Iceland, and at their parting King Olaf saw him off with friendly gifts. That same summer Eyvind Urochs-horn went into the West viking, and came in the autumn to Ireland to Konofogor the Erse-king. In the autumn the King of the Irish and Einar, the Earl of Orkney, met in Ulfreksfirth, and there was a great battle. King Konofogor had by far the bigger host, and got the victory ; but Earl Einar fled in one ship, and came back in autumn to Orkney in such a plight that he had lost well-nigh all his host and all the plunder that they had gotten afore ; and exceeding ill content was the earl with his journey, and laid his defeat on the Northmen who had been in the battle with the Irish king.

CHAPTER LXXXVIII. KING OLAF ARRAYETH HIS BRIDE-FARE.

NOW the story is to be taken up where afore it was turned from, that King Olaf the Thick fared his bridal journey to seek his betrothed, Ingigerd, the daughter of

Olaf the Swede-king. The king had a great company with him, and so picked it was, that in his following were all the great men he could get hold of; and every one of the mightier men had with him a chosen band, both as to kindred, and withal the goodliest that might be. Arrayed was the host with the best of goods, both of ships, and weapons, and raiment. The host held east to King's Rock. But when they came there, they got no news of the Swede-king, nor were any folk come there on his behalf. King Olaf tarried for a long while that summer at King's Rock, and set him much to asking, what men had to tell him of the goings of the Swede-king, and the mind of him; but no one knew aught for certain to tell him thereof. Then he sent his men up into Gautland to Earl Rognvald, to ask of him if he knew what might have brought it about that the Swede-king came not to the meeting according to what had been settled afore. The earl said he knew it not: "but if I get to know it," says he, "then shall I send my men to King Olaf, and let him know what is amiss; whether this delay is from any other sake than from the much business which oft brings about delay of the journeys of the Swede-king beyond what he himself may reckon."

CHAPTER LXXXIX. OF THE CHIL-DREN OF OLAF THE SWEDE-KING.

OLAF the Swede-king had first a con-cubine hight Edla, daughter of an earl in Wendland; she had been taken cap-tive, and therefore was she called the king's bond-maiden. Their children were Emund, Astrid, Holmfrid. Again he begat on his queen a son, who was born on the wake-day of James, and when the boy was to be baptized, the bishop gave him the name of James. This name the Swedes liked ill, and they cried out that never a Swede-king had hight James. All King Olaf's children were goodly to look upon, and well furnished with wits. The queen was masterful of mood, and not kind to her step-children. The king sent Emund, his son, to Wendland, where he was brought up among his mother's kindred; nor did he keep to Christ's faith for a long while. Astrid, the king's daughter, was brought up in West Gautland at a noble lord's, who hight Egill; she was the fairest of women and the most deftly spoken, glad of talk and humble-minded, and open-handed withal. But when she was of ripe age she would often be with her father, and was well looked to of every man.

King Olaf was of masterful mind, and unmild of speech. It liked him exceeding ill that the folk of the land had made throng on him at the Upsala Thing and threatened him mishandling, and that he laid chiefly on Earl Rognvald. No bridal journey did he cause to be arrayed according to what had been settled the winter before, to wit, that he should give his daughter Ingigerd to Olaf the Thick, King of Norway, and fare this tide of summer to the marches of the lands.

Now as the summer wore, many folk grew right wistful to know what mind the king might have, or whether he would keep his covenant with the King of Norway or was minded to tear up the settlement and the peace withal. Many were mind-sick hereover; but none was so bold as to question him concerning it by word of mouth, though many bewailed hereof to Ingigerd, the king's daughter, and bade her get to wot what the king would. She answers: "Unwilling am I to have converse with the king, and talk with him on his dealings with Olaf the Thick, for therein neither is the other's friend; and one time he answered me ill, when I put forth the cause of Olaf the Thick." For Ingigerd, the king's daughter, this matter gat much forthinking, and she was sick at heart and unmerry; and full wistful she was as to what the king would take up. But she misdoubted rather that he would not keep his word to the King of Norway, for that was found of him, that ever he grew wroth when Olaf the Thick was called a king.

CHAPTER XC. OF THE SWEDE-KING'S HUNTING-CATCH.

BEFELL it early on a day that the king rode abroad with his hawks and hounds, and his men with him. But when they flew the hawks, the king's hawk slew in one swoop two heath-cocks; and forthwith he made another swoop, and then slew three heath-cocks. The hounds ran beneath it so as to catch up every fowl that fell to earth. The king gallopped after them, and took his own catch to him, and boasted much thereof, saying: "Long will ye have to wait, most of you, before ye make such a catch." They said that true it was, and that they were minded to think that no king would bear about such good luck in hunting. Thereupon the king rode home, and all they together, and was in a right merry mood. Ingigerd, the king's daughter, was as then coming out of her chamber, as it happed, and when she saw the king come riding into the court, she turned round his way, and greeted him. He greeted her, and laughed, and straightway he held forth the fowl to her, and tells her of his hunting, and said: "Where knowest thou of a king who hath got so mickle a catch in so little while?" She answers: "A good morning's catch is this, lord, that ye have gotten five heath-cocks; but greater was that when Olaf, Norway's king, in one morning caught five kings, and took to him all their dominions."

Now when he heard this, he leapt from his horse, and turned about, and said: "Know this, Ingigerd, that for all the great love thou hast bestowed on that Thick Man, thou shalt never enjoy him, nor either of you the other. For I shall wed thee to such a lord as I shall deign to have friendship withal; but never can I be friends with a man who has taken my realm as war-gettings, and done to me manifold harm in robberies and manslayings. Therewith they sundered, and went each their own way.

CHAPTER XCI. INGIGERD'S MESSAGE TO EARL ROGNVALD.

NOW Ingigerd, the king's daughter, had come to know all the truth about the mind of King Olaf, and sent forthwith men down to West Gautland to Rognvald the earl, and let tell him the news of the Swede-king, that all the covenant with the King of Norway was broken; and bade the earl and other West Gautlanders to beware, for peace at the hands of the men of Norway would now be unsure. And when the earl heard these tidings, he sends word throughout all his dominion, bidding the people beware, lest the men of Norway should be minded to make war on them. The earl also sent messengers to King Olaf the Thick, and let tell him the words he had heard, and this withal, that he will have peace and friendship with King Olaf; and he prayed this thereto that the king should forbear harrying his dominion. Now when this message came to King Olaf he was very wroth and sick at heart, and it was for some days, that no man gat a word of him.

Thereafter he held a House-thing with his host; and first of all stood up Biorn the Marshal, and first began his speech, how he had fared east for peace-making in the winter; he says how Earl Rognvald had given him a goodly welcome, and how thwartly and heavily the Swede-

king had taken these matters at first. " But the
covenant that was made," he said, " was brought
about rather by the might of the many, and
through the power of Thorgnyr and the avail of
Earl Rognvald, than by the goodwill of the
Swede-king; for this cause we deem that we wot
that it is the king who has brought it about that
the covenant is broken, and that it is not to be laid
on the earl soothly, for we found him to be a true
friend of King Olaf." Now the king will know of
his captains and other folk, what rede he shall
take, whether he shall go up into Gautland and
harry there " with such host as we now have, or
whether it seem good to you to take up another
rede." He spake long and deftly. Thereupon
many of the great men had their say, and it came
much to one point at last, that all letted war. And
thus said they : " Though we have a great host,
yet here are gathered together mighty men and
noble; but for warfare are no less meet young men
who deem it good to gain for them wealth and
honours. Moreover, it is the manner of mighty
men, if they fare into war or battle, that they have
with them many men to go before them and to
shield them ; but oft it happens that men of little
wealth fight no worse than those who are brought
up wealthy."

Now from their talk hereover the king made up
his mind to break up the muster, and he gave each
one leave to fare back home; but he gave it out
that next summer he should have out the folk
from all the land, and go meet the Swede-king
and avenge him of this fickleness. This was well

liking to all. So King Olaf went again north into the Wick, and in the autumn took up his seat in Burg, and let draw thither all goods that he needed for his winter-quarters; and there he sat with a great throng through the winter.

CHAPTER XCII.   SKALD SIGVAT'S JOURNEY TO THE EAST.

FOLK spake very diversely about Earl Rognvald. Some would have it that he was a true friend of King Olaf, while to some that seemed untrustworthy, for they said he might well have prevailed with the Swede-king that he should hold the word and covenant betwixt him and King Olaf the Thick.

Now Sigvat the Skald was a great friend of Earl Rognvald in all he said about him, and on that matter he would often be talking before King Olaf. He offered the king to go to see Earl Rognvald, and to spy what he might learn about the Swede-king, and to try if he might bring about peace in any way. This the king liked well, for he deemed it good to talk oft concerning Ingigerd, the king's daughter, to his trusty men. Early in the winter Skald Sigvat, he and his, three together, fared from Burg east over the Marklands, and so to Gautland. But before they parted, King Olaf and Sigvat, he sang this stave:

> Now sit thou hail, King Olaf,
> Until again we twain meet
> And have our talk together,
> And I come thine hall to look on.

The skald meanwhile thus prayeth,
That the stem of the drift of war-helm
Hold life, and withal the land here.
Life to thy fame! Thus end I.

O king, the words are spoken
Which most of every matter
To us were heedful; nathless
Of more things have we cunning.
Heart-hardy king, may God now
Do thee to keep thy land whole,
For thou wert born thereunto.
This do I will full surely.

Then they went east to Eid and gat an ill ferry
over the river, an oak dug-out to wit, and came
hardly over the water. Sigvat sang a ditty:

Wet let I drag the crank tub
To Eid, and feared I sorely
The coming-back; so drave we
Toward folly in that shipping.
May the howes'-host take the fool-ship;
Ne'er saw I worser. Let I
Risk all on yonder sea-ram;
All was better than I looked for.

Thereafter they went through Eid-wood, and
Sigvat sang a stave:

Nought longed I for the running
Twelve miles and one through wild-wood
From Eid; and well man wotteth
That hurts enow I had there.
Yet thither, as meseemeth,
I went that day full keenly,
Though on both feet of the king's men
In flakes the sores were falling.

Thereupon they went through Gautland, and
came at eve of a day to the stead hight Hof; the

door was fast and they might not get in ; the
serving-man said that there was it hallowed, and
so they turned away thence.   Sigvat sang :

> For Hof I made unslothful.
> The door was locked, I louted,
> And thrust in nose, and speered I
> Of matters from without-ward.
> Few words gat I of folk there ;
> The heathen lads thence thrust me,
> For holy-tide they called it,
> And I bade the trolls to take them.

Then he came to another stead, where the
housewife stood in the door, and bade him not
come inside there, for Elf-worship was toward.
Sigvat sang :

> "O wretch," cried out the woman,
> "No further in, for I fear me
> To win the wrath of Odin ;
> Here be we heathen people."
> The hideous hag, O folk-friend,
> Me as a wolf drave outward.
> She said that now Elf-offering
> Was toward within her homestead.

Next evening he came to three bonders, each
of whom hight Olver, and they all drove him out.
Sigvat sang :

> Now drave me out three name-sakes :
> Those fir-trees of the hone-bed,
> Who turned their head-backs on me,
> Honour themselves in nowise.
> But this I fear that henceforth
> Each loader of the sea-skate
> Who hath the name of Olver
> Will most of all drive guests out.

So they fared on still that same evening, and happened on a fourth bonder, who was accounted of as the best thane of them all. But out he drave Sigvat also, and Sigvat sang :

> Then fared I next to find him,
> That breaker of waves'-glitter,
> Whom all the folk were calling
> The friendliest; peace I hoped there.
> He the hoe's-heeder surly
> Heeded me little : bad then
> Is worst, if this the best is.
> The folks' blame here I bear forth.
>
> Of kindly quarters lacked I
> On the way to the east of Eid-wood,
> When I asked the churl unchristened
> To give me nought but guesting.
> The son of mighty Saxi
> Nought found I : in one evening
> Four times they bade me outward;
> Nought fair abode within there.

But when they came to Earl Rognvald, the earl says that they had had a toilsome journey. Sigvat sang :

> The sent-men of the chieftain
> Of the Sogn-folk, they who sought forth
> Their ways with the kings' own errands,
> On hand had mickle faring.
> Great outfit need men ganging,
> But few of things were grudged us.
> The worthy Norway's warder
> So ruled, when he went northward.
>
> Hard going 'twas through Eidshaw
> For the men on the East-ways wending
> To the thruster down of king-folk.
> The king's praise make I greater.

Nought due was my out-thrusting
By the Earl's groves of the fire-flame
Of the field of the deer of rollers,
Ere I gat me to my good lord.

Earl Rognvald gave Sigvat a golden ring. One
of the women said he had come his ways to some
purpose with those dark eyes of his.　Sigvat
sang :

Yea, these swart eyes of Iceland,
O woman, surely showed us
The steep way wending longsome
Unto the ring, the bright one.
Mead-Nanna ! this my foot here
Full bravely hath been ganging
Over the ways of old time,
Whereof thy man nought knoweth.

Sigvat the Skald was in good cheer with the
earl for a long while.　Then he learnt this from
writ-sendings of Ingigerd, the king's daughter, that
messengers from King Jarisleif from Holmgarth
in the Eastlands had come to Olaf the Swede-king
to woo Ingigerd his daughter on behoof of King
Jarisleif, and this moreover, that King Olaf took
it up as a matter most likely.　Therewithal came
to the court of the earl, Astrid, the daughter of
King Olaf, and thereon a great banquet was
arrayed.　Now Sigvat soon got to know the
king's daughter to talk to, and she called to mind
who he was and of what kin, whereas Ottar the
Skald, the sister's son of Sigvat, had been for a
long while in good liking with Olaf the Swede-
king.　Now many things were talked over, and
Earl Rognvald asked Sigvat if Olaf, Norway's
king, would have Astrid, the king's daughter, to

wife: "And if he has a will thereto," says he, "then I ween we shall not ask the King of Sweden about that wooing."

Astrid, the king's daughter, said the same thing.

Thereafter Sigvat and his turned back home, and came a little before Yule to Burg, and met King Olaf. But when Sigvat came home to King Olaf, and went into the hall and looked on the walls thereof, then he sang:

> Here courtmen, they that fatten
> The wound-swan, dight the king's hall
> With helms and byrnies: see I
> On the walls good choice of either;
> For no young one of the king-folk
> May boast of house-gear braver:
> That is a thing past doubting.
> Dear is the hall in all wise.

Then he told the tale of his journeys and sang these staves:

> I bid the guards high-hearted
> Of the eager king, to hearken
> How brisk I bore my travel;
> These staves I made on the faring.
> Sent was I in the harvest
> Up from the skates of swan-mead
> To fare far east to Sweden.
> Sithence slept I but little.

But when he got to talk to the king, he sang:

> Olaf the king! uprightly
> I let hold word betwixt us,
> Whenas I came and met there
> The famed and mighty Rognvald.
> I learnt of many a matter
> Of the good gold-ward in Garthrealm,
> And never courtman heard I
> More clear in dealing speech-word.

O drowner of the Rhine-sun,
The earls'-kin prayed thee ever
Hold well each of his house-carles,
Whoe'er should get him hither.
But, Listi's lord, whoever
Of thine shall go see thither—
This shall be e'en as surely—
Hath safe hold under Rognvald.

King, when from out the west land
I came, most folk were deeming
That Eric's kin already
Had whet these wiles against them.
But the brother's help (I say it)
Of the Wolf's kin hath nathless
Propped thee, to gain the earls' land
That erst from Svein thou tookest.

"Wise Wolf, let take betwixt you,
Ye twain, the deed of peace-word."
Such answer there we gat us;
Both ye, lay down your guilts now!
The minisher of thief-kin,
Rognvald, said unto thee, king,
'Twas given nought to wreak thee
For the bond of peace late riven.

Soon telleth Sigvat to the king the tidings whereof he had heard; at first the king was all unmerry, when Sigvat told him of the wooing of King Jarisleif, saying that for nought but evil might he look from the Swede-king: "But one day we may get the luck to pay him with some remindings."

But as time past away, the king asked Sigvat for many tidings from the east of Gautland. Sigvat told him much about the fairness and sweet-speech of Astrid, the king's daughter, and therewith that every man there said she was in no way worse than Ingigerd her sister. The king took that well into his ears ; and Sigvat told him all the converse they had holden betwixt them, he and Astrid ; and the king found that right good, and said : " The Swede-king will not think that I shall dare wed his daughter without his will." But this matter was not given out to any more folk. But King Olaf and Sigvat the Skald spoke often about it. The king asked Sigvat heedfully, what he had found out about Earl Rognvald : " What like friend he be of ours ? " said he. Sigvat said the earl was the greatest friend of King Olaf, and sang withal :

> O mighty king, thy friendship
> Hold fast with mighty Rognvald,
> A friend in need he standeth
> Both night and day before thee.
> O Thing's crafts-master, wot I
> That in him still thou ownest
> The best friend of all East-ways,
> All downlong the green salt-sea.

CHAPTER XCIII. CONCERNING THE JOURNEY OF EARL ROGNVALD AND ASTRID TO THE KING.

AFTER Yule, they two, Thord Skotakoll, a sister's son of Sigvat the Skald, and another foot-swain of Sigvat, went secretly from the court, and went east to Gautland, whither they had fared in company with Sigvat the harvest-tide before. But when they came to the court of Earl Rognvald, they brought forth tokens before the earl such as Sigvat and the earl had

done between them at parting; withal they brought
the earl the tokens which King Olaf himself had
sent the earl in trust.   Forthwith the earl maketh
ready at once for faring, and with him Astrid, the
king's daughter, having with them nigh an hundred
of men, a picked company, both of the body-guard
and of sons of mighty bonders, with all array of the
choicest, both weapons and raiment and horses.
So they rode north into Norway unto Sarpsburg,
whereto they came at Candlemas.

CHAPTER XCIV.   THE WEDDING OF KING OLAF.

KING OLAF had caused all things to
be made ready there; there was all kinds
of drink, the best that might be gotten,
and all other goods there were of the best.   He
had also summoned to him, from the countrysides
around, many great men.   And when the earl with
his company came there the king welcomed him
wondrous well, and big and good chambers were
gotten for the earl, dight most stately; serving-men
withal were appointed to him, and therewith they who
should look to it that nought should be lacking
whereby the feast might be glorified.   But when
this banquet had stood for certain days, the king
and the earl and the king's daughter met at a
parley, and the upshot of their talk was this, that
they settled that Earl Rognvald should betroth
Astrid, the daughter of Olaf the Swede-king, to
Olaf, Norway's king, with the same dowry which
afore had been covenanted that Ingigerd, her

sister, should take with her from home.   The king
withal was to give to Astrid such a jointure as he
was to have settled on Ingigerd her sister.   Then was
the banquet eked, and the bridal of King Olaf and
Queen Astrid was drunk with mickle glory.   After
this Earl Rognvald went back to Gautland, and at
parting the king bestowed good gifts and great upon
the earl, and in the dearest friendship they parted,
and to that they held as long as they lived.

CHAPTER XCV. PEACE WITH NOR-WAY'S KING SUNDERED.

THE next spring there came to Sweden
messengers from King Jarisleif east away
from Holmgarth, and they fared to see
to the matter of King Olaf's promise from the
past summer to give Ingigerd his daughter to King
Jarisleif.   King Olaf put the matter before Ingigerd,
and said it was his will that she should wed King
Jarisleif; she answers : "If I am to be wedded to
King Jarisleif, then," she says, " will I have for my
jointure Aldeigia-burg   and   the   earldom   that
thereto appertaineth."   But the Garthrealm messengers yeasaid this on behalf of their king.   Then
spoke Ingigerd : " If I am to go east into Garthrealm, then will I choose that man out of the realm
of Sweden to go with me whom I deem most meet
thereto ; and I also claim that east there he have a
title nowise lesser than here, and a right and
honours in no way worser or lesser than here he
has."   This the king yeasaid and the messengers
in like wise ; and the king plighted his troth,

and the messengers withal, to this matter. Then the king asked Ingigerd who the man was within his realm whom she is minded to choose for her following. She answers: "That man is Rognvald the earl, son of Wolf, my kinsman." The king answers: "Otherwise I have made up my mind to reward Earl Rognvald for the betrayal of his lord, in that he took my daughter to Norway and handed her over for a whore to the Thick Man, and whereas he knew, moreover, that he was our greatest unfriend; for that deed he shall hang aloft this summer." Ingigerd bade her father keep to the faith he had handselled her. And by reason of her praying, the matter came to this, that the king says, that Rognvald shall go in peace out of Sweden, but not come before his eyes, nor back to Sweden while Olaf was king. So Ingigerd sent men to meet the earl and to tell him these tidings, and appointed time and place with him where they should meet. So the earl made ready forthwith for his journey, and rode up into East Gautland, where he got him ship, and so went on with his company to the meeting with Ingigerd, the king's daughter; and in the summer they went all together east into Garthrealm, and Ingigerd was then wedded to King Jarisleif. Their sons were Valdimar, Vissivald, Holti the Nimble. Queen Ingigerd gave to Earl Rognvald Aldeigia-burg and the earldom thereunto appertaining, and a long while Earl Rognvald was there and was a renowned man. The sons of Earl Rognvald and Ingibiorg were the Earl Wolf and the Earl Eilif.

CHAPTER XCVI. THE STORY OF EMUND THE LAWMAN.

THERE was a man named Emund of Skarar; he was Lawman there in West Gautland, wisest of men, and the most deft of speech. He was of great kin, had many kindred, and was exceeding wealthy. He was called a man of underhand dealings, and but middling trusty. He was the mightiest man in West Gautland, now when the earl was gone away. The same spring that Earl Rognvald went away from Gautland, the Gautland folk had a Thing between them, and murmured oft amongst themselves as to what the Swede-king would take up. They heard that he was wroth with them for having become friends with Norway's king rather than to uphold the strife with him. He also laid guilt on the men who had followed Astrid, his daughter, to Norway. So some urged that they should seek for avail at the hands of Norway's king, and offer him their service. But some letted this, and said that the West Gautlanders had no strength to uphold strife with the Swedes. " Norway's king will be afar from us," said they, " for the main of his land is far away from us ; and so the first thing to look to is to send men to the Swede-king, and try to bring ourselves into peace with him. But if that is not to be brought about, then there is the choice before us to seek for aid of Norway's king." So the bonders bade Emund fare on this message, and he said yea thereto, and went with thirty men, and came forth into East

Gautland ; there were many of his kinsmen and friends, and he gàt good welcome there. Here he talked this troublous matter over with the wisest men, and they deemed it contrary to custom and law, what the king was doing to them. So Emund went up into Swede-realm, and had there talk with many men of might, and there everything came to one and the same point.

He held on his journey till such time as he came on eve of a day to Upsala ; there they got good quarters for them, and rested the night over. But the next day Emund went to see the king as he sat in his law-court, and a throng of folk with him. Emund went up before the king, and bowed to him, and greeted him. The king looked up at him, and greeted him, and asked him of tidings. Emund answered : "Small are the tidings àmongst us Gautlanders ; but news we deem it, that Atti the Fool, of Vermland went last winter up into the Mark with his snowshoes and bow ; in our esteem he is the greatest of hunters. He had gotten on the mountain so many furs, that he had filled his sleigh with as much as he could bring after him. Then he turned homeward from the Mark, but in the wood he saw a squirrel, and shot at it, and missed it ; then was he wroth, and let loose the sleigh, and ran after the squirrel ; but the squirrel would ever keep there whereas the wood was thickest, whiles running by the roots, whiles up into the limbs ; then would he sail between the limbs into another tree. But whenever Atti shot at him, the arrow flew ever above or below him, but never went the squirrel where Atti did not see him. Now he got so eager for this prey, that he crept after it all day long, but none the more might he catch that squirrel. But when mirk night fell, he threw himself down on the snow as he was wont, and lay there the night through, but the weather was drifty. The next day Atti went to look for his sleigh, but never found it after, and in this plight fared home. These are my tidings, lord."

The king said: " Little enough tidings these, if there be nought more to tell."

Emund answers: "Well, a short time agone there happened another matter which well may be called news, in that Gauti, son of Tovi, went with five warships down the Elf; and as he lay amidst the Oak-isles, there came the Danes with five large cheaping-ships. Then Gauti and his folk swiftly overcame four of the ships, losing not a man, and gaining measureless wealth. However, the fifth ship got away into the main, and gat under sail. But Gauti went after them with one ship, and at first drew in upon them, but then the wind fell to wax, so that there was greater way on the cheaping-ship, and they gat them into the main. Now would Gauti turn back, but the weather grew to a storm, and he wrecked his ship on Les-isle, and all the goods were lost and the greater part of the men. Now he had bidden his company await him at the Oak-isles, but anon came the Danes upon them there with fifteen cheaping-ships, and slew them all, and took all the wealth they had gotten afore. Thus by greed had they speed."

The king answered : "These be great tidings, and taleworthy. But what is thine errand hither?" Answers Emund : "I am about this, lord, to get unravelled those knotty points wherein our laws and Upsala laws are diverse."

Asks the king : "What is it whereof thou wilt bewail thee ?"

Emund answers : "There were two men, of noble birth, equal of kindred, but unequal of wealth and temper ; they strove concerning lands, and each wrought scathe to the other, but he the more who was the mightier, until their strife was ended and doomed at an All-folk's Thing. Then had he to pay who was erst the mightier ; and for the first handsel he yielded a gosling for a goose, a sucking-pig for an old swine, and for a mark of burnt gold he delivered half a mark of gold and another half-mark of clay and rubble, and threatened him, to boot, with hard dealings, who had to take this payment of his debt. What doom ye hereon, lord ?"

The king answered : "Let him yield to the full what was awarded, and to his king the amount thrice over. And if it be not yolden at the term appointed, he shall fare away and be outlaw of all that is his own ; and let one half of his wealth fall to the king's garth, and the other to him whose wrong he had to boot."

Emund took witness to this award of all those who were the mightiest there, and laid it to the laws that prevailed at the Upsala Thing.

Thereupon he saluted the king, and went out thereafter. Thereupon other men set forth their plaints before the king, and for a long time that day he sat over the affairs of men.

Now, when the king came to table, he asked where Lawman Emund was, and was told he sat at home in his quarters. Said the king: "Go fetch him; he shall be my bidden guest to-day." Now came in the courses, and thereafter fared in the players with harps, and gigs, and song-tools, and then the skinkers of the drink. The king was exceeding merry; he had many mighty men at his guest-bidding, and gave no heed to Emund. All that day the king drank, and slept through the night; but on the morrow, when he awoke, he called to mind what Emund had spoken the day before. And when he was clad, he had his wise men called in to him.

King Olaf had always with him twelve men of the wisest, who sat over the dooms with him, and gave counsel in knotty matters; but that was nought without trouble, for the king misliked greatly if dooms were thrust away from right, and it would nowise do to gainsay him.

Now at this parley the king took up the word, and bade Lawman Emund be called in thither. But when the messenger came back, "Lord," said he, "Lawman Emund rode off yesterday, as soon as he had had his meal." Then said the king: "Tell me this, good lords, what way pointed that question at law that Emund asked yesterday?"

They answered: "Lord, thou must have taken that to heart, if it pointed to aught else than what he spake."

The king said: "Those two nobly-born men, of

whom he then told the tale, that they had been at unpeace with each other, whereof one was the mightier, and yet each did scathe to the other, therein he told a tale of us two, me, and Olaf the Thick." "So it is, lord," said they, "even as thou sayest." Answereth the king: "The doom in our case was adjudged at the Upsala Thing. But what did it point to, when he said that so ill paid it was, that a gosling was given for a goose, a sucking-pig for an old swine, and half clay for all gold?"

Arnwith the Blind answers: "Lord," says he, "most unlike to each other are red gold and clay, but yet further sundered is king from thrall. Thou didst promise to Olaf the Thick thy daughter Ingigerd, who is king-born in all branches from the race of the Up-Swedes, the noblest stock in the North-lands, inasmuch as all that kindred hath come down from the gods themselves. But now King Olaf hath gotten for wife Astrid, who, though she be a king's child, hath for mother a bondwoman, and her a Wendish one withal. Wide apart are those kings, forsooth, one of whom taketh such a matter with thanks; yea, a thing it is to be looked for, that a mere Norwegian should not hold himself equal to the King of Upsala. Let us all give thanks that so it may endure, for the gods have for a long time recked mickle of their offspring, though now many folk be reckless of that faith."

There were three brothers of them: Arnwith the Blind; his eyesight was so little, that he was scarce war-worthy, though he was the nimblest-minded of men; the second was Thorwith the Stammerer,

who might not get out two words one after the
other, but he was the boldest man there, and the
most freespoken; the third was Freywith the
Deaf, who was hard of hearing. All these brothers
were men of might, wealthy, of high kin, and
exceeding wise, and all in good liking of the king.

Then spake King Olaf: "What does it point
to, that which Emund said about Atti the Fool?"
Then answered none, but all looked on each
other. The king said: "Speak up now!" Then
said Thorwith the Stammerer: "Atti, griping,
greedy, ill-willed, doltish, foolish." Spake the
king: "At whom is this thrust?" Answered Freywith the Deaf: "Lord, men will be barer spoken
if they have thy leave thereto." The king said:
"Tell now, Freywith, by my leave, whatever thou
willest speak." Then Freywith took up the word:
"Thorwith, my brother, who is called the wisest
of us, calls such an one as Atti griping, doltish, and
foolish; thereby calleth he him so, who is loth
to peace, so that he striveth after small things, yet
reacheth them not, and for this sake forfeiteth
things profitable and great. Now 'tis true that I
am deaf, but so many have now spoken out, that
I have gotten to wot that men like it ill, mighty
men no less than the commonalty, that thou,
lord, dost not keep word with Norway's king. But
this yet worse, that thou breakest the All-folk-
doom, which was done at the Thing of Upsala. Thou
needest nought fear Norway's king, nor the
Dane-king, or never another, while the Swede-
host will follow thee; but if the folk of the land
turn against thee with one accord, then we,

thy friends, see no rede which shall verily avail
thee."

The king asketh : "Who will be made head-
men herein to bewray me of my lands ? "

Answered Freywith : " All Swedes will have
their ancient laws and their full right. Look ye now
to this, lord, how many of your chiefs are sitting
here together in counsel with you. I am minded to
think that it be sooth to say, that now are we six here
together, whom ye call your counsellors, but all the
others, methinketh, have ridden away and gone
into the countrysides, there to have Things with
the folk ; and sooth it is to tell thee, that the war-
arrow has been shorn up and sent all over the
land for the summoning of a Thing of Escheat.
All we brethren have been bidden to have part
in this rede, but none of us will have the name to be
called Lord-betrayer ; for nought such was ever
our father."

Then the king took up the word, saying :
"What rede shall we now take to ? Mickle
trouble is now borne in at our hands ; now therefore, good lords, give me such counsel as that
thereby I may hold to the kingdom and to the
heritage of my forefathers ; for I am not minded to
deal in strife with the whole host of the Swedes."
Arnwith the Blind answered : " Lord, meseemeth
rede, that thou ride down to Riveroyce with such
company as will follow thee, and take ship there,
and so fare out into the Low, and then summon
the folk to thee. Fare stubbornly no more, but bid
men law and lands-right, and thus get the war-
arrow dropped ; as yet it will not have fared wide

over the land, for the time hath been short thereto ; send thou such men of thine as thou trustest in to see the men who have this rede on hand, and try if this murmur may be laid."

The king saith he will take that rede. "And my will is," says he, "that ye brothers fare this errand for me, for I trust you best of all my men."

Then said Thorwith the Stammerer : "I shall abide behind : let James go ; this needeth."

Then said Freywith : "Do we, lord, even as Thorwith says ; he will not sunder him from thee in this peril ; but I and Arnwith shall fare."

Now this counsel was carried out, that King Olaf went to his ships and held into the Low ; and speedily a multitude of folk gathered to him. But those brothers, Freywith and Arnwith, rode out to Ullers-acre, and had with them James, the king's son, though they kept his journey privy. They were speedily ware that there was before them a gathering and running to arms, whereas the bonders were holding Thing day and night. And whenas Freywith and his brother came there upon many kinsmen and friends, they said they would betake them to that flock, and thereof they all were full fain. Forthwith all counsels were made over to those brothers, and the throng drew to them. Now men spake, all of them, one and the same thing, saying that they would have Olaf for king over them no longer, and would not suffer at his hands his lawlessness and insolence ; whereas he would listen to no man's word, nay, not even though mighty lords should tell him the very truth.

Now when Freywith found the eagerness of
people, he saw into what hopeless plight things
were gotten. So he had meetings with the great
men of the land, and set forth the matter before
them and spoke thus : " Meseemeth, if this great
business shall come to pass, to wit, to take Olaf
Ericson from his realm, we, the Up-Swedes, shall
have to be at the head of it ; for so it hath alway
been, that whatsoever the Up-Swede lords have
made fast between them, that same counsel hath
hearkened the other folk of the land. Never
needed our forefathers to beg the West-Gauts for
counsel of the land-steering. Now we shall not
be such outcasts among our kindred that Emund
must needs learn us rede. And I will that we
bind us rede together, we kinsmen and friends."

This they all yeasaid, and deemed it well
spoken. Thereafter all the throng of folk joined
the bond that the Up-Swede lords made among
them, and now Freywith and Arnwith were chiefs
over the company. But when Emund saw this,
he misdoubted him if this rede would be carried
through. So he went to meet those brothers, and
they had talk together, and Freywith asked
Emund : " What mind have ye hereover, if Olaf
Ericson be bereft of life, to wit, what king ye will
have to you ? "

Emund answered : " Him who we deem the
fittest thereto, no matter whether he be of a high
degree or not."

Freywith answered : " We Up-Swedes will nowise have it that in our days the kingship should
sunder from the lineage of the ancient kings while

there is so good avail thereto as now is. King Olaf hath two sons, and one or the other we will have for king ; yet wide is the sundering betwixt them, whereas one is wedlock-born and a Swede of either kin, the other a son of a bondwoman and half a Wend."

At this word there was great cheering, and all would have James for king.

Then said Emund : " As for this time ye Up-Swedes have the might to rule the matter. But this I tell you, as will come to pass hereafter, that some of those who now will listen to nought but that the kingdom in Sweden go in the ancient lineage, will themselves live to yeasay the kingdom passing into other kindred which certes will better avail."

Thereafter the brothers Freywith and Arnwith let lead forth James, the king's son, there at the Thing, and let give him the king's name ; and therewithal the Swedes gave him the name of Onund, and thereby was he called ever afterwards as long as he lived. At this time was he ten or twelve years old.

Thereafter King Onund took him a body-guard and chose him his captains, and they all together had as large a company as he deemed needful. But he gave leave to all the throng of the bonders to go home.

After this messengers went about between the kings, and presently it came about that they met, themselves, and made peace together : Olaf should be king over the land as long as he lived ; he was to hold peace and friendship with the King of Norway, and with all those men who had woven themselves into that matter between them. But Onund was to be king also, and to have of the land as much as father and son should agree upon ; but he should be bound to back up the bonders if King Olaf should do aught which they would not endure of him.

CHAPTER XCVII.   PEACE-MEETING OF THE KINGS; AND THE CASTING OF THE DICE.

HEREAFTER messengers went to Norway to meet King Olaf with the message that he should come to King's Rock to meet the Swede-king, whereto was added that it was the will of the Swede-king that they make pledge of peace together. But when King Olaf heard this message, he was, as ever, willing for peace, and so went with his company according as had been afore-settled.   Now the Swede-king came there, and when they, father- and son-in-law, met, they bind peace and friendship betwixt them ; and now Olaf the Swede-king was good to speak with and meek of mood. So says Thorstein the Learned, that in Hising there was a dwelling that had whiles gone with Norway, whiles with Gautland.   Then the kings spoke between them that they should go to lots for that having, and cast dice thereto ; and he was to have it who cast the strongest. Then the Swede-king threw two sixes, and said that King Olaf had now no need to throw. He answered : " There are still two sixes on the dice, and 'tis but little for the Lord my God to let them turn up." So he cast, and had two sixes uppermost. Then Olaf the Swede-king threw, and still up came two sixes. Then Olaf, Norway's king, threw, and there was six on one, but the other brake asunder, and thereon were seven. Thus he came by that dwelling. No more tidings of that meeting have we heard. But the kings parted in peace.

CHAPTER XCVIII.   OF OLAF, NORWAY'S KING.

AFTER these tidings whereof we have just been telling, King Olaf turned back with his company to the Wick; and first to Tunsberg, and tarried there a little while, and then fared into the North-country, and in harvest all the way north to Thrandheim, where he had all things arrayed for winter-abode; and there he sat the winter through. Then was King Olaf Haraldson sole ruler over all that realm which Harald Hairfair had swayed; with this, moreover, that he was king alone in the land. By peace and covenant he had then gotten him that part of the land which Olaf the Swede-king had had before. But the part of the land which the Dane-king had had he took by force, and ruled over that as otherwhere in the land. Knut the Dane-king ruled at this time both over England and Denmark, and himself sat mostly in England, but set chieftains to rule over Denmark, and he laid no claim to Norway at that time.

CHAPTER XCIX. THE STORY OF THE EARLS OF ORKNEY.

SO is it said, that in the days of Harald Hairfair, King of Norway, the Orkneys were builded. Before that time they were but a viking-lair. Sigurd was the name of the first Earl of Orkney; he was the son of Eystein Glumra, and brother to Rognvald the Mere-Earl. But after Sigurd, Guthorm his son was earl for one winter. After him Turf-Einar took the earldom; he was the son of Earl Rognvald, and was for a long time earl and a mighty man withal. Halfdan High-leg, son of Harald Hairfair, went against Turf-Einar, and drove him away from Orkney, but he came back again and slew Halfdan in Rinansey; whereupon King Harald went with a war-host to Orkney, and Einar fled into Scotland, while Harald let the Orkneyings swear him all their odal lands. But after this king and earl made peace between them, and the earl became the king's man and took the lands in fief of the king, but was to pay no scat, whereas they lay so open to war. The earl paid the king sixty marks of gold. Hereafter King Harald harried into Scotland, as is told of in Glymdrapa.

After Turf-Einar the rule over those lands came to his sons Arnkel, Erlend, and Thorfin Skull-cleaver. In their days came from Norway Eric Bloodaxe, and to him the earls were a-feoffed. Arnkel and Erlend fell in war, but Thorfin ruled the lands and became an old man. His sons were these: Arnfin, Howard, Hlodver, Liot, Skuli.

Their mother was Grelad, daughter of Dungad, Earl of Caithness, but her mother was Groa, the daughter of Thorstein the Red.

In the latter days of Earl Thorfin there came from Norway the sons of Bloodaxe, whenas they had fled out of the land before Earl Hakon; mickle was the tyranny of them all over Orkney. Earl Thorfin died of sickness, and after him his sons ruled over the land, and many be the tales told of them. Hlodver was the longest-lived of them, and ruled alone over the land when the others were no more. His son was Sigurd the Thick, who took the earldom after him, and was a mighty man and a great warrior.

In his days fared Olaf Tryggvison from western viking together with his company, and hove in to Orkney and laid hands on Earl Sigurd in Rognvaldsey, who lay there before him with but one ship. King Olaf offered the earl this ransom of his life, that he should take christening and the right faith, and become his man and bid christening throughout all Orkney. King Olaf took for hostage his son, who hight Hound or Whelp. Thence Olaf went to Norway and became king there. Hound tarried with King Olaf for some winters and died there. But thereafter Earl Sigurd did no service to King Olaf. He went and wedded the daughter of Malcolm, the King of the Scotch, and their son was Thorfin; but besides him there were these older sons of Earl Sigurd: Summerlid, Brusi, Einar Wrongmouth. Five winters or four after the fall of Olaf Tryggvison Earl Sigurd fared to Ireland, but he set his elder sons to the ruling of the lands ; Thorfin he sent to the Scottish king, his mother's father. In that journey Earl Sigurd fell in the Brian battle. But when the news thereof came to Orkney, then were taken to earls those brethren, Summerlid, Brusi, Einar, and they shared the islands into thirds between them. Thorfin Sigurdson was five winters old when Earl Sigurd fell. But when the Scottish king heard the news of his fall, he gave to his kinsman Thorfin Caithness and Sunderland and an earl's name therewithal, and got men to rule over his dominion with him. Earl Thorfin was from his youth up speedily wrought with all pith ; he was mickle and stark ; a man ill-favoured ; and so soon as he waxed in years, it was easily seen of him that he was a grasping man, hard and grim and exceeding wise. So saith Arnor the earls' skald :

> No man beneath the cloud-hall
> Younger than Einar's brother
> Was held more nimble-minded
> To ward land or to war land.

CHAPTER C. OF EARLS EINAR AND BRUSI.

THE brothers, Einar and Brusi, were unlike in mind. Brusi was meek and peaceful, wise, deft of speech, and well-beloved. Einar was stubborn, sullen, and gruff, grasping and griping, and a great warrior. Summerlid was like to Brusi in his ways ; he was the oldest and the shortest-lived of those brethren, and died of sickness. After his death Thorfin laid claim to his share of Orkney. Einar answered that Thorfin held Caithness and Sunderland, that dominion which their father Earl Sigurd had had before, and this he deemed to be much more than a third part of Orkney, and therefore he would not yea-say Thorfin's sharing; but Brusi, for his part, granted the sharing: "for I will not," said he, "hanker after more of the lands than the third which I own of right." Then Einar took under him two-thirds of the islands, and became a mighty man, and had many folk about him; in summer he would oft be a-warring, and had out mickle gatherings from the land, but all uneven were his viking-gettings. Then the bonders began to be weary of this toil, but the earl upheld with exceeding masterfulness all that was laid on them, and let it avail no man to speak thereagainst. Earl Einar was the most overbearing of men. Then befell dearth in his dominion by reason of the toil and money-cost which the bonders were put to; but in that deal of the land which Brusi had was mickle increase and sweet life for the bonders, and well-beloved that earl was.

CHAPTER CI. OF THORKEL, SON OF AMUNDI.

THERE was a man hight Amundi, a mighty man and wealthy, who dwelt in Rossey at Sandwick on Laupandaness. Thorkel was the name of his son, of all men the doughtiest in Orkney. Amundi was the wisest of men, and

one of the best accounted of in the islands.   Now
it befell one spring, when Earl Einar once more
bade out his folk as he was wont, that the bonders
made ill murmur thereat, and laid their case before
Amundi, and bade him speak up for them some
furtherance before the earl.   He answers : " The
earl is all unheedful ; " and he gave it out that it
would be of no avail to bid any boon whatsoever
of the earl in this matter ; "moreover, the friendship between me and the earl is good enough as
matters stand ; but meseemeth things would be at
the point of peril if we should get to wrangling,
looking to the mood of each of us ; so," says
Amundi, " I will have nought to do herein."

Then they spoke about this to Thorkel, but he
was unwilling, though at last, from the egging of
men, he promised.   Amundi deemed he had promised over-hastily.

. Now when the earl held a Thing, then spake
Thorkel on behalf of the bonders, and bade the
earl spare men of those burdens ; and he set forth
the need of men.   The earl answered well, and
said he will pay mickle honour to Thorkel's word :
" I was now minded to have six ships out of the
land, but now will I have no more than three.
But thou, Thorkel, ask such boons never again."
The bonders thanked Thorkel well for his aid.
The earl went on his viking and came back in
harvest.

But the next spring the earl had the same
bidding whereto he was wont, and held a Thing
with the bonders.   Now Thorkel spoke again and
bade the earl spare the bonders.   The earl

answers wrathfully, and says that the lot of the
bonders shall only be the worser for his speaking
up for them.   He made himself so wood-wroth
that he said that next spring they should not both
of them meet hale at the Thing ; and therewith he
broke up the Thing.

Now when Amundi knew for sure what words
Thorkel and the earl had had together, he bade
Thorkel get him gone, and he crossed over on to
Caithness to Earl Thorfin.   Thorkel was there
for a long time thereafter, and loved the earl well,
whereas he was young; and thereafter was he
called Thorkel the Fosterfather, and a fair-famed
man was he.

CHAPTER CII.   THE EARLS MAKE PEACE.

THERE were more mighty men who fled
away from their lands in Orkney before
the overmastery of Earl Einar ; the most
of them fled over to Caithness to Earl Thorfin ;
but othersome fled from Orkney to Norway, and
others again to sundry lands.   But when Earl
Thorfin grew into man's estate, he sent word to his
brother, Einar, and craved of him the dominion
whereto he had a title in Orkney, to wit, one-third
of the islands.   Einar was slow to minish his
realm.   But when Thorfin heard thereof, he bade
out folk from Caithness, and fared out into the
islands.   And when Earl Einar had news thereof,
he gathers an host and is minded to ward his lands.
Earl Brusi also gathers an host and fares to meet

them, and bears between them words of peace. And hereon they made such terms of peace, that Earl Thorfin should have one-third of the islands in Orkney, even as appertained to him by right. But Brusi and Einar joined their lots together into one, over which Einar was to rule alone; but if either should die before the other, then was the longest-lived to take to him the other's lands. But this covenant was deemed not to be fair, whereas Brusi had a son hight Rognvald, but Einar was without sons. So now Earl Thorfin set his men to look after his dominion in Orkney, while he abode mostly in Caithness. Earl Einar was for the most part in summer a-warring about Ireland and Scotland and Bretland.

CHAPTER CIII. THE SLAYING OF EYVIND UROCHS-HORN.

ONE summer, when Earl Einar was warring on Ireland, it befell that he had a fight in Ulfreksfirth with Konofogor, King of the Irish, even as is writ afore, that Earl Einar gat there a mickle overthrow and loss of men.

The next summer Eyvind Urochs-horn went away from the west from Ireland minded for Norway. But inasmuch as the weather was stormy, and the roosts could not be crossed, Eyvind turned to Asmundbay and lay there a while weather-bound. But when Einar the earl heard this, he drew thither with a mickle host, and laid hands there on Eyvind and let slay him, but gave life to most of his men; and they went east to

Norway in the autumn, and came to meet King
Olaf, and told him of the making away of Eyvind.
The king answered few words thereover, but it was
to be found that he deemed this mickle manscathe,
and a deed done sorely in his despite; and few-
spoken he was on most things which he took
greatly to heart.

Earl Thorfin sent Thorkel Fosterfather out into
the isles to gather his dues. Earl Einar wyted
Thorkel much of that uprising of Earl Thorfin to
claim lands out in Orkney. So Thorkel went
speedily away from the isles over to Caithness.
He told Earl Thorfin that he had made sure of this,
that Earl Einar had minded him death, if his kinsmen and friends had not brought him timely news.
" Now shall I," says he, "have the chance before
me, either to let such be the meeting between me
and the earl, that matters come to an end between
us; but the other choice is to fare further away, and
thither whereover his sway be not." The earl
urged that Thorkel should fare east to Norway to
meet King Olaf : "thou wilt be," says he, "much
accounted of wheresoever thou comest among men
of high degree, but I know the temper of you
both, thee and the earl, so well, that ye will
take short aim at each other." So then Thorkel
got ready and went in autumn to Norway, and then
to meet King Olaf, and he tarried there over the
winter in mickle good-liking. The king had Thorkel
much into his counsels, and deemed him, as sooth
was, a wise man, and mickle stirring in affairs. The
king found this in his converse, that he told a very
different tale of the two earls, whereas he was a

much friend to Thorfin, but laid heavy charges at the door of Earl Einar.   So early in the spring the king sent a ship west beyond sea for Earl Thorfin, and with it the word that the earl should come east to meet him.   And that journey the earl did not lay under his head, for friendly words went with the message.

CHAPTER CIV.   THE SLAYING OF EARL EINAR.

EARL THORFIN went east to Norway, and came to see King Olaf, and had a good welcome of him, and tarried there a while that summer.   And when he went back west, King Olaf gave him a long-ship great and good, with all gear.   Thorkel Fosterfather betook himself to the journey with the earl, and the earl gave him the ship he had had from the west that same summer.   The king and the earl parted in mickle good-liking.   Earl Thorfin came to Orkney in the harvest-tide, and when Earl Einar heard thereof, he had out a great company and lay aboard ship.   But Earl Brusi went to meet both those brethren, and to bear words of peace between them, and once again it came to this, that they were appeased and bound the peace with oaths.   Thorkel Fosterfather was to be in peace and friendship with Earl Einar, and it was settled that each should give a feast to the other, and that the earl should first seek to Thorkel's at Sandwick.

But when the earl was there a-feasting the cheer was of the noblest, yet the earl was nowise merry.

A great hall was there with doors at either end. Now the day whereon the earl was to go away Thorkel was to go home with him a-feasting. Thorkel sends forth men a-spying the road whereby they were to fare that day; and when the spies came back, they told Thorkel that they had come upon three waylayings and armed men in each. "And we are minded to think," say they, "that treason is toward." Now when Thorkel heard this he tarried his arrayal, and gathered his men to him. The earl bade him get ready, saying it was high time to ride off. Thorkel said he had many things to give heed to; and whiles he would be going out and whiles he went in. Fires were burning on the floor; and now he came in through one of the doors, and behind him a man called Hallward, an Iceland man, an Eastfirther; he locked the door after them. Thorkel walked up the hall between the fire and the place where the earl was sitting. The earl asked: "Art thou not ready yet?" Thorkel answers: "Now am I ready." And therewith he hewed at the earl and smote his head; and the earl fell on the floor.

Then spake the Iceland man: "Never saw I such drop-handed ones as you, whereas ye drag not the earl out of the fire." Therewith he thrust in a stake under the nape of the neck of the earl and hove him up towards the daïs.

Then Thorkel, he and his fellow, went out swiftly through another door than that whereby they had come in, and there without stood Thorkel's men all-weaponed.

The earl's men took hold of him, and by then

he was dead; but their hands fell down all from avenging him, whereas, moreover, this was done so suddenly, and none looked for such a deed from Thorkel, inasmuch as they all thought that so would things be still, as they had been settled before, to wit, that friendship yet was between the earl and Thorkel; moreover, most of the men within were weaponless, and many of them were already good friends of Thorkel. This also went toward the hap, that to Thorkel was fated a longer life. And now when he came out, he had a company no less than the men of the earl.

Then Thorkel fared to his ship, and the earl's men went their ways. That day Thorkel sailed straight away and east into the main; it was after Winter-nights, and he came safe and sound to Norway, and fared at his swiftest to meet King Olaf, of whom he had a right good welcome. The king was well pleased with this work, and Thorkel tarried with him through the winter.

CHAPTER CV. PEACE BETWEEN KING OLAF AND EARL BRUSI.

AFTER the fall of Earl Einar, Earl Brusi took that deal of the islands which Earl Einar had had afore, for there were many folk witnesses thereto, under what covenant those brothers, Einar and Brusi, had made fellowship. But Thorfin thought it most just that each of them should have half of the islands, yet that winter Brusi had two-thirds thereof. The next spring Thorfin laid claim against Brusi to those lands, saying that he would have one-half with Brusi, but Brusi would not give yeasay hereto. Now they had Things and parleys over this business, and their friends went between to settle the matter, but so it came about, that Thorfin said he would like nought but to have one-half of the islands; and said this, moreover, that Brusi needed to have nought more than one-third, seeing the mind of him. Brusi answers: "I was content," says he, "to have that one-third of the land which I took in heritage after my father, nor did any one lay claim to it at my hands; but now I have taken a second third in heritage after my brother, according to rightful covenant. But though I be unmighty to try masteries with thee, brother, yet will I seek otherwhere than to yeasay my lands from me as yet." And thus they broke off this parley.

But when Brusi saw that he would not have avail to stand on an even footing with Thorfin, whereas Thorfin had much greater might, and trust in the King of Scotland his grandfather, therefore Brusi a-reded him to sail away east and meet King Olaf, and he had with him Rognvald his son, who was then ten winters old. But when the earl met the king, he had good welcome of him. And when the earl put forth his errand and told the king all the matter between him and his brother, and asked the king to give him strength to hold his dominion, and offered in return his full friendship, the king answered and took up his tale there whereas Harald Hairfair had made his own all odal land in the Orkneys;

but the earls had ever since held those lands in fief, but never as their own ; and in token thereof, he says that when Eric Bloodaxe and his sons were in the Orkneys, the earls were his liegemen. "But when Olaf Tryggvison my kinsman came there, Earl Sigurd thy father became his man. Now I have taken all the heritage after King Olaf, and I will give this choice, that thou become my man, and then will I give thee the islands in fief, and we shall thus try, if I give thee my strength, whether that shall be of more avail to thee, or the backing-up of the King of Scotland to Thorfin thy brother. But if thou wilt not take this choice, then shall I go seek those havings, and the odal lands which my kinsmen and forefathers have owned west-away."

These words the earl brought home to his mind, and laid them before his friends, and sought counsel of them as to what he should say yea to, whether he should as the matter stood make peace with King Olaf and become his man. "But the other thing is unseen to me, what my lot shall be at our parting, if I say no thereto, whereas the king has laid bare the claim which he deems him to have to the Orkneys ; but because of his masterfulness, seeing that I have come here, it will be but little for him to deal with my affairs even as it seemeth good to him."

Now although the earl found drawbacks in either case, he took the choice to lay all his case in the hand of the king, himself and his dominion withal. Thus King Olaf took over from the earl power and sway over all the heritage lands of the earl.   So the earl became his man, and bound it with sworn oath.

CHAPTER CVI. PEACE BETWEEN THE EARLS AND KING OLAF.

EARL THORFIN heard that Brusi his brother was gone east to meet King Olaf and to seek avail of him.   But for this reason, that Thorfin had been before to see King Olaf, and had gotten himself into friendship with him, he thought he had there a safe enough place, and he wotted moreover that there would be many furtherers of his case, but more would they be, if he himself came thereto.   So Earl Thorfin took that rede, that he got him ready at his swiftest and went east to Norway, and was minded that betwixt his coming and Brusi's should be as short a space as might be, and that Brusi's errand should not come to an end before Thorfin met the king.   But this came otherwise to pass than the earl was minded, for when Earl Thorfin came to see King Olaf, then was ended and done the covenant between the king and Earl Brusi.   And Earl Thorfin wotted not that Earl Brusi had given up his dominion until he was already come to King Olaf.   Now when they met, Earl Thorfin and King Olaf, then hove up King Olaf the very same claim to the dominion over Orkney which he had set forth to Earl Brusi, and he bade Thorfin the same thing, to wit, that he should will away to the king that deal of the islands which was the earl's already.   The earl gave a good and a quiet answer to the words of the king, and said that he set a right great store by the friendship of the king. "And if thou, lord, deem thyself in need of my aid against other chieftains, thou hast fully earned it already; but it is not handy for me to give thee homage, because I am already an earl of the Scottish king and his liege-man."

But when the king found that the earl hung back in his answers to these claims of his which he had already set forth, then spake the king : "If thou, earl, wilt not become my man, then is the choice open to me to set what man I will over Orkney; but I will that thou make me oath not to lay claim to those lands, and to leave them in peace whom I set thereover. But if thou wilt take neither choice, then he who rules the lands will deem that unpeace shall be looked for of thee, nor mayst thou deem it wonderful then though dale meet knoll."

The earl answers and prayed the king for respite to think the matter over. The king did so, and allowed the earl a while to take counsel on this choice with his men.

Then he prayed the king to give him time until next summer, that he might first go West-over-sea, because his counsellors were at home, but he was but a child of years. But the king bade him make his choice there and then.

Now Thorkel Fosterfather was at that time with King Olaf. He sent a man privily to Earl Thorfin, and bade him, whatsoever were in his heart, not to set his mind on parting as at this

time from King Olaf without coming to peace,
seeing that he had gotten into the hands of the
king. By this reminder the earl thought he saw
the only choice of good hap was to let the king have
his will as then. But this seemed to him nowise
choice-worthy, to wit, that himself should have no
hope of his heritage, and withal that he swear
oath that they should hold his dominion in peace,
who had no birthright thereto. But whereas he
misdoubted him as to his getting away, he chose
to come under the hand of the king and become
his man, even as Brusi had done.

The king found that Thorfin was a man much
more high-mettled than Brusi, and could away
worse with this penalty; wherefore he trusted in
Thorfin worse than in Brusi, for the king saw
through it, that Thorfin would deem that he
might look for the backing of the Scottish king
if he should break this covenant. The king
wotted this of his wisdom, that Brusi came loth
into all the peace-covenant, but that he said
that only which he was minded to hold. But as
to Thorfin, when he had made up his mind as to
what to agree to, he came cheerfully into all the
terms, and hung back in nought which the king
was the first to settle. But this the king misdoubted, that the earl would be minded to throw
over some of the covenant.

CHAPTER CVII.　THE DEPARTURE OF THORFIN, AND HIS PEACE WITH THORKEL.

WHEN King Olaf had thought out all this matter, he let blow to a thronged assembly, and called thither the earls. Then said the king: "Now will I make clear the covenant between me and the earls of Orkney unto all people. They have now yeasaid my being the owner of Orkney and Shetland, and have become my men, both of them, and have bound all this with sworn oaths, and now I give the dominion to them as a fief, one-third of the lands to Brusi, another third to Thorfin, even as they had had before. But that third which Einar Wrongmouth had, I claim to have fallen into my court in return for his having slain Eyvind Urochs-horn, my courtman and fellow and dear friend; to that deal of the islands I will look in the manner that seemeth good to me. This also do I crave of you brethren, my earls, that I will ye take peace of Thorkel Amundson for the slaying of your brother Einar, and I will that doom thereof be under me, if ye will say yea thereto." As in other matters, so also in this, the earls yeasaid all that the king spake. Then came forth Thorkel and handselled the king's doom in this case; and so the Thing broke up. King Olaf awarded were-gild for Earl Einar equal to were-gild for three landed-men, but because of his guilt one-third of the gild should fall through. Then Earl Thorfin prayed the king for leave to go away, and when he had got it, the earl got ready at his swiftest.

Now when he was all-boun and was drinking on board his ship, on a day Thorkel Amundson came before him all of a sudden and laid his head on the earl's knees, and bade him do with him what he would. The earl asked why he fared thus. "We be men already at peace by the king's doom; so stand up, Thorkel."

Thorkel did so, and said : " The peace that the king has made I shall abide by, as concerning the matter between me and Brusi, but the part therein that concerneth thee thou shalt rule alone; for though the king has awarded me lands and land-dwelling in Orkney, yet can I of thy temper so well, that I have no business to those islands unless I go under thy given troth, earl. Therefore will I," says he, "bind myself to thee in this, never to come into Orkney, whatever the king may say." The earl held his peace, and was slow to fall to speech. Then he said : " If thou wilt, Thorkel, that I doom in our matter rather than we abide by the king's doom, then this shall be the beginning of our peace-making, that thou shalt fare with me to Orkney and be with me, nor ever sunder from me but with my leave and freedom thereto. Thou shalt be bound to ward my land and to do all such works as I will let do while we are both alive."

Thorkel answers : " This shall rest in thy power, earl, as all else wherein I may have my say."

Then Thorkel stood forth and handselled all this

to the earl as he had quoth it. The earl said
that as to were-gild he would set forth that matter
later on, and then he took sworn oath of Thorkel
hereto.

Now Thorkel betook himself forthwith to the
journey with the earl, who went away as soon as
he was ready, and he and King Olaf never saw
each other again.

CHAPTER CVIII. EARL BRUSI'S DE-PARTURE.

EARL BRUSI tarried behind there, and
got ready more at his leisure, but before
he went away King Olaf had certain
parleys with him and spoke on this wise: "I am
minded to think, earl, that I shall have in thee
the man to trust and trow in West-over-sea
yonder, and my mind is that thou have two-thirds
of the lands to rule over, even as thou hast had
before; for my will it is that thou be in no way a
lesser or a less mighty man, now that thou art my
liege-man, than thou wert before. But I will
make fast thy troth to me, in that I will that
Rognvald thy son shall be left behind here with
me. I see then that when thou hast both my
backing and two-thirds of the islands, thou mayest
well hold thine own against Thorfin thy brother."

Brusi took that with thanks, the having two-thirds
rather than one-third of the islands; and
after this he tarried but a little while or ever he
went away, and he came in the harvest-tide to
Orkney.

Rognvald, Brusi's son, was left behind in the east with King Olaf; he was the goodliest of all men to look upon, his hair thick and yellow as silk ; he was of early days big and strong, and of all men was he the likeliest, both by reason of his wits and his courteous manners. He was for a long time thereafter with King Olaf. Hereof telleth Ottar the Swart in that drapa which he wrought on King Olaf:

> The Shetlanders, grown leal now,
> To thee for thanes are counted ;
> Now keep thou ward on the power,
> On the good ones of the folk-kings.
> Ne'er yet was seen an Yngling
> In Eastland, who beneath him
> Brake down the isles of Westland,
> Ere thee we gat, O fight-swift.

CHAPTER CIX. OF EARLS BRUSI AND THORFIN.

WHEN the brethren, Thorfin and Brusi, came west to Orkney, Brusi took two-thirds of the islands to rule over, and Thorfin one-third. He was ever in Caithness and in Scotland, and set his men over the islands. So now Brusi alone had the warding of the islands, which at that time lay much open to war, in that Northmen and Danes harried much in western viking, and oft came on the Orkneys as they fared to and fro the west, and ness-liftings they made. Brusi wyted his brother Thorfin, whereas he had no folk out for the warding of Orkney and Shetland, but yet took scat and dues therefrom as appertained to his share.   Then Thorfin bade him the choice to have one-third of the land, and that Thorfin should have the other two and uphold the land-warding on behalf of both of them.   Now although this shifting did not speedily befall then, yet it is so told in the Earl-tales that it came to pass, and that Thorfin had two-thirds and Brusi one-third whenas Knut the Rich had laid Norway under him, and King Olaf was gone out of the land.

Earl Thorfin, the son of Sigurd, was the noblest of all earls of the islands, and had more dominion than other Orkney earls ; he gat to him Shetland and Orkney and the South Isles, and had withal a great dominion in Scotland and Ireland.   Thereto quoth Arnor the earls' skald :

> Folk hearkened to Ring-hater :
> From the Giant-isles to Dublin
> Each man was counted Thorfin's ;
> Truth tell I to the people.

Thorfin was the greatest of warriors ; he took the earldom when he was but five winters old, and ruled for more than sixty winters, and died of sickness in the latter days of Harald Sigurdson. But Brusi died in the days of Knut the Rich, a little after the fall of King Olaf the Holy.

CHAPTER CX.   OF HAREK OF THI-OTTA.

NOW fare forth two stories; and now shall we take up the matter where we left it afore, whereas it was told how King Olaf Haraldson had made peace with Olaf the Swede-king, and how he had gone that same summer north to Thrandheim.   At that time he had been king for five winters.   That autumn he made all things ready for a winter dwelling in Nidoyce, and there he abode the winter through.   That winter abode with King Olaf Thorkel Foster-father, the son of Amund, as was written before.

King Olaf set himself much to asking how Christ's faith might be holden in the land; and what he learnt thereof came to this, that Christian faith would not be holden to when one came north into Halogaland, and yet it fell far short of being well done both throughout Naumdale and Upper Thrandheim.   Now there was a man named Harek, son of Eyvind the Skald-spiller, who dwelt in the island called Thiotta, which lies in Haloga-land.   Eyvind had been a man not of great wealth, but of high kin and mickle manhood.   In Thiotta there lived at this time small bonders not a few.   Harek bought him a stead first, not right great, and moved his household thither; but after a few seasons he had cleared off all the other bonders who had dwelt there before, so that now he alone owned all the island, and reared for himself there a right great manor.   Harek speedily became right wealthy; he was of mickle wisdom

and a man of great ado.   He had long been held
in great honour by men of high degree.   He was in
the tale of kindred with the kings of Norway ; so
for that sake Harek had much worship of the
lords of the land.   For Gunnhild, the mother of
Harek's father, was the daughter of Earl Halfdan
and Ingibiorg, the daughter of Harald Hairfair.
By the time that these things befell Harek was
somewhat stricken in years.

Harek was the man most accounted of in all
Halogaland.   He had for a long while held the
Fin-cheaping and the king's bailiwick over the
Mark ; whiles he had it alone, whiles in fellowship
with others.   As yet he had not come to meet
King Olaf, but words and messengers had gone
between them, and all in loving wise.   And the
same winter that King Olaf sat in Nidoyce men
went yet again between him and Harek of Thiotta.
And then the king made it known that in the
following summer he was minded to fare north
into Halogaland and all the way north to the
land's end.   But of this journey the Halogalanders
had right many misgivings.

CHAPTER CXI.   OF THE HALOGA-
LANDERS.

NOW King Olaf gat him ready in spring
with five ships, and had three hundred
men.   And when he was all-boun, he
dight his journey north along the land, and when
he came into Naumdale-folk he summoned a
Thing with the bonders, and at every Thing he

was taken for king.   There, as elsewhere, he let be read out the laws whereby he bade the folk of the land to hold to the Christian faith, at the peril of life and limb, or forfeiture of all goods for every man who would not go under Christ's law. There on many a man the king laid heavy penalties, and let them go alike over rich and unrich ; and in such a way he left things in every part, that all folk avowed they would hold to the holy faith.   But most of the mightier men and many great bonders made banquets against the king's coming, and in this wise he went on all the way north to Halogaland.   Harek of Thiotta made a feast for the king, and there was right mickle throng and the feast of the bravest.   Therewithal Harek became King Olaf's landed-man, and King Olaf gave him the same grants as he had held of the former lords of the land.

CHAPTER CXII. OF ASMUND, THE SON OF GRANKEL.

A MAN is named Grankel, or Granketil, a wealthy bonder, and now somewhat on in years.   But while he was in his young days he had been in viking and a mickle warrior. He was a man of great prowess in most things concerning manly deeds.   Asmund was the name of his son, and was in all things like to his father, or somewhat further he went.   It was the say of many men that by goodliness, strength, and prowess, he was the third best endowed man in Norway.   But named the first therein were King Hakon, Athelstan's Fosterson,. and Olaf Tryggvison.

Now Grankel bade King Olaf to a banquet, and the feast there was full noble, and Grankel saw the king off with great gifts. The king prayed that Asmund come with him, and laid many words thereto. Asmund deemed he might not thrust his own honour away from him, so he betook himself to the journey with the king, and thereafter became his man and came into the greatest good-liking with the king.

King Olaf tarried in Halogaland for the most part of the summer, and went into every Thing-round, and christened there all the people. In those days there dwelt in Birchisle Thorir Hound, the mightiest man north there, and he now became King Olaf's landed-man. Then many sons of mighty bonders betook themselves into King Olaf's company out of Halogaland. But when the summer wore on, the king came from the north and turned inward up Thrandheim unto Nidoyce, and sat there through the winter after ; and that winter Thorkel Fosterfather came west-away from Orkney whenas he had slain Earl Einar Wrongmouth.

That autumn there was dearth of corn in Thrand-heim, but before for a long while had been plenteous years ; but now the dearth was over all the North-country, and was the greater the further northward one was. But east in the land the corn was good, and all over the Uplands withal. But this helped the Thrandheim folk that they had mickle old corn.

CHAPTER CXIII. OF THE BLOOD-OFFERINGS OF THRANDHEIM FOLK.

THAT harvest were the tidings told to King Olaf from Inner Thrandheim, that the bonders there had had thronged feasts at Winter-nights, and that there were great drinkings. The king was told that all cups there were signed to the Æsir after ancient wont. This followed the tale withal, that neat were slaughtered there and horses, and the stalls reddened with blood, and blood-offering was done, with this word set forth, that that was for the booting of the year. This followed, moreover, that all folk deemed it was clearly to be seen, that the gods had gotten wroth whereas the Halogalanders had turned to Christ's faith. Now, when the king heard these tidings, he sent men up into Thrandheim, and summoned to him the bonders whom he thought good to name.

There was a man named Olvir of Eggja, known by the name of the stead whereat he dwelt; he was a mighty man and of high kindred, and was at the head of those who went on this journey to the king on behalf of the bonders. And when they met the king he laid against them these charges. But Olvir answered on behalf of the bonders, and said that they had had no feasts that autumn, out-taken their own gilds, or drinkings turn and turn about; and some but biddings of friends. " But, as to what has been told thee," said he, " concerning the ways of talk of us Thrandheim folk, when we are a-drinking, that wot all wise men to beware of such

IV.   O

talk; but I may not answer for men foolish and ·
men ale-wood, what they may say."

Olvir was a man deft of speech and bold-spoken,
and warded all these guilts from off the bonders.
And at last the king said that the Up-Thrandheimers would bear witness to themselves as to
how well they stood in their faith. Then the
bonders got leave to go home again, and forthwith
when they had arrayed them they departed.

CHAPTER CXIV.   OF THE BLOOD-OF-
FERINGS OF THE UP-THRANDHEIM
FOLK.

LATER on in the winter the king was told
that the Up-Thrandheimers were gathered
together in multitudes at Mere, and that
great blood-offerings had been there at midwinter ;
and that there they had made blood-offerings for
peace and a good winter season. And when the
king deemed he knew for sure the truth of this, he
sent men and messages up into Thrandheim, and
summoned the bonders down to the town, still
naming by name such men as he deemed the wisest
among them. So now the bonders had a parley and
talked over this message between them ; and they
were all the least willing to go this journey who had
fared the winter before. But at the prayer of all the
bonders Olvir undertook the journey. And when he
came down to the town, he went straightway to see
the king, and then fell to talk. The king laid it on
hand to the bonders that they had had a midwinter
blood-offering. Olvir answered and said that the

bonders were sackless of that guilt. "We had," said he, "Yule-biddings and drinking-bouts far and wide about the countrysides. The bonders are not minded so to pinch them in their cheer for the Yule-feast, as that a good deal be not left over ; and this it was, lord, that men were a-drinking of long after. At Mere there is a great chief-stead and big houses, and mickle dwelling round about, and there folk deem it good glee to drink together a many."

The king answered little, and was rather cross-grained, deeming that he wotted that other things were truer than that which was now set forth. The king bade the bonders go back. "But yet," says he, "I shall get to know the truth, to wit, that ye hide the matter and do not face it ; but however things have gone hitherto, do no such things again."

So the bonders fared home again, and told of their journey that it had been none of the smoothest, and that the king was somewhat wroth.

CHAPTER CXV. THE SLAYING OF OL-VIR OF EGGJA.

KING OLAF had a great feast at Easter, and had many men of the town bidden and many bonders withal. But after Easter the king let run out his ships, and bear thereto rigging and oars. He let deck the ships, and tilt them and bedight them ; he let the ships float thus arrayed by the gangways. King Olaf sent men into Verdale forthwith after Easter. Now a man is named, Thorald, a king's steward ; he warded the

king's manor at Howe, and the king sent him word
to come to him at his speediest. Thorald did not put
the journey under his head, but went forthwith out
to the town together with the king's messengers.
The king called him for a privy talk, and asked after
it : "What truth is in that which is told me about
the ways of the Up-Thrandheimers, whether it be
so that they are turning them to blood-offerings.
I will," says the king, "that thou tell me things
as they are, and as thou knowest them most truth-
fully; this is thy bounden duty, for thou art my
man."

Thorald answers : "Lord, this will I tell thee
first, that I flitted hither to the town my two sons
and my wife, and of my chattels all that I might
bring with me; now if thou wilt have a true story
of me, that shall be at thy will, but if I tell thee
things as they are, then must thou look after mine
affairs."

The king said : "Tell thou the truth of what I
ask thee, but I shall so look after thine affairs that
thou shalt take no hurt."

Thorald answered : "This is the truth to tell,
king, if I am to tell things as they are, that throughout Upper Thrandheim wellnigh all the folk are all-
heathen in their faith, though some men be there
who are christened. Now it is their wont to have
a blood-offering in autumn to welcome the winter,
and another at midwinter, and the third at summer
for the welcoming of summer. These are the ways
of the Isle-folk, the Sparebiders, the Verdale-folk,
and the Skaun-folk. There are twelve men who
take upon themselves to carry out the blood-feasts ;

and now next spring it is Olvir's turn to uphold the feast, and now he is in much ado at Mere, and thither have been brought all the goods which are needed for the feast."

Now when the king knew the truth, he let blow together his host, and let tell men to go aboard ship. The king named captains of ships and leaders of companies withal, and the ship on which each company should go. The arrayal was speedy; the king had five ships and three hundred men, and therewith stood up the firth. The wind was fair, and the cutters made no long way of it before the wind. But no man was ware that the king would so speedily come up thither.

The king came by night to Mere, and there a man-ring was straightway cast about the houses. There was Olvir laid hand on, and the king let slay him, together with very many other men. The king seized all the goods of the feast, and let bring them aboard his ships, and all that wealth withal, both house-decking and garments and dear-bought things, which folk had flitted thither, and let share them as war-getting amongst his men. The king also let set upon those men in their houses who he deemed had the most share in these doings ; some of whom were laid hands upon, and laid in irons, and othersome got away by running off, but of many were their goods seized.

Then the king summoned a Thing with the bonders. And whereas he had by then laid hands on many of the mighty men, and had them in his power, their kinsmen and friends were minded to yeasay obedience to the king ; so that, as at this time, there was no uprising against the king in Thrandheim. All the folk there he turned to the right faith, and set there teachers, and let make churches and hallow them.

The king laid down that Olvir was not to be atoned for, and laid hand on all the wealth which he had owned. But as to other men whom he deemed to be the most guilt-bitten, some of them he let slay and some maim, othersome he drove out of the land, and from others again he took fines. Thereafter the king fared back again down to Nidoyce.

CHAPTER CXVI. OF THE SONS OF ARNI.

A MAN is named, Arni, son of Arnmod. He had for wife Thora, the daughter of Thorstein Gallows. These were their children: Kalf, Finn, Thorberg, Amundi, Kolbiorn, Arnbiorn, Arni; their daughter was Ragnhild, and Harek of Thiotta had her to wife. Arni was a landed-man, mighty and well renowned, a great friend of King Olaf. At this time his sons Kalf and Finn were of King Olaf's company, and were held there in great honour. The woman whom Olvir of Eggja had had to wife was young and fair, of high kin and wealthy; she was deemed an exceeding good match, but her warding was then in the hands of the king. She and Olvir had two sons, both young. Kalf, son of Arni, prayed the king to give him in wedlock the wife that Olvir had had, and for the sake of friendship the king granted him this, and therewithal the wealth that Olvir had owned.

Then the king made him a landed-man, and the king gave him his stewardship about Up-Thrandheim. So now Kalf became a great lord, and an exceeding wise man was he.

CHAPTER CXVII. KING OLAF'S JOURNEY TO THE UPLANDS.

AND now had Olaf been for seven winters king in Norway. That summer came to him the Earls of Orkney, Thorfin and Brusi. Those lands King Olaf had made his own, as is afore writ. That summer King Olaf went over either Mere, and in harvest he went into Raumsdale, where he went aland from his ships, and fared on to the Uplands and came forth unto Lesiar. There he let hands be laid on all the best men, both about Lesiar and Dofrar, and they must needs either take to Christ's faith or else suffer death, or flee away if they could bring that about; but they who took to Christ's faith gave their sons into King Olaf's hands as hostages of their troth.

The king abode the night over at the place called the Steads in Lesiar, and set a priest thereover. Then he went across Loradale and came down to a place called Staffbrent; along that valley there runs a river called Otta, and fair built it is on either side of that river, and is called Loar. And the king might see all the dwelt country endlong.

"Scathe is it," says the king, "that we needs must burn so fair a dwelling."

Therewith he made his way with his company down into the dale, and took night quarters at a homestead hight Ness; and there the king chose his chamber in a certain loft, where he slept himself, which stands yet to-day, and nought hath been done to it since. There the king tarried for five nights, and sheared up a Thing-bidding, summoning to him both the folk of Vagi, and of Loar, and of Hedale, and let the message go with the summons that they should either fight with him and abide fire at his hands, or take christening and bring him their sons for hostages. So they came to the king and gave themselves up to him; but some fled south to the Dales.

CHAPTER CXVIII. THE STORY OF GUDBRAND A-DALES.

THERE was a man hight Gudbrand a-Dales, who was as a king over the Dales, though he were but hersir by title. Sigvat the Skald accounted him as even with Erling Skialgson for might and wide lands. And thus Sigvat sang about Erling:

> One other Jalk-board's waster
> Have I wotted like unto thee,
> Herder of men, hight Gudbrand;
> Wide over lands he rulèd.
> O loather of the worm's land,
> I call ye twain deemed even.
> That bower of snake-seat lieth
> Who deems himself the mightier.

Gudbrand had one son who is here told of.

Now when Gudbrand heard of these tidings, that King Olaf had come to Loar, and drave men against their will to take christening, he sheared up the war-arrow and summoned all the Dale-folk to the stead which is called Houndthorp to meet him there. Thither they all came, and a countless host was there, whereas anigh thereto is the water called the Low, so that folk could come together by ship as well as by land. So Gudbrand had a Thing with them, and said that into Loar was come a man hight Olaf, "who will bid us another faith than that which we have already, and will break asunder all our gods, and sayeth that he hath a god much greater and mightier. It is a marvel that the earth doth not burst asunder under him whereas he dareth to say such things, and that our gods suffer him to walk about any longer. And meseemeth, if we bear Thor out of our gods'-house when he standeth here at this homestead, and he hath ever been our avail, that when he seeth Olaf and his men then will his god melt away, and he and his men come to nought."

Thereat they lifted a whoop all together, and said that Olaf should never come away thence, if he came to meet them. "And he will not dare," they say, "to go farther south through the Dales."

Then they set apart seven hundred men to go a-spying north to Broad; and the leader of that company was the son of Gudbrand, then eighteen winters old, and many renowned men with him, and they came to the stead which is hight Hof, where they tarried three nights, and where many folk flocked to them, such as had fled from Lesiar and Loar and Vagi, they, to wit, who would not go under christening.

But King Olaf and Bishop Sigurd set up clerks behind them in Loar and Vagi. Thereupon they crossed the Vagi-roost and came down to Sil, and were there for the night, and learnt the tidings that a great host was there before them. Thereof withal heard the bonders who were at the Broad, and arrayed them for a battle with the king. And so when the king was arisen he did on his war-gear and went south along the Sil-walls, and stayed him not till he was within the Broad, and saw there a great host before him arrayed for battle. Then the king arrayed his folk, and rode himself at their head, and cast word at the bonders and bade them to take christening.

They answered : " To-day thou wilt have to be about something else than mocking us." And therewithal they whooped the war-whoop and smote their weapons on their shields. Thereat the king's men leapt forward and shot their spears ; and forthwith the bonders turned to flight, so that but few men held their ground. The son of Gudbrand was laid hand on, and the king gave him peace and kept him with him. The king tarried there four nights.

Then spake the king to the son of Gudbrand : " Go thou now back to thy father, and tell him that speedily shall I come thither." So he went home again and tells his father hard tidings, how they had met with the king and fallen to a fight with him ; " but all our host broke into flight forthwith at the first ; but I was laid hands upon," says he, "and the king gave me my life, and bade me go tell thee that he cometh hither speedily. Now we have no more here than two hundred of all that host which we then had to meet him withal ; therefore, I counsel thee, father, not to fight with that man." " That is easily heard," says Gudbrand, "that all the pith hath been knocked out of thee ; on an evil day thou wentest away from home, and for a long while will that journey be told against thee ; for thou trowest already that madness wherewith that man goeth about, and who hath done a right evil shame to thee and to thy company."

But in the night after, Gudbrand dreamed that a man came to him bright-shining, and great awe there went out from him, and he spake to Gudbrand : "No journey of victory was it that thy son went on against King Olaf, but much less wilt thou have, if thou art minded to give battle to the king ; for thou wilt fall thyself and all thy company, and wolves will drag thee, and all of you, and ravens will tear you."

At this terror he was exceeding adread, and telleth it to Thord Bigbelly, who was a lord over the Dales. He answers and says : " The self-same thing came before me," says he.

But on the morrow's morn they let blow for a Thing, and said that they deemed it good rede to have a parley with the man who came from the north with a new word of bidding, and to wot with what truth he fareth.

Then spake Gudbrand to his son : "Now thou

shalt go, and twelve men with thee, to see the king that gave thee thy life." And so it was done. And to the meeting of the king they came and told him their errand, that the bonders would have a Thing with him, and make truce between the king and the bonders. The king was well enough pleased at this, and they settled this with him on their word of honour, as long as the meeting should last. And this done, they went back and told Gudbrand and Thord that truce was made.

Then fared the king to the stead which was called Lidstead, and tarried there for five nights; whereupon he fared to meet the bonders and held a Thing with them; but much wet was there day-long.

So soon as the Thing was set, the king stood up and said that the folk of Lesiar and of Loar and of Vagi had been christened and had broken down their houses of blood-offerings, and now believe in the true God who shaped Heaven and Earth, and who knoweth all things.

Thereupon the king sat down, and Gudbrand answers: "We know not of whom thou art speaking; thou callest him a god whom neither thou seest nor any other man. But we have a god who can be seen every day, but who is not abroad to-day because the weather is wet; and awful will he seem to you and mighty enough to look on; and I ween if he come to the Thing that fear will shoot through the breasts of you. But inasmuch as thou sayest that thy God is so mighty, then let him do so much as that to-morrow the weather be

cloudy but no rain, and then we shall meet here
again."

Thereafter the king went home to his chamber,
and with him went the son of Gudbrand in
hostage ; but the king gave them another man in
his stead.

In the evening the king asked the son of Gudbrand what like their god was made. He says
that he was marked after the likeness of Thor, and
had a hammer in his hand; great of growth and
hollow within ; under him there is it done as
it were a stall, and thereon he stands when he is
without doors ; on him there is no lack of gold
and silver ; four loaves of bread are brought to
him every day, and flesh-meat withal.

Thereafter they went to bed, but the king
waked all the night through, and was at his
prayers. But when it was day again the king
went to mass, and then to meat, and thereafter to
the Thing.

But the weather had gone even so as Gudbrand
had bespoken. Then stood the bishop up in his
choir-cope, with a mitre on his head and a staff in
his hand, and set forth the faith to the bonders,
and told them many tokens which God had done ;
and made goodly end of his speech.

Then answers Thord Bigbelly : " Much sayeth
he, the horned one yonder, who hath a staff in hand,
the upper end whereof is crooked after the fashion
of a wether's horn. Now, inasmuch as thou,
fellow, claimest that thy God doeth so many marvellous things, then say thou to him to-morrow
before the sun rises, that he let it be clear and

sunshine; then let us meet and do one of two things, either be of one mind on this matter, or give battle." And so for that time they parted.

CHAPTER CXIX. GUDBRAND A-DALES CHRISTENED.

THERE was with King Olaf a man hight Kolbein the Strong, a man of Firth-folk kin. He was always so arrayed that he was girt with a sword, and had in his hand a great stake of wood which some men call a club. The king said to Kolbein that he should stand next to him in the morning. Thereafter he spake to his men : " Go ye this night to where the ships of the bonders are and bore holes in them all, and ride ye their yoke-beasts away from the homesteads whereas they are abiding." And so was it done. All that night the king was at his prayers, and prayed God to loosen this trouble by his grace and mercy.

But when Hours were done, towards the dawn of day he went to the Thing. And when he came to the Thing, there were come some of the bonders ; and therewith they saw a great throng of bonders faring to the Thing, bearing between them a mickle man-shape, all gleaming with gold and silver. Now when the bonders who were at the Thing already saw this, they all leapt up and bowed to the monster ; and sithence was he placed in the midst of the Thing-mead. On one side sat the bonders, on the other the king and his company.

Then Gudbrand a-Dales stood up and spake:
"Where is now thy God, king? I am minded to
think now that somewhat low he beareth his chin-
beard; and it seemeth to me that less now is
the swagger of thee and of the horned one yonder
whom thou callest a bishop, and that sitteth there
beside thee, than yesterday it was; for that now
our god is come, he who ruleth all things, and
looketh on you with keen eyes, and I see, that now
ye are full of fear, and scarce dare to lift up your
eyes. Now, drop your folly, and trow in our god
who hath all your ways in his hand." And thus he
closed his speech.

The king spake to Kolbein the Strong, without
the bonders wotting thereof: "If so it befall, the
while of my speech, that they look away from their
god, then give him that stroke, the most that thou
mayst, with thy club."

Then the king stood up and said: "Many
things hast thou said to us this morning; thou
deemest it a wonder that thou mayest not see our
God, but we hope he will soon come to us. Thou
threatenest us with thy god, who is blind and deaf,
and may neither help himself nor others, and may
get him nowhither away from his place, save he
be borne; and now I look for it that he will be but
a little way from ill. Lo! look ye now and gaze
eastward, there now fareth our God with a great
light."

Then ran up the sun and all the bonders looked
towards him. And in that same nick of time laid
on Kolbein so well on their god, that it burst
all asunder, and out of it leapt mice as big as cats,

and adders and worms. But the bonders were so afeard, that they fled away, some to the ships, but whenas they ran out their craft, the water rushed in and filled them, so they might not go a-board them. But they that ran to the yoke-beasts found them nowhere.

Thereafter the king let call the bonders, saying that he wished to have a talk with them, and thereat they turned back and held a Thing. Thereon stood up the king and spake : " I know not," says he, " what betokeneth this hubbub and running about which ye are making; but now ye may see what might your god hath, on whom ye laid gold and silver, meat and victuals ; and e'en now ye saw who the wights were that enjoyed this, mice, to wit, worms, adders, and paddocks ; and in a sorry case are they, who trow in such things, and will not forsake their folly. Now take ye back your gold and precious things which are scattered here over the mead, and give them to your wives, but no more bedeck therewith stocks and stones. But now two choices lie between you and me : either that ye take christening now and here, or else give me battle now to-day, and let him this day bear the victory from the other, unto whom that God willeth it, in whom we trow."

Then stood up Gudbrand a-Dales and said: " Mickle scathe have we now fared about our god ; and yet, seeing that he had not the might to help us, we will now trow in the God in whom thou trowest." And they all took Christ's faith ; and the bishop christened Gudbrand and his son. King Olaf and Bishop Sigurd left teachers there behind them; and as friends they parted who before were unfriends, and Gudbrand let make a church there in the Dales.

CHAPTER CXX. HEATHMARK CHRISTENED.

KING OLAF fared thereafter down to Heathmark and christened folk there; for whereas he had laid hands on the kings there, he did not venture to go far afield over the country with little folk, after such a mighty deed, whereas Heathmark was nought widely christened. But in this journey the king did not hold his hand till all Heathmark was christened, and churches were hallowed and teachers appointed thereto. Then he fared down to Thotn and Hathaland, and there righted the faith of the folk, and left it so that there was all-christened. Thence he fared into Ringrealm, and there all folk were christened. Thereafter heard the Raumrealm folk that King Olaf got ready for a journey up thither, and called out a mickle gathering, and said amongst themselves that it was ever in their minds concerning that progress when Olaf fared afore over the land, and said that never again should he so fare thereover. But the king arrayed himself for the journey none the less.

But when King Olaf fared up into Raumrealm with his host, a gathering of bonders came against him at the river called Nitia, and a whole host had the bonders. But when they met, the bonders fell to battle forthwith, but speedily it grew too hot for them, and aback they shrunk forthwith, and were beat to their bettering, for they all took christening then and there.

The king fared over that folkland, and did not depart therefrom till all men had taken to Christ's faith.

Thence he went east to Sol-isles, and christened that dwelling.

There came to him the skald Ottar the Swart, and prayed to go under the hand of King Olaf. The winter before Olaf the Swede-king had died, and now was Onund, son of Olaf, king in Sweden.

Thence King Olaf turned back to Raumrealm, and by that time the winter was all but passed. Then King Olaf summoned together a thronged Thing in the place where ever since the Heidsævis Thing has been holden; and he set up the law that to this Thing all Uplanders should seek, and that the law of Heidsævi should prevail throughout all the folks of the Uplands, and as far afield elsewhere as they have done since.

But when it was spring he made down towards the sea, and let array his ships, and went in the spring down to Tunsberg, and sat there through the spring, when it was most thronged there, and ladings were being brought to the town from other countries. The year's increase was good as then all about the Wick, and likewise of good avail all the way north to Stad; but to the north thereof there was mickle dearth.

CHAPTER CXXI.   PEACE BETWEEN KING OLAF AND EINAR THAMBAR-SKELFIR.

IN the spring King Olaf sent word west through Agdir, and all the way north through Rogaland and through Hordland, that he would have neither corn nor malt nor meal brought away thence, nor sold ; and let this go therewith, that he would be coming thither with his company, and would be faring about feasting according to old custom.   Now this message went throughout all these folklands.   But the king tarried in the Wick through the summer, and went all the way east to the land's end.

Einar Thambarskelfir had been with Olaf the Swede-king all the time since the death of Earl Svein, his brother-in-law, and had become Olaf the Swede-king's man, and got great grants from him.   But when the king was dead, Einar yearned to seek him peace with King Olaf the Thick, and to that end messages had gone between them in the spring.   But whenas King Olaf was lying in the Elf, Einar Thrambarskelfir came there with certain men, and he and the king talked over their peace-making, and it was settled between them that Einar should go north to Thrandheim, and have all his lands, and also those estates that had gone to Bergliot's dowry.   So Einar went on his way to the north, but the king tarried in the Wick, and was for a long time at Burg through the harvest and the first part of the winter.

CHAPTER CXXII. PEACE BETWEEN KING OLAF AND ERLING SKIALGSON.

ERLING SKIALGSON held his dominion suchwise, that all the way from the north from Sogn Sea and east to Lidandisness he had his will in all things with the bonders, but of kingly grants he had much less than before. Then people stood in such awe of him that no one put his lot into another scale than he willed. The king deemed that the mastery of Erling was exceeding.

A man was hight Aslak Skull o' Fitjar, a man of high kin and mighty. Skialg, the father of Erling, and Askel, the father of Aslak, were brothers' sons. Aslak was a great friend of King Olaf, and the king set him down in South Hordland, and gave him there a large fief and great grants, and the king bade him hold his own to the full against Erling. But nought was it that wise so soon as the king was no longer anigh ; for Erling must have it all his way between them, according to his will alone, and nowise meeker did he show himself, though Aslak would draw up with him. So fared their dealings that Aslak might not hold it out in his bailiffry ; so he fared to see King Olaf, and told him of his dealings with Erling. The king bade Aslak be with him, "until I and Erling shall meet."

Then the king sent word to Erling that he should come to Tunsberg in the spring to meet him. And when they met, they had parleys together, and the king said : " So it is told me of thy dominion, Erling, that there is no man from the north downward from Sogn Sea unto Lidandisness who may hold his freedom for thee; yet many men are there who deem them odal-born to even rights with men of like birth with themselves. Lo here is now Aslak, thy kinsman, who deemeth that he verily hath enough and to spare of thy cold shoulder in your dealings. Now I know not which of the two it may be, whether he hath any guilt thereto, or whether he must needs pay for my having appointed him to look after my affairs there. And though I name him herein, yet many others bewail themselves in like wise before me, both those who sit in bailiffries, and stewards withal, who look after our manors, and who have to array manor-feasts for us and our company."

Erling says: "Speedily shall I answer this, that I naysay that I wyted with guilt either Aslak or any other man because they be in thy service; but this shall I yeasay, that it is now as it has long been, that each one of us kinsmen will be greater than the other. This other thing shall I yeasay to thee: I bow the neck of a good will to thee, King Oláf; but this shall I deem a troublous matter, to lout before Seal-Thorir, who is thrall-born through all his kin, although he be now thy steward, or to bow to other such as are his peers of kindred, although thou lay honour on them."

Then the friends of both sides took up the speech, praying that they should come to peace; they said that in no man could the king have such strengthening as in Erling, "if he may be thy full friend." On the other hand, they said to

Erling that he should be yielding with the king, saying that if he hold him in friendship with the king, then it would be an easy matter for him to bring about whatso he would with any other man.

So ended this parley, that Erling was to have the same grants as he had had before, and all charges which the king had against Erling came to nought. Moreover, Skialg, the son of Erling, should go to the king and be with him. Then Aslak went back to his manors, and they were at peace, so to say. Erling also went home to his manors, and held to his wont as to his masterfulness.

CHAPTER CXXIII. THE BEGINNINGS OF ASBIORN SEAL'S-BANE.

THERE was a man hight Sigurd, son of Thorir, and brother to Thorir Hound of Birchisle. Sigurd had to wife Sigrid, the daughter of Skialg, and sister to Erling. Their son was Asbiorn, who was deemed to have in him much of the makings of a man when he was growing up. Sigurd abode at Thrandness in Omt, and was a man of mighty wealth, a man of mickle worship; he had not done homage to the king, and Thorir was the more accounted of of the brothers in that he was the king's landed-man. But at home at his house Sigurd was in no way a man of lesser state. While heathendom was, he was wont to have three blood-offerings every year, one at winter-nights, another at midwinter, the third against summer. And when he took christening, he held to the same wont in the matter of the feasts. In autumn, then, he had mickle bidding of friends, and in winter a Yule-bidding, and bade yet again many men to him ; and a third feast he had at Easter, and had then also a multitude. And to this wont he held as long as he lived. Sigurd died of sickness. Then was Asbiorn of eighteen winters. He took the heritage after his father; and he too held to the old wont, and had three feasts every year, even as his father had had. Now it was but a short while after Asbiorn took the heritage of his father, that the year's increase took to worsening, and the sowings of folk failed. But Asbiorn held to the same wont as to his feasts, and in good stead it stood him then, that there was old corn and other old stores that were needed. But when this season wore and the next came round, the corn was no whit better than it had been afore. Then would Sigrid have the feasts done away with, some or all of them. But this Asbiorn would not have; so in harvest-time he went to see his friends, and bought corn whereso he might, and got it as gift from some. And so it came to pass that year, that he upheld all his feasts. But the next spring but little sowing was to be got done, for no one could buy any seed-corn. Wherefore Sigrid counselled that the house-carles should be minished ; but this Asbiorn would not, and in all matters he kept to the same wont as before. That summer the corn looked like to be scarce, and on the top of that came the tale told from the south of the land, that King Olaf banned the flitting of corn and malt and meal

from the south up into the North-country. Then
Asbiorn deemed that the gathering in of household stuff was growing a troublous matter. So
then that was his rede, that he let run out a ship of
burden which he owned, a ship seaworthy for the
main as for its growth. The ship was good, and
all its rigging was of the very best, and there went
with it a sail striped with a bend.

Asbiorn fell to his journey, and twenty men
with him. They fared away from the north in
the summer-tide, and of their journey nought is told
until they hove into Kormtsound at eve of day and
lay to at Ogvaldsness. A great stead there stands
a little way up on the island of Kormt, and is
called Ogvaldsness; a king's manor it was, a noble
stead, and the steward thereof was Thorir Seal;
he was the steward of the king there. Thorir was
a man of small kin, but had been well brought up;
he was a good craftsman, deft of speech, showy of
array, froward and stubborn, and all this stood him
in stead after he had gotten him the backing of the
king. Swift he was of speech, and ready thereto.

Asbiorn, he and his, lay here over-night; but in
the morning, when it was full daylight, Thorir
went down to the ship and certain men with him.
He asked who was the master of that brave
craft, and Asbiorn told of himself, and named
his father. Thorir speers what was the furthest
he was minded to go, and what was his errand.
Asbiorn says he will buy him corn and malt; and
says, as sooth was, that mickle dearth there was
north in the land: " But it is told us that good is
the season here. So wilt thou, goodman, sell us

some corn ? I see that here be big ricks, and an easement it were to us if we need go no further afield." Thorir answers : " I shall do thee the easement that thou needest not fare any further corn-cheaping, or wider about Rogaland. I can tell thee this, that thou mayst well turn back hence and fare no further ; whereas thou wilt get no corn here nor otherwhere ; for the king banneth the selling of corn hence into the North-land. So fare thou back, Halogalander ; that will be best for thee."

Asbiorn answers : " If it be so as thou sayest, goodman, that we shall get here no corn-cheaping, then my errand will be nought less than to go kin-seeking to Soli, and see the abode of my kinsman Erling."

Thorir answers : " How mickle kinship hast thou with Erling ? " He answers : " My mother is his sister." Thorir says : " Maybe then that I have not spoken warily, if thou art the sister's son of the King of the Rogalanders." Then Asbiorn and his men cast off the tilt, and turned the ship seaward. Thorir called after them, and said : " Fare ye now well, and come here as ye fare back." Asbiorn says that so it should be.

So they fare on their journey and come to the Jadar one day at eve ; fared Asbiorn up aland with ten men, and ten gave heed to the ship. So when Asbiorn came to the stead he got there a good welcome, and Erling was as merry as might be to him. Erling seated him next to himself, and asked many tidings from the North-country. Asbiorn told him of his errands all clearly. Erling

answered, that it had not well befallen them, that
the king had banned the selling of corn. " I know
no men hereabouts," says he, " of whom it may be
hoped that they will dare to break the word of the
king ; and I have trouble enough in heeding the
king's temper, for there be many who try to undo
our friendship."

Asbiorn says : " Late may truth be learned ; in
my youth I was taught that my mother was free-
born on every half, and this, moreover, that Erling
of Soli was now the noblest of all her kindred ; but
now I hear thee say that thou hast not so much
freedom for the king's thralls on Jadar here, as that
thou mayest do with thy corn whatso pleaseth
thee."

Erling looked on him, and grinned till his teeth
showed, and said : " Less wot ye Halogalanders of
the king's might than we Rogalanders ; but rash of
word thou wilt be at home, and no long descent
hast thou to tell up hereunto. Drink we now
first, kinsman ; let us see to-morrow how thine
errand shall speed."

So did they, and were merry that night. Next
day they talk together, Erling and Asbiorn, and
Erling said : " I have somewhat thought over thy
corn-cheaping, Asbiorn. Now, how hard to please
wilt thou be about thy sellers ? " He said he cared
never a whit from whom he bought the corn if it
were fairly sold him. Said Erling : " It seemeth
to me most like that my thralls own so much corn
as that thou wilt have a full cheaping ; and they
be not within laws or lands-right with other men."

Asbiorn says he will take this. Then the thralls

were told about the bargain, and they gave forth corn and malt, and sold it to Asbiorn, who loaded his ship even as he would. And when he was ready to go away Erling saw him off with friendly gifts, and in love they parted.

Asbiorn had a good wind at will, and hove into Kormtsound and lay to off Ogvaldsness in the evening, and there they tarried for the night.

Now Thorir Seal had already tidings of the journey of Asbiorn; of this withal, that his ship was deep-laden. Thorir summoned folk to him in the night-tide; so that before day he had over sixty men, and went to meet Asbiorn in the first of the dawn. They fared straightway aboard the ship. Asbiorn and his were clad by then, and Asbiorn greeted Thorir. Thorir asked what sort of lading Asbiorn had on board ship; he said that corn and malt it was. Thorir says: " Then will Erling be at his old wont, to take for fooling all words of the king. Forsooth, he wearieth not of that, to withstand him in all wise; and a marvel it is that the king letteth him have his way in all."

Thorir was mad of speech for a while. But when he held his peace Asbiorn said that this corn had been owned by Erling's thralls. Thorir answered snappishly that he heeded no whit any tricks of Erling and his folk. " But it is either this or that, Asbiorn, either ye go aland, or we put you all out-board, for we will not have you thronging us while we are clearing out the ship."

Asbiorn saw that he had no strength of men against Thorir, and he and his men went up aland, and Thorir let clear all the lading out of the ship.

But when the ship was cleared, Thorir walked along it and said : " A mighty good sail have these Halogalanders ; go ye, fetch that old sail of my ship of burden and give it to them ; it is quite good enough for them, whereas they be sailing with a loose keel." And so it was done that the sails were shifted.

In this plight Asbiorn with his men went their ways and made for the north along the land, and letted not till he came home early in winter ; and great was the fame of that journey.

So now all the toil of feast-dighting was taken off Asbiorn's shoulders for that winter. Thorir Hound bade Asbiorn to a Yule-feast and his mother, and such of their men as they would take with them. Asbiorn had no will to go, and sat at home. That was found, that Thorir deemed that Asbiorn had dealt uncourteously with the bidding in that he would not go. So Thorir jeered about Asbiorn's journey. Says he : " There is both great diversity of honour between us, the kinsmen of Asbiorn, and he moreover so maketh it, such toil as he was at last summer to go and seek out a meeting with Erling all the way to Jadar, but now will not fare here to me unto the next house. I wot not but he may deem that Seal-Thorir is waylaying him in every holm."

Such words heard Asbiorn of Thorir and other suchlike. Asbiorn was mightily ill content with his journey ; all the worse when he heard it held at such laughter and mocking. So this winter he abode at home, and went nowhither to any biddings.

CHAPTER CXXIV. THE SLAYING OF SEAL-THORIR.

ASBIORN had a longship, a twenty-benched cutter which stood in a great boat-house. After Candlemas Asbiorn let the ship be launched, and its gear borne down thereto, and let array the ship. Then he summoned to him his friends, and had wellnigh ninety men, all well weaponed. But when he was ready and a wind at will befell, he sailed south along the land; and they fare on their ways, going somewhat slow. But when they got south along the land, they kept to the outer road rather than the highway, when they might. Nought is told of their faring till they hove in to Kormt from the west in the evening of the fifth day after Easter. But the land goes such-wise there, that it is a great isle, and long, and for the most part nought broad, and lies on the high-way on the western side thereof. There is mickle dwelling, but on the side that turneth towards the main sea the island is widely undwelt. Asbiorn and his men landed on the western side of the island, where it was undwelt. And when they had tilted them, Asbiorn said: "Now shall ye be left here behind and abide me, but I shall go into the island to spy what is toward, for we have heard no tidings as yet." Asbiorn had but evil raiment, and a slouch-hat; he had a fork in hand, and was girt with a sword under his garment. He went up a-land and across the island. And as he came upon a certain heath whence he might look on the stead of Ogvaldsness and further out over Kormtsound, he saw mickle faring of men both by sea and by land, and all those crowds were making for the homestead of Ogvaldsness. He deemed this wondrous. So he went home to the stead, and there whereas serving-men were dighting meat. And straightway he heard and understood from their talk that King Olaf had come there to a feast, and this withal, that the king had gone to table. So Asbiorn turned to the hall. And as he came into the porch one man went out and another in, and no man gave any heed to him. The hall-door was open, and he saw that Thorir Seal stood before the board of the high-seat. By now the evening was far spent. Asbiorn hearkened and heard how men were asking Thorir about his dealings with Asbiorn, and also that Thorir told a a long story thereof, and Asbiorn deemed he clearly told an unfair tale. Then he heard how a man said: " How did Asbiorn take it when ye were clearing the ship ? " Thorir says : " He bore up in a way, but not right well, while we were a-clearing the ship, but when we took the sail from him he wept." But when Asbiorn heard this, he drew his sword hard and swift, and sprang into the hall and straightway hewed at Thorir, and the stroke came on the outward of his neck and the head fell on the board before the king, but the trunk on his feet, and the table-cloths were all bloody up and down. The king spake and bade take him and lead him out, and even so it was done, and Asbiorn was laid hands on and led out of the hall. But the table-array and the cloths were taken and brought away, and Thorir's body was carried off withal, and all was cleansed on which blood had fallen. The king was mighty wroth, yet kept his words well in, as his wont ever was.

CHAPTER CXXV. OF SKIALG ERLING-SON.

SKIALG ERLINGSON stood up and went before the king, and spoke thus: "Now it will be, as oft before, king, that one must look to thee for making good what has fallen amiss. I will offer money for this man that he may hold his life and limbs; but thou, king, shape ye and shear all the rest."

The king says: "Is it not a guilt unto death, Skialg, if a man break the Easter-peace? And is it not another, that he slew a man within the king's hall; and the third one, which thou and thy father will deem of little account, that he had my feet for hewing-block?"

Skialg answers: "Ill it is, king, that it misliketh thee; for otherwise had the work been done at the best. But, king, if thou take this deed amiss and deem it a great matter, yet I have hope that I shall have of thee something great for my service, and many will say, that thou mayest well so do."

The king answers: "However much thou be worth, Skialg, I shall not for thy sake break the law or cast down kingly honour."

Then Skialg turned away and went out of the hall. With Skialg there had been twelve men, and they all followed him, and many others went away with him.

Skialg spoke to Thorarin Nefiolfson : " If thou wilt have my friendship, then lay thine whole mind hereto, that the man be not slain before Sunday."

Thereupon fared Skialg and his men, and took a rowing-cutter which he owned, and rowed south as hard as they might make it, and came at the kindling of day to Jadar, and went straightway up to the stead and into the loft wherein slept Erling. Skialg ran against the door so that it broke off the nails, whereat awoke Erling and those others who were there within. He was the quickest on foot, and caught up his shield and sword, and sprang to the door and asked who fared so fiercely. Skialg named himself and bade open the door. Erling says : "That was likeliest, that thou wouldst be the man, if a fool were astir ; or fare any men after thee ? "

Then the door was opened, and Skialg said : "This I ween, that though thou think that I am faring madly, Asbiorn thy kinsman deems that I fare none too speedily, now that he sits in fetters north at Ogvaldsness ; and that were manlier to fare now and avail him." Then father and son had a talk together, and Skialg told Erling all the tidings at the slaying of Seal-Thorir.

CHAPTER CXXVI. OF THORARIN NEFIOLFSON.

KING OLAF sat him down in his seat when things had been put straight in the hall, and exceeding wroth he was. He asked what were the tidings of the slayer. He was told that he was out in the porch, and was watched there. The king says: "Why is he not slain?" Answers Thorarin Nefiolfson: "Lord, callest thou not that a deed of murder, to slay men by night?"

Then said the king: "Put him in fetters and slay him the morrow's morn."

Then was Asbiorn fettered and locked up in a house through the night. Next day the king hearkened matins, and then went to council, where he sat till high mass. Then he went to the mass, and when he came from the service he spoke to Thorarin: "Will the sun perchance be high enough now, so that Asbiorn thy friend may hang?"

Thorarin answered and louted to the king: "Lord, that said the bishop last Friday, that the king, who hath might over all, both bore with them that grieved his heart, and blest is he who may rather liken himself to him, than to them who then doomed the Man to death, or them who had his death fulfilled. Now it is no long while to wait for the morrow, and that is a working day."

The king looked around at him, and said: "Thou shalt have thy will herein, that he shall not be slain to-day. So now shalt thou take him to thyself and guard him ; and know this for sure, that thereon lies thy life if he get away, no matter how."

Thereupon the king went his ways, and Thorarin thither where Asbiorn sat in irons. Then Thorarin did off him the fetters, and brought him into a certain little chamber, and let fetch him meat and drink, and told him what the king had laid upon himself in case Asbiorn should run away. Asbiorn says that Thorarin had no need to fear of that. So Thorarin sat with him long through that day, and slept there the next night withal.

On the Saturday the king arose and went to matins, and then he went to the council, and a multitude of bonders was come there, and they had many plaints to set forth. There the king sat for a long while of the day, and went somewhat late to the high mass ; whereupon he went to meat, and when he had partaken thereof he drank for a while with the tables still standing.

Now Thorarin went to the priest who looked after the church, and gave him two ounces of silver to ring in the holy-tide so soon as the king's tables were taken up. Now when the king had drunk for as long as he deemed seemly, then was the board taken up. Then spoke the king, saying that now it was meet that the thralls should take the manslayer and slay him. But at that nick of time the holy tide was rung in.

So Thorarin went before the king, and said : " That man will belike have respite the holy-day over, though he have done evil."

The king says : " Heed him, Thorarin, that he may not get away."

So the king went to church to nones, and Thorarin sat still that day with Asbiorn. On the Sunday the bishop went to Asbiorn and shrived him, and gave him leave to go and hearken high mass. Then Thorarin went to the king, and bade him get men to guard the manslayer. " I will now," says he, " be quit of his matter." The king bade him have thanks for what he had done, and got men to guard Asbiorn, and then he was put into fetters. But when folk went to high mass, Asbiorn was led to the church, and outside the church he stood, together with those who warded him. The king and all the people stood at the mass.

CHAPTER CXXVII. PEACE BETWEEN ERLING AND KING OLAF.

NOW must we take up the tale whereas afore we turned from it, that Erling and Skialg his son took counsel together on this troublous matter, and through the whetting of Skialg and other of the sons of Erling it was settled to gather an host together and to shear up the war-arrow. And soon there came together a great company and went aboard ship, and when the score of the tale of the folk was told, there were wellnigh fifteen hundred men. With this company they fared, and came on Sunday to Ogvaldsness in Kormt, and went with all the host up to the stead, and came there at the time when the gospel was done; they went forthwith up to the church and took Asbiorn, and broke the fetters away from him.

But at this din and crash of weapons rushed all into the church who had erst stood without; but they who were in the church looked all out, save the king alone, who stood and looked not about. Erling and his sons arrayed their host on either side of the street that led from the church to the hall; and Erling and his sons stood next to the hall.

Now, when all the hours had been sung, then straightway the king went forth out of the church; he went forth the first into the fold, and then his men one after the other. Straightway when he came home to the door, then went Erling before the door and louted before the king, and greeted him. The king answered and bade God help him. Then Erling took up the word: "So is it told me that a great folly hath overtaken Asbiorn my kinsman, and ill is it, king, if so it hath been brought about that thou art ill content thereat. For this therefore have I now come to offer for him peace, and suchlike boot as thou thyself wilt have done, and to take in return his life, and limbs, and land-dwelling."

The king answers: "So meseemeth, Erling, as if thou and thine deem ye now to have the might in the matter of Asbiorn; and I know not why thou so givest it out that thou wouldst bid peace for him; for I am minded to think that for this cause hast thou drawn together an host of men, that thou meanest now to rule matters between us."

Erling says : " Thou shalt rule, king ; and rule so that we part appeased."

The king says : " Dost thou mean to put me to fear, Erling ? and hast thou this mickle company to that end ? Nay," says he, " but if there be aught else in it, I shall not flee now." . . . .

Erling answereth : " Thou needest not mind me of that, that our meetings have hitherto gone in such wise that I have had but a little might of folk against thee. But now I will not hide it from thee what is in my mind : to wit, that I will we part in peace; otherwise I look for it that I shall not risk our meeting any more." And Erling ·was red as blood in the face of him.

Then came forth Sigurd the Bishop and said to the king : " Lord, I command thee in obedience to God's cause, to make peace with Erling even according to his bidding, to wit, that this man have peace of life and limb, but that thou alone frame the peace-covenant."

The king answered : " Thou shalt rule." Then spoke the bishop : " Thou, Erling, give the king such surety as liketh him ; and let Asbiorn then take his truce and go into the power of the king." Erling got the sureties, and the king took them. Then Asbiorn went to take truce, and gave himself up to the king, and kissed him on the hand. Whereupon Erling turned away with his company ; but no greetings there were.

The king went into the hall, and Asbiorn with him ; whereupon the king laid open the peace-award : " This shall be the beginning of our peace, Asbiorn, that thou shalt undergo this law of the land, that whoso slayeth a servant of the king, he shall undertake that same service if it be the king's will. Now will I that thou take on thee this same stewardship that Seal-Thorir had, and to rule over my manor here at Ogvaldsness." Asbiorn said that so it should be as the king would. "But first would I fare home to my house, and set it in order." The king said he was well content therewith, and he went thence to another feast which had been arrayed for him thereby; but Asbiorn gat him away to meet his fellows. They had lain in hiding-bights all the while that Asbiorn was away. They had had news of all that had betid him over his matters, and would not go away until they knew what might be the upshot thereof.

CHAPTER CXXVIII. OF THORIR HOUND AND ASBIORN SEAL'S BANE.

THEN Asbiorn turns to his journey, and letted not the spring through, until he comes north to his stead. Ever thereafter he was called Asbiorn Seal's-bane. But when Asbiorn had been home no long while, the two kinsmen met, he and Thorir, and talked together. Thorir asked him carefully about his journey, and all the things that had betid therein; and Asbiorn told the tale as it had come to pass. Said Thorir: "Then, belike, thou deemest thou hast wreaked the shame that was done to thee when thou wast robbed last autumn?" "So is it," said Asbiorn, "or what deemest thou thereof, kinsman?" "That is soon said," quoth Thorir; "thy first journey, whereas thou faredst south into the land, was of the shamefullest, yet one that stood to some booting ; but this journey is the shame both of thee and thy kinsmen if that come to pass that thou be made a king's thrall, and peer of Thorir Seal, the worst of men. Now do thou so manly that thou rather sit here on thine own lands, and we, thy kinsmen, shall give thee strength so much that thou shalt come never again into such a jeopardy."

Asbiorn deemed this seemly, and before he and Thorir parted, this counsel was settled upon, that Asbiorn should sit at home, and not go to the king or into his service. And so did he, and sat at home at his steads.

CHAPTER CXXIX. HOW KING OLAF CHRISTENS VORS AND VALDRES.

AFTER that King Olaf and Erling Skialgson had met at Ogvaldsness, ill-will arose anew betwixt them, and waxed hereto that it came to utter enmity betwixt them.

In the spring King Olaf fared manor-eating about Hordland, and thence fared up to Vors, whereas he had heard that the folk there were but little in the faith. He held a Thing with the bonders at a place called Vang ; thither came the bonders thronging all-armed. The king bade them take christening, but the bonders bade him battle in return, and it came to this that either side drew up the battle in array. But this befell the bonders that fear shot through their breasts, and no one would stand the foremost ; so that was the end of

it, which served them better, that they gave themselves up to the king and took christening.　Nor
did the king depart from thence till all folk were
christened there.

On a day it befell that the king was riding his
ways and singing his psalms; but when he came
over against the Howes, he took his stand and said:
"Now let man tell man these words of mine, that
it be my counsel that never again a king of
Norway fare betwixt these Howes."　And men say
that most kings have taken heed thereto ever
since.

Then fared King Olaf out into Osterfirth, and
there met his ships, and then went north into Sogn,
and there went feasting the summer through.　But
when harvest-tide set in, he turned up into the
firth and fared thence up to Valdres, where the
folk were yet heathen.　The king went as fast as
he might drive up to the Water, and came there
unawares upon the bonders and took all their ships,
and went aboard with all his host.　Then he
sheared a Thing-bidding, and the Thing was set so
near to the water that the king had all the ships to
fall back upon if he deemed he needed it.　The
bonders sought to the Thing with an host of men
all-weaponed.　The king bade them christendom,
but the bonders whooped against him and bade
him hold his peace, and forthwith made huge din
and clatter of weapons.　But when the king saw
that they would not hearken to what he had to teach
them, and also that they had such a multitude of
folk that there was no withstanding them, he
turned his speech and asked them if there were

any men at the Thing who had such causes against each other as they wished that he should settle between them. It was soon found in the words of the bonders, that there were many but ill at peace with each other, who had run together to gainsay all christening. But so soon as the bonders began to set forth their plaints, each one gathered folk to him to back up his suit. Thus matters went on all that day, and at eve the Thing broke up.

But so soon as the bonders had heard that King Olaf had fared over Valdres and had come into the peopled parts, they had let fare abroad the war-arrow, and summoned together thane and thrall, and with this host they fared against the king, so that many places there were empty of people.

The bonders held together the gathering whenas the Thing broke up, and the king was ware thereof. So when he came to his ships, he bade row right across the water in the night, and let go up into the dwelling, and let burn and rob there. Next day they rowed from ness to ness, and the king let burn all the dwelling. But the bonders who were in the gathering, when they saw the reek and low of their homesteads, became loose in the gathering; so each one took himself away and made for home, to see if he might find his household. And so soon as the rift came into the host, each fared after other, until it was all split into small flocks. And now the king rowed across the water and burnt on either shore thereof. Then came the bonders to him and prayed for mercy, and bade allegiance to him. And he gave life to every man who came to him and craved therefor, and their goods therewithal.   And now no man gainsaid christening, so the king let christen the folk and took hostages from the bonders.

The king tarried there long through the autumn, and let draw the ships over the necks between the waters.   The king fared but little up country away from the waters, for he trusted the bonders but ill.

He let build and hallow churches there, and appointed clerks thereto.   But when the king deemed that frosts might be looked for, he made his way up inland and came down upon Thotn. Hereof telleth Arnor the earls' skald how King Olaf had burnt in the Uplands, whenas he sang concerning Harald his brother :

> It goes in the kin, that the king burned
> The homes of those Uplanders.
> There folk paid for the king's wrath,
> Who of all men was foremost.
> Folk would not give obedience
> To the furtherer of things gainful,
> Till things were plunged in peril :
> For the king's foes got but gallows.

Thereafter King Olaf went north through the Dales all the way up on to the fell, nor made a halt until he came to Thrandheim, and all the way down to Nidoyce.   He arrayed there for winter sojourn, and sat there winter over.   That was the tenth winter of his kingdom.

CHAPTER CXXX. OF EINAR THAMBARSKELFIR.

THE summer before, Einar Thambarskelfir fared away from the land, and first went to England, where he met Hakon his brother-in-law, and dwelt there with him a while. Sithence Einar went to meet Knut the king, and got great gifts of him. Thereafter he fared south over sea and all the way south to Romeburg, and came back the summer after, and went to his steads; and that time he and King Olaf did not meet.

CHAPTER CXXXI. THE BIRTH OF MAGNUS THE GOOD.

THERE was a woman hight Alfhild, who was called King's-bondmaid, though she was come of good stock. She was the fairest of women, and lived at the court of King Olaf. But that spring the tidings were that she was with child, and the bosom-friends of the king knew that he would be father to that child. It so befell on a night that Alfhild fell ill, and few people were nigh; there were some women, and a priest, and Sigvat the Skald, and some few others. Alfhild was heavily beset, and was brought wellnigh to death's door. She gave birth to a boy bairn, and for a while they knew not for sure whether the child were alive. And when he gave forth a breath, but all unmightily, the priest bade Sigvat go and tell the king. He answers: "I dare in nowise go wake the king, for he banneth any man to break his sleep ere he awake of himself."

The priest answers: "Hard need calls for it now that this child be christened, for meseems it is right unlike to live." Sigvat answers: "Rather dare I risk this, that thou christen the child, than that I wake the king, and I will take the blame on myself and give name to it." And so they did, and the boy was christened and hight Magnus.

The next morning, when the king was waked and clad, he was told of these tidings, and let call Sigvat to him, and said: "Why wert thou so bold to let christen my child before I knew thereof?" Sigvat answers: "Because I would rather give two men to God than one to the devil." The king said: "Why should all that be at stake?" Answered Sigvat: "The child was at death's door, and that had been a devil's man had it died heathen; but now is it a God's man. And, on the other hand, I knew, though thou shouldst be wroth with me, nought more would lie on it than my life; and if it be thy will that I lose it for this sake, then I look to it that I be God's man."

The king said: "Why lettest thou hight the boy Magnus? that is no kin-name of us." Sigvat answered: "I called him after Karla-Magnus the king, for him I knew to be the best man of this world."

Then said the king: "A man of great good-luck art thou, Sigvat! but it is nought to wonder at, though good-luck and wisdom go together; but that is more wondrous which whiles can be, that such good-luck follows unwise men, that even unwise redes turn to good-luck." Then was the king right glad. The swain was reared, and was soon a likely lad as age went over him.

CHAPTER CXXXII. THE SLAYING OF ASBIORN SEAL'S-BANE.

THIS same spring King Olaf gave to Asmund Grankelson one-half of the bailiwick of Halogaland against Harek of Thiotta, who before had had the whole of it, part as grant, part as fief. Asmund had a cutter, and wellnigh thirty men on board her, all well weaponed. And when Asmund came north they met, he and Harek, and Asmund told him how the king had ordained concerning the bailiwick, and let the tokens of the king follow therewith. Harek says that the king must rule as to who was to have the bailiwick; "yet the lords of aforetime did not so, to minish the right of us who are kinborn to holding dominion of kings, and to hand it over to sons of bonders, such as never have had the like affairs on hand before."

Now, though it might be found in Harek that he took the matter to heart, he let Asmund take over the bailiwick, even according as the king had sent words to him.

So Asmund went home to his father and tarried there for a little while, and afterwards went to his bailiffry north in Halogaland. And when he came north into Longisle, there lived there at that time two brothers, one called Gunnstein, the other Karli; they were wealthy men, and of mickle account. Gunnstein was a man of husbandry, and the older of the two brothers. Karli was goodly to look upon, and full showy of attire, and either was of great prowess in many ways.

Asmund had good welcome there and tarried for a while, and gathered from the bailiffry what he could get. Karli put that before Asmund that he would go with him south to meet King Olaf, and seek him there court-service. Asmund egged him on much to¹ this, and promised his furtherance before the king hereto, so that Karli might get done the errand he besought. So Karli became Asmund's fellow-farer.

Asmund heard that Asbiorn Seal's-bane had gone south to the fair of Vaga, and had a great ship of burden which he owned, and nigh twenty men thereon, and that he was as then like to be coming from the south. Asmund, he and his, went on their way south along the land, and had a head-wind, though but little thereof. They met ships a-sailing which were of the Vaga-fleet, and they asked privily about the goings of Asbiorn. It was told them that by then he would be on his way from the south.

Now Asmund and Karli were bedfellows and the dearest of friends. So on a day it befell that Asmund with his company rowed along a certain sound, and a ship of burden came sailing up to them. An easy-to-know ship it was : a ship of painted bows, and stained with white stone and red, and a sail striped with bends they had withal.

Then said Karli : " Oft talkest thou hereof, how thou wouldst be full fain to set eyes on Asbiorn

Seal's-bane; now I wot not how to ken a ship if
he be not sailing there."

Asmund said: "Do me a good turn, good fellow, and tell me if thou kennest him."

Then the ships ran past each other, and Karli
said: "There sits Seal's-bane at the tiller in a blue
kirtle." Asmund answers: "I shall fetch him a
red kirtle." And therewith Asmund shot a spear
to Asbiorn Seal's-bane, and it smote him amidward,
and flew through him, so that it stuck fast in the
head-board, and Asbiorn fell dead from the tiller.
Thereupon either of them went their own way.

They brought the dead body of Asbiorn north
to Thrandsness. Then let Sigrid send after Thorir
Hound from Birchisle, and he came thereto whenas
Asbiorn's body was laid out according to their
wont. But when they went away Sigrid chose
gifts to her friends, and led Thorir off to his ship.
But before they parted she spake: "So it is now,
Thorir, that Asbiorn my son hearkened to thy
loving redes. Now his life did not last long
enough to reward it as it was worth, and though
I be worse fitted thereto than he would have been,
yet have I good-will thereto. Here is now a gift
that I will give thee, and which I would might
stand thee in good stead."—But it was a spear.—
"Here is now that spear which stood through
Asbiorn my son, and the blood is still thereon;
thereby thou mayest the better bear in mind that
it will tally with the wound which thou sawest on
Asbiorn, thy brother's son. Now it would be a
manly deed of thee if thou shouldst so let this
spear go out of thine hand that it should be stand-

ing in the breast of Olaf the Thick. Now I speak this word hereon," says she, "that thou be every man's dastard if thou avenge not Asbiorn." And therewithal she turned away.

Thorir was so wroth at her words, that he might answer nothing, and he heeded not though he let go the spear, nor did he heed the bridge, and into the deep would he have gone, if men had not caught hold of him and steadied him as he went aboard the ship. That was a bar-spear and no great one, and the socket thereof inlaid with gold.

So Thorir and his folk rowed away, and home to Birchisle.

Asmund and his company went on their way until they came south to Thrandheim and met King Olaf, and Asmund told the king what tidings had befallen in his farings. Karli became one of the king's body-guard, and he and Asmund held well to their friendship. But as to the words which Karli and Asmund had spoken to each other before the slaying of Asbiorn betid, they were nowise kept hidden, for they told them to the king themselves. But there befell as is said : Each hath his friends amongst unfriends; for there were certain men there who bore the words in mind, and hence they came back again to Thorir Hound.

CHAPTER CXXXIII. OF KING OLAF.

AS the spring wore on, King Olaf bestirred himself and arrayed his ships; and later in the summer he went south along the land, holding Things with the bonders, atoning men, and mending the faith of the land. Wherever the king went he called in his dues. This summer the king went all the way south to the land's end; and by this time he had christened the land everywhere whereas were the wide countrysides. He had also framed laws over all the land. He had moreover brought under him the Orkneys, even as is aforetold. He had also been sending out messages, and made many friends both in Iceland and Greenland, and likewise in Faroe. King Olaf had sent to Iceland timber for a church, and that church was made at Thingwall whereas is the Althing, and therewith he sent a great bell, which is there still. That was after that the Icelanders had changed their law and set up Christian right, even according to the words that King Olaf had sent them thereanent. Sithence there went from Iceland many men of worship, who served in the household of King Olaf. There was Thorkel, son of Eyolf, Thorleik, son of Bolli, Thord, son of Kolbein, Thord, son of Bork, Thorgeir, son of Havar, and Thormod Coalbrow-skald. King Olaf had sent friendly gifts to many chiefs in Iceland, and they sent him such things as there were to be had, and which they thought he would deem most worthy of being sent him. But in these tokens of friendship which the king was showing to the

IV.   R

Icelanders there lay hidden other matters which afterwards were laid bare.

CHAPTER CXXXIV. OF KING OLAF'S MESSAGE TO ICELAND AND THE COUNSEL TAKEN BY THE ICELANDERS.

THAT summer King Olaf sent to Iceland Thorarin Nefiolfson on his errands; and when the king set off, Thorarin steered his own ship out of Thrandheim, and bore him fellowship as far south as Mere. Then Thorarin sailed out into the main, and had so fair a wind that he sailed for four days until he made the Eres in Iceland. He went straightway to the Althing, and came there when men were on the Law-burg, and forthwith went to the Law-burg. But when men had done their law-business there, Thorarin Nefiolfson took up the word: "Four nights ago I parted from King Olaf Haraldson, and he sendeth hither to this land, unto all chieftains and men who bear rule in the land, and therewithal to all folk, carles and queans, young men and old, men of weal and men of woe, God's greeting and his own, and therewith that he willeth to be your lord, if ye be willing to be his thanes, and either to be friends and furtherers of the other unto all good things." Men answered his word well, and all folk quoth that they would fain be friends of the king, if he were the friend of folk here within the land. Then Thorarin took up the word: "This goeth with the message of the king, that for friendship's sake he prayeth

the Northlanders to give him that island or out-
skerry which lieth off Eyiafirth and men call
Grimsey; in return therefor he willeth to pay such
goods from his own land as men may crave
of him. But more, he sendeth word to Gudmund
of Maddermead to further this matter, for he hath
heard that Gudmund has most to say in those
parts."

Gudmund answered: " I am fain of friendship
with King Olaf, for I am minded to think that
that will profit me a mickle more than that out-
skerry which he biddeth. But the king has not
heard aright that I have more might thereover
than other men, for that hath now been made
common. But now shall we have a meeting on
this matter between ourselves, we who have most
gain of the island."

Then go men to their booths; and thereupon
the Northlanders hold a meeting between themselves and talk this matter over, and each one had
his say according as he looked upon the matter.
Gudmund flitted the case, and many turned towards
it after his way. Then folk asked why Einar, his
brother, said nought thereon, "for we deem," they
say, "that he can see clearest through most
things."

Then answered Einar: "I am few-spoken on
this matter because no one has called upon me to
speak. But if I am to speak my mind, then I am
minded to think that it will be for the folk of this
land not to go under any scat-gifts to King Olaf,
nor any suchlike burdens as he layeth on men in
Norway; that unfreedom we should not bring

upon our own hands only, but both upon ourselves and our sons, and our sons' sons, yea, and all our offspring dwelling within this land, and that thraldom should never go nor turn away from this land. Now though this king be a good man, which I well trow he be, yet it will go henceforth as hitherto, when there is a change of kings, that they be uneven, some good, some ill. But if the folk of the land are minded to hold to their freedom, which they have had ever since this land was dwelled in, then thus must it be done, to let the king get no hold, neither as to owning land here, nor as to the matter of paying him fixed dues such as may be reckoned for liege duty. But that I deem well fitting, that men send friendly gifts to the king, they who will that, such as hawks, or horses, tilts, or sails, or such other things as may be fit to be sent. That would be well bestowed if friendship came in return. But as to Grimsey, this is to be said, that if nothing be brought thence wherein is meat-getting, yet may an host of men be fed there; and should an host of outland men be sitting there, and they fare thence in their longships, then I ween that many a cot-carle might deem his door bethronged."

And forthwith when Einar had spoken this, and set forth the whole way out of it, then all the people had turned round with one accord that this should not be done; and thus Thorarin saw what was the end of his errand in this affair.

CHAPTER CXXXV. OF THE ANSWERS OF THE ICELANDERS.

THE next day Thorarin went again to the Law-burg, and again spake his errand, and began in such wise : " King Olaf sendeth word to his friends hither in the land— and he named thereof Gudmund, son of Eyolf, Snorri the Priest, Thorkel, the son of Eyolf, Skapti, the Speaker-at-law, Thorstein, the son of Hall— he sendeth you word to this end, that ye should fare to meet him, and seek thither a friendly bidding ; and this he said, that ye should not put this journey under your head, if ye deemed his friendship of any worth."

They answered this matter, and thanked the king for his bidding, and said that they would later on let Thorarin know about their journeys, when they had taken rede with themselves and their friends.

Now when the chiefs fell to talking the matter over between themselves, each one spake what seemed good to him concerning this journey. Snorri the Priest and Skapti letted this, to run the risk, in face of the men of Norway, that thither should fare all those men from Iceland who bore most rule in the land. They said that from this message they deemed that misgivings might be drawn, concerning that which Einar had guessed, to wit, that the king was minded to pine some of the Icelanders, if he might have his will. Gudmund and Thorkel, son of Eyolf, urged much that men should bestir themselves according to the word of

King Olaf, and said that that would be a journey
of great honour.   And as they were thrashing out
this matter between them, that seemed to be held
most fast among them, that they themselves should
not fare, but each one to send on his behalf some-
one who was deemed well fitted thereto.   And
with things thus done they parted from the Thing;
and there befell no outfarings that summer.   But
Thorarin made a double journey of it that summer,
and came in harvest-tide to meet King Olaf, and
told him what was the upshot of his errand, and
this withal, that the chieftains would come from
Iceland according to the word he had sent thereto,
or their sons else.

CHAPTER CXXXVI.   OF THE FOLK OF FAROE.

THIS same summer came out to Norway
from the Faroes, at the bidding of King
Olaf, Gilli, the Speaker-at-law, Leif
Ozurson, Thoralf of Dimon, and many other sons
of bonders.   Thrand o' Gate also arrayed him for
the journey, but when he was all but ready he fell
sick of a sudden, so that he might fare nowhither,
and so tarried behind.   And when the Faroe men
came and met King Olaf, he called them for a talk
and had a meeting with them, and unlocked to
them the errand that underlay the journey, and
tells them that he will have scat of the Faroes,
and therewithal that the Faroe folk should abide
by such laws as King Olaf should frame for them.
At this meeting, moreover, that was found from

the words of the king, that for this matter he would take surety of the Faroe men, who were then come there, if they would bind the covenant by sworn oaths. And he bade those men of them whom he deemed to be the noblest there, to become men of his household, and take at his hand honours and friendship. The Faroe men accounted so much of the words of the king, as that it might be doubtful whereto their matter might turn, if they would not take upon them all that the king bade them. And although sundry meetings were held anent this matter or ever it came to a close, it came at last to this, that the king prevailed in all he bade. And Leif and Gilli and Thoralf became of the household of the king, and were made of his body-guard. And all these fellow-travellers swore oaths to King Olaf to the end that in the Faroes should be holden such law and land-right as he should frame for them, and such scat be paid as he should settle. Thereupon the Faroe men arrayed them for the journey home; and at parting the king gave friendly gifts to those who had become his men. And whenas they were ready, they went on their way. But the king let array a ship and got him men thereto, and sent them to the Faroes to gather there such scat as the Faroe folk should yield him. They were not early boun, but they fared when boun they were; and of their journey this is to be told, that they came never back, nor any scat to boot the next summer; for they had never come to the Faroes, nor had any man craved scat there.

CHAPTER CXXXVII. THE WEDDING OF KETIL AND THORD.

KING OLAF went up into the Wick in autumn, and sent word before him to the Uplands, and had manor-feasts arrayed, whereas he was minded that winter to fare about the Uplands; and therewith he arrayed his journey and fared into the Uplands. King Olaf tarried that winter about the Uplands, going from feast to feast, and setting right all such matters as he deemed needed booting, and amending Christian law once more wherever he deemed it needful.

Now that tidings befell, while King Olaf was in Heathmark, that Ketil Calf of Ringness fell to wooing and bade for Gunnhild, the daughter of Sigurd Sow and Asta; and Gunnhild being the sister of King Olaf, it fell to the king to answer and to settle that matter. He took it in a likely manner; for this cause forsooth, that he knew about Ketil that he was high-born and wealthy, a wise man and a great lord; moreover he had long since been a mickle friend of King Olaf, even as herein is aforesaid. All these things together brought it about that the king granted the suit to Ketil. And so it came to pass that Ketil gat Gunnhild for wife, and at that bridal was King Olaf himself.

Thereafter King Olaf went north to Gudbrandsdales, going a-feasting there. There dwelt the man who is hight Thord Guthormson, at a stead called Steig. Thord was the mightiest man in the northern parts of the Dales. And when he

and the king met, Thord hove up his wooing, and
bade for Isrid, daughter of Gudbrand, the sister of
King Olaf's mother; and to the king it came to
give answers to that suit. And as they sat over
that matter, it was settled that that betrothal
should take place, and so Thord gat Isrid for wife.
Afterwards he became the dearest friend of King
Olaf, and with him many of his kinsfolk and friends
who turned after his ways.

Then King Olaf went back south over Thotn
and Hathaland, and then to Ringrealm, and thence
out into the Wick. In the spring he went to
Tunsberg, and tarried a long while there while the
fair was most and the shipping of goods. Thereupon he let array his ships, and had with him a
mickle many men.

CHAPTER CXXXVIII. OF ICELAND-ERS.

THIS summer there came from Iceland,
according to King Olaf's message, Stein,
the son of Skapti, the Speaker-at-law,
Thorod, the son of Snorri the Priest, Gellir, the
son of Thorkel Eyolfson, Egil, son of Hall o' Side,
and brother of Thorstein. The winter before,
Gudmund, the son of Eyolf, had died.

The Iceland men went straightway to meet
King Olaf when they might bring it about. And
when they met the king, they had a good welcome,
and were all with him.

That same summer King Olaf heard that the
ship he had sent to Faroe for the scat the summer

before had been lost, and had made land nowhere
that men had heard of. So the king got another ship
ready, and men, and sent it to Faroe for the scat.
And these men set off and put to sea, but nought
was heard of them sithence any more than of the
others, and many were the guesses as to what
might have become of these ships.

CHAPTER CXXXIX. THE BEGINNINGS OF KNUT THE RICH.

KNUT the Rich, whom some call the
Ancient Knut, he was king at that tide
over England and over Denmark. Knut
the Rich was the son of Svein Twibeard, the
son of Harald. Those forefathers had ruled over
Denmark for a long time. Harald Gormson,
the grandfather of Knut, had gotten Norway after
the fall of Harald Gunnhildson, and had taken scat
thereof, and set up for the warding of the land Earl
Hakon the Mighty. Svein the Dane-king, the son
of Harald, also ruled over Norway, and set thereover for the guarding of the land Earl Eric Hakon-
son. And the brothers, Eric and Svein Hakon-
son, ruled over the land, until Earl Eric went west
to England at the word of Knut the Rich, his
brother-in-law; but he set to rule over Norway,
and left behind Earl Hakon, his son, the sister's
son of Knut the Rich. But sithence, when Olaf
the Thick came to Norway, he first laid hand on
Earl Hakon, and drove him from the sway, as is
aforewrit. Then fared Hakon to Knut, his
mother's brother, and had been with him sithence

all the time till where the story has now come. Knut the Rich had won England with battles, and fought thereto, and had long toil or ever the folk of that land had become obedient to him. But when he deemed himself fully come into the governance of the land, he turned his mind to what title he might deem he had to that dominion, the rule whereof he had not himself in his hand, Norway, to wit. He deemed that he owned all Norway by birthright; but Hakon, his sister's son, deemed that he owned some, and that, moreover, he had lost it in shameful wise. One matter went hereto, why Knut and Hakon had held them quiet about laying claim to Norway, that, first when King Olaf Haraldson came into the land, upsprang all the throng and multitudes of the people, and would hear of nothing but that Olaf should be king over the whole land. But sithence, when folk deemed they might not have their freedom on account of his masterfulness, some betook them out of the land; and a great many mighty men, or sons of powerful bonders, had fared to meet King Knut, on sundry errands as they gave out. And each and all who came to King Knut and would obey him, got their hands full of wealth from him. Withal, there might be seen mickle more lordliness than in other places, both as to that multitude of people that were about there daily, and in the arrayal of the chambers that were his, and wherein he himself abode. King Knut the Rich took scat and dues of those lands which were the wealthiest in northern lands, but at the same rate that he had more revenue to take

than other kings, he also gave away all the more
than any other of the kings.   In all his dominion
there was peace so good, that no one dared transgress it, and the folk of the land themselves kept
peace and ancient land-right.   For this sake he
gat mighty renown in all lands.   But they who
came from Norway, a many bemoaned them of
their loss of freedom, and some set it forth to Earl
Hakon, and others to King Knut himself, that the
men of Norway would now be ready to turn back
under the sway of King Knut and the earl, and
have their freedom again.   This talk was much
after the heart of the earl, and he bewailed it before
the king, and bade him see to it, whether King
Olaf would give up to them the realm or share
it with them under some covenant.   And many
men furthered this matter along with the earl.

CHAPTER CXL. OF KING KNUT'S MES-
SENGERS.

KNUT the Rich sent men from the west
out of England to Norway, and right
gloriously was their journey arrayed ;
they had letters with the seal of the King of the
English.   They came and met Olaf Haraldson,
the King of Norway, in the spring at Tunsberg.
And when people told the king that there were
come messengers from King Knut the Rich, then
waxed he cross-grained thereat, and said thus,
that Knut would be sending no men thither with
errands wherein would be gain either to him or
his men ; and the while of some days the mes-

sengers could not get to see the king.   But when
they got leave to speak to him, they went before
the king and bore forth the letters of King Knut,
and gave out the errand that went therewith, to
wit, that King Knut craved all Norway for his
own, and tells that his forefathers had had that
realm before him; "But inasmuch as King Knut
desireth to deal peacefully in all lands, his will is
not to fare with war-shield to Norway, if other
choice may be found; but if Olaf Haraldson
will be king over Norway, then let him fare to
meet King Knut and take the land in fief of
him, and become his man, and pay him such dues
as the earls paid aforetime."   Then they bore
forth the letters, which said altogether the same
thing.

Then answered King Olaf: "I have heard it
told in ancient tales that Gorm the Dane-king was
deemed to be a mighty enough king of the people,
and he ruled over Denmark alone.   But this the
Dane-kings that have been since deem not enough.
And now it has come to this, that Knut rules over
Denmark, and over England, and, moreover, has
broken a mickle deal of Scotland under his sway,
yet now he layeth claim to my lawful heritage at
my hands.   He should wot how to have measure
in his grasping in the end; or is he indeed minded
alone to rule over all the Northlands, or does he
mean, he alone, to eat all kale in England ?   Yea,
he will have might thereto or ever I bring him my
head or give him any louting soever.   Now shall
ye tell him these words of mine, that I mean to
ward Norway with point and edge whiles my life-

days last thereto, and not to pay any man scat for my own kingdom."

After this downright answer the messengers of King Knut got ready to depart, in nowise pleased how their errand had sped.

Sigvat the Skald had been with King Knut, and the king gave him a ring that weighed half a mark. Thenwithal was with King Knut, Bersi, the son of Skald-Torva, and King Knut gave him two gold rings, each of which weighed half a mark, and therewithal a fair-dight sword. So sang Sigvat:

> O Cub! this Knut the famèd
> Right deed-noble, full stately
> Bedight the hands of us twain,
> Then when the king we came on.
> To thee a gold mark gave he
> Or more, and a war-sword bitter,
> To me a half-mark. Throughly
> God ruleth all much wisely.

Sigvat got himself acquainted with the messengers of King Knut and asked them of many tidings. They told him all he asked for of the parley between them and King Olaf, and also of the end of their errand. They said that the king had taken their business heavily. "And we wot not," they say, "unto whom he trusteth so much, as to gainsay it to become King Knut's man, and to go see him; for that would be the best thing he could do, for King Knut is so merciful that never do lords so bigly to win his enmity, but that he will give all up, so soon as they fare to meet him and do him louting. It was but a little since that to him came two kings from the north from Scotland out of Fife, and he gave up all his anger to them, and gave them back all the lands which they had owned before, and therewithal great friendly gifts." Then sang Sigvat:

> Yea, kings full well renownèd
> Have brought King Knut their heads then
> From Mid-Fife of the Northland.
> That was peace-cheaping soothly.
> But Olaf sold head never
> To any man of this world.
> Full often hath the Thick one
> Well fought him out the victory.

King Knut's messengers went back on their way, and had fair wind over the main. Afterwards they went to meet King Knut, and told him to what end their errand had sped, and therewith also the winding-up words which King Olaf spoke to them at the last.

King Knut answered: "Olaf guesseth not aright, if he be minded that I want to eat up, myself alone, all kale in England; but I would rather that he find that there is more stuff within the ribs of me than kale alone; from henceforth cold rede shall come to him from under every rib of mine."

That same summer came from Norway to King Knut, Aslak and Skialg, the sons of Erling of Jadar, and gat a good welcome there, for that Aslak was wedded to Sigrid, the daughter of Earl Svein, son of Hakon, and she and Earl Hakon, the son of Eric, were brothers' children. King Knut gave those brethren great grants there under him, and they were held in great honour.

CHAPTER CXLI. BOND BETWEEN KING OLAF AND ONUND THE SWEDE-KING.

KING OLAF summoned to him his landed-men and had great multitude of folk about him that summer ; for the word went that Knut the Rich would be faring from the west from England in the run of the summer. Folk deemed with themselves that they learnt from cheaping-ships which came from the west, that Knut would be drawing together a mickle host in England; but as the summer wore, one would yeasay, another gain-say that the host would be coming. But that summer through King Olaf was in the Wick and had his spies out if King Knut should be coming to Denmark.

In autumn King Olaf sent men east to Sweden to King Onund his brother-in-law, and let tell him the message of King Knut and the challenge he laid against King Olaf to Norway; and this he let follow, that he was minded to think that if Knut laid Norway under, then Onund would have peace in Sweden but a little while thereafter, and therefore he deemed it a good rede that he and Onund should bind covenant together and rise up against him ; and he said that they nowise lacked might to uphold strife with King Knut.

King Onund took King Olaf's message in good part, and sent word in return that he will strike fellowship on his part with King Olaf, on the terms that each should grant the other help out of his realm whichsoever should need it first.

This was in the messages between them withal,

that they should have a meeting together and make up their minds as to what was to be done. King Onund was minded to fare the next winter over West Gautland, but King Olaf made things ready for a wintering at Sarpsburg.

CHAPTER CXLII. MESSENGERS SENT BY KNUT THE RICH TO KING ONUND.

KING KNUT came that harvest-tide to Denmark, and sat there through the winter with a great multitude of people. It was told him that men and messages had gone betwixt Norway's king and the Swede-king, and that behind it were big redes toward. King Knut sent in the run of that winter men over to Sweden to see King Onund, and he sent him great gifts and friendly messages, saying that he might well sit in quiet over the quarrels of him and Olaf the Thick : "whereas King Onund," says he, "and his realm shall be in peace for me." And when the messengers came to see King Onund, they bore forth the gifts that King Knut sent him and his friendship therewith. King Onund did not turn a ready ear to their parleys, and the messengers deemed they saw this therein, that King Onund will have much turned to friendship with King Olaf. So back they went and told King Knut how their errands had sped, and that therewithal, that they bade him look to no friendship from King Onund.

CHAPTER CXLIII. JOURNEY INTO BIARMLAND.

THAT winter King Olaf sat in Sarpsburg and had a many men about him. At this time he sent Karli the Halogalander north into the land with his errands. Karli fared first to the Uplands, and then north over the mountains, and came down in Nidoyce, and took there the king's money, so much as he had word to, and a good ship which he deemed well fitted for such a journey as the king had been minded for him, to wit, to fare north to Biarmland. The matter was so laid down, that Karli should be the king's partner, and each should have one-half of all the goods against the other.

Karli steered the ship north into Halogaland early in the spring, and then Gunnstein, his brother, betook himself to the journey with him, and had to him cheaping-wares. They were nigh five-and-twenty men aboard that ship ; and they went early that spring north into Finmark.

Thorir Hound heard the news of this, and sent men and messages to those brethren, and that withal, that he is minded himself to fare that summer to Biarmland, and that he would they should sail in fellowship and share their gettings evenly. Karli and his brother sent word in return that Thorir should have five-and-twenty men even as they had ; and then they would that of the goods that might be gotten there should be equal sharing between the ships, not counting therein the cheaping-wares men had. But when Thorir's messengers came back, he had let launch a longship, a huge buss which he owned, and had let array it. This ship he manned with his house-carles, and aboard the ship were wellnigh eighty men. Thorir ruled alone over this company, and to him belonged whatever gain might be come by in the journey.

And now when Thorir was arrayed, he steered his ship north along the land, and happened on Karli and his, north in Sandver. Sithence fared they all in company, and had a fair wind.

Gunnstein said to his brother Karli, so soon as they and Thorir met, that he deemed Thorir had altogether too great a company of men. "And my mind is," says he, "that it would be wiser to turn back, and not to fare in such wise as that Thorir may do with us whatsoever he pleaseth, for I trust him but ill."

Karli says: "I will not turn back; yet this is true, that if I had known, when we were at home in Longisle, that Thorir Hound would come into our journey with so great an host as he now has, then we should have taken more men with us."

The brothers talked hereon with Thorir, and asked how it came about that he had so many more men with him than had been bespoken. He answereth thus: "We have a big ship that needeth many hands; and methinketh that in such a venturous journey a good man is not one too many." The summer through they went mostly as the ships would go: for when the wind was light the ship of Karli and his made more way, and then they sailed on ahead; but when it blew harder Thorir and his would overhaul them. Seldom were they all together, but each knew always of the other.

So when they came to Biarmland, they hove into a cheaping-stead, and there befell a market, and those men who had money to spend got wealth in plenty. Thorir got some grey wares, and beaver-skins, and sables ; Karli also had a right mickle of money, wherewith he bought much of peltries.

Now, when the market came to an end, they sailed down the river Vina ; and then the peace with the folk of the land was proclaimed to be ended. So when they came out into the main there was a meeting of the crews, and Thorir asked if the men were at all minded to go up aland and get wealth for themselves. The men answered that they were fain thereof, if wealth was certain to be gained. Thorir said that wealth there would be for the getting, if the journey should turn out well, but that it was not unlike that there would be man-risk in the faring. They all said that they would venture on it, if wealth was to be looked for. Thorir said that this was a wont of the land when wealthy men died, that the chattels should be shared between the dead man and his heirs : he to have one-half or one-third, or whiles less ; that wealth should be carried out into woods, or whiles into howes, and mould should be poured upon it ; but that whiles houses would be reared thereover. He said that they should array themselves for the journey at the eve of day. So was it given out that no one should run away from the others, and that none should lag behind when the shipmasters called out that they should be off again. They left some men behind to heed the ships, and the rest went up aland.

At first there were flat fields, and next a mickle woodland. Thorir went ahead, but the brothers Karli and Gunnstein went last. Thorir bade the men fare silently: "And strip ye the trees of their bark so that one tree may be seen from the other."

Now they came forth into a great clearing in the wood, and in the clearing was a high faggot-garth, with a door therein locked. Six men out of the folk of the land should watch the fence every night, each two for one-third thereof. When Thorir and his men came to the garth, the watchers were gone home, but those who next should watch were not yet come to the watch. Thorir went to the fence and hooked his axe on the top of it, and hauled himself up hand over hand, and so in over the garth on one side of the gate; and by that time Karli also had gotten him over the fence on the other side of the gate; and Thorir and Karli came both at one and the same time to the door, and pulled the bolts aside and opened the door, and the men went into the garth.

Spake Thorir: "In this garth is a howe in which all is mixed together, gold and silver and mould, and for this men shall make; but in the garth stands the god of the Biarms, which hight Jomali; and let no one be so daring as to rob him." Then they made for the howe and took there wealth as they most might and bare it in their raiment, and much mould went with it, as was to be looked for. Then Thorir gave out the word that the men

should go back, and spake thus : "Now shall ye
brothers Karli and Gunnstein go first, and I shall
go last." Then turned they all out towards the
gate. Thorir turned back to Jomali, and took a
silver bowl which stood in his lap and was full of
silver pennies, and he poured the silver into his
cloak, but slipped upon his arm the bow which
was over the bowl, and then went out to the
gate.

By that time all those fellows had got out
through the faggot-fence, and then became ware
that Thorir had tarried behind. So Karli turned
back to look for him, and they met inside the gate,
and Karli saw that there had Thorir got the silver
bowl. Then Karli ran up to the Jomali, and saw
that a thick collar was about his neck; he reared
up his axe and smote asunder the string at the
back of the neck whereto the collar was fast; the
stroke was so mickle, that off flew Jomali's head ;
then came a crash so great, that they all deemed
it a wonder. But Karli took the collar, and they
went their ways.

But straightway when the crash befell, the
warders came forth into the clearing, and forthwith
blew on their horns ; and thereon the others heard
trumpets go on every side about them. So they
made for the wood and got into it, but heard from
the clearing behind them whooping and crying,
for now the Biarms were come.

Thorir Hound went the last man of his company; before him walked two men carrying a bag
between them, and what was therein seemed most
like unto ashes. Thorir dipped his hand therein,

and sowed this about their slot, and whiles he cast it forth over the company.

Thus they fared out of the wood, and unto the fields. They heard how the host of the Biarms went after them with crying and yelling full ugsome. Then came they rushing after them out of the wood, and on two sides of them. Yet nowhere came the Biarms or their weapons so near them that any hurt befell thereof; and they kenned that of it, that the Biarms saw them not. But when they came to the ships, Karli and his went first aboard, for they were the foremost as they came down, but Thorir was farthest up aland. Forthwith when Karli and his got aboard their ship, they swept off the tilts and cast off the moorings; then they drew up sail, and the ship soon sped off into the main.

But with Thorir and his things went more slowly, their ship being more unwieldy. And when they bore a hand to the sail, Karli and his were already long from the land. So both sailed across Witchwick.

The nights were still bright, and both sailed day and night until Karli and his hove into certain islands one day at even; there they struck sail and cast anchor, waiting for the ebb of tide, for there was a strong roost before them. Thereafter, thither came Thorir and his, and to anchor also. Then they put out a boat, and thereon went Thorir and men with him, and rowed over to Karli's ship. Thorir went aboard it, and the brothers greeted him well, but Thorir bade Karli handsel him the collar: "For I deem myself worthiest to have the most

precious things which were taken there, inasmuch
as I deemed that ye had to thank me for that the
coming away thence was without loss of life; but
thou, Karli, meseemeth, didst run us into the
greatest peril."

Then said Karli: "King Olaf is the owner of
one-half of all the goods that I may come by in
this journey; now I mean the collar for him. Go
see him, if thou wilt, and it may be that he will
give the collar over to thee, if so be he will have
nought of it, because I took it off the Jomali."

Then answered Thorir and said that he would
they should go up on the island and share their
gains. Gunnstein said that now was the turn of
the tide, and it was time to sail. Therewith they
drew in their cables, and when Thorir saw that,
he went down into the boat, and he and his rowed
back to their ship. Karli and his men had hoisted
their sail and were gotten afar, before Thorir and
his were under sail. And they fared in such wise,
that Karli and his always sailed ahead, and either
of them did the utmost they could. In this wise
they fared on until they came to Geirsver, the first
place where, coming from the north, one may lie
at a pier. Thither they came both one day at
eve, and lay in haven there off the pier. Thorir
and his lay up the haven, and Karli and his
further out in it.

Now when Thorir and his had tilted their
ship, he went up aland, and a great many of his
men with him, and went to Karli's ship, which he
and his had already made snug. Thorir hailed the
ship, and bade the masters come aland, and the

brothers went ashore together with certain of their men. Then Thorir set forth again the same speech as before, bidding them go up on land and bear up their wealth for sharing, such as they had taken as war-prey. The brothers answered there was no need for this until they came home to the builded land. Thorir said that was no men's wont not to share war-spoil till they were back home, and so risk men's uprightness. They had sundry words about this matter, each looking at it in his own way.

So Thorir turned away; but when he had gone but a little way, he turned back and said that his fellows should bide him there. Then he called to Karli, and said: " I will speak with thee privily." So Karli came to meet him. But when they met Thorir thrust a spear to the midmost of him, so that it stood through him. Then spake Thorir: " There mayst thou ken, Karli, one of the Birch-isle men, and I thought it good withal that thou shouldst ken the spear, Seal's-avenger." Karli died at once, and Thorir and his went back to their ship.

Gunnstein and his men saw the fall of Karli, and ran thither forthwith to the spot, and took up his body, and bore it to their ship; they struck the tilts straightway and cast off the gangways, and thrust out from the land; sithence they hoisted sail and went their ways. Thorir and his saw this, and strike their tilts, and array themselves at their utmost speed. But as they hauled up the sail the halliard broke asunder, and down came the sail athwart the ship, and a long while

Thorir and his must needs tarry there, or ever
they got up their sail a second time; and far in
the offing were Gunnstein and his by the time that
Thorir's ship was under way; and both things did
Thorir and his men : sail, to wit, and help sail by
rowing, and the same thing Gunnstein and his did.
And thus either went at their utmost speed day
and night. Slowly it drew together between them,
for when the island sounds began, Gunnstein's
ship was much the handier for steering; yet Thorir
and his drew up to them so much, that when
Gunnstein and his came off Longwick they turned
there to land, and ran away from the ship up on
to the land. And a little after Thorir and his
came thither, and leapt up ashore after them and
gave them chase. A certain woman gat help to
Gunnstein and hid him, and it is said that she was
much cunning in wizardry. Then Thorir and his
went back to the ship and took to them all the
wealth aboard Gunnstein's ship, and bore stones
on it instead thereof, and brought it out into the
firth and scuttled it, and sank it down, whereupon
Thorir and his went their way home to Birchisle.

Gunnstein and his fared at first with head much
hidden; they ferried them forth in small boats,
and fared a-night and lay still by day; and fared
thuswise till they were come past Birchisle, and
were clear out of the bailiwick of Thorir.

Gunnstein fared first to Longisle, and tarried
there but a short while. Then straightway he
set off on his journey to the south, and letted
not till he came south to Thrandheim, and there
fell in with King Olaf, and told him all tidings

such as had befallen in the journey to Biarmland. The king took this journey of theirs sorely to heart, but bade Gunnstein be with him, and says he will right Gunnstein's case as soon as he might bring it about. Gunnstein took that bidding with thanks, and abode with King Olaf.

CHAPTER CXLIV. MEETING OF THE KINGS OLAF AND ONUND.

SO is it aforesaid that King Olaf was east at Sarpsburg that winter whenas King Knut sat in Denmark. That winter Onund the Swede-king rode over West Gautland with more than thirty hundred men. Then fared men and word-sendings between him and King Olaf; and they made tryst between them to meet in the spring at the King's Rock. They tarried the meeting thus for this cause, that they would know, before they met, what undertakings King Knut might have on hand. But as the spring wore King Knut got ready with his host to fare west to England. He set up behind him in Denmark Hordaknut his son, and with him Wolf the Earl, the son of Thorgils Sprakalegg. Wolf was wedded to Astrid, the daughter of King Svein and sister of King Knut, and their son was that Svein who was sithence king in Denmark. Wolf the Earl was a man of the greatest mark.

Now Knut the Rich went west to England, and when the Kings Olaf and Onund heard that, they went to the tryst and met in the Elf at King's Rock. A merry meeting was this, and of much friendly

ways, so far as it was bare before all folk. Yet they
bespoke many things between them, whereof only
they two knew; sundry of which counsels came to be
gone on with, and were then clear for all folk to see.
But at sundering the kings gave gifts one to the
other and parted friends. Then King Onund went
up into Gautland, but King Olaf went north into
the Wick and thence out to Agdir, and thence
again north along the land, and lay a much long
while in Eikundsound and abode a wind. He heard
that Erling Skialgson and the folk of Jadar with
him were laying a gathering, and had a mickle
host.

That was on a day that the king's men were
talking of the weather, if it were blowing south or
south-west, or whether such a wind were weatherly
to sail about the Jadar or not. Most said that un-
weatherly it was. Then answers Haldor Bryn-
iolfson: "I am minded to think," says he, "that it
would be deemed fair weather enough for fetching
Jadar, if Erling Skialgson had arrayed a feast for
us at Soli."

Then said King Olaf that the tilts should
be struck, and the ships be put to sea, and so it
was done. So that day they sailed and doubled
the Jadar, and the weather was of the fairest, and
at night they hove into Whitings-isle. Then the
king went north to Hordland, where he went about
feasting.

CHAPTER CXLV. THE SLAYING OF THORALF.

THAT spring a ship had fared from Norway out to the Faroes, and with that ship went words from King Olaf to the end, that from the Faroes there should come to him some one of his men, Leif, the son of Ozur, to wit, or Gilli the Speaker-at-law, or Thoralf of Dimon. But when this word-sending came to the Faroes and was told to these same, they had a parley between them as to what might lie under this message; and they were of one mind in deeming that the king would be of will to ask of the tidings, which some men held had verily befallen in the islands concerning the misgoing of the king's messengers, those two crews, to wit, whereof not a soul had been saved. They settled between them that Thoralf should go; and he betook himself to the journey, and arrayed a ship of burden which he owned, and gat him men thereto; and they were ten or twelve together aboard. But when they were boun and abiding fair wind, that betid at the house of Thrand o' Gate in East-isle one fair-weather day, that Thrand went into the hall while there lay on the daïs two of his brother's sons, Sigurd and Thord, sons of Thorlak; but the third man was Gaut the Red, who was also a kinsman of theirs. All these fostersons of Thrand were doughty men; Sigurd was the eldest, and ahead in all matters. Thord had a to-name, and was called Thord the Low; for all that he was the highest of men; and yet more, he was both exceeding stout and mighty of strength.

Then said Thrand: " Much will change in a man's life. Unoft it betid when we were young, that on fair-weather days they should be sitting or lying who were young and of able body in all matters. Nor would that have seemed like to the men of aforetime, that Thoralf of Dimon should be a man of more pith than ye; but the ship of burden which I have had this while, and here stands in her shed, methinks, it is now become so ancient that she rots under her tar. Every house here is full of wool, and one cannot so much as get it aired. This would not be if I were but a few winters younger."

Now Sigurd sprang up and called upon Gaut and Thord, saying he could not stand the mocking of Thrand. And out they go to where were the house-carles. They go to the shed and run out the ship of burden; they let flit a lading, and loaded the ship; for no lack of lading was there at home; and withal all gear for the ship. So in a few days they arrayed her, and they too were ten men or twelve aboard.

They and Thoralf had one and the same weather, and always knew of each other on the main sea. They took land in Herna at eve of a day, and Sigurd and his lay-to further west along the strand, yet there was short space between them.

Now it befell in the evening, when it was dark, and Thoralf and his were minded for bed, that Thoralf went up aland, and another man with him, and sought for them a place of easement. And when they were about to go down again, says he who followed him, a cloth was cast over his head, and he was lifted up from the earth, and in that same nick of time he heard a crash ; then he was brought along and heaved up for a fall where was the sea under him, and into the deep he was plunged ; but when he got aland again, he fared thither whereas he and Thoralf had parted, and found Thoralf, who was cloven down to the shoulder, and was then dead. And when his shipmates were ware hereof, they bore his body out on board ship and waked it.

Now at that time was King Olaf in Lygra at a feast, and word was brought thither ; then was an Arrow-Thing summoned, and the king was at the Thing. He had let summon thither the Faroe crews from both the ships, and to the Thing they had come. Now when the Thing was set, the king stood up and spoke : " Tidings have befallen here, whereof it is better that such are seldom told of. Here has a good man been bereft of his life, and a sackless one we deem him to be ; or is there any man at the Thing who knows and can tell who is the doer of this deed ? "

But no one came forth thereto.

Then said the king : " It is nought to lain what my misdoubting is about this work, that in my mind it lies on the hands of the Faroe men ; and I misdoubt me that it is most like that in this way it hath been done ; to wit, that Sigurd Thorlakson must have slain the man, and Thord the Low must have cast the other into the deep ; and furthermore I would make this guess, that the grudge found against Thoralf must have been, that they did not wish that he should be a tell-tale of those ill-doings of theirs, which he must have known of as true, whereof we have long misdoubted us, concerning the murders, and those ill-deeds whereby my messengers have been murdered there."

But when the king came to the end of his speech, Sigurd Thorlakson stood up and said : "Never have I spoken at Things before, and I doubt I shall not be deemed deft of word, and yet, meseems, there is cause enough why I should answer somewhat. Now I will guess that this rede which the king hath put forth, will have come from under the tongue-roots of such men as are much unwiser than he, and worser; and it is no hidden matter that they have fully made up their minds to be our foes. Now that is a word unlikely, that I should have the wish to be Thoralf's scather, whereas he was my fosterbrother and my good friend. But if there had been other matters thereto, and that there had been guilts betwixt me and Thoralf, yet I am stored with wits enough, that I should rather risk such work at home in Faroe than here, under thy very hand, king. Now will I gainsay this matter for myself and for all us shipmates; and I offer to take oath thereon, even as thy laws stand thereto. But if ye deem another thing more trustworthy in aught, then will I bear iron, and I will that thou thyself see to the ordeal."

Now when Sigurd had made an end of his speech, many men came forward in his furtherance, and bade the king that Sigurd get chance to clear himself; they deemed that Sigurd had spoken well and quoth that that would be unsooth whereof he was wyted.

The king says : "Concerning this man great

will be the difference. If he be belied in this case, he will be a good man, but otherwise he must be foolhardy beyond example, and that is rather my misgiving; but I guess he will himself bear witness thereof."

Now because of the prayers of men the king took surety of Sigurd for the ordeal of iron-bearing, and he was to come the day after to Lygra, and there the bishop should do him the ordeal; and thus the Thing broke up. The king fared back to Lygra, and Sigurd and his shipmates to their ship.

And now it speedily grew dark with night, and Sigurd said to his shipmates : " Sooth to say it is, that we have come into mickle trouble, and are in face of a mickle false witness; and this is a king tricky and guileful, and it is easily seen what our lot will be if he shall rule it; for he first let slay Thoralf, and now will he make us out of the laws. It is a small matter for him to bewilder this bearing of iron, and I am minded to deem that he will come by the worse who will run this risk with him. Now withal there setteth down the sound a flaw from the mountains, and my counsel is that we up sail, and sail out into the main sea. Let Thrand fare next summer with his wool if he will let sell it; but if I get away now, methinks it is to be looked for of me, that I shall never be coming again to Norway."

His shipmates deemed this deft rede, and fell to setting their sail, and let go through the night into the main as fast as they might drive. They letted not ere they came to the Faroes, and home to Gate. Thrand took it ill of their journey; but they

IV.   T

gave him back no good answers, though they were biding at home with Thrand. Speedily heard King Olaf that Sigurd and his men were gotten away, and therewith rumour lay heavy on them of that case. There were many who said then that it was like that Sigurd and his men had been spoken of truly, even of them who before had denied the matter on Sigurd's behalf, and spoken against it. King Olaf was few-spoken about this matter, but deemed he now knew that it was true what before he had but misdoubted. So the king went on his way, and took banquets where they were arrayed for him.

CHAPTER CXLVI.   OF THE ICELAND-ERS.

KING OLAF called to a parley with him those men who had come from Iceland, to wit, Thorod, the son of Snorri, Gellir, son of Thorkel, Stein, the son of Skapti, and Egil, son of Hall. And the king took up the word: "Ye have waked up to me this summer a matter, to wit, that ye will dight you for the Iceland-faring, and I have not as yet given out my last word thereon ; now I will tell you what I am minded to. Gellir, thee am I minded for Iceland, if thou wilt bear my errands thither ; but the other Iceland men who are here now, they shall not fare to Iceland, ere I hear how those matters are taken, which thou, Gellir, shalt bear thither."

But when the king had put this forth, they who were fain of the journey, and to whom it was banned, deemed they had but a sour lot, and thought their sitting there a matter ill, and savouring of unfreedom.

Now Gellir gat ready for his journey, and fared in the summer to Iceland, and had thither with him those words sent, which he gave forth the summer after at the Thing. But this was the word sent by the king, that he bade this of the Icelanders, that they should take to those laws which he had set in Norway, and give him from the land thane-gild and nose-gild, for every nose a penny, ten whereof should go to an ell of wadmal. That went herewith, that he behight men his friendship if they would yeasay this, but a hard lot otherwise, on to whomsoever he might bring it. Men sat long over this matter, and took counsel thereon between them, and at last they were all agreed, with one accord to naysay all scat-gifts and taillages such as were craved of them.

And that summer Gellir fared abroad to meet King Olaf, and happened on him that same autumn east in the Wick, whenas he had come down from Gautland ; whereof I ween the story shall be further told later on in the saga of King Olaf.

As the harvest-tide wore on, King Olaf sought north to Thrandheim, and drew with all his company down to Nidoyce ; there he let dight his wintering. King Olaf sat that winter in the Cheaping-stead. That was the thirteenth winter of his kingdom.

CHAPTER CXLVII. OF THE IAMTLAND-ERS.

KETIL IAMTI hight a man, the son of Earl Onund of Spareby in Thrandheim. He had fled before King Eystein the Evil-minded east over the Keel. He cleared the woods and built there whereas it is now hight Iamtland. Eastways thither fled also crowds of folk from Thrandheim before that unpeace; for King Eystein made the Thrandheim folk yield him scat, and set up for a king there his own hound hight Saur. The son's-son of Ketil was Thorir the Helsing, after whom is Helsingland named, and there he builded. But when King Harald Hairfair ridded the realm before him, then a multitude of folk fled before him out of the land, both of Thrandheim and of Naumdale, and dwellings were made yet further east about Iamtland; and some fared to Helsingland from the eastern sea, and they were lieges of the King of Sweden.

But when Hakon, Athelstan's Fosterson, was king over Norway, then was set peace and chaffering from Thrandheim to Iamtland. And for the sake of their love of the king, the Iamtlanders sought from the east to see him, and yeasaid to him their allegiance, and yielded scat to him, and he set them law and land-right, and they were fain rather to obey his kingdom than that of the Swede-king, inasmuch as they were come of Norwegian kin; and this all the Helsings did who were sprung from folk living north of the Keel; and this prevailed for a long time afterward, right until King

Olaf the Thick and Olaf the Swede-king strove over the boundaries of their lands, and sithence the Iamtlanders and the Helsinglanders turned to the dominion of the Swede-king ; and therewith Eid-wood made the land-sundering from the east, and then the Keels all the way north to Finmark ; so then the Swede-king took scat of Helsingland and of Iamtland as well. But Olaf, Norway's king, held that it had been in the covenant between him and the King of Sweden, that the scat of Iamtland should go elsewhere than it had done heretofore, notwithstanding that for a long while the matter had stood so, that the Iamts had yolden scat to the Swede-king and that the bailiffs of the land had been appointed thence. But the Swedes would as then hearken to nought, but that all land lying east of the Keels should lie under the sway of the King of Sweden. And that went so, as oft is seen, that, in spite of the affinity and friendship there was between the kings, each wanted to have all that dominion to which he deemed he had any title at all. King Olaf had let the word go abroad in Iamtland that it was his will that the Iamts should do him fealty, and had threatened them with hard dealings otherwise. But the Iamts had made up their mind that they would yield obe-dience to the King of Sweden.

CHAPTER CXLVIII. THE STORY OF STEIN.

THOROD, son of Snorri, and Stein, the son of Skapti, were ill content at not being allowed to go about in freedom. Stein, son of Skapti, was the goodliest of men to look upon, and the best fashioned of prowess, a good skald, and a man of great show and yearning for honours. Skapti, his father, had wrought a drapa on King Olaf, and taught it to Stein, and it was so meant that he should bring King Olaf the song. Stein nowise kept himself tongue-tied in speaking out and finding fault with King Olaf, both in speech loose and in speech up-knitted. Both of them, he and Thorod, were men unwary of words, and they say so much as that the king's will was to deal worse with them than they had weened, who in trust of him had sent him their sons; whereas the king laid them in bondage. The king was wroth. Now on a day whenas Stein Skaptison was before the king, he asked the king to say whether he would listen to the drapa which his father, Skapti, had wrought on the king.

He answered : " The other thing must be first, Stein, that that thou give forth that which thou hast wrought on me." Stein said it was nothing that he had wrought. " I am not a skald, king," says he ; " but though I could make rhymes, thou wouldst deem that, as other matters concerning me, but of little account." And therewithal Stein went away, and deemed he saw whereto the king was speaking.

Thorgeir was the name of a steward of the king's who was over a manor of his in Orkdale; at this time he was with the king, and heard the talk between the king and Stein, and a little after he went home.

Now on a night it befell that Stein ran away from the town together with his servant. They went out upon Gauledge, and so westward till they came into Orkdale; and that evening they came to the king's manor that Thorgeir had in charge, and Thorgeir bade Stein abide there for the night, and asked him what was toward in his farings. Stein bade him let him have a horse and a sleigh; for he saw that they were carting home corn there. Thorgeir said: "I do not know how it stands with this journey of thine, whether thou farest at all by the king's leave; for methought the day before yesterday words nowise meek went between thee and the king."

Stein said: "Though I have to look for no free will from the king, that shall not be so before his thralls." And therewith he drew his sword and slew the steward. And the horse he took and bade the swain jump aback of it, and Stein set him in the sleigh, and so they went their way and drove through the whole night, and they went their ways till they came down into Sorreldale in Mere. Then they got themselves ferried across the firths, and at their very swiftest they sped on. They told no men where they came of this man-slaughter, but said they were the king's men; and therefore they were well furthered wheresoever they came.

At eve of a day they came into Gizki to the house of Thorberg Arnison. He was not at home, but there was his wife, to wit, Ragnhild, the daughter of Erling Skialgson. And Stein had here a good welcome, for between them there was already close acquaintance. It had happened before, in Stein's faring abroad from Iceland in a ship which he owned himself, when he hove in from the main to the western coast of Gizki, and he and his were lying by the island, that Ragnhild lay in and should be lighter of a child, and was heavy with sickness; but no priest was there in the island nor anywhere anigh. So they came to the cheaping-ship, asking if there were any priest aboard. A priest there was, hight Bard, a man of the Westfirths, young, but somewhat little of lore. The messengers bade the priest go with them to the house. He deemed that that would be a mickle hard matter, for he knew his lack of learning, so he would not go. Then Stein laid word on the priest, and bade him go. The priest answereth : " I will go if thou goest with me, for therein I deem I shall have avail for good counsel." Stein said that he would surely share him that. Then they go to the stead, and thereto where Ragnhild was.

A little sithence she gave birth to a child, which was a maiden and was deemed to be somewhat weakly. So the priest christened the child, and Stein held her at the font, and the maiden was hight Thora. Stein gave the maiden a finger-ring. Ragnhild behight Stein her full friendship, and bade him come thither to her, whensoever he deemed he had need of her help. Stein said that he would hold no more maiden bairns at the font, and therewith they parted.

But now were things come to such a pass, that Stein was come there to claim the keeping of this friendly promise of Ragnhild, and tells her what has befallen him, and therewith, that he must have fallen under the king's anger. She answers that her might and main would be in her help; but bade him abide Thorberg there. She seated him next to her son, Eystein Blackcock, who was then twelve winters old. Stein gave gifts to Ragnhild and Eystein.

Thorberg had heard all concerning the faring of Stein before he came home, and somewhat frowning was he. Ragnhild went to talk with him, and told him all about Stein's farings, and bade him take Stein to him and look to his case. Thorberg answers : " I have heard," says he, " that the king has let hold an Arrow-Thing after Thorgeir, and that Stein has been made an outlaw, and also this, that the king is exceeding wroth. Now I know better how to look to what behoves me than to take on hand but an outland man and have the wrath of the king therefor. Let ye Stein fare away at his speediest." Ragnhild answers and says that they would either both fare away together, or both abide there. Thorberg bade her go whithersoever she would. " For I ween," says he, " that though thou fare, thou wilt speedily come back, for here will be thy most honour." Then stood forth Eystein Blackcock their son ; he spake and said thus, that he would not abide behind if Ragnhild fared away.

Thorberg said they showed them mickle wilful and headstrong in this matter : "And it is most like now that ye will have your way in this, since ye set all this great store by it ; but thou walkest far too much in the way of thy kin, Ragnhild, whereas thou holdest the word of King Olaf as of little worth."

Ragnhild said : "If it be such a big thing in thine eyes, this holding of Stein, then fare thou thyself with him to find Erling my father, or give him such a faring-mate that he may get thither in peace."

Thorberg says that he will not send Stein thither ; for Erling will have enough on his hands that the king will mislike him of.

So Stein abode there the winter through. But after Yule there came to Thorberg messengers from the king, with these words, that Thorberg should come meet the king before Midlent ; and threats of sore pains went with this word. Thorberg bore this before his friends, and sought their rede whether he should risk it, to go to the king as things now stood ; but the greater part of them letted it, and called that rede rather, that he should let Stein go out of hand, rather than fare into the king's power. But Thorberg was rather minded not to lay the journey under his head.

Some while after Thorberg went to see Finn, his brother, and laid this matter before him, and bade him fare with him. Finn answers that he deemed such wife-mastery evil, whereby one should not dare for his wife's sake to hold faith with his liege lord. Says Thorberg : " Thou art free not to go, yet methinks thou hangest back more for fear-sake than out of goodwill to the king." And they parted wroth.

Then Thorberg went to see Arni Arnison, his brother, and tells him all, how things were, and bade him fare with him to the king. Arni says: "Wondrous methinketh it of thee, so wise a man and so heedful of thy ways, that thou shouldst ever have tumbled into so great a mishap, and have gotten the king's wrath, when no need was thereto. Thou wert excused if thou wert holding thy kinsman or a fosterbrother, but nought at all wherein thou hast taken in hand an Iceland man, and holdest the king's outlaw, and hast put thyself in peril, and all thy kinsmen." Says Thorberg: "So goes the saw, Every ilk has an outcast. That illhap of my father is easiest seen of me, how he blundered in the getting of his sons, that he should get him last, who hath no like of our kindred and is but deedless; and most true it would be to say, if it were not spoken to the shame of my mother, that I should never call thee our brother." And Thorberg turned away and went home somewhat joyless. Thereafter he sent word north to Thrandheim to his brother Kalf, bidding him to come and meet him at Agdaness. And when the messengers met Kalf, he behight his faring without another word.

Ragnhild sent men east to Jadar to Erling her father, and bade him send her folk. And thence fared the sons of Erling, Sigurd and Thorir, and had each of them a craft of twenty benches, and thereon ninety men. And when they came north to Thorberg, he welcomed them at his best and

fainest. He arrayed him for the journey, and had
a craft of twenty benches, and they went their way
northward.

And when they came off Thrandheim mouth,
there were lying there already the brothers of
Thorberg, Finn and Arni, with two twenty-
benched craft. Thorberg welcomed well his
brethren, and said that now had the whetting come
home to them. Finn said that for him seldom had
he need of such whetting.

Thereupon they went with all that band north
to Thrandheim, and Stein was in their company.
And when they came to Agdaness, there was
before them Kalf Arnison, with a keel of twenty
benches well manned.

Fared they with all this host in to Nidholm, and
lay there over night. The next morning had they
their talk. Kalf and the sons of Erling would
bring all the host up to the town, and then let
things go as shaping should. But Thorberg would
that at first they should go to work quietly, and let
bid terms. Hereto were Finn and Arni consenting.
So now it was settled that Finn and Arni fare first
to see King Olaf, but a few together.

The king had already heard of the throng they
had, and he was rather cross-grained in his talk
with them. Finn bade bidding for Thorberg, and
for Stein withal; he bade that the king should
award as great a fine as he wished, but Thorberg
to have dwelling in the land, and his grants, and
Stein to have peace of life and limb.

The king answers: " Meseemeth that ye have
made this journey from home in such wise, that now

ye deem ye may have your will half-way against me,
or more maybe; but for this do I least look from you
brethren, that ye would come with an host against
me. I ken these counsels, that they will have been
uphoven by the men of Jadar; but no need there
is to offer me money."

Then says Finn: "Nought have we brethren
had a gathering for this sake, that we bid thee
unpeace, king; rather this way beareth it, king, that
we will first bid thee our service; but if thou naysay it, and art minded for hard dealings on Thorberg, then will we all fare with that host we have,
and join Knut the Rich."

Then the king looked on him and said: "If ye
brethren will swear me oath hereto, to follow me in
the land and out of the land, and not to sunder
from me without my goodwill and leave, and ye
will not hide it from me if ye wot of treason
brewed against me, then will I take peace of you
brethren."

Then Finn went back to his company, and told
them the terms the king had made them. So they
take counsel together, and Thorberg said that he
will take this choice for his hand: "Loth am I,"
says he, "to flee from my own lands and seek to
outland lords. I am minded that to me will honour
ever be toward in the following of King Olaf, and
to be there whereas he is."

Then said Kalf: "I will win no oath to the
king, and that while only will I be with him
whereas I may hold my grants and other honours,
and whereas the king will be my friend; and that
is my will that all we do even so."

Finn answers : " My counsel it is to let King Olaf alone settle terms between us."

Arni Arnison sayeth thus : " If I have made up my mind to follow thee, brother Thorberg, even if thou wouldst fight with the king, all the less shall I sunder from thee, if thou follow better rede. I will follow thee and Finn, and take such choice as ye see handiest for you."

Then those three brethren went aboard one ship, Thorberg, Finn, and Arni, and rowed up to the town, and went sithence to meet the king. And then this covenant came about, that the brethren swore oath to the king. Then Thorberg sought peace for Stein of the king. But the king answered that Stein should go in peace as for him whithersoever he would. " But with me shall he never be henceforth."

Then Thorberg and his went back out to their company. Kalf fared up to Eggja, but Finn fared unto the king; Thorberg and the others of the company went home again south. Stein went south with the sons of Erling. But early in the spring he fared west to England, and thereafter into the hand of Knut the Rich, and was for a long while with him in good liking.

CHAPTER CXLIX. THE JOURNEY OF FINN ARNISON TO HALOGALAND.

WHENAS Finn Arnison had tarried for a little while with King Olaf, it happened on a day that the king called Finn to him for a talk, and more men thereto, whom he was wont to have in his counsels. Then the king took up the word and said : "That rede is growing fast in my mind, that I am minded to bid out an hosting of the whole land next spring, both men and ships, and fare therewithal, with all the host that I may get me, against Knut the Rich. For I wot of that claim which he hath set forth for the realm at my hands, that he will not deal with it as a vain matter. Now I have this to say to thee, Finn Arnison, that I will that thou fare mine errand north to Halogaland, and bid out an hosting there, and call out all the folk, both men and ships, and take with thee that host to meet me at Agdaness."

Then the king named for like errands other men, sending some up into Inner Thrandheim and some south into the land, so that this summons he let fare throughout the whole realm.

Now this is to be said of Finn's journey, that he had a cutter, and thereon wellnigh thirty men ; and when he was arrayed, he went on his journey till he came into Halogaland. Then he summoned a Thing of the bonders and set forth his errand, and craved the muster. The bonders had in the country big ships fit for war-muster, and at the word-sending of the king they bestirred them and arrayed their ships. But when Finn came farther north into Halogaland, he held there a Thing, but sent some of his men whereas it seemed good to him to crave the out-gathering. Finn sent men to Birchisle to Thorir Hound, and let crave the muster there as elsewhere. And when the bidding of the king came to Thorir, he arrayed himself for journeying, and manned that same ship

with his house-carles which he had had to Biarmland the summer before ; and he bedight it at his
own cost alone.

Finn summoned to Vagar all such Halogaland
folk as dwelt to the north of that place ; and there
gathered together a great host through the spring,
and all abode such time as Finn should come
from the north.

And therewithal was come Thorir Hound.

And when Finn came, forthwith he let blow all
the mustered host to a House-Thing. At that
Thing men showed their weapons, and then the
muster of each ship-rathe was ransacked.

But when all that was cleared, spoke Finn : " I
will call on thee hereto, Thorir Hound ; what
bidding wilt thou bid King Olaf for the slaying of
Karli his courtman ; or for that robbery whereby
thou tookest the king's gear north away in Longwick ? Now the full power of the king have I
in this matter ; and now will I have thine
answer."

Thorir looked about and saw standing on either
side of him men full-weaponed, and knew Gunnstein there, and a many other kinsmen of Karli.
Then said Thorir : " My offer is quickly done,
Finn ; I will lay all this matter for which he bears
me mispleasure under the king's wielding."

Finn answers : " More likely now, that thou
wilt be honoured less than that, for now thou must
abide my doom, if peace is to be made."

Thorir says : " Then I still deem my affair in a
good case, and for that shall I nowise draw aback."

Then Thorir stepped forward to give surety,

and Finn framed the terms of all that matter. Then Finn says out the peace, to wit, that Thorir shall yield the king ten marks of gold, and to Gunnstein and his kinsmen another ten marks, and for robbery and fee-scathe the third ten marks, "and yield it now forthwith," says he.

Thorir says : " This is a great fine to find."

" The other the choice is," says Finn, " that the peace be all done with."

Thorir says that Finn must give him time to seek loans from his fellows. Finn bade him yield the fine on the place, and give up withal the collar, the mickle one, which he took off Karli dead. Thorir said he had taken no collar.

Then came forth Gunnstein and said that Karli had had the collar round his neck when they parted, " but it was gone when we took up his dead body." Thorir said he had not searched his mind about that collar. " But though we should have some collar or other, it must be lying at home in Birchisle."

Then set Finn his spear-point against Thorir's breast, and bade him hand over the collar. Therewith Thorir took the collar off his neck, and handed it over to Finn. Then Thorir turned away and went aboard his ship, and Finn went after him out on to the ship, and a many of men with him. Finn went along the ship, and they opened the berths, and by the mast they saw down under the deck two great tuns, so that they deemed mickle marvel thereof. Finn asked what was in those tuns, and Thorir said therein lay his drink. Said Finn : " Why givest thou us not to drink, good fellow, seeing thou hast so much drink with thee?" Thorir ordered his man to tap the tun into a bowl, and then this was given to Finn to drink, and the best of drink it was.

Then Finn bade Thorir hand over the money, and Thorir bade him go aland and said he would pay it there. So Finn and his men went up aland. Then came there Thorir and paid the silver, and out of one purse there was handed ten marks by weight. Then he put forth many knit-up clouts; and in some was a mark by weight, in some half, or sundry ounces.

Then said Thorir: "This is borrowed money which sundry folk have lent me, for methinks all upcast now is the loose money which I had."

Thereafter Thorir went on board ship, and when he came back he paid out silver little by little, and thus the day wore.

But when the Thing broke up, men went to their ships and arrayed them for putting off, and under sail men got so soon as they were ready; and soon it came to this, that most men had sailed. So Finn saw this, that the company was thinning about him, and men called to him and bade him get ready; but not one-third of the money was paid up as yet.

Then said Finn: "This payment goes slowly now, Thorir. I see thou takest it greatly to heart to pay the money; so I shall leave the matter in quiet for a while, and thou canst pay to the king what is left." Therewith Finn stood up and went away.

Thorir says: "I am well pleased, Finn, that we

part; but I shall have right goodwill to pay this
debt in such wise that the king shall deem it not
under-paid, yea, and both of you."

So then Finn went to his ship and sailed after his
company. But Thorir was late boun from the haven,
but when their sail came up they held out of West-
firth, and so out into the main, and so south along the
land, in such wise that whiles was the sea on mid-
mountain, whiles the land under water. Thuswise
he steered on southwards, until he sailed into
England's main; and he fared therewith to see
King Knut, who gave him a good welcome. And
now it came out that Thorir had there right much
of chattels, all that wealth, to wit, which they had
taken in Biarmland, he and Karli, with their men.
But in those mickle tuns there was one bottom a
little way from the other; and betwixt the two was
drink, but the rest of either tun was full of grey
skins, and beaver, and sable. And now Thorir was
with King Knut.

Finn Arnison fared with that host to King Olaf,
and tells him all about his journey, and this withal,
that he doubts Thorir was gone out of the land and
west away to England to meet Knut the Rich,
"and I am of the mind that he will be all unprofitable to us." The king says: "I well believe that
Thorir will be our unfriend, yet ever I deem him
better afar from me than anigh."

CHAPTER CL. THE STRIFE OF HAREK AND ASMUND, THE SON OF GRANKEL.

ASMUND, son of Grankel, had been that winter in his bailiwick in Halogaland, and was at home with his father Grankel. There lieth out towards the main a haunt where was to catch both seal and fowl, an egg-lair and fish-lair withal; and this had of old gone with the stead now owned of Grankel. But Harek of Thiotta laid claim to the same, and to such a pass matters had come, that he had had of the lair all gain for several seasons. But now Asmund and his father deemed they might fall back upon the king's avail in all rightful causes. And so they fared, the twain of them, in the spring to see Harek and tell him King Olaf's words and tokens; to the end that Harek should leave off laying claim to the lair. Harek answered heavily thereon and said that Asmund went to the king with slander in this, as in other matters: "I have all the right on my side; and thou, Asmund, mightest well mind thee of measure, though now thou deem thee a man much of might, because thou hast the king's avail at thy back. And so is it, forsooth, if thou shalt be allowed to slay sundry chieftains and make of them men out of atonement, and to rob us, who whiles deemed we knew how to hold our own fully against men, even were they of equal birth with us; but now is that all far from it, that ye are mine equals for kin sake." Asmund answers: "This know a many of thee, Harek, that thou art of great kin and masterful; a many sit over a sharded lot because of thee; yet it is most like that thou, Harek, must seek another whereon to push forth thy wrong-dealings than on us, or to take up thy so great lawlessness."

Thereupon they parted. Harek sent his house-carles, ten or twelve of them, with a certain great row-ferry. They fared into the lair and took there every sort of catch and loaded the ferry therewith. But when they were ready to go back, there came on them Asmund Grankelson with thirty men and bade them let loose all that catch. Harek's house-carles answered somewhat unspeedily there-over, so Asmund and his set upon them, and soon the odds told their tale: some of Harek's house-carles were beaten, some wounded, some cast into the deep; and all the catch was borne out of their ship, and Asmund and his had it away with them.

In this plight the house-carles of Harek came home and told Harek of their journey. He answers: "New doings, new tidings; this has not been done before, the beating of my men."

But this matter lay quiet, and Harek said never a word thereto and was of the merriest.

In the spring Harek let array a cutter of twenty benches, and manned it with his house-carles; and right well found was that ship both of men and all gear.

This spring Harek went into the warfare; but when he met King Olaf, Asmund Grankelson was there already. Then the king brought about a meeting between Harek and Asmund, and appeased them; and the case was laid to the king's doom.

Then Asmund let call witness that Grankel had been owner of the lair, and the king doomed thereafter. And then the cases stood uneven, so that the house-carles of Harek were unbooted, and the lair was doomed to Grankel. Harek says it was no shame for him to abide by the king's judgment, however this matter might shape itself afterwards.

CHAPTER CLI. THE STORY OF THOROD.

THOROD, the son of Snorri, had tarried in Norway by the command of King Olaf when Gellir Thorkelson got leave to go to Iceland, as is aforewrit; and he was with King Olaf, and was ill content at abiding in such unfreedom, whereas he might not fare his ways whither he would.

Early in the winter whereas King Olaf sat in Nidoyce, the king made it known that he was minded to send men to Iamtland to gather the scat. But for this journey folk were uneager, because the messengers of King Olaf which he had sent before, Thrand the White, to wit, and they twelve together, had been cut off, as is written afore, and from that time the Iamtlanders had held to the Swede-king as their liege lord. Thorod Snorrison offered himself for this journey, whereas he recked but little what might befall him so he were free of his ways. The king took his offer, and they went twelve in company, Thorod and his.

So they came right east away to Iamtland, and

came to a man named Thorar. He was lawman there, and the most of honour. Here they had a good welcome, and when they had been abiding there a little while, they set forth their errands to Thorar. He said that the answers thereto were ruled no less by other folk of the land, and by chieftains than by him, but said that a Thing ought to be summoned. And so it was done: a Thing-bidding was up-shorn, and a crowded Thing was summoned, and Thorar fared to the Thing; but the king's messengers abode at his house the while. Thorar set this matter forth to the people; but they were all of one mind on this, that they would not pay scat to the King of Norway. The messengers some would have hanged, and others would have them for blood-offering; but it was settled that they should be held there until the bailiffs of the Swede-king should be coming, and these should determine concerning them what they would, by the counsel of the folk of the country; but that they should make a show of this, that the messengers being well holden, they were tarried for their abiding the scat, and they should part them and quarter them two and two together. Thorod was with another man at Thorar's; and there was mickle Yule-feast and gild ale-drinkings. There were many bonders living in that thorp, and they all drank together through the Yule-tide. Another thorp there was a little way thence; there dwelt a kinsman-in-law of Thorar, a mighty man and a wealthy. He had a son full grown. These kins-men-in-law were to drink half-Yule at each other's, beginning at Thorar's. The kinsmen-in-law drank against each other, and Thorod against the bonder's son. It was a champion drinking, and in the evening was mickle masterful talk and man-pairing betwixt the Norway men and the Swedes, and then betwixt their kings, both those who had been aforetime and those who now were, and also about the dealings there had been betwixt both countries in manslayings and liftings, such as had befallen betwixt the two lands.

Then spake the bonder's son: "If our kings have lost the more men, then the bailiffs of the Swede-king will square that up with the lives of twelve men, whenas they come from the south after Yule; and ye wot unclearly, wretched men, whereto ye are tarried."

Thorod thought about his case, and many would draw a jeer on them, and found words of shame for them, yea, and their king withal. And now it fared unhidden what the ale spake in the Iamts, and whereof Thorod had not misdoubted him afore. But the next day Thorod and his man took all their clothes and weapons, and laid them ready to hand; and the night after, when all folk were asleep, they ran away into the wood.

The next morning, when men were ware of their running away, they fared after them with sleuthhounds, and happened on them in the wood where they had hidden them, and brought them back home and put them into a bower. Therein there was a deep pit, and thereinto they were let, and the door thereof locked. Little meat they had, and no clothes save their own.

Now when mid-Yule was come, Thorar and all

his freedmen with him went to his kinsman-in-law, and there he was to drink the latter Yule; but the thralls of Thorar should guard the pit. Drink enow was minded for them, but they measured their drinking but little, and became ale-mad straightway that same night. And when they deemed they were full-drunk, then spake they betwixt them who were to bring food to the men of the pit that they should not be left short of food. Thorod sang a lay and made the thralls merry, and they said he would be a chosen man, and gave him a right mickle candle, which was lighted. Then came out thither the thralls who before were in the house, and called full eagerly to the others to come in. But either lot of them was ale-mad, so that they neither locked the pit nor the bower. Then Thorod and his fellow cut their cloaks up into ropes, and tied them together, and made a ball of the end, and cast it up on to the outhouse floor; and it twisted round the foot of a chest and stuck fast. Then they tried to get up; and Thorod lifted his fellow up until he stood on his shoulders, who then drew himself up hand over hand through the trap-door. And now there was no lack of ropes in the outhouse, and he let one drop down to Thorod. But when he was to haul Thorod up he might nowise get him astir. Then Thorod bade him cast the rope over the tie-beam which was in the house, and make a loop at the end and carry thereto timbers and stones, so as to outweigh the weight of him. He did even so. And then the weight sank down into the pit, and Thorod came up out of it. In the outhouse they took raiment for themselves such as they needed ; therein were sundry skins of reindeer, and they cut the shanks thereof, and bound them turned toe-to-heel under their feet. But before they fared away they set fire to a great corn-barn which there was, and then ran away amidst the pit-mirk. The barn was burnt up, and many other houses in the thorp withal.

Thorod and his fellow fared through the wilderness all that night, and hid themselves at dawn of day. In the morning they were missed, and folk went with sleuthhounds to seek them, every quarter away from the stead ; but the hounds tracked their steps back to the stead, for they knew them by the reindeer-shanks, and tracked the slot thither whereto pointed the hoofs of the shanks ; so that they might not be searched out.

Thorod and his fellow wandered through wildernesses for a long while, and came on an evening to a little homestead and walked inside. Within there sat a carle and a quean by the fire ; he named him Thorir, and said she was his wife who was sitting there, and withal that they owned the house-cot. The goodman bade them abide, and they took his bidding. He told them that thither was he come because he had had to flee from the dwelling for slaying's sake. Good cheer was gotten for Thorod and his man, and they all ate their meat round the fire. Then a bed was arrayed for Thorod and his man there on the settle, and they laid them down to sleep.

That while the fire was yet aflame. Thorod then saw that from another chamber came forth a man, and never had he seen a man like big. That man had on raiment of gold-broidered scarlet, and was of the goodliest to behold. Thorod heard that he blamed them for taking guests, when they had scarce meat enough to bless themselves withal. The housewife said : " Be not wroth, brother, seldom doth such a chance befall : do them rather something that may be to their profit, for thou art handier thereto than we be."

Thorod heard that the big man was named Arnliot Gellini, and also that the goodwife was his sister. Thorod had heard tell of Arnliot, and of this, moreover, that he was the greatest way-besetter and evildoer.

So Thorod and his man slept night over, for they were weary afore of their much walking. But when about one-third of the night was still left, thither came Arnliot and bade them stand up and array them for their journey. So Thorod and his man stood up and arrayed them, and break-fast was served them. Then Thorir gave snow-shoes to either of them, and Arnliot betook him-self to faring with them, and strode on the snow-shoes, which were both broad and long. But so soon as Arnliot plied his staff, he was off and afar from them. Then abided he, and said that in this wise they would get no-whither, and bade them step on the snowshoes along with him ; and so did they ; and Thorod stood next to Arnliot and held by his belt, while Thorod's fellow held on to him. Then Arnliot slid on as fast as if he were faring loose.

Now when one-third of the night was spent,

they came to a certain hostel, and made fire there, and dight their meat. But whenas they were at meat then spake Arnliot, and bade them cast down nought of the meat, neither bone nor crumb. Arnliot took out of his sark a silver dish, and ate therefrom. But when they were full, Arnliot gathered their leavings together, and thereupon they got ready for their beds.

At one end of the house there was a loft on the tie-beams, and up into that loft went Arnliot and the others, and there they laid them down to sleep. Arnliot had a mickle bill, the socket whereof was gold-driven, but its shaft was so high that one's hand could but just reach to the socket, and he was girt with a sword withal. They had both weapons and raiment up there in the loft with them.

Arnliot bade them hold their peace. He lay the foremost of them in the loft.

A little afterwards there came twelve men to the house; they were chapmen, who were faring to Iamtland with their wares. When they came into the house they made mickle din about there, and were very merry, and they made them big fires. But when they had their meat they cast out all the bones. Thereafter they got them ready for bed, and lay down on a settle before the fire there. But when they had sat there for a little while there came into the house a mickle troll-wife; and whenas she came in, she swept up fast, and took the bones and all things she deemed good to eat and cast them into her mouth. Then she seized the man that lay next to her, and tore and slit him all asunder, and cast him unto the fire. Then awoke the others to an evil dream forsooth, and leapt up. But she sent them to hell one after other, till only one was left alive; and he rushed up the floor under the loft, calling out for help if any were thereto in the loft who might be of avail to him. Arnliot stretched out his hand for him, and caught him by the shoulder and drew him up into the loft. Then she ran up to the fire and fell to eating of the men, those who were roasted. Then stood Arnliot up and gripped his bill, and thrust it between her shoulders so that the point ran out through the chest. She turned her hard thereat, and cried out evilly and ran out. Arnliot lost the hold of the spear, and she had it away with her. Then Arnliot bestirred himself and cleared out the bodies of the men, and set a door and door-posts before the hall, for she had broken it all loose when she went out.

And now they slept for what was left of the night. But when day dawned, they stood up and first ate their day-meal; and when they had eaten, Arnliot said: "Now shall we part here: ye shall follow this sledge-road whereby the merchants fared hither yesterday; but I will seek my spear. For my wages I shall take what I deem of money's worth among the chattels which these men owned. But thou, Thorod, shalt bear my greeting to King Olaf, and tell him this, that he is the man of all men whom I were fainest to meet; but he will deem my greeting nothing worth."

Therewith he took up the silver dish and rubbed it with a cloth and said: "Bring this dish to the king and say that it is my greeting."

Thereafter either of them got ready for the journey and parted, even as things were. And Thorod and his fellow, and the man withal out of the company of the merchants who had escaped alive, went each his own way; and Thorod went on until he met King Olaf in Chippingham, when he told him all about his journeys and brought him the greeting of Arnliot, and handed over to him the silver dish. The king says that it was ill that Arnliot should not have come to see him, "and it is a great scathe that so good a fellow and a man so noteworthy should have fallen into such evil ways."

After this Thorod abode with King Olaf for the rest of the winter, and sithence got leave of him to fare to Iceland next summer. He and King Olaf parted in friendship as at that time.

CHAPTER CLII. OF KING OLAF'S OUT-BIDDING.

IN the spring King Olaf got ready to leave Nidoyce; and mickle company drew together to him both from the parts of Thrandheim and withal from the North-country. And when he was boun for faring, he went with his host first south into Mere, and gathered together thence his folk-company, and also out of Raumdale. Then he went to South Mere, and a long while he lay in Her-isles, and abode his folk, and that while oft had he House-Things, for there many matters came to his ears which he deemed needed talking over. It befell at one of the House-Things which he held, that he had that speech in his mouth, and spake of

that manscathe which he had gotten of the Faroes.
"But the scat which they behote me is nowise
forthcoming. Now I am minded to send men
thither for the scat once more."

And the king stirred this matter to sundry men
that they should betake them to the journey. But
there came such answers in return, whereby all
begged off from that journey. Then stood up a
man in the Thing, a mickle man, and very stately of
look : he had on a red kirtle, helm on head, girt
with sword, a mickle bill in his hand. He took up
the word : "Sooth is it to say," quoth he, "that
here is wide diversity of men. Ye have a good
king, but he hath ill men, who naysay a mere
errand-faring which he biddeth you, though ye
have ere this taken at his hands friendly gifts and
many seemly things. But I have been hitherto no
friend of this king, and he hath been my unfriend ;
and he deemeth there be good causes hereunto.
Now I will offer thee, king, to fare this faring if no
better man be thereto forthcoming."

The king answereth : "Who is this valiant man
who answereth thus to my cause ? Thou makest
thee wide apart from other men who are here,
whereas thou offerest thee for this faring and they
excused them thereof, of whom I deemed that
they would well have buckled thereto. But I
can nought of thee, nor wot I even thy name."

He answereth thus : "My name is nought far
to seek, king ; meweeneth thou wilt have heard
me named : I am called Karl o' Mere."

The king answereth : "So it is, Karl, that I
have heard thee named afore ; and, sooth to say,

time has been when, if we had come together, thou
wouldst not have known how to tell the tidings
thereof. But now I will not have so much the
worser part than thou, since thou offerest me thine
aid, as not to return thee therefor my thanks and
favour. Therefore, Karl, thou shalt come to me
and be my guest to-day, and then we will talk this
matter out." Karl says it should be so.

CHAPTER CLIII. THE STORY OF KARL O' MERE.

KARL O' MERE had been a viking and
the greatest of lifters, and oft had the
king set men upon him, and would take
the life of him. But Karl was a man of great kin,
a man of mickle stir, a man of prowess and doughty
in many matters.

But now when Karl had bound him to this
journey, the king took him into his peace and
thereafter into his good love, and let array his
journey in the best wise. Nigh twenty men they
were on board the ship. The king made word
to his friends in the Faroes, and sent Karl for
trust and troth to Leif, son of Ozur, and Gilli
the Speaker-at-law, and to that end he sent his
tokens. Karl fared forthwith when he was ready,
and a fair wind they had, and came to Faroe, and
hove into Thorshaven in Stream-isle. Then a
Thing was summoned there, and folk came
thronging thereto. Thither came Thrand o' Gate
with a mickle flock, and thereto came Leif and
Gilli, and had with them a multitude of people.

Now when they set up their tilts and dight them their booths there, they went to see Karl o' Mere, and the greetings there were good. Then Karl bore forth to Gilli and Leif King Olaf's word and tokens, and his tale of friendship, and that they took well, bidding Karl to them, and offering him to flit his errand, and to give him whatsoever avail they had might to, and this he took thankfully. A little after came Thrand thereto and greeted Karl well. "Fain am I," said he, "that such a true man has come hither to our land with our king's errand, the which we be all bound to further. Nought will I, Karl, but that thou fare to me for winter-dwelling, and therewithal that of thy company which would make thine honour greater than afore."

Karl answers that he had already settled to fare to Leif; "otherwise," says he, "I were fain to have taken this bidding."

Thrand answers: "Then must Leif be fated to great worship hereof; but are there any other matters that I may do, wherein were furtherance to thee?"

Karl answers that he should deem it a great aid if Thrand would fetch in the scat throughout East-isle, and all the North-isles.

Thrand said it was due and welcome that he should give that much furtherance to the king's errand. Then Thrand goeth back to his booth; and at this Thing was nought more whereof to tell tidings. Karl fared to guesting with Leif Ozurson, and abode there the winter after. Leif fetched in the scat from out of Stream-isle and all the isles to the south thereof.

IV.   X

The next spring Thrand o' Gate gat failing health; he had pains in the eyes and other ailments besides, yet he got him ready to fare to the Thing after his wont. And when he came to the Thing and his booth was tilted, he let hang the inner part thereof with black cloth, for this sake, that the day-light might be less dazzling. But when some days were worn of the Thing, Leif and Karl went to the booth of Thrand, and had a great company; and whenas they came to the booth, there stood with-out certain men. Leif asked if Thrand were within the booth; they said he was there. Leif asked them to bid Thrand come out; " I and Karl have an errand with him," says he. But when these men came out again, they said that Thrand had such pain in his eyes that he might not go out, "and he bade thee, Leif, to go in."

Leif spoke to his fellows and bade them fare warily when they came within the booth, and not to throng together: "and let him go out first who last goeth in."

Leif went in first, and Karl next, and then his fellows, and they went fully weaponed, as if they must needs array them for battle. Leif went up to the black hangings, and there asked where was Thrand. Thrand answered and greeted Leif. Leif took his greeting and asked sithence, if he had gathered any scat from the North-isles, or how ready he was to pay the silver.

Thrand answered and said that never had it been out of his mind what he and Karl had spoken; and also, that the scat would be paid readily enough: " Lo, Leif! Here is a purse, which thou shalt take, and it is full of silver." Leif looked about and saw few men in the booth; most lay about the daïs, but a few were sitting up. Then Leif went to Thrand and took the purse to him, and bore it further out into the booth, where it was light, and poured the silver down upon his shield, and stirred it about with his hand, and said that Karl should look at the silver.

They looked on it for awhile, and Karl asked Leif, how the silver seemed to him. He answered: " Methinks that every bad penny to be found in the North-isles is here come together." Thrand heard this and said : " Seemeth the silver nought well to thee, Leif?" "Even so," says he. Said Thrand : " Forsooth, those my kinsmen are no middling dastards, whereas one may trust them in nought. I sent them in the spring north into the islands to gather up the scat, because last spring I was good for nothing myself; but they will have taken bribes of the bonders to take this false coin which is not deemed fit to pass. Thou hadst better, Leif, look at this silver wherewith my rents have been paid."

So Leif took back to him that silver, and took from him another purse, and bore it to Karl, and they ransacked it, and Karl asked what Leif thought of this money. He said he deemed it bad, but not so bad as that it might not be taken in payment for debts carelessly bespoken, " but on behalf of the king I will have nought of this money."

A certain man, one who lay on the daïs, cast a cloak off his head and said : " Sooth is said of old, ' Each irketh as he ageth;' and so it goes with thee,

Thrand, to let Karl o' Mere drive back thy money all day long."

This was Gaut the Red.

Thrand leapt up at Gaut's word, and was mad of speech and sore wyted his kinsmen.

At last he bade Leif hand him that silver back : " And take thou here this purse which my tenants have fetched me home last spring, and dim of sight though I be, still, 'Self hand the safest hand.'"

A man who lay on the daïs rose up on his elbow, Thord the Low to wit, and said : " No middling scoldings get we from that Mere-carle there ; it would be well to reward it him."

Leif took the purse and once more bore it to Karl, and they looked at the money, and Leif spoke : " No need to look long at this silver ; every penny here is better than the other, and this money will we have. Get thee a man, Thrand, to look to the weighing." Thrand says that he would take it best that Leif should oversee it on his behalf.

So Leif and Karl went out, and a little way from the booth, and there sat down and weighed the silver. Karl took the helm off his head and poured into it the silver when it was weighed.

They saw a man going beside them with a cudgel in his hand and a slouch-hat on his head, and a green cloak ; barefoot, in linen breeches strait-laced to the bone. He stuck the cudgel into the field, and went thence and said : " Look thou to it, Mere-carle, that thou take no hurt of my cudgel."

A little after there came a man running, and called out wildly to Leif Ozurson, and bade him fare at his swiftest to the booth of Gilli the Speaker-at-law ; "for there ran in to the door of the tent Sigurd Thorlakson, and hurt deadly a booth - man of Gilli's."

Leif stood up forthwith and went away to meet Gilli, and with him went all his booth-fellows. But Karl sat behind there, and the Eastmen stood in a ring about him. Gaut the Red ran up to them and hewed forward with a hand-axe over the shoulders of men, and the blow came on the head of Karl, and no great wound was it. But Thord the Low caught hold of the cudgel which stood stuck in the field, and smote down on the axe-hammer, so that the axe stood in the brain of Karl. And therewith a many men ran out of Thrand's booth, but Karl was borne away thence dead.

Thrand was ill pleased at this work, but bade money for atoning for his kinsmen. Leif and Gilli followed up the blood-suit ; and no fee-boot could be brought about for it. Sigurd was outlawed for the wound wherewith he had wounded Gilli's booth-mate, and Thord and Gaut were outlawed for the slaying of Karl. The Eastmen arrayed the ship wherein Karl had come thither, and went east to meet King Olaf. But it came never to pass that King Olaf might avenge this on Thrand or his kinsmen, because of that unpeace which now befell in Norway, and whereof further on will the tale be told. And hereby leaves the tale to tell of the tidings which sprung out of King Olaf's claiming

scat of the Faroes.   Yet later on strifes arose in
the Faroes out of the slaying of Karl o' Mere,
and the kinsmen of Thrand o' Gate and Leif, the
son of Ozur, had to do herein, and great tales are
told thereof.

CHAPTER CLIV.   KING OLAF'S WAR-FARING.

NOW is the tale to be told which afore was
uphoven, that King Olaf had called out
a muster of ships from all the land, and
every landed-man from the North-country followed
him, out-taken Einar Thambarskelfir.   He had
sat quiet at home at his manors sithence he came
into the land, and did no service to the king.
Einar had lands mickle broad, and held himself up
in a stately manner, notwithstanding that he had no
kingly fiefs.

King Olaf made with his host south about
Stad, and there again drew to him great host out
of the countrysides.   Then had King Olaf the
ship which he had let make the winter before,
and was called the Bison, the greatest of all ships.
On its prow there was a bison-head dight in gold.
This telleth Sigvat the Skald :

> The Ling-fish of the flight-shy,
> The Tryggvi's son, its lip bore,
> All with the tried gold reddened,
> Unto the prey, as God willed.
> Olaf the Thick another,
> A Bison, glorious gold-dight,
> Let tread the billows over.
> Brine plenty washed the beast's horn.

Then the king went south into Hordland. There he heard the tidings that Erling Skialgson had already fared away from the land, and had a great company and four ships or five. He himself had a great swift-sailing ship of war, and his sons three keels of twenty benches each, and had sailed west to England to find Knut the Rich. So now King Olaf went east along the land and had a very great company, and held on a-speering, if men had any news of the journey of Knut the Rich ; and all men could to tell that he was in England, but that was said withal, that he was having an hosting and was minded for Norway. But inasmuch as King Olaf had a mickle host, and he got not true tidings, as to whither he should steer to meet Knut, and whereas his men deemed withal that it was ill gain to tarry long in one and the same place with such a great host, he made up his mind to sail south to Denmark with the host, and took with him all thereof that he deemed most fight-worthy and best arrayed, but gave home-leave to the rest ; as saith the song :

> Word-nimble Olaf urgeth
> With oars the Bison southward.
> Another king from the southland
> With dragon breaks up wave-home.

Now fared those folk home by the following of which he set the lesser store ; and now King Olaf had a great and proud host, there being most of the landed-men of Norway therewith, out-taken those who, as is aforewrit, had either gone out of the land, or sat behind at home.

CHAPTER CLV. OF KINGS OLAF AND ONUND.

WHEN King Olaf sailed to Denmark he made for Sealand; and when he came there, he fell to harrying and lifting, and there were the folk of the land some robbed, some slain, some laid hand on and bound, and so brought on board ship; but all fled who might bring it about, and there was no withstanding. King Olaf did there the greatest warwork.

But while King Olaf was in Sealand he heard tidings that King Onund Olafson had out a muster, and went with a great host along the eastern shore of Skaney and was harrying there. And now was laid bare that plan which King Olaf and King Onund had had afore in the Elf, when they made their bond and friendship to withstand King Knut both of them. King Onund fared until he met King Olaf his brother-in-law; and when they met, they made it known, both to their own host and to the folk of the land, that they mean to lay Denmark under them, and to crave of the folk to be taken for liege lords of the land. But here it fared, as many an example proveth, that when the folk of the land is fallen upon by war and hath no strength to make a stand, most men are fain to say yea to whatsoever may be laid upon them, if it will buy them peace. And so it was that many men took service with the kings and yeasaid them obedience; far and wide where they went they laid the land under their sway, or else harried it. Sigvat the Skald

makes mention of this warfare in that drapa which
he wrought about King Knut the Rich.

> Knut was 'neath heaven . . .—
> Deem I by hearsay
> That for kinsman of Harald
> Heart in fight helpéd.
> Olaf, king of the wealth-year,
> Let the host fare
> Over the fish-path,
> South out of Nid.
>
> Cold keels from the North-land
> With the king were a-sweeping
> To Silund the level,
> E'en so was it rumoured.
> But forth fareth Onund
> With host yet another
> Of Swedes to do battle
> Against the Dane-people.

CHAPTER CLVI. OF KING KNUT THE RICH.

KING KNUT had heard west in England
that Olaf, Norway's king, had a folk-host
abroad, and that, withal, that he went
with all his host to Denmark, and that unpeace
was in his realm. Then King Knut fell to gathering folk, and speedily a mickle war-host was
drawn together, and a multitude of ships; and
Earl Hakon was a second captain over that host.
Sigvat the Skald came that summer to England
from the west from Rouen in Valland, and together
with him a man called Berg. They had gone
thither on a chaffering journey the summer before.

Sigvat wrought a " flock " which was called "West-faring-ditties," and whereof this is the beginning :

> Berg, many a morn we minded
> How I let moor the ship-prows
> To the western wing of Rouen,
> Erst in the chapmen's faring.

But when Sigvat came to England, he went straightway to see King Knut, and would ask him for leave to go to Norway. Now King Knut had laid a ban against all cheaping-ships sailing before he had arrayed his host. So when Sigvat came to him, he went to the chamber wherein was the king ; it was locked, and he stood a long while without; but when he saw the king he got the leave he craved, and then he sang :

> Needs must I ask from outside,
> Or ever gat I answer
> From the Jute-lord ; there beheld I
> The house-doors mailed before me.
> But Gorm's son well he lockéd
> Our errand in the hall there.
> Now so it is that often
> Mine arms bear sleeves of iron.

But when Sigvat was aware that King Knut was arraying warfare against King Olaf, and he knew how great a strength King Knut had, then sang Sigvat :

> The bounteous Knut, who hath out
> His whole host, he and Hakon
> Mean a doomed life for Olaf.
> For that king's death I fear me.
> Yet upheld be our warden,
> Though Knut and his earls scarce will it.
> If he get him clear, 'twere better
> Than a mote on furthest fell-side.

Still more rhymes Sigvat wrought about the journey of Knut and Hakon, and this one moreover:

> Should the famed earl be appeasing
> Olaf and those old bonders
> Who oft and oft refrained them
> From hearkening to the matter?
> Erst have they cheapened chieftains
> Ere Hakon gat hate bounden
> For Olaf's greater peril.
> Forward are Eric's kindred.

CHAPTER CLVII. OF THE DRAGON OF KING KNUT.

KNUT the Rich had arrayed his host for leaving the land; he had an exceeding might of muster, and ships wondrously big; he himself had that dragon, which was so mickle that it told up sixty benches, and on it were heads gold-bedight. Earl Hakon had another dragon: that had a tale of forty benches; thereon also were gilt heads; but the sails of both were banded of blue and red and green. These ships were all stained above the water-line, and all the array of them was of the bravest. Many other ships they had, great and well-found. This Sigvat mentions in Knut's drapa:

> Knut was 'neath heaven . . .—
> Here from east fareth
> The fair and the eye-bright
> Son of a Dane-king.
> The wood from the west glode
> All glistering was it,
> Bearing the foeman
> Of Ethelred out thence.

And the drakes of the land's chiefs
Blue sails were bearing
At yard in the breezes ;
Dear was the king's fare.
But those keels, a-coming
From west away, glided
Over the surf road
On to the Limfirth.

So it is said, that King Knut steered with that
great host from the west from England, and brought
his whole host safe and sound to Denmark and
hove into Limfirth, and there was before him a
great gathering of the folk of the land.

CHAPTER CLVIII.   HORDAKNUT TAKEN TO KING.

EARL WOLF, the son of Sprakalegg, had
been appointed to the warding of the land,
whenas King Knut went to England.
He had given into the hands of Earl Wolf his son,
who is called Hordaknut, and this was the summer
before, as is aforewrit. But the earl said straightway
that the king had bidden him that errand, at their
parting, that it was his will that the Danes should
take Hordaknut, son of Knut the King, to king
over the Dane-realm : "And for that reason he
handed him over to us. I have," says he, "together
with many men and chieftains of this land, often
made a plaint of it to King Knut, that the folk of
this land deem it mickle trouble to sit here king-
less ; whereas kings of the Danes of aforetime
deemed that they had their hands full in holding
kingdom over the Dane-realm alone. For in times

gone by many kings ruled this realm. But now hath that become a mickle more troublous matter than erst it was; whereas hitherto we have been left to abide in peace for outlandish lords; but now we hear it that the King of Norway is minded to come with war upon our hands, and moreover folk misdoubt them that even the King of Sweden is also minded for that journey, and to boot King Knut is now in England."

Then the earl brought forth sealed letters of King Knut which proved the truth of all this which the earl had set forth.

This business backed up many other lords of the land; and, by the counsel of all of them, the folk of the land was of one mind to make Hordaknut king, which was done even at this very Thing. But in this counsel had Queen Emma been first upheaver; for she had caused these letters to be written and sealed, having got guilefully at the seal of the king; but from him was all this hidden.

Now when Hordaknut and Earl Wolf were ware that King Olaf had come from the north from Norway with a mickle host, then fared they to Jutland, whereas there is the main might of the Dane-realm; there they sheared up a war-arrow and summoned together a mickle host. But when they heard that the Swede-king had come there also with his war-host, they deemed they had not strength to join battle with them both. Yet they held the gathered army in Jutland, being minded to ward that land from the kings; but the muster of the ships they drew all together in Limfirth, and thus abode the coming of King Knut.

And when they heard that King Knut had come from the west to Limfirth, they sent messengers to him and to Queen Emma, and bade her find out for sure whether the king was wroth with them or not, and give them a warning thereof. The queen talked this matter over with the king, and said that Hordaknut their son would atone in any wise that his father would, if he had done that which was not to the mind of the king. He answers and says that Hordaknut had not followed his own counsels. "It has befallen," says he, "as was to be looked for, whereas he is a child and witless, that, whenas he would be called king, trouble cometh on his hands ; for this land looked like to be all wended with war-shield, and be laid under outland lords, but if our strength came there between. Now, if he will make any peace with me, let him come to me and lay down this fool's name whereby he hath let him be called a king."

Thereafter the queen sent these same words to Hordaknut, and that withal, that she bade him not lay this journey under his head; and said, as was true, that he would get no help to withstand his father. And when these sent words came to Hordaknut, he took counsel with the earl and with other chieftains that were with him. And that was speedily found, that when the folk of the land heard that Knut the Old was come, then flocked to him all the throng of the land, and thought that all their trust was there. And Earl Wolf and other, his fellows, saw that they had two choices on hand, either to go and meet the king and lay everything in his power, or otherwise to get them gone out of the land. But all urged Hordaknut to go see his father; and so he did. And when they met he fell at the feet of his father, and laid on his knees the seal with which went the title of king. King Knut took Hordaknut by the hand and set him in a seat as high as that in which he had sat before. Earl Wolf sent Svein his son to meet King Knut; and Svein was the sister-son of King Knut. He sought truce for his father and peace at the hand of the king, and offered himself an hostage on behalf of the earl. They, Svein and Hordaknut, were equals in age. King Knut bade these words be told to the earl, that he should gather together an host and muster of ships, and then come and meet the king, but afterwards they should talk their peace over; even so did the earl.

CHAPTER CLIX. WAR IN SKANEY.

BUT when the Kings Olaf and Onund heard that King Knut was come from the west, and therewith that he had an host not to be dealt with, then they sail to the east coast of Skaney, and fall to harrying and burning the countrysides, and seek east along the land towards the realm of the Swede-king. But when the folk of the land heard that King Knut was come from the west, then was no fealty done to the kings. This Skald Sigvat telleth:

> The swift kings gat not
> Denmark luréd
> Underneath them
> By the warfare.

The Danes' undoer
Then let sharply
Harry Skaney.
—King far foremost.

Then the kings made their way east about the
land, and hove into the water which is called the
Holy River, and tarried there awhile. Then news
came to them that King Knut fared after them
with his host. Then they took counsel together
and settled on this, that Olaf with some of the war-
host should go up aland, and all the way up into
the mark-lands, to that water whence the Holy
River falls. There at the outfall of the river they
made a dam of timber and turf, and thuswise
stemmed the water; and then they cut great
ditches and ran together many waters, and thereby
wide flows were made. But into the river-bed
they cut down huge timbers. They were about this
work many days, and King Olaf had all the rule
over this contrivance; but King Onund bore rule
over the ship's host that while. King Knut got
news of the journeys of the kings and of all that
scathe which they had done to his realm; and
then he makes for a meeting with them where
they lay in the Holy River, and a great host he
had, yea, more by the half than they both. Hereof
Sigvat telleth :

Jutland's ruler
In land now lets him
Be eat up nowise ;
Man's kin well liked it.
The warding-shield
Of the Danes brooked fewest
Of the land's liftings.
—King far foremost.

CHAPTER CLX.   BATTLE OFF THE HOLY RIVER.

ON a day towards even it fell that the spies of King Onund saw the sailing of King Knut, and he had by then no long way to sail.   Then King Onund let blow the war-blast. Then the men struck the tents and clad them for war, and rowed out of the haven and to the eastern shore, and there laid their ships together, and laid out hawsers and arrayed them for battle.   King Onund slipped spies up aland, and they went to meet King Olaf and told him these tidings.   Then King Olaf let break the dykes, and send the river into its old road; but in the night he went down to his ships.   King Knut came athwart the haven and saw where the war-hosts of the kings lay boun for battle.   He deemed it would be over-late in the day to join battle by the time that all his host should be ready, whereas his fleet needed mickle sea-room to sail, and it was long between the first ship and the last, and that which sailed outermost and that which sailed nearest to the land; and withal the wind was little.

But when King Knut saw that the Swedes and the Northmen had cleared out of the haven, then made he into it, and all the ships that could find berth there, yet the main host lay out in the open sea.

In the morning, when it was high-day, much of their folk was up aland, some a-talking, and some at their sports.   Then know they nought till waters come rushing upon them like falling forces; there-

IV.   Y

withal came huge timbers, which were driven against the ships, that took great hurt thereat; but the waters flooded all the fields, and the folk that was aland did perish, yea, and many of those who were on board the ships. But all those who might bring it about cut their moorings and got loose, and the ships were driven all of a huddle. That mickle dragon, to wit, which the king himself owned, drave out before the stream; not easily was it turned with oars, so it drifted out to the fleet of the kings, Olaf and Onund. And straightway when they knew the ship, they set upon it all round. But whereas the ship was high of bulwark even as might be a castle, and a multitude of men was on board, and the company chosen of the best, and weaponed, and of the valiantest, the ship was nowise easily overcome; and short was the hour ere Earl Wolf thrust in with his host, and then uphove the battle. Thereupon the host of King Knut drew thereto from every side. Then saw the Kings Olaf and Onund that for that time they had won all the victory that was fated them. So they let back-water and got loose out of King Knut's host, and the fleets parted.

Now whereas this onset had not fallen suchwise as King Knut had ordered it, there was no rowing after them; so they took to arraying the host and put things in order.

Now after they had parted and each fleet went its own way, the kings kenned their host and found that they had gotten no man-spilling; then withal they saw that if they abode until King Knut should have arrayed all that mickle host of his, and he should then fall upon them, the odds against them were so mickle, that but little hope there was of victory for them. So that rede was taken, to row all the host east along the land. But when they saw that King Knut held not after them, they raised up their masts and set their sails. So says Ottar the Black in the drapa which he wrought on King Knut the Rich.

> King, for thy foemen eager,
> Aback the Swedes thou beatedst,
> But mickle bait gat she-wolf
> Where called 'tis the Holy River.
> Thou heldest, O awful fight-stall,
> Thy land by the kin of warriors
> Against two kings, where starved not
> The raven ; thou swift-ready.

So sang Thord, son of Siarek, in the death-song on King Olaf :

> Olaf, the lord of the people
> Of Agdir, had a steel brunt
> With the most noble Jute-lord,
> The cleaver of the gold rings.
> The king of the folk of Skanings
> Shot sharp enough against him ;
> Nought slow of proof was Svein's son.
> The wolf howled over corpses.

CHAPTER CLXI. THE COUNSELS OF THE KINGS OLAF AND ONUND.

THE Kings Olaf and Onund sailed east beyond the realm of the Swede-king ; and at the eve of one day they brought-to aland where it is hight Barwick, and there the kings lay

the night through. But it was found of the Swedes,
that they were homesick, for all the main host sailed
east along the land through the night, and letted
not their faring till each one came home to his own
abode. But when King Onund was aware of this
he let blow to a House-Thing. Then King Onund
took up the word: "So it is, King Olaf," says he,
" even as thou knowest, that this summer we have
fared all together, and harried far and wide about
Denmark; we have got together much wealth of
chattels, but nought of land. This summer I have
had four hundred and twenty ships abroad, but now
there is left no more than a hundred and twenty.
Now so it seemeth to me, that we shall win but
little for our furtherance with no more host than now
we have, although thou hast still the sixty ships
which thou hadst through the summer. Now therefore it seems to me the likeliest to go back into my
own realm, for it is good 'to drive the waggon home
whole;' for we have gained somewhat and lost
nought. Now will I bid thee, Olaf, my brother-in-
law, to come with me, and let us abide all together
this winter; and take thou so much of my goods as
thou wilt, and whereby thou mayst well maintain
thyself and thy host; and if thou wilt rather the
other choice, to have our land to fare over, and wilt
fare the land-road to Norway, that shall be welcome
to thee also."

King Olaf thanked King Onund for his friendly
bidding: "But if I shall rule, then somewhat else will
be settled, and we shall hold together what host is
left us. We have a chosen company and good ships
a many, and we may well lie on board our ships all

through the winter after the wont of war-kings, but Knut will no long time be lying in the Holy River, for there is no haven for all that many ships he hath. I wot withal that in that place the folk will be no less homesick than here, and I ween that we have so dealt with matters in the summer that the thorp-dweller shall know what is to do, both in Skaney and about Halland. King Knut's host will speedily be scattered far and wide, and then there is no telling to whom victory may be fated. So let us keep spies about first, as to what rede he takes."

And King Olaf closed his speech in such wise that men gave good cheer thereto, and that rede was taken which he would. So spies were held on the army of King Knut, but both the kings, Olaf and Onund, lay in the same place.

CHAPTER CLXII.   OF KING KNUT AND EARL WOLF.

KING KNUT saw that the Kings of Norway and Sweden steered with all their host east along the land. So he let his men ride the upper way, day and night, even according as the kings sailed out in the open. King Knut had ever spies in their army, and when he heard that a great part of the host had sailed away from the kings, he steered with his host back again to Sealand, and lay in Eresound with all the host; some of his folk lay over against Skaney, some over against Sealand. King Knut rode up to Roiswell the day before Michaelmas with a great following. Earl Wolf, his son-in-law, had arrayed a banquet for him. The earl gave him entertainment full noble, but the king was unjoyous and scowling. The earl wrought many ways to make him gleesome, but the king was short and fewspoken. The earl bade him play at the chess, and that he yeasaid, so they got them a chessboard and played. Earl Wolf was a man quick of word and unyielding in all things ; he was the mightiest man in Denmark next after King Knut. A sister of Earl Wolf was Gyda, whom Earl Godwin, son of Wolfroth, had to wife, and their sons were King Harald and Earl Tosti, Earl Waltheow, Earl Morkar, and Earl Svein ; their daughter was Gyda, whom Edward the Good, King of England, had to wife.

CHAPTER CLXIII. THE SLAYING OF EARL WOLF.

NOW when they had been playing a while at the chess Earl Wolf checked the king's knight. The king put his move back, and bade him play another. The earl got angry, cast down the table and went away. The king said : " Runnest thou away now, Wolf the Craven ?" The earl turned back in the door and said : " Further wouldst thou have run in the Holy River if thou mightest have brought it about ; nor didst thou call me Wolf the Craven when I thrust in to the helping of thee when the Swedes were beating you like hounds."

Therewith the earl went out and went to sleep, and a little afterwards the king himself went to sleep.

The next morning as the king clad himself he said to his foot-swain, "Go thou to Earl Wolf," says he, "and slay him." The swain went and was away a while and came back. The king said: "Didst thou slay the earl?" "I did not slay him, for he had gone to Lucius' church."

There was a man hight Ivar the White, a Norwegian of kin. The king said to Ivar: "Go, and slay the earl." Ivar went to the church and up into the choir, and thrust a sword through the earl, and forthwith Earl Wolf lost his life. Then went Ivar to the king and had his bloody sword. Said the king: "Slewest thou the earl?" "I slew him," says he. The king said: "Then thou hast well done."

But after the murder of the earl the monks let lock the church; but the king sent men to the monks, bidding them to open the church and to sing the Hours there, and they did even as the king bade. And when the king came to the church he endowed it with great estates, so that they made a wide countryside, and thereafter this stead arose greatly.

King Knut rode down to his ships, and lay there long through harvest with a very great host.

CHAPTER CLXIV. OF KING OLAF AND THE SWEDES.

WHEN Kings Olaf and Onund heard that King Knut had gone back to Eresound they had a House-Thing, and spoke many things concerning their business.

King Olaf's will was that they should lie there with the whole host, and abide what rede King Knut should take; but the Swedes said it was nought redy to abide the frosts there. It was settled at the last that King Onund fared home with all his host, but King Olaf lay behind there.

CHAPTER CLXV. OF EGIL AND TOVI.

ON a night Egil Hallson and Tovi Valgautson had to hold watch aboard the king's ship. As they sat on the watch, it befell that they heard a mickle greeting and wailing amongst the folk taken of war, which a-nights was kept bound up aland. Tovi says that he deemed it ill to hearken this wailing, and bade Egil come with him to loose the folk. So they took to this trick, that they sheared the bonds, and let the folk run away; and work ill-favoured of the host was this. But the king was so wroth that they were in very peril of their life; and thereafter, when Egil was sick, the king would not see him for long, until many men had prayed for him. Then Egil rued him much of his deed, and bade the king forgive him. And the king gave up his anger to Egil, and put his hand over the side of him where the pain lay beneath, and he sang thereover, and forthwith Egil bettered. Tovi got himself into peace, as the tale goes, whereas he brought Valgaut his father to a meeting with the king. He was a hound-heathen man, and was christened through the words of the king, and straightway died thereafter.

CHAPTER CLXVI. TREASON AGAINST KING OLAF.

KING KNUT had ever spies in the army of King Olaf, who got into talk with many men, and would be holding forth offers of money and of matters of friendship on behalf of King Knut; and many were led away by this means, and sold him their faith, to the end that they should vouchsafe him the land if he came to Norway. Many became bare hereof later on, though then at the first it fared all hidden. Some men took gifts of money straightway, others were promised money thereafter; but there were very many others who had aforetime taken great friendly gifts from him; for it was indeed the truth to say of King Knut, that whoso came to him on whom he deemed he saw the stamp of a man, and who was fain to obey the king, even such man had of him his hands full of fee; and therefor was he greatly beloved. His bounteousness was greatest to outland men, and that most to such as were come from furthest.

CHAPTER CLXVII. THE PLANS OF KING OLAF.

KING OLAF had often parleys and meetings with his men, and asked for their counsel. But when he found that one uttered this, another that, then he misdoubted him that there would be some amongst them that spoke other than what they deemed to be of most rede, and thus it would not be sure that all of them would be yielding him their rightful debt of good faith. Many egged him to this, that they should take a fair wind and sail to Eresound and so north to Norway, saying that the Danes would not dare to set upon them, although they were lying there before them with a great host. But the king was a man so wise that he saw that this was nowise to be tried. He knew, moreover, that with Olaf Tryggvison, when he had few folk and joined battle, and a great host was before him, it fell another way than that the Danes durst not fight. The king knew, moreover, that in King Knut's host there was a great many of Norwegians. Therefore the king misdoubted him that those who gave him such counsel must be more leal to King Knut than to him. So King Olaf made this decision, saying so, that men should array them, those who had will to follow him, and fare the upper road through the parts of Gautland, and thus all the way to Norway; "but our ships," says he, "and all the heavy ware which we may not flit after us, will I send east into the realm of the Swede-king, and let it be guarded there on our behalf."

CHAPTER CLXVIII. THE JOURNEY OF HAREK OF THIOTTA.

HAREK of Thiotta thus answereth the speech of the king: "It is easily seen that I may not fare afoot to Norway: I am an old man and heavy, and little wont to walk.

I am minded that perforce only I shall part from my ship; I have laid out such care on that ship and the arraying thereof that I were loth to let my unfriends have prey thereof."

Says the king, "Fare thou with us, Harek; we shall bear thee after us, if thou mayst not walk." Then sang Harek:

> Ground of the Rhine's flame, surely
> Have I reded me to ride hence
> On my long mare of the din-road,
> Rather than walk hence homeward,
> Though Knut, the grove of arm-rings,
> Be lying with his war-ships
> Out in the Eresound yonder.
> The folk my stout heart knoweth.

Then King Olaf let array his faring; men had their daily garments and their weapons, and what they could get together of nags was packed with raiment and chattels. But he sent men and let flit his ships east to Kalmar, where they hauled them aland, and had all their shrouds and other goods put into safe keeping.

Harek did as he had said; he abode a fair wind, and then sailed west about Skaney until he came east of the Knolls, and that of the evening of a day, and with a wind behind blowing a breeze. Then he let strike sail and mast, and take down the vane, and wrap all the ship above the water in grey hangings, and let men row on a few benches fore and aft, but let most of the men sit low in the ship.

Now King Knut's watch saw the ship, and they spoke among themselves as to what ship it could be, and guessed that there would be flitted

salt or herring, whereas they saw few men, and
little rowing, and moreover the ship seemed
grey and untarred, like a ship bleached by the
sun, and withal they saw that the ship was much
low in the water.

But when Harek came forth into the sound past
the host, he let raise the mast and hoist sail, and
let set up gilded vanes, and the sail was white as
snowdrift and done with red and blue bends.

Then King Knut's men saw the sailing of him,
and tell the king that it was most likely that King
Olaf had sailed thereby.   But King Knut sayeth
so, that King Olaf was so wise a man that he
would not have fared on board one ship through
the host of King Knut, but saith that he deemed
it more like that there would have been Harek of
Thiotta or his make.

But men have it for sooth of the matter, that
King Knut will have known of the faring of
Harek, and that he would not have so fared, if
there had not gone friendly words between him
and King Knut; and this, men deemed, came out
clearly thereafter, when the friendship between
King Knut and Harek became all-known.   Harek
sang this song when he sailed north past Weather-
isle :

> Shoot we the oak withoutward
> Of the isle of heaven's shift-ring.
> I let not the Lund widows
> Nor the Dane-maids laugh thereover,
> O land of falcon's long-ship !
> That I durst not this autumn
> Fare back with the Scantlings' falcon,
> On the level ways of Frodi.

So Harek went on his way, and letted not till he came north to Halogaland, to his manor in Thiotta.

CHAPTER CLXIX. KING OLAF'S JOURNEY FROM SWEDEN.

KING OLAF beginneth his journey, and fared first up through the Smallands, and came down into West Gautland; he fared quietly and peacefully, and the people of the land gave them good furtherance. The king fared till he came down into the Wick, and then north along the Wick until he came to Sarpsburg. And there he took up his dwelling, and let array for wintering there. Then King Olaf gave home-leave to the most part of his company, but kept by him as many of the landed-men as seemed good to him. There were with him all the sons of Arni Arnmodson, and they were held in most honour of the king. Then there came to the king Gellir Thorkelson, and had come from Iceland the summer before even as is aforewrit.

CHAPTER CLXX. OF SIGVAT THE SKALD.

SIGVAT THE SKALD had been long with King Olaf, even as is here writ, and the king had made him his marshal. Sigvat was not a fast speaker in loose-hung words, but skaldship was so handy to him, that he rhymed out from the tongue just as if he spoke aught else.

He had been in chaffering voyages to Valland, and
in one of them he had come to England and met
Knut the Rich, and got of him leave to go to
Norway, even as is aforewrit. But when he came
into Norway, he went at once to meet King Olaf,
and found him in Burg, and went before the king
as he sat at table. Sigvat greeted him, but the
king looked over his shoulder at him and held his
peace. Sigvat sang :

> Here we are come home hither,
> Thy marshals ! Now behold it,
> King of the folk ! Let men learn
> My sayings that I utter.
> Folk-king, say, where thou mindest
> A seat for me withinward,
> For all thine hall with wealth-stems
> Is pleasing to thy warriors !

Then came true the saw said of old, that many
are a king's ears. King Olaf had heard all about
the farings of Sigvat, that he had met King Knut.
King Olaf said to Sigvat : " I know not whether
thou be minded now to be my marshal, or hast
become King Knut's man." Sigvat sang :

> Knut, of the dear rings bounteous,
> Asked me, would I to him be
> A servant as I had been
> Unto the heart-keen Olaf.
> I said that to me 'twas seemly
> To have one lord at one time,
> And I deemed that sooth I answered.
> Good pattern here to each man.

Then said King Olaf that Sigvat should go to
his seat, even the same he had been wont to have

aforetime. And once more Sigvat got himself into the same good liking which he had had afore.

CHAPTER CLXXI. OF ERLING SKIALG-SON AND HIS SONS.

ERLING SKIALGSON and all his sons had been through the summer in the host of King Knut, and of the company of Earl Hakon ; there, too, was Thorir Hound, and had mickle worship. But when King Knut heard that King Olaf had gone overland to Norway, then he broke up the muster, and gave all men leave to array for wintering. At this time was in Denmark a great host of outland men, both Englishmen and Norwegians, and from yet more lands, who had come to join the hosting in the summer. Erling Skialgson went in the autumn with his folk to Norway, and took great gifts of King Knut at their parting. Thorir Hound stayed behind with King Knut.

In company with Erling there went north into Norway King Knut's messengers, and had with them exceeding store of money; and that winter they went far and wide about the land, and paid out the moneys that King Knut had promised men in the autumn for their aid to him ; and gave also to many others whose friendship to King Knut they got bought with money. But they fared over the land in the trust of Erling Skialgson.

Now things went so that a multitude of men turned them for friendship to King Knut, and

behote **him** their service, and this, moreover, **to**
withstand King Olaf; that did some openly, but
the others were many more who hid it from the
people.   King Olaf heard these tidings, **for** many
knew how to tell him thereof, and it was much
brought into talk there at the court. Skald Sigvat
sang this :

> The king's foes there are ganging
> With purses loose; that people
> Bids heavy metal often
> For the head of the king we sell not.
> For down-adown each wots him
> In the swart hell, who would sell him,
> His own good lord, for gold-pay :
> For such men such is worthy.

And again **Sigvat** sang this :

> Sore price was got in heaven,
> When they who smote down lealness
> With treason needs must seek to
> The deep home of high fire.

Often was the word heard in mouth there, how
ill it behoved Earl Hakon to bring an host against
King Olaf, seeing that he had given him his life
when **the** earl had gotten into **his** power.   But
Sigvat was the greatest friend **of** the earl ; and then
again, **when** he heard **the** earl wyted, he sang :

> O'er-yielding waxed the house-carles
> Of the Hord-folk's king to the earl then,
> If so be that they took money
> Against the life of Olaf.
> Nought to his court 'tis noble
> To have such wyte upon them.
> To all us seemlier is it
> If we be clean of treason.

CHAPTER CLXXII.   OF THE YULE-GIFTS OF KING OLAF.

KING OLAF had a great Yule-feast, at which there was gathered to him a many great men.   On the seventh day of Yule it fell that the king went a-walking, and a few men with him.   Sigvat followed the king day and night, and at this time he was with him.   So they went to a certain house, wherein were guarded the precious . things of the king.   He had then had great store arrayed, as his wont was, and fetched together his precious things for this sake, to give gifts of friendship on the eighth eve of Yule. There stood in the house swords gold-wrought nowise all few.   Then sang Sigvat :

> Stand swords there the most trusty,
> All gold bedight ; here praise we
> The wound-sound's oar.   Host-ruler,
> Now do I need thy good-will.
> All-wielder, I would take it,
> If one to the skald thou gavest.
> O sender-forth of wicks' flame,
> With thee I whiles was wending.

The king took some one of the swords and gave it to him ; the grip thereof was wound with gold, and the hilts inlaid with gold, and a right good keepsake it was.   But an un-envied gift it was not, and that was heard thereafter.

Now forthwith after Yule King Olaf began his journey to the Uplands ; for he had a mickle throng, but no revenues had come to him from the North-country this autumn ; whereas the host had been

IV.   z

out through the summer, the king had expended thereon all goods that he might get. Then, too, there were no ships whereon to bring his company into the North-country. Moreover, such news only he had from the north as seemed to him to look nought peaceable, unless he went with mickle folk. For the sake of these things, the king made up his mind to fare across the Uplands. But now it was not so long since he had fared there a-feasting, even as the law stood or the wont of kings had been. But when the king got further on into the land, landed-men and mighty bonders bade him to their houses, and thus lightened him his costs.

CHAPTER CLXXIII. OF BIORN THE STEWARD.

THERE was a man named Biorn, of Gautland kindred, a friend and acquaintance of Queen Astrid, and in somewhat akin to her; and she had given him stewardship and bailiwick in the Upper Heathmark, and he also had in charge the Eastern Dales. Nought was Biorn dear to the king, nor was he in good-liking of the bonders. That also had come to pass, in the countryside over which Biorn had rule, that there had been big loss of the neat and swine. Biorn had let call a Thing thereto, whereat was sought after vanishings. He claimed that the men likeliest to do such things, and such evil tricks were those who abode in woodland dwellings far away from other men, and he laid the guilt for this at the doors of those who dwelt in the Eastern Dales. That dwelling was very straggling, the abodes of men being along waters or in clearings in the woods, and in few places any thronged dwellings together.

CHAPTER CLXXIV. OF THE SONS OF RED.

RED was the name of a man who dwelt in the Eastern Dales; his wife was called Ragnhild, and his sons Day and Sigurd, both the likeliest of men. They were standing at that Thing and upheld the answers on behalf of the Dale-dwellers, and thrust the charges from them. Biorn deemed that they had gone on bigly, and were mickle of pride, both as to weapons and clothes. Biorn turned his speech against those brethren, and said that they were nowise unlike to have done such a thing. But they gainsaid this on their behalf, and therewith the Thing broke up.

A little after King Olaf came to Steward Biorn with his band, and took guesting there. Then was the matter bemoaned to the king, which was had before at the Thing, and Biorn said that he deemed the sons of Red were likeliest to be at the bottom of this unhap. Then the sons of Red were sent for; and when they met the king, he took them for men unthieflike, and declared them free of these charges. Then they bade the king to their father to a feast of three nights, with all his folk. Biorn letted the journey; but the king went none the less.

At Red's was the feast of the stateliest.   Then
the king asked of what men was Red, and his wife
withal.   Red said he was a Swedish man, wealthy
and of high birth, " but I ran away thence," he says,
"with this woman, whom I have had for wife
sithence, and who is a sister of King Ring, the son
of Day."   Then the king awoke to the kinship of
them both.   Withal he found this, that father and
sons were men exceeding wise, and he asked them
concerning their prowess and crafts; and Sigurd
says that he can to arede dreams, and to tell the
hours of day and night though no light of heaven
be seen.   The king tried this art in him, and it all
tallied with what Sigurd had said.   Day found
that of his craft that he could to tell what was gain
and lack in every man on whom he set his eyes,
if he would but put his mind and thought to it.
The king bade him tell what mind-lack he saw
in him, and Day hit upon what the king deemed
right.   Then the king asked concerning Biorn
the Steward, what heart-lack he had.   Day said
that Biorn was a thief; therewithal he told, where
Biorn had hidden at his stead, bones and horns
and hides of the neat which he had stolen that
same harvest.   " He is," said he, " at the bottom
of all those thefts which have befallen this autumn,
wherewith he hath wyted other men."   And Day
told the king all marks thereto, whereas the king
should let seek.   And when the king went away
from Red, he was seen off with great friend-gifts,
and in his company were the sons of Red.   Fared
the king first to Biorn's, and made proof of him in
all things, even as Day had said.   Then the king

let Biorn fare away from the land, and it was of the queen's avail that he held life and limb.

CHAPTER CLXXV. THE SLAYING OF THORIR.

THORIR, the son of Olvir of Eggja, the stepson of Kalf, the son of Arni, and sister's son to Thorir Hound, was the goodliest of all men, a mickle man and a strong, and by this time eighteen winters old. He had gotten good wedding in Heathmark, and good wealth therewith. He was a man full well-beloved, and was deemed to be likely of a lord. He bade the king together with his company to a feast at his home ; and this bidding the king took, and went to Thorir's house, and there got right good welcome. There was a feast most brave, and entertainment of the noblest, and goods the best that might be. The king and his men talked among themselves how well went together Thorir's housing, plenishing, board-array, drink, and the man who gave the entertainment, so that they wotted not which was the foremost. Day had but little to say thereto. King Olaf was wont often to have converse with Day, and asked him of sundry matters, and of all that Day said the king proved the sooth, whether it were bygone or yet to come ; and thus the king would put great trust in his redes. Then the king called Day to a privy talk, and spoke with him concerning very many matters. Thither came down the speech of the king, that he set forth to Day how stately a man was Thorir, who had made them so noble a feast. Day had little to say to this, but said it was all true what the king had spoken. Then the king asked Day, what blemish of mind he saw in Thorir. Day said he deemed that Thorir would be well fared of mind, if he were so endowed as to all folk was upcome. The king bade him tell him all he asked, saying, he was in duty bound thereto. Day answers: "Then wilt thou, king, grant me that I rule the feud, if I find out the fault." The king answers that he will not hand his doom over to other men, but bade Day tell him what he asked.

Day answered: "Dear is the lord's word! This is the mind-lack I must find in Thorir's heart, as to many befalleth,—that he is a man over fee-lustful."

The king answers: "Is he a thief or a robber?" Day answers: "Not that," says he. "What is it, then?" says the king.

Day answers: "He won that for money, that he became his lord's traitor; he has taken money of Knut the Rich for thine head."

The king answered: "How makest thou this true?" Day spoke: "He has on his right arm, above the elbow, a thick gold ring, which King Knut hath given to him, and he letteth no man see it."

Thereafter Day and the king sundered their talk, and the king was exceeding wroth.

So when the king sat at table, and men had drank for a while, and were right merry, and Thorir went about the entertaining, then the king let call Thorir to him. He came up to the outside edge of the table and laid his hands upon the table. The king asked : " How old a man art thou, Thorir ? " " I am eighteen winters old," says he. The king says : " A mickle man art thou for thine age, Thorir, and well knit." And therewith the king took his right arm and stroked it up above the elbow. Thorir said : " Touch it gently there ; I have a boil on the arm." The king held his hand still, and felt something hard underneath. The king spake : " Hast thou not heard that I am a leech ? Let me see the boil."

Thorir saw that then there was no good in hiding it any longer, and so he took the ring and gave it forth. The king asked if that was King Knut's gift. Thorir said that was a thing could not be hidden. The king let lay hands on Thorir, and set him in irons.

Then Kalf came forward and prayed for peace for Thorir, and bade money for him ; and many men furthered the matter and bade their moneys. But the king was so wroth, that no words could be brought to bear on him, and he said that Thorir should have the like doom which he had minded for the king, and thereafter the king let slay Thorir. But this work was for the greatest ill-will both there about the Uplands, and no less north about Thrandheim, where the most of Thorir's kindred abode. Kalf withal accounted the slaying of this man an exceeding great matter, for in his youth Thorir had been his fosterson.

CHAPTER CLXXVI.   THE FALL OF GRIOTGARD.

GRIOTGARD, son of Olvir and brother of Thorir, was the elder of the two brothers ; he was the goodliest of men, and had a following of men about him.   Eke was he at this time abiding about Heathmark.   And when he heard of the slaying of Thorir, he raised the feud on the king's men and goods wheresoever they were in his way, but otherwhiles he kept himself in woods or in other lairs.   But when the king heard of this unpeace, he let hold spies on the farings of Griotgard.   So the king gets to know ot his farings ; and Griotgard had night-abode at a place not far from where the king was.   King Olaf went thither forthwith that same night, and came there about the dawn of day, and they threw a ring of men around the chamber wherewithin was Griotgard.   Griotgard and his awoke at the din of men and clatter of weapons, and sprang straightway to their weapons ; and Griotgard sprang into the fore-hall and asked who was at the head of that company.   He was told that there was come Olaf the king, and he asked if the king could hear his words.   The king stood before the door and said that Griotgard could say whatever he pleased ; "for I can hear thy words," said the king.   Griotgard said : "Nought will I pray thee peace."   Then Griotgard rushed out, and had a shield over his head and a drawn sword in his hand ; little light there was, and he saw unclearly.   He thrust his sword at the king, but there before it was Arnbiorn

Arnison, and the thrust took him under the byrny, and ran up into his belly, and thereof gat Arnbiorn his bane. But Griotgard was slain forthwith, and the most part of his band. After these haps the king turned his ways back south to the Wick.

CHAPTER CLXXVII. OF KING OLAF'S MESSENGERS.

NOW when King Olaf came to Tunsberg, he sent out men into all bailiwicks and craved for him host and muster of ships. At that time he had but a few ships, and no other ships he had then but craft of the bonders; but the host drew well in from the countrysides about, but few came from afar, and it was soon found that the folk of the land must have turned away from their faith to the king. King Olaf arrayed his host east in Gautland, and sent them after the ships and goods which they had left behind in the autumn. But the journey of these men sped slowly, whereas it was no better then than in harvest to fare through Denmark; for King Knut had an host out in the spring throughout all the Dane-realm, and had no less than twelve hundred ships.

CHAPTER CLXXVIII. KING OLAF'S COUNSEL.

THOSE tidings were heard in Norway that Knut the Rich was drawing together in Denmark an host not to be dealt with, and that he was minded to make for Norway with all that host and to lay the land under him. But when suchlike was heard, then were the men yet worse for King Olaf to fall back upon, and thereafter he gat him but little help of the bonders. On this his men would often be talking between themselves. Then sang Sigvat this :

> England's all-wielder biddeth
> His hosts out : and we gat us
> Men lesser and ships littler ;
> But the king nought see I fearsome.
> Right ugly are the redes now,
> If the folk of the land be letting
> This king go lack for war-host.
> Fee letteth folk lack faith now.

The king had meetings of his body-guard, and sometimes an husting with his whole host, and asked men as to what seemed to them best to take to : "We need not hide from us," said he, "that King Knut will come to see us this summer, and a great host he has, even as ye will have heard, but we have but a little company to set against his, as matters stand, and the folk of the land are now no longer looking true to us." But this speech of the king men answered diversely, such as he had put forth his word to. But here is set forth what Sigvat answered :

Flee can we ; but it layeth
Wyte on our hands.   Yet the foemen
Of All-wielder pay forth money.
I face the word of dastard.
Each thane himself shall heed now
Himself as far as may be,
Since all avail now faileth ;
Shoots up the king's friends' treason.

CHAPTER CLXXIX. THE BURNING OF GRANKEL.

THAT same spring befell the tidings in Halogaland that Harek of Thiotta called to mind how Asmund Grankelson had robbed and beaten his house-carles. That ship which Harek owned, of twenty benches, floated off his homestead tilted and decked. He gave out word that he was minded to fare south to Thrandheim. So on an evening Harek went aboard ship with the company of his house-carles, and had nigh on eighty men. They rowed the night through, and when it was morning they came to the homestead of Grankel, and cast a ring of men around the houses ; then they fell on, and sithence laid fire in the houses. And therein burned Grankel and his home-men with him, but some were slain without ; thirty men in all lost their lives there. Harek fared home after this work, and sat on his manor. Asmund was with King Olaf ; but as to the men who were in Halogaland, no one of them either bade Harek of atonement, neither did he offer any.

CHAPTER CLXXX. KING KNUT'S FARING TO NORWAY.

KNUT the Rich drew his host together, and made his way to Limfirth. But when he was arrayed, he sailed thence away with all his folk to Norway. He fared swiftly, nor lay by the land on the east side of the firth. So he sailed across the Fold and hove into Agdir, and there called Things together, and the bonders came down and had meetings with King Knut. And there Knut was taken for king over the whole land. So then and there he appointed men to bailiwicks, and took hostages of the bonders, and no man spake against him.

King Olaf was in Tunsberg when the host of King Knut fared across the Fold further out. King Knut went north along the land, and men flocked to him out of the countrysides, and they all swore him fealty. King Knut lay in Eikund-sound a while, and there came to him Erling Skialgson with a great host, and then he and King Knut bound their friendship together anew; and it was among the promises to Erling on behalf of King Knut that Erling should have all the land between Stad and Rygsbit to rule over. Thereupon King Knut went his ways northward, and that is shortest to tell of his faring, that he letted not till he came north to Thrandheim, and hove into Nidoyce. Then he summoned an Eight-folks-Thing, and at that Thing was King Knut taken to king over all Norway. Thorir Hound had fared from Denmark with King Knut, and he was there; there, too, was come Harek of Thiotta, and he and Thorir became King Knut's landed-men, bound by sworn oaths. King Knut gave them great grants, and handed to them the Finn-fare, and gave them great gifts to boot. All landed-men, who were fain to turn them towards him, he endowed both with grants and chattels, and let them all have more dominion than they had had before.

CHAPTER CLXXXI. OF KING KNUT.

NOW had King Knut laid under him all the land of Norway. Then had he a crowded Thing both of his own host and of the folk of the land; and King Knut made it known that his will was to give Earl Hakon, his kinsman, all the land to rule over which he had won in that journey. That went therewith, that King Knut led to the high-seat beside him Horda-knut his son, and gave him the name of king, and with it all the realm of Denmark. King Knut took hostages of all landed-men and mighty bonders; he took their sons or brothers, or other near kinsmen, or such other men as were dearest to them, and he deemed most meet. The king bound to him the faith of men in this wise, as is now said. Forthwith, when Earl Hakon had taken to him the rule of Norway, Einar Thambarskelfir, his kinsman-in-law, joined fellowship with him, and took over all those grants which aforetime he had had, when the earls ruled the land. King Knut gave to Einar great gifts, and knit him to himself in dear liking, and behote him that he should be

the greatest and noblest of all men untitled in
Norway, while his sway stood in the land ; and this
he let follow, that he deemed Einar best fitted to
bear a name of dignity in Norway, or his son else,
Endridi, for the sake of his kin, if there should be
no earl to choose. These behests Einar accounted
mickle, and promised his faith in return. Then
hove up anew the lordship of Einar.

CHAPTER CLXXXII. OF THORARIN PRAISE-TONGUE.

THERE was a man called Thorarin Praisetongue; he was an Icelander of kin, a
great skald, and had spent long time in
fellowship with kings or other lords. He was with
King Knut the Rich, and had wrought on him a
"flock"; but when the king knew that Thorarin had
done a flock on him, he grew wroth thereat, and
bade him bring him a drapa the next day, when
he should be sitting at table. But if he did not do
this, then, says the king, should Thorarin hang
aloft for his boldness, whereas he had done but a
"drapling" on King Knut. So Thorarin wrought
a refrain, and put it into the song, and eked it out
with a few staves. This is the refrain :

> Knut wards the land, as wardeth
> The ward of Greece heaven's kingdom.

King Knut rewarded the song with fifty marks of
silver. That drapa is called the Head-Ransom.
Thorarin wrought another drapa on King Knut,
which is called Togdrapa, wherein the tale is told

of these journeys of King Knut, when he fared
from Denmark north to Norway, and this is one
group of staves betwixt two refrains :

Knut 's neath the sun's . . . .
The high-mannered with host
Mickle fast farèd
My friend, up thither.
Fetched out of Limfirth,
The king, right nimble,
An all unlittle
Fleet of the otter-home.

The much-strong of fight,
The Agdir folk, fearèd
The faring of fierce craver
Of heaps of the fight swan.
The king's ship all over
With gold was bedighted.
Of such thing was to me
Sight richer than saw.

And forth off Listi
Hard over sea glided
The coal-black timbers
Of the beast of thole-pin.
All Eikund-sound
Down in the south was
All full-furnished
With the surf-boar's sea-skates.

And the house-fast
Peace-men swift glided
Past the ancient
Howe of Hjornagli.
Shaft-bidder's faring
Was nowise puny,
Where the stem-cliff's stud
Past Stad was driven.

The wind-strong surf-deer
Bore their longsome

Boards of hull-belly
On beyond Stim.
The cold-home's falcons
From the south so glided,
That the host-bier mighty
North into Nid came.

Gave then the nimble
Lord of the Jute-way
Unto his nieve
Norway all over.
To his son he gave,
So say I, Denmark,
Of the swan-dales' dim-hall.

Here it is said, that to him, who sang this, that
sight was richer than saw, concerning the journey
of King Knut; for Thorarin praiseth this, that he
was himself in the faring with King Knut when
he came into Norway.

CHAPTER CLXXXIII. OF THE MESSENGERS OF KING OLAF.

THE men whom King Olaf had sent east
into Gautland for his ships took away
those of them which they deemed the
best, but the rest they burnt; but took with them
the rigging and the other goods withal which
the king owned and his men. They sailed from
the east when they heard that King Knut had
gone north into Norway, and from the east they
sailed through Ere-sound, and so north to the
Wick to meet King Olaf, and brought him his
ships, when he was then in Tunsberg. But when
King Olaf heard that King Knut held with

his host north along the land, King Olaf hove
with his host into Oslofirth and up into the water
called Drafn, and held him about there until King
Knut was gone south again.

But in the journey which King Knut made
north along the land he had a Thing in every folk-
land, and at every Thing the land was sworn him
by oaths, and hostages were given him. He went
east across the Fold unto Burg, and there he had
a Thing, and the land was sworn to him there as
elsewhere. After that King Knut went south to
Denmark, and had made Norway his own without
battle. He ruled then over three realms. So
says Hallward Hareksblesi when he sang about
King Knut:

> Reddener of bark of boon-ship!
> Yngvi fight-bold sole ruleth
> O'er England and o'er Denmark;
> The straighter peace then waxeth.
> The Frey of the din of troll-wife
> Of points thrust too beneath him
> Norway; the lavish of the war-din
> Allays the falcon's hunger.

CHAPTER CLXXXIV. OF KING OLAF AND HIS FARING.

KING OLAF steered his ships out for Tunsberg forthwith when he heard that King
Knut was gone south to Denmark. Then
he arrayed his faring with what company would follow him, and he had then thirteen ships. Then he
held on down the Wick, and got but little of wealth
and even so of men, out-taken that there followed

him they who dwelt in islands or on outermost nesses. The king then never went up into the land, but got of wealth or men only what was in his way; and he found this, that the land had been beguiled from under him. He went on as wind would blow; and this was in early winter. Their journey sped rather slow, and they lay in Seal-isles for a long while, and there had tidings of chapmen from the north of the land; and the king was told then that Erling Skialgson had a great host gathered together on Jadar. His longship lay off the land and a crowd of other ships owned by bonders, and they were cutters and net-boats and big rowing-boats. Then the king held on with his company from the east, and lay for a while in Eikund-sound; and then each had news of the other. And then Erling thronged up to his utmost.

CHAPTER CLXXXV. OF THE SAILING OF KING OLAF.

ON Thomas-mass before Yule in the very first dawn, the king put out of the haven, there being a right good fair wind somewhat sharp. So then they sailed north coasting Jadar; the weather was wet, and some fog driving about. News went about up aland in Jadar so soon as the king came sailing in the offing. And when Erling was aware that the king came sailing from the east, then let he blow all his host for the ships; and all the people drifted on board the ships, and the battle was arrayed. But the ships of the king were borne on swiftly north past Jadar; and then he turned inward, being minded so to shape his journey as to fare into the firths, and there to get for him both men and money. Erling Skialgson sailed after him and had an host of men and a multitude of ships. Their ships glided on swiftly, since they had on board nought but men and weapons, and Erling's longship went faster by much than the other ships. Then he let reef the sail and waited for his host. Then King Olaf saw that Erling and his men pursued him eagerly, but the ships of the king were very water-logged and soaked, whereas they had been afloat on the sea all through the summer and the autumn and the winter to boot. He saw that the odds would be great if they met all the host of Erling at once. Then he let call from ship to ship that men should lower the sails and somewhat slowly, and take one reef out of them, and so it was done. Erling and his men found this. Then called out Erling, and urged his host, and bade them to sail faster: " Ye see," says he, " that now their sails lower and they draw away from us." So then he let fly the sail from the reefs on his longship, and speedily it drew away from the other ships.

CHAPTER CLXXXVI. THE FALL OF ERLING SKIALGSON.

KING OLAF steered inside of Bokn, and then hidden from each was the sight of the other. Sithence the king bade strike sail and row forth into a strait sound which was there; and there they laid the ships together, and

on their outer side there jutted out a rocky ness.
Men were then all clad for war.

Then Erling sailed into the sound, and they
were unware of an armed host lying before them,
till they saw the king's men row all their ships at
once against them. Erling and his struck sail
and gripped their weapons, but the king's host
beset the ship from every side. There befell a
battle, and was of the sharpest. Then speedily
turned the fall of men to the side of Erling. Erling
stood in the poop of his ship; he had a helm on his
head and a shield before him, and was sword in
hand.

Sigvat the Skald had been left behind in the
Wick, and there he learnt these tidings. Now Sigvat was the greatest friend of Erling, and had taken
gifts of him and been with him, and he wrought a
"flock" on the fall of Erling, and therein is this
stave :

> Erling, e'en he who reddened
> The bleak foot of the eagle—
> Doubtless is that—did run out
> The oak against the king there.
> His longship lay then sithence
> All close aboard the king's ship,
> Amidst the mickle war-host;
> Fought there with sword brisk warriors.

Then the company of Erling began to fall, and
as soon as they were over-borne and there was
boarding of the longship, then every man fell in
his place. The king himself went forth hard. So
says Sigvat :

> The strong king hewed the warriors,
> Wroth strode he o'er the longships;

> On the decks the slain lay throngèd;
> Off Tongues was heavy onset.
> The broad board-acre reddened
> The king there north of Jadar;
> Warm blood the wide sea into
> Came. There the famed king battled.

So throughly fell the folk of Erling that no man stood up on the longship save he alone. It was both that men craved little peace, nor got aught when they craved; and there was no turning to flight, for ships lay on every side around the longship. And it is told for truth that no man sought to flee away. Even so says Sigvat:

> All the ship's crew of Erling
> By Bokn's coast was fallen,
> For there the youthful Shielding,
> North of Tongues cleared the longship.
> The swift and the guile-loathing
> Skialgson stood up alone there,
> And far away from all friends,
> In the poop of the voided war-ship.

Then was onset made at Erling both from the fore-room and from the other ships. In the poop there was a great room, and it towered much high above the other ships, and nought might be got on him save shot and somewhat of spear-thrust, and all that he hewed away from him. Erling fought so nobly, that no man knew example of any one man standing so long before the onset of so many; but never sought he to get away or to crave peace. So says Sigvat:

> The stout-heart Skialg's avenger
> No peace for him was naming,

> Though from the king's men lacked not
> Showers of the axes' skerries.
> Spear-warder, no more bold-heart
> Comes ever on the guardian
> Cask of the winds, wide-bottomed,
> Washed by the sea-deep ever.

King Olaf then made aft for the fore-room and saw what Erling was at. Then the king cast the word at him, and said: " Forward thou facest us to-day, Erling." He answered : " Faceward shall eagles claw each other." Of these words Sigvat telleth :

> Glad Erling, who a long while
> Well the land heeded, neither
> Was lame in land-ward, bade he
> Ernes claw each other faceward,
> Whenas he fell to Olaf
> With true words, in brunt yonder
> At Outstone ; there already
> With fight-rede was he furnished.

Then said the king : " Wilt thou gang under my hand, Erling ? " " That I will," says he. Therewith he took the helm off his head, and laid down his sword and shield, and went forth into the fore-room. The king thrust at him with the horn of his axe and into his cheek, and said : " We shall mark the lord's traitor." Then leapt thereto Aslak Pate o' Fitiar and hewed with an axe into the head of Erling, so that it stood deep in the brain, and that was forthwith a bane-sore.

Then said King Olaf : " Of all men wretchedest of thy hewing ! So hast thou hewn Norway from out my hand."

Aslak answered : " That is ill then, king, if

there be hurt to thee in the stroke. Methought I hewed Norway into thy hand; but if I have done harm to thee, O king, and I have done a thankless work for thee, then am I foredone, whereas I shall have so many men's unthank and enmity for this work, that I should the rather stand in need of thine avail and friendship." The king said it should be so.

Then the king bade every man go on board his ship and array for the journey at his speediest. "We shall not," he said, "plunder the slain here; let either have what they have gotten." So men went back on board the ships, and arrayed them at their speediest. But when they were boun, then the ships with the bonder-host hove from the south into the sound. And then it befell, as oft is tried, that, though a great host be gathered, when men get heavy blows and lose their captains, and be then chieftainless, they are nought for bold deeds. The sons of Erling were not there, and the onset of the bonders came to nought, and the king sailed north on his way. But the bonders took the body of Erling, and laid it out and brought it home to Soli, and all the slain withal that had fallen there. Erling was sore bewailed, and that has been the saying of men, that Erling Skialgson was the mightiest and the noblest man in Norway among those who bore no higher title of dignity. Sigvat the Skald sang this moreover:

> Erling fell: no better
> Man's son his death abideth;
> But that all-rich one soothly
> With might and main he wrought it.

`I wót all-swiftly no man`
Other than he who could it
To hold his own more fully,
Life-long to his life-losing.

Then sayeth he that Aslak had brought about a
kin-slaying and a deed much unmeet:

Slain is the ward of the Hords' land;
Aslak has ekèd kin-guilt.
But few there be meseemeth
Would waken stour in such wise.
Now nought may he gainsay it,
Kin-slaying.   Sure born kinsmen
From anger should refrain them,
And heed the saws of old time.

CHAPTER CLXXXVII. WAR RUSH OF THE AGDIR-FOLK.

THE sons of Erling were, some north in
Thrandheim with Earl Hakon, some
north in Hordland, some up in the firths,
and were gathering folk there.   But when the fall
of Erling was heard, there followed the tale thereof a bidding-out from the east about Agdir and
Rogaland and Hordland.   An host was bidden
out, and the greatest multitude that was, and
all that host went with the sons of Erling north
after King Olaf.   Now whenas King Olaf fared
from the battle with Erling, he sailed north through
the sounds, and by then was the day far spent.   So
say men that he wrought this lay then:

But little the white goodman
Will joy to-night at Jadar.
The clash of Gunn we won us;
Flesh gotten eats the raven.

All evilly hath the robbing
Of me for him betided.
Wroth strode I o'er the ships there.
'Tis the Land that makes men's murder.

Thereafter the king fared north along the land
with his host, and heard all the truth told about
the gathering of the bonders.

At that time there were with King Olaf many
landed-men; there were all the sons of Arni.
This is set forth by Biarni Goldbrow's-skald
in the song which he wrought on Kalf, son of
Arni:

'Gainst very Bokn wert thou,
Kalf, when the Heir of Harald
Sword-bold bade men to battle;
Thy valour known to men is.
Ye gat for the steed of troll-wife,
Good store for Yule.   Then wert thou
Kenned first man at the meeting
Of the flint-stones and the war-spears.

Ill share from the strife the folk gat;
For a prey was Erling gotten.
In blood the black boards weltered
All to the north of Outstone.
The king, now clear 'tis proven,
Bewrayèd of his land was;
'Neath Agdir-folk were the lands laid.
Heard I that their host was greater.

King Olaf fared on till he came north beyond
Stad and hove into Her-isles, where he learnt the
tidings that Earl Hakon had a great host out
in Thrandheim.   Then the king took counsel with
his company, and Kalf Arnison egged on much
that they should make for Thrandheim and there
fight with Earl Hakon, the mickle odds notwith-

standing. This rede many backed up, while othersome letted it, so the matter was left to be settled
by the king.

CHAPTER CLXXXVIII. THE SLAYING OF ASLAK PATE O' FITIAR.

SITHENCE King Olaf held into Stonebight
and lay there over-night. But Aslak Pate
o' Fitiar took his ship into Borgund, and
tarried there through the night. Vigleik, the son
of Arni, was there before him, and in the morning,
when Aslak was about going aboard his ship,
Vigleik set upon him, being minded to avenge
Erling; and there Aslak fell. Then came men to
the king, his courtmen to wit, from the north,
from Frek-isle Sound, of them who had sat at home
through the summer, and they told the king the
tidings that Earl Hakon and many landed-men
with him had come in the evening to Frek-isle
Sound with a much throng. " And they are minded
to take the life of thee, king, and of thy folk, if
they have might thereto."

Now the king sends his men up on to the fell
which there is ; and when they came up on to the
fell, then saw they Bear-isle to the north, and they
saw that from the north there fared a great host
and many ships. Then they come down again and
tell the king that the host was coming from the
north.

The king was lying here before them with
twelve ships, and now he let blow up, and unship
the tilts, and they took to their oars ; and when they

were all arrayed and were putting out of the harbour, then the host of the bonders fared from them north past Thiotandi, and had five-and-twenty ships. Then the king steered on the inside of Nyrfi, and up past Houndham. But when King Olaf came off Borgund, then came to meet him the ship which Aslak had owned, and when they saw King Olaf they told him their tidings, that Vigleik, son of Arni, had taken the life of Aslak Pate o' Fitiar for that he had slain Erling Skialgson. The king took these tidings sorely to heart, yet he might not tarry his journey for this unpeace ; so he fared on in through Way-sound and through Skot. Then sundered his company from him ; there fared from him Kalf Arnison and many other landed-men and shipmasters, and made their way to the earl. But King Olaf held on his journey and letted not till he came to Todar-firth, and lay-to at Wall-dale, and there went from his ships ; and there he had but five ships, and he drew them ashore, and left the sails and shrouds to be kept there. Sithence he pitched his land-tent on the ere called Sult, where there be fair meads, and he raised a cross therebeside on the ere.

Now there dwelt a goodman hight Brusi, and he was the headman there in the valley. After a while Brusi and many other bonders came down to see King Olaf, and welcomed him well, as was meet ; and he made himself blithe to their welcome. Then the king asked if there were any pass up from the dale unto Lesiar. Brusi told him that there was a scree which was called Skerf-scree : " but that is passable neither for man nor horse."

King Olaf answered him : " That must we now
try, goodman ; by God's will it shall do. So come
ye here now to-morrow with your yoke-beasts and
yourselves, and let us see what the growth thereof
may be when we come to the scree, whether we
may see any device for overcoming it with our
horses and men."

CHAPTER CLXXXIX.   OF A ROAD
ACROSS THE SCREE.

SO when day came, the bonders went down
with their yoke-beasts, as the king had bade
them.   Then they flit by the yoke-beasts
their goods and garments, but all the folk went
afoot, even the king himself. He walked along
until he came to the place called Cross-brent, and
rested when he came on to the brent, and sat there
a while, and looked down upon the firth, and spake :
" A hard journey have they gotten me in hand,
those my landed-men who have shifted their faith,
but who for a while were my friends, and full-
trusted."   There are now standing two crosses on
the brent where the king sat.

Then the king got a-horseback and rode up
along the dale, and letted not till they came to the
scree ; then the king asked Brusi if there were any
mountain-bothies there wherein they might dwell.
He said there were. And the king pitched his
land-tent, and was there the night through.

But in the morning the king bade them go to
the scree and try if they might get wains across
it. Then they fared thereto, and the king sat at

home in his land-tent; and in the evening the king's men and the bonders came home, and said they had had great toil and got nothing done, and said that never would a road be laid thereover. So here they tarried another night, and all night was the king at his prayers. And forthwith when the king found that day was dawning, he bade men go to the scree, and try again if they could get wains thereover. They went, but all unwilling; they said that they should not get aught done. But when they were gone away, then came to the king the man who had to look to the victuals, and he said there was no more victual than two carcasses of oxen. "But thou hast four hundred of thine own band, and there be an hundred bonders besides." Then said the king that he should put up all the kettles, and let come into each kettle somewhat of flesh-meat; and so it was done. But the king went thereto, and made the sign of the cross thereover, and bade serve the meat. But the king fared to Skerf-scree, wherethrough they were to break the road. And when the king came there, all sat and were mithered with hard toil. Then said Brusi: "I said thee, king, and thou wouldst not trow me, that we might get nought done with this scree."

Then the king laid down his cloak, and said that they should all fall to and try again. And so was it done, and then twenty men would flit whithersoever they pleased stones which an hundred men before could nowise get stirred, and by midday the road was broken so that it was passable to men and pack-horses no worse than on a plain field.

Then the king went down again to the place where the victuals were, which is now called Olaf's-cave A well was there anigh to the cave, and therein the king washed himself. And if the household creatures of men fall sick in the dale, and drink of that water there, they are bettered of their sickness.

Now the king went to meat, and they all. And when he was full, he asked if any mountain-bothy were in the valley up beyond the scree and anigh to the fell, wherein they might abide the night through. Brusi says: "There are bothies which are called Grænings; but there may no man abide nightlong because of the hauntings of trolls and evil wights which are there about the bothies."

Therewith the king said that they should array their journey, for that he would be the night through at the bothies.

Then came to him the man who looked after the victual, and told him there was an exceeding plenty of victual, and "I know not whence they have come." The king thanked God for his sending, and he let make loads of meat for the bonders, who went adown the valley, but he himself abode at the bothies through the night. But at midnight, whenas men were asleep, a hideous crying was heard at the milking-stead, and it said: "So burn me now the prayers of King Olaf," says that wight, "that now I may not abide in my own home; and now must I flee, and never again come to this milking-stead."

But in the morning when men awoke, the king went up towards the fell, and spake to Brusi: "Here a homestead shall be reared, and whatso

bonder shall abide here will ever have his where-
withal, and never shall corn freeze here, though it
freeze above the stead and below." Then King
Olaf went over the fells, and came down to Oneby,
and was there through the night. By then had
King Olaf been king over Norway fifteen winters,
counting that winter when they were both in the
land, he and Earl Svein, and this one, whereof for
a while now the tale hath been told, and which had
worn already past Yule when he left his ships and
went up aland, as is aforewrit. This part of his
kingdom first wrote Priest Ari Thorgilson the
Wise, who was both a teller of truth, of good
memory, and so old a man that he minded those
men, and had stories of them, who themselves
were so old, that for eld's sake they might well
remember these tidings; even as he hath himself
said in his books, where he has named the men
by name of whom he had gotten his lore. But the
common tale is that Olaf was king over Norway
for fifteen winters before he fell; but they who so
say, count to the reign of Svein that winter which
was his last in the land; for after that Olaf was
king for fifteen winters, while he lived.

CHAPTER CXC. KING OLAF'S FORE-TELLING.

WHEN King Olaf had been the night
through at Nesiar, he fared with his
folk day after day, first to Gudbrands-
dales and thence on to Heathmark. Then was it
shown who were his friends, for now they followed

him ; but the others then sundered from him who with less uprightness had served him ; but some turned about to ill-will and full enmity, even as became clear.   And now it was found in many Uplanders, that they had liked right ill the slaying of Thorir, as is aforesaid.

King Olaf gave leave to go home to many of his men who had children to look after ; for these men deemed it unclear what peace would be given to the goods of such men as might fare out of the land with the king.

And now the king made it clear to his friends that he had made up his mind to fare away out of the land, first east into the Swede-realm, and there to take counsel whither he should turn thence. But he bade his friends bear in mind, that he was yet minded to seek to the land and back again to his realm, if God should grant him long life ; and he said that it was his foreboding that all folk in Norway would still be bound to his service. " But I am minded to think," says he, " that Earl Hakon will but a little while rule over Norway ; and to many men no wonder will that seem, whereas Earl Hakon has come short of good luck against me before.   But this, few men will trow, though I tell what my mind forebodeth me, which toucheth Knut the Rich, that he will be a dead man within the space of few winters, and all his realm will be come to nought, and there will be no uprising of his kindred, if so it fare whereas my words point."

So when the king made an end of his tale, men dight their journey ; and the king turned with what company followed him east to Eidwood.

That tide was with him Astrid the queen, Ulf-hild, their daughter, Magnus, son of King Olaf, Rognvald, son of Brusi, those sons of Arni, Thorberg, Finn, and Arni, and more landed-men yet; he had a company of chosen men. Biorn the Marshal had gotten leave to go home. He fared back home to his house; and many other friends of the king went back to their homesteads with his leave. The king bade them let him know if such tidings should befall in the land as it was needful for him to know of. And so the king turned off upon his ways.

CHAPTER CXCI. THE FARING OF KING OLAF TO HOLMGARTH.

IT is to be told of the journey of King Olaf, that he went first from Norway east over Eidwood unto Vermland and then out to Waterby, and thence through that wood whereas the road lieth, and came down on to Nerick. There he happened on a rich man and wealthy, called Sigtrygg. His son hight Ivar, who thereafter became a noble man. There King Olaf tarried with Sigtrygg through the spring. But when summer came on, King Olaf arrayed his journey and got him a ship. And he fared that summer, and letted not till he came east to Garthrealm to the meeting of King Jarisleif, him and his queen, Ingigerd. Queen Astrid, and Ulfhild the king's daughter, were left behind in Sweden, but the king took Magnus his son, with him to the east. King Jarisleif gave King Olaf a hearty welcome,

IV.   B B

and bade him abide there with him and have land
as much as he needed for the costs of holding of
his company. That King Olaf took with thanks,
and tarried there. So it is said, that King Olaf
was devout and prayerful unto God all the days of
his life. But from the time that he found his reign
was waning, and his enemies were waxing mightier,
then he laid all his heart to the serving of God ; he
was then hindered herefrom no more by other cares,
or the toil which aforetime he had had on hand.
For he had throughout all that time whenas he
sat in kingdom, toiled for that which he deemed to
be the most needful : first to free and deliver the
land from the thraldom of outland lords ; and
next to turn the folk of the land to the right faith ;
and therewithal to frame laws and land's-right ;
and this part did he for righteousness' sake to
punish them who were of a wrongful will.

CHAPTER CXCII. THE UPHEAVING OF THE UPRISING AGAINST KING OLAF.

IT had been greatly the wont in Norway, that
the sons of landed-men or of mighty bonders
would fare aboard warships and gain for them
wealth by harrying both inland and outland. But
from the time that Olaf took kingdom, he made
his lands so peaceful that he brought to nought all
robbing there in the land. Though sons of rich
men should break the peace, or do what the king
deemed unlawful, and if punishment could be
brought upon them, then let he nought else befall

them than losing life or limb; and there availed
against it neither prayers of men nor money-bidding.
So says Sigvat the Skald :

> They who wrought out-raids often
> Bade to the king rich-minded
> Red gold to buy guilt off them :
> Ever the king naysaid it.
> The hair of the men there bade he
> Shear with the sword : they bided
> Pains manifest for lifting ;
> Suchwise shall the land be warded.

And moreover he sang thus :

> The much-dear king, who full fed
> The wolves most, therewith maimèd
> The kin of thieves and reivers.
> Thuswise he cut short thievings.
> The good king let each bold one
> Of the thieves go thenceforth lacking
> Both hands and feet.   In suchwise
> Is the peace of the landsfolk bettered.
>
> That most to high might pointed,
> That there did do the land's-ward
> Shear pates of a fearful-many
> Of vikings with keen weapons.
> The bounteous Magnus' father
> Let wield much work was gainsome.
> I say that the most of victories
> Thick Olaf's fame did further.

Men mighty and unmighty he let abide by one
and the same penalty; but this the men of the
land deemed over-mastery, and were fulfilled of
hatred in return therefor, when they lost their kinsmen by a rightful doom of the king, though soothful
were their guilts.   This was the upheaving
of that uprising which the folk of the land made

against King Olaf, that they would not thole his
justice, but he would rather let go his dignity than
his rightwise dooms. Now nought rightly found
was the charge laid to him, that he was niggard of
wealth to his men ; he was the most bounteous of
men to his friends. But this was the cause why
folk upraised unpeace against him, that to men he
seemed hard and given to punishment, whereas
King Knut bade forth money measureless. But the
great lords were hereby hoodwinked, in that he promised to each of them dignity and dominion ; and
therewithal men in Norway were fain to take Earl
Hakon, whereas he had been a man most beloved
of the landfolk when aforetime he ruled over the
land.

CHAPTER CXCIII. OF JOKUL, SON OF BARD.

EARL HAKON had held his host out of
Thrandheim, and fared south to Mere to
meet King Olaf, as is aforewrit. But
when the king steered up the firths the earl made
for him thither ; and then came to meet him
Kalf, the son of Arni, and more men who had
parted company with King Olaf ; and a good
welcome was given to Kalf. Sithence the earl
held up thither, whereas the king had set up his
ships, in Walldale, to wit, of Todar-firth. There
the earl took the ships which the king owned, and
let run them out and array them, and then men
were allotted to the masterships thereof. With
the earl there was a man who was called Jokul, a

man of Iceland, son of Bard, the son of Jokul, out
of Waterdale. Jokul was allotted to the steering
of the Bison, which King Olaf himself had had.
Jokul sang this stave :

> 'Twas my lot from Sult to steer it,
> Thick Olaf's own ship. Look I
> For the storm 'gainst the bow's reindeer,
> But late shall hear the home-wife
> Of my quailing. O ye hill-sides
> Of the flame of bow's-stand, soothly
> Robbed was the king, the keen-one,
> Of victory in the summer.

This is the swiftest to tell hereof, which befell a
very long time after, when Jokul fell in the way
of King Olaf's host in Gotland and was taken, that
the king let lead him out to the hewing, and a
wand was twisted into his hair, and held by a
certain man ; and Jokul sat down on a certain
bank. Then a man made ready to hew him. But
when he heard the whine of the stroke, he raised
himself up, and the blow came on to his head and
was a mickle wound. The king saw that it was a
bane-sore, and bade them then leave him alone.
Jokul sat up, and wrought this stave :

> Now smart the wounds a-weary,
> 'Midst better things oft sat I.
> The wound is on us, that one
> Unsluggish, red stream spouting.
> From this same wound blood gusheth :
> I am grown wont to toiling ;
> Helm-glorious king wage-bounteous
> Warps over me his anger.

Thereupon Jokul died.

CHAPTER CXCIV.　OF KALF ARNISON.

KALF ARNISON fared with Earl Hakon north to Thrandheim, and the earl bade him be with him and do him service. Kalf says he would first go up to Eggja, to his house, and thereafter take rede thereover. So did Kalf. But when he came home he speedily found it out that Sigrid his wife was somewhat big-hearted, and told up her griefs which she said she had had of King Olaf; that first, that he had let slay her husband, Olvir; "and now thereafter," she says, "two of my sons, and thou, Kalf, wert at their doing away; that was the last thing I had looked for of thee."

Kalf says that it was mickle against his will that Thorir was taken from life; "and," says he, "I offered ransom for him, and when Griotgard was felled, I lost Arnbiorn, my brother."

She says: "Well it is that thou shouldst have such a lot from the king, for maybe thou wilt avenge him, though thou wilt not avenge me of my sorrows; thou sawest, when Thorir, thy foster-son, was slain, of what worth the king accounted thee."

Suchlike tales of woe had she up ever to Kalf. Kalf oft answered in surly wise; yet at last it turned out that he was led on by her urging, and gave his word to become the earl's liegeman if the earl would eke his grants. Sigrid sent word to the earl, and let tell him where things were gotten in the matter of Kalf. And forthwith when the earl knew thereof, he sent word to Kalf to the end that he should come out to the town and see him. Kalf nowise laid that journey under his head, and a little sithence fared out to Nidoyce, and there found Earl Hakon, and had a right good welcome there; and he and the earl talked their affairs over, and there in all things they were of one mind, and settled this between them, that Kalf became the earl's liegeman, and took from him big grants. Sithence fared Kalf home to his house, and he had the rule then of the greatest part of Inner Thrandheim.

But so soon as spring came, Kalf arrayed a ship which he owned, and so soon as he was boun, he sailed into the main sea, and held his ship west to England, for he had heard tell of King Knut, that he had sailed early in the spring from Denmark west to England. Then had King Knut given earldom in Denmark to Harald, the son of Thorkel the High.

Kalf Arnison went straightway to meet King Knut when he came to England. So says Biarni the Goldbrow-skald:

> The king with stem did doubtless
> Shear the main sea to eastward.
> Fight-weary Harald's brother
> · Must needs go visit Garthrealm.
> But after ye twain parted
> Swiftly to Knut thou soughtest.
> Unwont am I to gather
> Light lies about men's doings.

But when Kalf came to meet King Knut, the king gave him a wondrous good welcome, and had him to talk with him. And this was in the talk of

him and King Knut, that the king bade Kalf to bind
him to make an uprising against Olaf the Thick, if
he should seek aback to the land; "but I," says
the king, " shall give thee earldom then, and let
thee rule over Norway; but Hakon, my kinsman,
shall fare back to me, for that is most handy to
him, seeing that he is so true of heart, that I think
he would not shoot a shaft against King Olaf if
they should happen to meet."

Kalf gave ear to what King Knut said, and was
fain enough of the dignity; so this plan was settled
between them, King Knut and Kalf, and Kalf
arrayed himself for his home-journey, and at parting King Knut gave him gifts most honourable.
Of this Biarni the Skald telleth :

> Thou hadst, O fight-bold earl's son,   ·: :
> To thank the lord of England
> For gifts : forsooth most meetly
> Thou laidst thy case before him.
> The London's king let find thee
> Land, ere from the West thou faredst;   :
> Yet herein was there dallying,
> And thy life is nowise little.

Thereafter Kalf fared back to Norway and
came home to his house.

CHAPTER CXCV.   THE DEATH OF EARL HAKON.

THAT summer Earl Hakon fared from the
land and west to England. And when he
came there, King Knut gave him a good
welcome. The earl had a troth-plight in England,

and he went to fetch his bride, being minded to make his bridal in Norway, but gathered in in England such goods as he deemed were hardest to come by in Norway. The earl arrayed him in the harvest-tide for the home-journey and got somewhat late boun ; but he sailed off into the main when he was boun. But of his journey this is to be said, that that ship was lost, and no man was saved thereof. But it is the saying of some people that the ship was seen north off Caithness one day at eve in a great storm, and the wind blowing out into the Pentland firth. And those who will follow this tale, say that the ship must have been driven into the whirl. However, folk know for certain that Earl Hakon was lost at sea, and nothing came to land that was on board that ship. That same autumn chapmen told there that tidings went about England, how that men deemed the earl would be lost ; anyhow all folk knew that that autumn he came not to Norway. And then the land was without a lord.

CHAPTER CXCVI. OF BIORN THE MARSHAL.

BIORN the Marshal had sat at home at his house from the time he parted from King Olaf. Biorn was a man of renown, and that was soon told of far and wide, that he had sat him down in quiet. Earl Hakon and other men of rule in the land heard the same. Then they sent men and messages to Biorn ; and when the messengers came to their journey's end, Biorn gave them a good welcome.

Sithence Biorn called the messengers to him for
a talk, and asked them of their errand. But he
who was at the head of them spoke, and bare to
Biorn the greetings of King Knut and Earl Hakon,
and of yet more lords; "and this follows," says
he, "that King Knut hath heard mickle of thee,
and this thereto, that thou hast long followed Olaf
the Thick, and been a great unfriend to King
Knut. That he deemeth ill, whereas he will be
thy friend, as of all other doughty men, so soon as
thou wilt turn away from being his unfriend; and
the one thing for thee to do now, is to turn thither
for avail and friendship, whereas is most plenty to
look for, and which all men in the world's northern
parts have in worship. Ye, who have been following Olaf, may now see for yourselves, how he hath
parted from you : ye are all left with nought to
fall back upon in face of King Knut and his men.
Seeing that last summer ye harried his lands and
slew his friends, then is this to be taken with
thanks, that the king biddeth you friendship; for
more befitting were it, that thou shouldst pray
therefor, or bid wealth therefor."

But when he had closed his harangue Biorn
answered thus : " I am now of will to sit at home
at my house and not to serve lords."

The messenger answers: "Such as thou are
men for kings. And I can tell thee this : that thou
hast two choices in thine hand ; one, to fare abroad
an outlaw from thy lands, even as now fareth Olaf,
thy fellow ; the other may well be deemed better
worth looking at, to wit, to take the friendship of
King Knut and Earl Hakon, and become their

man ; to give them thy faith to this end, and here to take thy guerdon." Therewith he poured forth English silver out of a great pouch.

Biorn was a man eager of money, and mickle mindsick was he, and grew silent, when he saw the silver. He turned it over in his mind what rede he should take. He deemed it a great matter to lose all he owned, and deemed it uncertain that King Olaf would ever rear his head again in Norway. And when the messenger saw that Biorn's mind veered about at the sight of the money, he cast forth two thick golden rings and said: "Take the money, Biorn, and swear the oath. I behight thee that this wealth will be of little worth besides that which thou wilt have, if thou go to see King Knut." But by the greatness of the money, and by the fair behests of great gifts of wealth, he let himself be turned to avarice, and took up the money, and then went into fealty and oaths for troth to King Knut and Earl Hakon. And therewithal the messengers fared away.

CHAPTER CXCVII. THE JOURNEY OF BIORN THE MARSHAL.

BIORN the Marshal heard the tidings which were told, how that Earl Hakon was lost. Then his mind turned, and he rued him sorely of having broken his faith to King Olaf, and deemed he was free of the vows he had given of fealty to Earl Hakon. For Biorn now thought there might be some hope of uprearing the dominion of King Olaf, should he come back to Norway, so

that it lay lordless before him. So Biorn arrayed
his journey speedily, and had certain men with
him, and went his ways day and night, a-horseback where he might, a-shipboard where he needs
must. He letted not his journey till he came east
into Garthrealm to King Olaf in winter, about
Yuletide. The king was right glad, when Biorn
met him, and asked for many tidings from the
north from Norway. Biorn said the earl was lost,
and the land left without a ruler. At these tidings
the men were right glad who had followed King
Olaf out of Norway, and had had there lands and
kinsmen and friends, and who were sorely sick for
home. Many other tidings from Norway Biorn
told to the king, such as he was greatly wistful to
know. Then the king asked after his friends as to
how they kept faith with him, and Biorn said that
was all with ups and downs ; and therewith Biorn
stood up and fell at the feet of the king, and took
his foot about, and said : " All in God's power and
thine, O king ! I have taken money from the men
of Knut, and sworn oaths of fealty to them ; but
now will I follow thee, and never sunder from thee
while we are both alive."

The king answers : " Stand up speedily, Biorn ;
thou shalt be in peace with me. Boot this to God.
I may well wot that few men will be now in Norway who will keep their faith with me, when such
as thou turn off. And true it is, that men sit
there in great trouble, because I am far off, and
they sit before the unpeace of my foes."

Biorn told the king who mostly took the lead in
raising up hatred against the king and his men.

Thereto he named the sons of Erling of Jadar, and other kinsmen of theirs, Einar Thambarskelfir, Kalf Arnison, Thorir Hound, and Harek of Thiotta.

CHAPTER CXCVIII. OF KING OLAF.

SITHENCE King Olaf came to Garthrealm he had great imaginings, and turned it over in his mind what rede he had best take. King Jarisleif and Queen Ingigerd bade King Olaf dwell with them, and take over the dominion called Vulgaria, and that is one part of Garthrealm ; and there in that land the folk was heathen. King Olaf bethought him in his mind of this offer ; but when he laid it before his men, they all were loth to take up their abode there, and egged the king on to betake himself north to Norway to his own kingdom. The king would be still further thinking of this, to lay down his kingdom, and fare out into the world unto Jerusalem, or into some other holy places, and there to go under the Rule.

Hereunto, howsoever, his mind would mostly turn, to think if any means might betide, whereby he should get him his kingdom in Norway.

But when he had this in his heart, he would bring it to mind that for the first ten winters of his kingdom all things turned out profitable and happy to him, but afterwards all his redes were to him heavy to work, and hard to carry through, and all ventures for good luck went against him. Now for this reason he misdoubted him whether it

would be wise rede to try luck so much as to
fare with a little strength into the hands of his
foes, seeing that all the multitude of the folk
of the land had gathered them together to withstand him.   Such imaginings oft he bore, and he
put his case upon God, and bade him let that
come up, which he saw would be of best gain.   He
would be turning these matters over in his mind,
and knew not what he should take to; for however he told the matter up before him, ever was
trouble easy to see therein.

CHAPTER CXCIX.   KING OLAF'S DREAM.

IT was on a night, that King Olaf lay in his
bed, and kept awake long through the night
thinking over his plans, and being filled with
great imaginings in his mind.   But when his mind
grew over-mithered, sleep sank upon him, yet so
light that he thought he was awaking and saw all
that was betiding in the house.   He saw a man
stand at his bed, mickle of worship, clad in glorious
raiment; and the king's thought boded him most,
that there would be come King Olaf Tryggvison.
This man spoke to him : " Art thou very sick at
heart over thy plans, what thou shalt take up ?   It
seemeth marvellous to me, that thou shouldst be
turning this about in thy mind; and this withal,
that thou shouldst be minded to lay down the
kingdom which God hath given thee; and that
thou shouldst have this mind withal, to abide here
and to take over dominion from kings outland and

unknown to thee. Fare thou, rather, back to thy realm which thou hast gotten by heritage, and ruled long over with what power **God** hath granted thee, and let not thine underlings affright thee. It is a king's fame to conquer his enemies, and a glorious death to fall in battle with his war-host; or dost thou doubt at all having the right on thy side in this thy contest? Nought shalt thou do it, to hide the truth from thyself: for that cause boldly mayst thou seek to the Land, whereas God will bear thee witness that that is thine own."

And when the king awoke, he thought he saw the countenance of the man as he went away. So thenceforth he hardened his heart and made strong that mind alone of faring back to Norway, even as he had been eagerest for all along; and he found that all his men would the rathest that he should so do. So he talked it into his mind that the land would be easily won, since it lay lordless, even as he had heard. And he was minded to think that if he came thereto himself, many would be minded to give him help. And when the king made clear this rede to his men, they all took it right thankfully.

CHAPTER CC. OF THE LEECHCRAFT OF KING OLAF.

SO it is said that, while King Olaf tarried in Garthrealm, this hap befell there, that the son of a noble widow got a boil of the throat which grew so large that the boy might get down no food, so that he was thought to be at death's

door. The mother of the boy went to Queen
Ingigerd, whereas she was of her acquaintancy, and
showed the boy to her. The queen said she had
no leechdoms to lay thereto: " Go thou," says she,
"to King Olaf; he is the best leech here, and bid
him fare his hands over the hurt of the boy, and
tell him these words of mine, if otherwise he will
not do it.'

She did even according to the words of the
queen; and so when she found the king, she told
him that her son was at death's door from a throat-
boil, and bade him fare his hands over the boil;
but the king said he was no leech, and bade her
fare thither where leeches were to be found. She
said the queen had shown her thither: " And she
bade me bare her word to thee, that thou shouldest
lay leech-craft hereto, what thou couldest; and told
me withal, that thou art the best leech in the
town."

Then the king bestirred him and fared his
hands over the throat of the boy, and stroked the
boil much long, until the boy could move his
mouth. Then took the king bread, and brake it,
and laid it in the shape of a cross in his hollow
palm, and syne laid it in the mouth of the boy, but
he swallowed it down. And from that nick of
time all pain went from the throat, and the boy
was in a few days all whole, and the mother and
other kinsmen and acquaintance of the boy were
right fain at heart thereat. And then first folk
deemed that King Olaf had such great hands of
healing, as is said about those men who are much
endowed with that art, that they have good hands.

But later, when his working of wonders became known to all folk, this was taken for a true miracle.

CHAPTER CCI. KING OLAF BURNETH THE CHIPS.

THIS hap befell on a Sunday, that King Olaf sat in his high-seat at table, and was so deep in imaginings that he heeded not the hours. He had a knife in one hand, in the other a piece of firwood wherefrom he whittled certain chips. A boy in waiting stood before him and held a board-bowl. He saw what the king was doing, and knew that he himself was thinking of other things. He said : " Monday it is to-morrow, lord." The king looked to him, when he heard this, and it came into his mind what he had done. So the king bade bring him a lighted candle, and he swept up into his hand all the chips he had whittled, and set light thereto, and let the chips burn in the hollow of his hand ; whence it might be seen that he would hold fast all laws and commandments, and had no will to transgress wherein he wotted most right to be.

CHAPTER CCII. OF KING OLAF.

NOW when King Olaf had made up his mind to turn back home, he set the matter forth before King Jarisleif and Queen Ingigerd. They letted him of that journey, and said this, that within their realm he should have such dominion as he might deem seemly, and bade him not fare into the power of his foemen with such a little fellowship as he had there. Then King Olaf told them his dreams, and this therewithal, that he was minded to think it was the will of God. So when they found that the king had made up his mind to fare back to Norway, they offered him any avail for his journey which he would take from them. The king thanked them with fair words for their good will, saying he would be fain to take from them whatever he stood in need of for his journey.

CHAPTER CCIII. KING OLAF'S FARING FROM THE EAST OUT OF GARTH-REALM.

FORTHWITH on the back of Yule King Olaf was busy at his arrayal. He had wellnigh two hundred of his own men, and King Jarisleif fetched them all yoke-beasts and gear, such as they needed. And when he was ready, then he fared off; and King Jarisleif and Queen Ingigerd saw him off full worshipfully. But his son Magnus he left behind with the king.

Now King Olaf fared from the east, first over ice all down to the main sea; and when spring came on and the ice loosened, they arrayed their ships. And when they were boun and a fair wind came, they set sail, and their journey sped well, and King Olaf hove with his ships into Gotland, where he learnt tidings both from Sweden and Denmark, and all the way from Norway. By that time folk had learnt for sure that Earl Hakon had been lost, and that the land of Norway was lord-less. Both to the king and his men their journey seemed likely. And when a fair wind befell they sailed thence and made for Sweden. The king sailed with his company into the Low, and stood on further into the land even to Riveroyce, and then sent his men to see Onund the Swede-king, and appointed a meeting with him. King Onund gave good ear to the message of his brother-in-law, and fared to meet King Olaf according to the word he had sent thereto. Queen Astrid withal, with those men who had followed her, came to see King Olaf, and a meeting of great joy there was betwixt all these. The Swede-king gave a hearty good welcome to Olaf his brother-in-law when they met.

CHAPTER CCIV. OF THE LANDED-MEN.

NOW shall be told what they were at in Norway through these days. Thorir Hound had had the Finn-journey these two winters, and had been both winters for long on the fells, and had gotten him measureless wealth. He had had many kind of chafferings with the Finns. He had let make for himself twelve coats of reindeer-skin with so mickle wizardry that no weapon could bite on them, yea, mickle less than on a ring-byrny.

But in the latter spring Thorir arrayed a long-ship of his and manned it with his house-carles. He summoned bonders together and craved a

muster from out of all the northernmost Thing-
lands, and drew there together great multitudes of
folk, and fared from the north in the spring with
all that host.

Harek of Thiotta had a great hosting, and got
mickle company, and to that faring there betook
them many more men of worship, though these
were the most renowned thereof. Then they gave
it out that this war-host should fare against King
Olaf, and ward the land against him if he should
come from the east.

CHAPTER CCV.　OF EINAR THAMBAR-SKELFIR.

EINAR THAMBARSKELFIR had most
to say in the rule of Outer Thrandheim,
from the time that the death of Earl
Hakon was heard of; for he deemed that he and
his son Eindridi had the best title to those lands
and chattels which the earl had owned. And now
Einar called to mind those promises and friendly
words which King Knut had given him at their
parting. Then let Einar array a good ship he owned,
and went thereon himself with a great company.
But when he was boun, he set off south along the
land, and then west over sea, and letted not his
journey till he came west to England, and straightway went to King Knut. The king welcomed him
well. Sithence Einar bare forth his errand before
the king, and said as much as that he was come
for those promises which the king had bespoken
him, that Einar should bear a title of dignity over

Norway if it were no matter of Earl Hakon. King Knut said that that matter now turned altogether another way; "for now," says he, "I have sent men and tokens to Denmark to Svein my son with this message, that I have behight him dominion in Norway. But I will hold friendship with thee, and thou shalt have name-boot from me as thou hast birth thereto, and be a landedman, and have mickle grants, and be as much before other landed-men as thou art a man of greater deeds than other landed-men."

Then Einar saw concerning his matter how his errand would speed, and arrayed himself to go back home. But whereas he knew the purpose of the king, and that, if King Olaf should come from the east, it would not look like peace in the land, it came into Einar's mind that nought would be gained by hurrying on the journey beyond what was of the gentlest, if they should have to fight King Olaf, and have then no more furtherance of dominion than erst. So Einar sailed into the main sea, when he was ready, and came to Norway just when the greatest tidings that befell in Norway that summer had already come to pass.

CHAPTER CCVI. OF THE CHIEFTAINS IN NORWAY.

THE chieftains of Norway kept out spies east towards Sweden and south to Denmark, lest King Olaf come from the east from Garthrealm; and forthwith they heard, as fast as men could speed, that King Olaf had come

to Sweden.   And when that was known for truth,
a war-bidding went throughout all the land, and
all the folk were called out to the hosting, and thus
drew an host together.   But the landed-men of
Agdir and Rogaland and Hordland parted in two
ways : some turned north, some east, deeming
that both ways an host was needed toward.   The
sons of Erling of Jadar turned eastward with all
the host that was to the east of them, and were
captains over that host.   But northward turned
them Aslak of Finn-isle and Erlend of Gerdi, and
such landed-men as were to the north of them.
These who were now named were all oathsworn
to King Knut to take the life of King Olaf if hap
thereof should be given them.

CHAPTER CCVII.   THE JOURNEY OF
HARALD, SON OF SIGURD.

BUT when that was heard in Norway that
King Olaf had come from the east to
Sweden, then gathered together such of
his friends as were minded to give him aid.   The
noblest man in that company was Harald Sigurdson, brother to King Olaf.   He was then fifteen
winters old, a big man of growth, and manly to
behold.   But there were many other noble men
besides.   They had got together six hundred men
in all when they left the Uplands, and with that
company they made their way east through Eid-
wood unto Vermland, and thence they held on east
across the woodlands all the way to Sweden, and
then asked about the journeyings of King Olaf.

CHAPTER CCVIII. THE JOURNEY OF KING OLAF FROM SWEDEN.

KING OLAF was in Sweden through the spring, and had spies thence north away to Norway, and gat thence but one hearing, to wit, that all unpeaceful would it be to go thither; and the men who came from the north letted him much from faring into the land. But he had set his heart on the one thing, to go, as much as ever.

King Olaf asked in speech with King Onund what aid he would give him to seek to his land. King Onund answers thus, and says that it was not much to the mind of the Swedes to fare a warfare into Norway. "We know," says he, "that the Norwegians be hard and mickle men of battle, and ill to seek to with unpeace. Now I shall not be slow to tell thee what I will lay to thee : I will get thee four hundred men, and do thou choose out of the companies of my guard good warriors and well arrayed for fighting. Thereto will I give thee leave to fare over my land, and get thee all company, whatsoever thou mayest gather, or which is willing to follow thee." This offer King Olaf took, and arrayed him for his journey. But Astrid the queen, and Ulfhild, the king's daughter, were left behind in Sweden.

CHAPTER CCIX. KING OLAF'S JOUR-NEY TO IRONSTONE-LAND.

NOW when King Olaf hove up his journey, there came to him the host that the Swede-king had given him, four hundred men, to wit. The king fared such ways as the Swedes knew how to point out. They made their way up inland into the marches, and came to the country called Ironstone-land. There came to meet the king that folk which had fared from Norway to join him, as is aforesaid. Here he met Harald his brother, and many other kinsmen of his; and a meeting of the greatest joy was that. And now they had altogether twelve hundred men.

CHAPTER CCX. OF DAY, THE SON OF RING.

THERE was a man named Day, of whom it is told that he was the son of that King Ring who had fled away from his land before King Olaf. But men say that Ring was the son of Day, the son of Ring, the son of Harald Hairfair. Day was a kinsman of King Olaf, and father and son, Ring and Day, had taken up their abode in Sweden and got there dominion to rule over. In the spring, when King Olaf was come from the east to Sweden, he sent word to Day his kinsman, that Day should betake himself to the journey with him, with all the strength that he might muster; and if they should make the land of Norway their own, Day was to have there dominion no less than his forefathers had had. But when this word came to Day, it fell well to his mind, for he was greatly wistful of faring to Norway, and there to take over the dominion which his kinsmen had had aforetime. He gave a swift answer to this matter, and behight his journey. Day was a man swift of word and swift of rede, exceeding eager and of great valour, but naught sage of wits. Sithence he gathered together a company for himself, and got wellnigh twelve hundred men; and with this host he went to join King Olaf.

CHAPTER CCXI. OF THE JOURNEY OF KING OLAF.

KING OLAF sent out word into the dwelled land to those men to come to him and follow him, who would have that for wealth-getting, to gather plunder, and have such forfeit wealth as the unfriends of the king might hold their hand over.

Now King Olaf flitted forth his host and fared whiles through the woodland, whiles through wilderness, and often over big waters. They drew or bore their boats after them betwixt the waters. A crowded company of mark-men and some way-layers drifted to the king; and many places are sithence called Olaf's booths where he had his quarters a-night-time. He letted not his journeys till he came into Iamtland, whence he then went north on to the Keel. His host sundered about the dwelled land and went scatter-meal, so long as they wotted of no unpeace ahead. But always when they parted their host, the band of the Northmen followed the king, but Day went another way with his band, and the Swedes a third one with theirs.

CHAPTER CCXII.   OF THE WAY-LAYERS.

TWO men are named, one hight Gowk-Thorir, and the other Afrafasti; they were way-layers, and the most of robbers, and they had with them thirty men of their fashion. These brethren were bigger and stronger than other men, nor did they lack for boldness and stout heart. They heard of the host that was faring over the land there, and they said between them, that it would be handy rede to fare to the king and to follow him to his own land, and there to go into a folk-battle with him, and thus to approve themselves; for erst had they never been in battles such as were of hosts arrayed, and they were wistful exceeding to see the battles of the king. This rede their fellows liked well, and so they made their journey to find the king.

And when they came there, they went with their band before the king, and all these fellows stood all-weaponed. They greeted him, and he asked what men they were. They named themselves, and said that they were men of that land. And therewithal they upbore their errand and bade the king to fare with him.

The king said that it seemed to him that of

such men there would be good following; "therefore I am fain," says he, "to take such men; but are ye Christian men?" says he.

Answers Gowk-Thorir, saying that he was neither Christian nor heathen: "We fellows have no other faith than this, that we trust to our might and main, and our victory-goodhap; and that worketh enough for us." The king answers: "It is great scathe that men of such valiant bearing trow not in Christ, their Shaper." Answered Thorir: "Is there anyone in thy company, king, of the men of Christ, who hath waxed more in one day than we brethren."

The king bade them be christened and take the right faith therewith: "And follow me thereafter, and I shall make you men of mickle worship; but if ye will not this, then fare ye back about your business."

Afrafasti answers, saying that he will take no christening; and therewithal they turn away. Then said Gowk-Thorir: "It is a great shame indeed that this king should make us castaways of his company; for I never was before whereas I was not partaker against any other man; never shall I go back as things now stand."

So they threw themselves in company with the other mark-men, and followed the host.

And now King Olaf maketh his way westward towards the Keel.

CHAPTER CCXIII. OF KING OLAF'S VISION.

NOW when King Olaf fared from the east over the Keel, and won on to the western part of the mountain, so that the land fell away thence westward towards the sea, then beheld he thence the land.   Much folk went ahead of the king, and much after him ; he rode there whereas was room about him, and he was hushed and spoke not to men. In such wise he rode on for a long while of the day, that he looked little about him. Then rode the bishop up to him and spoke to him, and asked whereof he was thinking, seeing he was so hushed. For the king was ever glad and of much speech with his men in the journey, and thus gladdened all who were anigh him.   Then answered the king with mickle care : " Wondrous things have been borne before me a while.   I saw now over Norway when I looked west over the bent of the mountain ; and I called to mind how that I had many a day been glad in that land.   Then I had a sight so that I saw over all Thrandheim, and then over all Norway ; and the longer that sight was before my eye, then saw I ever the wider, right until I saw over all the world, both land and sea. I knew clearly those steads where I had been before and had seen ; but even as clearly saw I steads I had never seen before, some whereof I have heard tell of ; and even as well those which I have never erst heard tell of, both dwelt and undwelt, as wide as is the world."   The bishop said that this was a vision of holy fashion and of right great mark.

CHAPTER CCXIV. A TOKEN ABOUT THE ACRE.

WHENAS the king sought down from the fell, there was there in their way a homestead called Sula, in the upper dwelling of the Verdale folk. Now when they drew down towards the homestead, there were acres lying beside the way, and the king bade his men fare quietly, and not to spoil for the bonder what was his own. And this men did well, while the king was anigh ; but the companies that came after gave no heed to this, and men so overran the acre that it was all laid down to earth. The bonder who dwelt there was called Thorgeir Fleck. He had two sons well grown toward manhood. Thorgeir gave to the king a right good welcome, and to his men withal, and offered him all the cheer that he had stuff to. The king took this in good part, and asked Thorgeir for tidings, what was toward in the land, or whether any gathering would be made against him. Thorgeir said that a great host had been drawn together there in Thrandheim, and that landed-men had come there both from the south of the land, and from the north from Halogaland ; "but I wot not," says he, "whether they be minded to set that host against thee, or otherwhere." Then he made plaint to the king of his scathe, and of the unquiet of the king's men, in that they had beaten down and trodden all his acres. The king said it was ill hap that harm had been done to him. Thereafter the king rode to where the acre had been upstanding, and saw that it was all laid to the ground. He rode round about it and said: " I look forward to this, goodman, that God will right thy loss, and that this field will be better in another week's time." And even as the king had said, that acre was of the best. The king tarried there the night, and arrayed his journey the next morning. He says that goodman Thorgeir shall fare with him, but Thorgeir bade his two sons for the journey. The king says they should not fare with him, but the lads would go, and the king bade them abide behind. But whereas they would not be letted, the king's courtiers would bind them. The king said when he saw that: " Let them fare ; they will come back again." And it went with the boys even as the king had said.

CHAPTER CCXV.   THE MARK-MEN CHRISTENED.

THEN they brought their host out to Staff. And when the king came upon the Staff-mere he made a halt ; and there he heard of a truth that the bonders fared with an host against him, and that he would have battle speedily. Then the king took the muster of his host, and the tale of the men was scored, and there were found to be in the host nine hundred heathen men. So when the king knew this he bade them let themselves be christened, saying that he will not have heathen men in his battle. " We will not," said he, " trust in the multitudes. In God will we trust, for by his might and mercy shall we gain the victory; but I will not blend heathen folk up with my men."

But when the heathen heard this, they took counsel together, and at last four hundred took christening, but five hundred gainsaid Christ's law, and that host turned back to their own country. Then stepped forward the brethren Gowk-Thorir and Afrafasti with their band, and offered the king their aid once more. He asked if they had already taken christening, and Gowk-Thorir said it was not so. The king bade them take christening and the true faith, or go their ways otherwise. So then they turned away and had a talk between them, and took counsel together what rede they should take up. Then spake Afrafasti: "So is it to be said of my mind, that I will not turn back. I will fare to the battle, and give my aid to one side or other; but to me it makes no odds on which side I be." Then said Gowk-Thorir: "If I shall fare to the battle, then will I give aid to the king, for he stands in the greatest need of help; but if I am to trow in some god or other, why should it be worse to me to trow in White-Christ than in any other god? Now it is my counsel that we should let us be christened, if the king deemeth that a great matter, and let us afterwards go into the battle with him." This they all yeasaid, and go to the king to tell him that they are willing to take christening. So they were christened of the clerks and confirmed thereafter, and the king took them into the laws of his body-guard, and said they should be under his banner in the battle.

CHAPTER CCXVI. THE SPEECH OF KING OLAF.

NOW King Olaf had heard it for sure that but a little while it was to this, that he would have battle with the bonders. And when he had taken muster of his host, and scored the tale thereof, he found he had more than thirty hundreds of men, which was then deemed to be a mickle host on one field.

Then the king spoke to the host, saying : " We have a great host and a brave company ; and now I will tell men what array I will have in our host. I shall let fare my banner forth in the midmost of the host, and therewith shall follow my Bodyguard and Guests, and therewithal that band which came to us from the Uplands, and, moreover, that company which came to us here in Thrandheim. But on the right hand of my banner shall be Day Ringson with all that host which he brought to our aid, and he shall have another banner. But on the left of mine array shall be the band which the Swede-king gave us, and all the company that came to us in Sweden, and they shall have the third banner. My will is that men shall be arrayed in companies, and that kinsmen and acquaintance flock together, for thus each will heed the other best, and each ken the other. We shall mark all our host, and make a war-token on our helms and shields, and draw thereon in white the holy cross. And if we come into battle then shall we all have one and the same word-cry : ' Forth, forth, Christ's-men, Crossmen, King's-men !' We shall have thinner ranks if we be the fewer folk, for I will not that they ring us round with their host. Now let men array them into companies, and sithence the companies shall be drawn up in battles, and let then every man wot his stead, and give heed to which side he stand of the banner whereunder he is arrayed. Now we shall keep up our battle-array, and let men have all weapons day and night until we know where the meeting shall be betwixt us and the bonders."

Sithence, when the king had thus spoken, they arrayed their host and set it out even according as the king had ordered.

CHAPTER CCXVII. SPEECH-MEETING OF KING OLAF.

AFTER this the king had a meeting with the captains of companies. By then were come back the men whom the king had sent into the countrysides to crave help of the bonders. They had these tidings to tell from the peopled parts where they fared, that far and wide all was waste of wight men, and all that folk had fared into the gathering of the bonders ; but where they came upon men, but few would follow them, and the most answered that they sat at home for this cause, that they would follow neither side ; they had no will to fight against the king, or against their own kinsmen ; they had got but a scanty company. Then the king asked his men for rede, what seemed likeliest to take up. Finn Arnison answered the king's speech and said : " I

will tell thee," says he, " what would be done, if I
should rule : we should fare the warshield over all
the peopled parts, rob all wealth and burn down
the abodes so throughly that never a cot should be
left standing, and thus pay the bonders for their
betrayal of their lord. Methinks many a one
would get loose from the flock, if he saw home to
his house, and the reek and flame thereof, and
wotted unclearly what tidings were to tell of his
bairns and women and old folk, their fathers,
mothers, and other kindred. And this I ween,"
says he, " that if some of them make up their mind
to break away from the gathering, then their ranks
will speedily thin. Thereto are bonders given, that
such rede as is newest, that is the dearest to them."

But when Finn had done his speech, men gave
it a good cheer ; for to many it liked well to turn
to wealth-lifting, and all deemed the bonders well
worthy of scathe, and thought what Finn said
was like enough to happen, that many of the
bonders would be loose from the gathering. Then
Thormod the Coalbrow-skald sang this stave :

> Burn we all lands we find there
> That inward be of In-isle ;
> The host would ward with war-sword
> Against the king men's homesteads ;
> The yew's grief should be quickened
> In thorn-wood, might I wield it.
> All men of Upper Thrandheim
> Cold coals should have their houses.

But when King Olaf heard the eagerness of the
folk, he craved hearing, and said : " Forsooth the
bonders are full worthy of being dealt with, even

as ye will; they know this withal, that I have done as much as burning them in their abodes, and have laid upon them other heavy punishments. I have done this, that I have burnt them within, when they had gone away from their faith, and taken up blood-offerings, and would not yield to my words; but then had we God's right to awreak; whereas now is this treason much less of worth, though they hold not their troth to me; though forsooth it is, that it will not be deemed beseeming to those who will be men of mandom. Yet I am here somewhat more free to grant them some release, when they misdo against me, than then, when they did hatefully against God. Therefore it is my will that men go forth peacefully, and do no deeds of warwork. I will fare first to meet the bonders, and if we make peace, it is well. But if they hold battle against us, then there will be two ways before us: if we fall in the fight, it will be well done not to fare thither with wealth robbed; but if we gain the victory, then will ye be the heirs of those who are now fighting against us; for some of them will fall in the fight, and some will flee, and both alike will have forfeited all their havings. Then it is good to go into big households and stately manors, but to no man is there any avail in what is burnt down. Likewise of liftings, the more part by far fares to spilling, than what is turned to any use. So now let us go scatter-meal down along the dwellings, and have with us all men meet for fight which we may find. Withal men shall hew beasts, or take other victual, according as men need for their feeding; but let no other ill deeds be done.

Yet I deem it well that the spies of the bonders be slain if ye take them. Day and his company shall fare down along the dale on the north side; but I shall follow the highway, and at night we shall meet, and let us all have one night-lair."

CHAPTER CCXVIII. OF THE SKALDS OF KING OLAF.

SO it is said, that when King Olaf arrayed his host in battle-array, he told off men for a shield-burg, which should hold itself before him in the battle, and thereto he chose out such men as were the starkest and keenest. Then the king called to him his skalds, and bade them go into the shield-burg. Said he: " Ye shall be here, and see the tidings which here shall be done; then there will be no need for others to tell you the tale, for ye shall be the tellers thereof, and sing of it thereafter."

Then were there Thormod Coalbrow-skald and Gizur Goldbrow, the fosterfather of Templegarth-Ref; and the third was Thorfin Mouth. Then said Thormod to Gizur: "Stand we nought so thronged, bedfellow, but that Sigvat may get to his place, when he comes; he will wish to stand in front of the king, and with nought else shall the king be well-liking."

The king heard that and answered: " No need to jeer at Sigvat for not being here. Oft has he followed me well; now will he pray for us, and we shall yet stand in right sore need thereof."

Thormod says: " It may be, king, that now

thou standest most of all in need of prayers, but
thin would it be about the banner-staff, if all thy
courtmen were now on the Rome-road ; and indeed
it was true, that we would be talking then how
that no one might get place because of Sigvat,
howsoever one might wish to speak to thee."

Then the skalds spake together between themselves, saying that it would fall well to frame some
staves of upheartening concerning the tidings which
would speedily be borne on their hands. Then
sang Gizur :

> For throng at the Thing of war-board
> Busk we ! let folk that word hear.
> But never shall thane's daughter
> Hear tell of me grown unglad,
> Though the deft war-groves tell us
> Hope is of the wife of Hedin.
> Be we to the king all helpful
> East in the gale of Ali.

Then sang Thorfin Mouth a stave :

> Toward the mickle rain it darkeneth
> Of the hard storm of war-shield.
> The host of the Verdalers
> With the keen king will battle.
> Ward we All-wielder bounteous,
> And merry feed the blood-mew !
> In Thund's storm fell we Thranders !
> To that same do we egg on.

Then sang Thormod :

> Shaft-thrower ! on it gathers
> To the mickle gale of Ali ;
> And now the sword-age waxeth ;
> Nought blenching should men fumble ;

Busk we for onset, ganging
To the mote of spears with Olaf;
But sure the fight-brisk warrior
Should shun the word of sluggard.

These songs men learnt then and there.

CHAPTER CCXIX. KING OLAF'S SOUL-BOOTING GIFT.

THEN the king arrayed his journey and sought down along the dale; and he took night-harbour, and there came together all his host; and they lay nightlong out under their shields. But forthwith when it dawned of day, the king arrayed the host; and when they were ready thereto, they held still on their way down along the dale. Then came to the king very many bonders, and the more part went into his host; and they all knew how to tell him one tale, that the landed-men had drawn together an host unfightable, and meant to go and give battle to the king. Then the king took many marks of silver, and gave them into the hand of a bonder, and said withal: "This money shalt thou guard and share it hereafter; allot some to churches, give some to clerks, some to almsfolk, and give it for the life and soul of the men who shall fall in battle fighting against us."

The bonder answers: "Shall this money be given for the soul-booting of thy men, king?"

Answered the king: "This money shall be given for the souls of the men who are in battle with the bonders, and who shall fall before the weapons of our men. But those who follow us in the fight, and who fall in it, shall all be saved together, they and I."

CHAPTER CCXX. OF THORMOD COAL-BROW-SKALD.

THE night that King Olaf lay among his host as is aforesaid, he waked long, and prayed to God for himself and his host, and slept but little. Against dawn there fell heaviness upon him, and when he awoke, up ran the day. The king deemed it somewhat early to rouse the host. Then he asked where was Thormod the Skald. He was anigh there, and gave answer, and asked what the king would with him. The king said: "Tell us some song." Thormod sat up and sang out right high, so that it was heard throughout all the host. He sang Biarklay the Ancient; whereof this is the beginning:

> Day is come up again,
> Din the cock's feathers;
> Time, sons of trouble,
> The toil to be winning.
> Wake aye, and wake aye,
> Heads of the friend-folk!
> All ye of the foremost
> Fellows of Adils!
>
> High, the hard-gripping,
> Hrolf of the shooting,
> Kin-worthy men
> Who will not of fleeing.
> To wine nought I wake you,
> Nor whispers of women;
> But up do I wake you
> To Hilda's hard play.

Then awoke the host.   And when the lay was
done, men thanked him for it, and set mickle store
by it, and deemed it was well chosen, and called
the lay "Housecarles'-whetting."   The king
thanked him for his glee, and sithence the king
took a gold ring weighing half a mark and gave it
to Thormod.   Thormod thanked the king for his
gift, and said: "A good king have we, but it is a
hard matter now to see through, how long-lived
the king may be; and it is my boon, king, that
thou let us part nevermore, alive or dead."

The king answered: "All we shall fare together, while I rule over it, if ye choose not to
part from me."

Thormod said : "This I look for, king, whether
the peace be better or worser, that I shall be
standing near to you, while I have the choice,
whatever we may hear of Sigvat, where he may
be faring with Goldenhilt."   Then sang Thormod :

> Fight-bold all-wielder! ever
> About thy knee I turn me,
> Till other skalds thou get thee.
> When hopest thou for these then?
> Though we give the greedy raven
> Corpse meat, off shall we get us,
> Or else here shall be lying.
> Soothly is this unfailing,
> O reddener of the wave-steeds.

CHAPTER CCXXI. KING OLAF COMES UNTO STICKLESTEAD.

KING OLAF brought the army down along the valley; and Day still fared with his host another way. The king letted not his faring until he came down to Sticklestead. Then they saw the host of the bonders, and that folk went much scatter-meal, and was so mickle a multitude, that along every path were folk drifting in, and wide about it was, that big flocks fared together. They saw where a company of men came on down from Verdale, who had been out a-spying, and fared nigh to where was the host of the king, and found nought, before there was so short a space between them both, that men might know each other. And there was Ram of Vigg with thirty men.

Then the king ordered the Guests to fare against Ram and take his life, and ready enough were men for that work.

Then spoke the king to the Icelanders: "So is it told me, that it is a custom in Iceland that bonders be bound in harvest-time to give their house-carles a slaughter-wether. Lo, there I will give you a ram for the slaughter."

The Icelanders were easily egged on to this deed, and fared forthwith on Ram with other men, and he was slain and all the company that followed him.

The king took a stand and stayed his host, when he came to Sticklestead; and the king bade men get off their horses and make ready there, and men did as bade the king.

Then the host was cast into battle-array, and the banners were set up. Day was not yet come with his host, so that wing of the battle was lacking. Then spake the king that the Uplanders should go forth and take up the banner; "but I deem it rede," says the king, "that Harald my brother be not in the fight, for he is but a child of age."

Harald answers: "I shall surely be in the fight; but if I am so unstrong that I may not wield the sword, then can I good rede thereto, to wit, that my hand be bound to the grip thereof. No man shall be of better will than I to be unprofitable to those bonders; and I shall follow mine own fellowship." So men say, that Harald sang this song therewith:

> That wing shall I dare warding
> Wherein to stand my lot is.
> In wrath the shield we redden.
> 'Tis a thing that woman loveth.
> The war-blithe youngling warrior
> Before spears nowise fareth
> To heel, where strokes are striking.
> To the murder-mote men hasten.

Harald had his will and was in the battle.

CHAPTER CCXXII. OF THORGILS HALMASON.

A MAN is named Thorgils, son of Halma, and he was the bonder who then dwelt at Sticklestead, and was the father of Grim the Good. Thorgils offered the king his help, and to be in the battle with him. The king bade him have thanks for his offer: " But I will, bonder, that thou be not in the battle. Grant us rather that other help, to save our men after the fight, such as be wounded; and lay out the bodies of the others, who fall in the fray. Likewise, should such hap be, bonder, that I fall in this battle, then do what service may be needful to my body, if it be not forbidden thee."

And Thorgils avowed to the king to do his behest.

CHAPTER CCXXIII. THE TALK OF KING OLAF.

NOW when King Olaf had arrayed his host, he spake to them, and said that men should harden their hearts, and go forth boldly, if a battle befall. Says he: "We have an host good and great, and although the bonders have an host somewhat more, yet will fate rule the victory. I have to make known unto you that I shall not flee from this battle; I shall either overcome the bonders, or shall fall here else. And this I pray, that that lot come up which God sees will be for me the gainfullest. We shall trust in this, that we have a more rightful cause to plead than the bonders; and this furthermore, that God will make free our own to us after this battle, or else will give us a reward mickle more for the loss that we here get, than we ourselves know how to pray for. But if it be my lot to have aught to say after the battle, then shall I reward each one of

you according to his work's-worth, and according
to the way whereas each goeth forth in the battle;
for then, if we gain the victory, there will be enough
to share between you, both of lands and chattels,
which are now in the hands of my foemen. Let us
make the hardest of onslaughts at first; for swiftly
then will be a shifting, though odds be mickle, and
we have to hope for victory from speedy dealings;
whereas that will fall heavy on us, if we have to
fight unto weariness, so that men thereof become
unfightworthy. For we shall have less fresh folk
than they, to go forth in turn, while some shield
themselves and rest. But if we make the brunt
so hard that they turn aback who are foremost,
then will each fall across the other, and their mishap will be the greater, the more they are together."

And when the king left off speaking men gave
a great cheer to his speaking, and each egged on
the other.

CHAPTER CCXXIV. OF THORD, THE SON OF FOLI.

THORD, the son of Foli, bore the standard
of King Olaf. So says Sigvat the Skald
in that death-song which he wrought on
King Olaf, and fashioned after the Uprising
story :

> Heard I that Thord with Olaf
> Hardened the fight begun there
> With sword; then throve the onset,
> Good hearts there fared together.

The bold-heart Ogmund's brother
Toiled sorely, high upbearing
The fair-gilt staff before him,
The fight-worn king of Ringfolk.

CHAPTER CCXXV. OF THE ARRAY OF KING OLAF.

KING OLAF was so arrayed, that he had a helm all-gilded on his head; but a white shield, and thereon done in gold the Holy Cross; in one hand he had that spear which now standeth beside the altar in Christ's Church. He was girt with that sword which was called Hneitir, the keenest of swords, the grip wrapped around with gold. He had on a ring-byrny. Hereof telleth Sigvat the Skald:

Olaf the Thick won felling
Of folk; the lord fight-daring
Went forth all in his byrny
To fetch a victory mighty.
But the Swedes, who came from the eastland
With the bounteous lord, rushed onward
Into the bright blood-eddies.
There then the battle waxèd;
Much things I tell all naked.

CHAPTER CCXXVI. KING OLAF'S DREAM.

BUT when King Olaf had done arraying his host, then were the bonders come nowhere nigh as yet. Then said the king that the whole host should sit down and rest them. And King Olaf himself sat him down, and all his host, and they sat at their ease. He leaned back and laid his head on the knee of Finn Arnison. Then sleep ran over him, and that was for a while.

Then they saw the heap of the bonders, how their host sought on to meet them, and had set up its banners; and the greatest multitude of men was that. Then Finn roused the king, and told him the bonders were making for them. And when the king awoke, he said: "Why didst thou wake me, Finn, nor leave me to have my dream out?"

Finn answered: "Thou wouldst not be dreaming such, as that it should not be more due for thee to wake, and be ready for the host that fareth upon us. Or dost thou not see now whereto the bonder-crowd hath gotten?"

The king answers: "They are not so near yet, as that it were not better that I had slept."

Then said Finn: "What didst thou dream, king, whereof thou deemest it so mickle amiss, that thou shouldst not wake up of thyself?"

Then the king told his dream; he thought he saw a high ladder, and that he walked up the same, up aloft so long, that he deemed he saw the heavens open, and even thither the ladder reached: "And I was even then come to the topmost rung, when thou didst call me."

Finn answers: "To me nought seemeth the dream so good as thou deemest it; for I am minded to think that this forebodeth thee for fey, if that which came before thee were aught else than mere dream-fooling."

CHAPTER CCXXVII.   THE CHRIS-TENING OF ARNLIOT GELLINI.

IT befell again, when King Olaf was come to Sticklestead, that a certain man came to him. But this was nought wondrous, in so far that many men came to the king out of the country-sides there, but it was deemed for new tidings, whereas this man was unlike unto other men of them who had come to the king as then. He was a man so high, that none of the others were more than up to the shoulder of him; he was a very goodly man to look upon, and of fair hair. He was well weaponed, and had a full fair helm and a ring-byrny, and a red shield, and was girt with a fair-wrought sword; he had in hand a gold-inlaid great spear, the shaft whereof was so thick that a good handful it was. This man went before the king and greeted him, and asked if he would have help of him. The king asked what was his name and kindred, and whence of lands.

He answers: "I have kindred in Iamtland and Helsingland; I am called Arnliot Gellini; and that most I can to tell thee, that I gave some furtherance to those men of thine whom thou sentest to Iamtland to crave scat there; and I handed over to them a silver dish which I sent thee for a token that I was willing to be thy friend."

Then asked the king if Arnliot were a man chris-tened or not. But he said this of his troth, that he trowed in his might and main. "And that belief has served me full well hitherto; but now I am minded rather to trow in thee, O king."

The king answered : " If thou wilt trow in me, then thou shalt believe in what I teach thee. Thou shalt believe this, that Jesus Christ has created heaven and earth and all men, and that to him shall fare after death all those who are good, and who believe aright."

Arnliot answered : " I have heard tell of the White-Christ, but I am not well learned in his doings, nor where he ruleth ; so I will now believe all that thou hast to tell me, and I will leave all my matter in thine hand."

Then Arnliot was christened, and the king taught him as much of the faith as he deemed was most needful, and arrayed him to the vanward battle-array, and before his own banner. There, too, were Gowk-Thorir and Afrafasti and their fellows.

CHAPTER CCXXVIII. OF WAR GATHERING IN NORWAY.

NOW is to be told the tale that was dropped afore, that landed-men and bonders had drawn together an host, not to be dealt with in battle, so soon as they heard that the king had fared from the east from Garthrealm, and was come to Sweden ; and when they heard that he was come from the east to Iamtland, and that he was about to fare from the east over the Keel to Verdale, they brought the host into Thrandheim, and there gathered together to them all the folk, thane and thrall, and so fared up to Verdale, and had there so great a gathering, that no man who was there had ever seen so great an host gathered in Norway.

But there it was, as always will be in so big an host, that the company was all diverse; there was a mickle of landed-men, and a great crowd of mighty bonders, but there was also the whole heap of villeins and workmen, and they made the main host which had been gathered together in Thrandheim; but that host was most fierce in foeship against the king.

CHAPTER CCXXIX. OF BISHOP SIGURD.

KING KNUT the Rich had laid under him all the land of Norway, as is afore writ, and therewithal had set Earl Hakon up for a ruler there. He gave the earl a court bishop, named Sigurd, a Dane by kindred, who had been with King Knut for a long time. That bishop was a man masterful, and pompous of speech; he gave King Knut all the word-propping he might, and was the most unfriend of King Olaf. That same bishop was with this host, and oft would speak to the bonder-folk, and egged on mickle the uprising against King Olaf.

CHAPTER CCXXX.   THE   TALK   OF BISHOP SIGURD.

NOW Bishop Sigurd spoke at a certain House-Thing whenas was a mickle throng. And thus he took up the word : " Here is now come together a great multitude of folk, so that in this poor land might by no chance ever be seen a greater host of inlanders. Now this strength of men should stand you well in stead, for now is need enough thereto, if this Olaf is yet minded not to lay by his harrying of you. When he was yet but a youth he became wont to rob men, and to slay, and hereto fared he wide over lands; and at last turned hither toward this country, and began his business by becoming the greatest unfriend of those who were the best men and the mightiest, (such as is King Knut, whom all are bound to serve to their best;) and he set himself down in his scat-land. The same wise he dealt too with Olaf, the Swede-king; and the earls, Svein and Hakon, he drave away from the lands of their birthright; and yet to his own kin he was grimmest of all, in that he drave away all the kings of the Uplands; yet that was well enough in some way, for they had already broken their faith and oaths to King Knut, and backed this Olaf up in what folly soever he took up. Now meetly sundered their friend-ship; he maimed them, and took to himself their dominion, and thus voided the land of all men of dignity. But thereafter ye must be wotting how he hath dealt with landed-men; the most renowned of them are slain, and many have become land-waifs before him. He hath also fared wide over this land with robber flocks, burnt the country-sides, and slain and robbed the people; or which of the men of might will be here, who hath not sore wrongs to avenge on him? Now he fareth with an outland host, of which the most part are woodland-men and waylayers, or robbers of other sort. Deem ye that he will be soft with you, now that he fares with this rout of evil-doers, seeing what deeds of ravage he did when even all who followed him letted him? I call that your rede, that ye mind you now of the words of King Knut, whereas he counselled you, if Olaf should make his way to the land again, how ye should hold your freedom even as King Knut hath behight it you. He bade you withstand and drive off your hands such lawless rabble. And this is now to hand, to go meet them, and to smite down this evil folk to the eagle and the wolf, and let each one lie whereas he is hewn; unless ye will it rather, to drag their carcases into holt and warren. But let no man be bold enough to bring them to churches, for all these be but vikings and evil-doers." And when he had made an end of this talk, men gave it a mickle cheer, and they all said yea to doing as he bade.

CHAPTER CCXXXI. OF THE LANDED-MEN.

THE landed-men who were come there together had their meeting, and talk and outspeaking, and then ordered the array of the battles, and who should be captain over the host. Then said Kalf, the son of Arni, that Harek of Thiotta was best fitted to become the chief of this army: "For he is come of the kin of Harald Hairfair; and the king has against him a right heavy grudge for the slaying of Grankel, and he will sit under the most of evil dealings, if Olaf should once more come to his might; moreover, Harek is a man much proven in battles, and a man all eager for renown."

Harek answers that those men were better fitted for this, who then were in the nimblest of their age: "But I am now," says he, "an old man and a tottering, and nowise well meet for battle; withal, there is kinship betwixt King Olaf and me; and, of howsoever little worth he counts that to me, yet it beseems me nowise to thrust me forth in this unpeace against him more than any other man in our flock. But thou, Thorir, art well fitted to be the head-man in holding battle against King Olaf, and grievance enough hast thou against him: thou hast to avenge on him loss of thy kinsmen, and this, moreover, that he drave thee into outlawry from all thy goods, and thou hast behight King Knut, and thy kinsmen withal, that thou wouldst avenge Asbiorn; or deemest thou that a better chance of Olaf will be given thee, than that which now is, for avenging thee of all that mighty shame ? "

Thorir answered his speech : " I trust myself nought to raise up banner against King Olaf, or to become chief over this host. Here have the Thrandheim folk the most throng of men ; and I know their pride, that they will not obey me or any other man of Halogaland. But there is no need to call to my mind the wrongs whereof I have to pay Olaf ; I mind me of that loss of men, how that Olaf has cut off from life four men, all of them noble of honours and kin, Asbiorn, my brother's son, Thorir and Griotgard, my sister's sons, and their father, Olvir, and I am in duty bound to avenge each one of them. Now, this is to tell of me, that I have chosen out eleven men of my house-carles, they who are briskest, and I am minded to think that we shall not haggle with other men as to dealing in blows with King Olaf, if we shall get us the chance thereof."

CHAPTER CCXXXII. THE SPEECH OF KALF, SON OF ARNI.

THEN Kalf Arnison took up the word : " This need we in the work which we have taken up, not to make it a fool's errand now that the host is gathered together. We shall need something else, if we are to give battle to King Olaf, than that each one back out of undertaking the trouble. For we may be fast in this mind, that though King Olaf have no great host beside that which we have, yet there is the leader dauntless, and all his host will be trusty for fight and following. But if we now be wavering at all, who should be most chiefly the leaders of our host; and if we will not put the host in heart, nor egg it on, nor lead it to the onset, then forthwith in a many of them that be faltering, the heart will fail them, and then each one will be looking to himself. Now albeit a mickle host is here come together, we shall none the less come into such a trial, when we meet King Olaf with his host, that worsting shall be certain for us, unless we, the captains, be ourselves keen-hearted, and the whole throng fall on with one accord. But if this come not about, then would it be better for us not to risk battle; and then will our choice be deemed easy to see, that we risk the mercy of Olaf, howsoever hard he was then thought, when there were less guilts against us than he will now deem there be. And yet I know that such men are arrayed in his host, that I shall have the chance of my life if I will seek for it. Now if ye will, as I will, then shalt thou, Thorir, my brother-in-law, and thou, Harek, go under the banner which we shall all upraise and follow after. Be we all hard-set and keen about this rede we have taken up, and lead we on the host of bonders in such wise that they find no flutter of fear in us; and that will stir up the folk, if we go glad to the arraying of the host and the egging-on of it."

And when Kalf had done giving forth his errand, they all with one consent turned them to his rede, saying they would have all things even as Kalf should deem best for them. So they all willed that Kalf should be captain of the host, and should order each one into what company he would.

CHAPTER CCXXXIII. CONCERNING LANDED-MEN BEARING BANNERS.

KALF set up his banner and arrayed thereunder his house-carles, and therewith Harek of Thiotta and his folk. Thorir Hound with his following was in the onward breast of the array before the banners. And there, on either side of Thorir, was a picked company of the bonders, of all that was briskest and best-weaponed. That array was made both long and thick, and in that line were Thrandheimers and Halogalanders. But on the right-hand side to this array there was set another such, and on the left hand from the main battle was the battle of the men of Rogaland, Hordland, Sogn, and the Firths, and they had there the third banner.

CHAPTER CCXXXIV. OF THORSTEIN SHIPWRIGHT.

THERE was a man named Thorstein Shipwright; he was a chapman and a great smith, and a man mickle and strong, exceeding eager-hearted in all things, and a mickle slayer. He had fallen into the king's enmity, and the king had taken from him a cheaping-ship, a new and big one, which Thorstein had made. That was for Thorstein's brawlings and for a thane's weregild which the king had against him. Thorstein was there in the host; and he went forth before the line of war, to where stood Thorir Hound, and spoke thus : " Here will I be in this company, Thorir, with thee ; whereas I am minded, that if we two, Olaf and I, meet, to be the first to bear weapon on him, if I may be standing so nigh him ; so that I may pay him for the taking of the ship, when he robbed me of that craft which is the one only best that is brooked in cheaping-fare." So Thorir and his folk took Thorstein, and he went into their fellowship.

CHAPTER CCXXXV. OF THE ARRAYING OF THE BONDERS.

NOW when the bonders had been set in battle-array, the landed-men gave out the word, and bade the folk give heed to their places, whereas each one was marshalled, or under what banner they were each to be, or how nigh to the banner he was set, and which way from it. They bade the men be watchful and swift to fall into line, when the horns should sing out, and the war-blast come up, and then to go forth in array ; for they had still a much long way to flit the host onward, and it was to be looked for, that the lines should be broken on the march.

Then they egged on the host. Kalf said that all men, who had grief and hatred whereof to pay King Olaf, should go forth under those banners which should fare against the banner of King Olaf, and that they should be mindful then of the wrong-doing he had dealt them ; and he says that they would never hit upon a better chance for avenging of their sorrow, and to free themselves from that bondage and thraldom under which he had laid them. " He is now," says Kalf, " a blencher who fighteth not at his boldest, for no-wise sackless are they whom ye fight against, neither will they spare you if they get the chance." To his speech there was made right mickle cheer. And therewithal there was a mighty great shout and egging-on throughout the whole host.

CHAPTER CCXXXVI. THE HOSTS OF THE KING AND OF THE BONDERS.

THEN the bonders flitted their host on to Sticklestead, whereas King Olaf was before them with his host. At the head of the host Kalf and Harek fared onward with the banner. But when they met, the onset befell not right speedily, for the bonders tarried the onfall, whereas not all their host had come forth any-where nigh evenly; so they abode that folk which lagged behind. Thorir Hound had fared last with his company, for he was to watch that the host should not slink back, when the war-whoop came up and the foemen's folk were seen. So Kalf and his waited for Thorir.

The bonders had this watchword for egging on their host to battle : " Forth, forth, Bonder-men !"

King Olaf made no onfall because he waited for Day and the folk which followed him. But now the king and his saw where Day's host was coming. So it is said, that the bonders had an host nothing less than an hundred hundreds of men. But thus sayeth Sigvat :

> Wild unto me the woe is
> That the king had little gathering
> From eastward, e'en the lord king,
> Who grasped the grip gold-twinèd.
> I heard that there the bonders
> By the half were more than he was.
> So gat they gain ; that somewhat
> Betrayed the battles' urger.

CHAPTER CCXXXVII. THE KING AND THE BONDERS MEET.

NOW when either host stood face to face and men knew each other, the king said : " Why art thou there, Kalf ; whereas we parted friends south in Mere ? It beseems thee but ill to be fighting against us, or to shoot death-shot into our host, whereas here be thy four brethren ? "

Kalf answers : " Much fareth otherwise now, king, than were best beseeming. In such wise didst thou part from us, that need was to make peace with them who were left behind ; and now must each be whereas he is set. But we two should yet make peace together, if I might rule."

Then said Finn : " That is a mark of Kalf, that if he speaketh well, he is minded to do ill."

The king said : " Maybe, Kalf, that thou willest peace now ; but meseemeth that nought peacefully now ye bonders are doing." Then answereth Thorgeir of Kviststead : " Ye shall now have such peace as many a man hath had afore of you, and now shall ye pay therefor."

Answered the king : " Thou needest not be so eager for our meeting—for nowise shall victory over us be fated for thee to-day—whereas I have raised thee up to might from a little man."

CHAPTER CCXXXVIII. THE BEGINNING OF THE BATTLE OF STICKLESTEAD.

THEREWITH came Thorir Hound with his company, and went forth before the banner, and cried out: " Forth, forth, Bonder-men!" And the bonder-men let out the war-whoop and shot both arrows and spears. And then the king's men set up the war-whoop; and when that was over, they egged each other on as they had been taught to do before, and said : " Forth, forth, Christ's men, Cross-men, King's men!" And when the bonders heard that, even they who stood out in the wing, they cried the same cry as they heard these call out. And when the others of the bonder-host heard this, they thought that these last were the king's men, and bore weapons upon them, so that they fought between themselves, and many men fell before they were ware how it was.

Fair was the weather, and the sun shone in the clear heaven. But when the battle began, the heaven was besmitten by redness, and the sun withal ; and before it cleared off, it grew mirk as night.

Now King Olaf had arrayed his folk whereas

was a certain bent, and they plunged adown upon
the battle of the bonders, and gave them so hard
an onfall that the line of the bonders bent before
them, so that there stood the breast of the king's
array, whereas they had had their stand erewhile,
who were hindmost in the host of the bonders;
and at this while much of the bonder-host was
ready to flee; but the landed-men and their house-
carles stood fast, and a right hard brunt then
befell.   So says Sigvat:

> Wide must the field with feet din;
> To men was banned the peace-tide.
> The byrny-clad betook them
> Into hot brunt of battle;
> When they that ply the bow-draught,
> Bright-helmed rushed down all early,
> And mickle was the steel-storm
> At Sticklestead befallen.

The landed-men egged on their host and thrust
on hard to onset; thereof Sigvat telleth:

> Now farèd forth the banners
> In the mid host of the Thrand-men.
> There nimble men were meeting;
> That work the bonders rued them.

Then set on the bonder-host from all sides.
They hewed who stood the foremost; but they,
who there were next, thrust with spears; but all
those, who were further back, shot spears, or
arrows, or hurled stones, or hand-axes, or shaft-
flints.   And soon there befell a battle man-
scathing, and much folk fell on either side.
In the first brunt fell Arnliot Gellini, Gowk-

Thorir, and Afrafasti, and all their company, but each had slain his man first, or two, or some more.

Then grew thin the array before the king's banner. So the king bade Thord bear forth the banner, but he himself followed the banner, and that company withal which he had chosen to be anigh him in the battle. And those men were the aldermost of daring and the best arrayed in his company. Thereof telleth Sigvat:

> I heard that my Lord for the most part
> Went nighest his own banner;
> The staff before the king rushed,   .
> Enough the stour was toward.

When King Olaf went forth out of the shield-burg, and into the vanward of his battle, and the bonders might look into the face of him, then they were filled with dread and their hands dropped. This Sigvat telleth:

> For throwers of flame of spear-pond
> 'Twas given to look, meseemeth,
> Into the keen-set eyen
> Of Olaf brisk in battle.
> The Hersir's Lord full awful
> Was deemed; the Thrandish warfolk
> They durst not look with eyen
> Into his eyes worm-gleaming.

Then was a right hard battle, and the king went himself fast forth into the brunt of handy-strokes. So says Sigvat:

> The men's host, shield in hand there,
> Reddened the swords all gory

In warriors' blood, where fell they
On the dear king of the people.
And the king, in iron-play eager,
Let the red-brown sword be seeking
The meadows of the hair-path
Of the dwellers of Up-Thrandheim.

CHAPTER CCXXXIX. THE FALL OF THORGEIR OF KVISTSTEAD.

THEN fought King Olaf all dauntlessly. He hewed on Thorgeir of Kviststead, a landed-man, who is afore-named, athwart the face, and sheared asunder the nose-guard of the helm of him, and clave the head below the eyes, so that it nearly flew off. And when he fell, the king said: "Yea! is that true, which I said thee, Thorgeir, that thou wouldst have no victory in our dealings?"

In this brunt Thord smote down the banner-staff so hard, that the staff stood upright of itself; for then had Thord got his bane-wound, and there he fell under the banner. Therewith fell also Thorfin Mouth, and Gizur Goldbrow; but on him had two men set, and one he slew and the other he hurt, or ever he fell himself. So saith Templegarth-Ref:

The ash-tree of the battle,
The bold one in the steel-rain,
With two brisk thanes had war-din.
Uproared the flame of the High one.
The plunger in bow's river,
Hewed Frey of the dew of Draupnir
A bane-stroke; and another
Wrought wound for; steel he reddened.

Then it was, as is said before, that the heaven was clear, but the sun vanished from sight, and it grew mirk.   As says Sigvat:

> For not a little wonder
> Men deem it, when unclouded
> Was the sun, yet had no warming
> For the Niordings of the shroud-horse.
> On the day-tide fell great portent,
> When its fair hues the day gat not.
> From east away then heard I
> How it went, the Lord-king's battle.

At this nick of time came up Day, the son of Ring, with the host he had led, and fell to arraying his battle, and set up his banner.   But because that mickle was the mirk, their onset was nought speedy, whereas they knew not surely what might be before them.   Howsoever they turned thither where before them were the men of Rogaland and Hordland.

Now all these haps fell at one and the same time, though some happened a little before or a little later.

CHAPTER CCXL. THE FALL OF KING OLAF.

KALF and Olaf are named two kinsmen of Kalf, the son of Arni, who stood on one side of him, mickle men, and valiant. Kalf was the son of Arnfinn, the son of Arnmod, and brother's son of Arni, the son of Arnmod. On the other side of Kalf Arnison went forth Thorir Hound.   King Olaf hewed on Thorir Hound

right across the shoulders; the sword did not
bite, but it seemed as if dust flew out of the reindeer skin. Hereof tells Sigvat:

> The bounteous king most clearly
> Himself found how the wise-work
> Of the witchcrafty Finn-folk
> Saved the big-fashioned Thorir;
> When the scatterer of the fire
> Of the mast-knop smote the shoulders
> Of Hound, and the sword gold-broidered,
> Blunted, would bite in nowise.

Then Thorir smote at the king, and sundry
blows they gave and took; but the sword of the
king bit not, whereas the reindeer-skin was in the
way, yet was Thorir hurt in the hand. As again
Sigvat sings:

> The wealth-pine, taunting Thorir,
> Owns not the soothful valour
> Of Hound. From home that wot I;
> Who e'er saw deeds were doughtier.
> The Thrott of the storm of thwart-garth
> Of the fight-shed, he who thrust him
> Forth on there, dared to hew back
> At one who was a king-man.

The king said to Biorn the Marshal: "Smite
thou the hound whom iron will bite not." Biorn
turned the axe in his hand and smote with the
hammer thereof, and the blow took Thorir on
the shoulder and was a full mighty blow, and
Thorir staggered thereat. And in that same nick
of time the king turned against Kalf and his kinsmen, and gave a bane-wound to Olaf, a kinsman
of Kalf. Then Thorir Hound thrust a spear at
Biorn the Marshal, and smote him in the midst,

and gave him a bane-wound. Then spake Thorir:
"Thus bait we the bears."

Thorstein Shipwright smote at King Olaf with
an axe, and the blow struck the left leg anigh the
knee and above it. Finn Arnison smote Thorstein down forthwith. But at this wound the
king leaned him up against a stone and threw
away his sword, and bade God help him. Then
Thorir Hound thrust a spear at him. The
thrust came on him below the byrny, and ran
up into the belly. Then Kalf hewed at him, and
that blow took him on the left side of the neck.
But men are sundered on the matter, where Kalf
gave the king the wound. These three wounds
the king got towards the loss of his life. But
after his fall, then most all the company fell which
had gone forth with the king. Biarni Goldbrow-
skald sang this on Kalf, the son of Arni:

> Fight-nimble, thou by battle
> Didst ward the land 'gainst Olaf;
> Thou daredst the king most valiant,
> That, say I, I have heard of.
> To Sticklestead, deed-mighty,
> Thou wentst: forth rushed the banner;
> Forsooth thou gavest onset
> Till the valiant king was fallen.

And of Biorn the Marshal, Sigvat sang this:

> Eke heard I that erst Biorn
> Learned marshals throughly whatwise
> 'Twas due to hold liege-fealty:
> He, too, was in the onset.
> He fell in the host of battle
> At the head of the king fame-wealthy;
> That death is all be-praisèd
> 'Mongst the faithful men king-warding.

CHAPTER CCXLI. THE BEGINNING OF DAY'S BRUNT.

THEN Day, the son of Ring, upheld the battle, and made the first onset so hard that the bonders shrank before him, and some turned to flight. Then there fell a multitude of the host of the bonders, and these landed-men besides, Erlend of Garth, Aslak of Finn-isle ; and therewith was hewn down the standard which they had fared with before. Then was the battle of the fiercest, and this they called Day's Brunt. Then turned against Day these : Kalf Arnison, to wit, Harek of Thiotta, and Thorir Hound, with the array which followed them. Then Day was overborne by sheer might, and he turned to flight, and all the host that was left. There was a certain dale there, up along which the main rout went, and there fell at this time a many of the host. Drifted then the folk away to two sides ; many were sorely hurt, and many so weary that they were good for nought at all. The bonders drove the chase but a short way, for the captains soon turned back, and thither where lay the fallen ; for many had there to look for their friends and kinsmen.

CHAPTER CCXLII. TOKENS OF KING OLAF ON THORIR HOUND.

THORIR HOUND went thereto where was the body of King Olaf, and gave lyke-help to it, laying the body down and straightening it and spreading a cloth thereover. And when he wiped the blood off the face, he said thereof afterwards, that the face of the king was so fair, that the cheeks were even as ruddy, as he were asleep; but a mickle brighter than it was afore, while he was yet alive. Then came the blood of the king on to the hand of Thorir, and ran up unto the grip where he had afore gotten his hurt; and there was no need of any binding up of that hurt thenceforth, so speedy was the healing thereof. Thorir bore witness to this hap himself, when the holiness of King Olaf became known to all folk; and Thorir Hound was the first among the mighty men who had been of the host of his foes to uphold the holiness of the king.

CHAPTER CCXLIII. OF THE BRO-THERS OF KALF, THE SON OF ARNI.

KALF, the son of Arni, sought for his brothers who were fallen there. He came upon Thorberg and Finn, and it is the say of men that Finn hurled a sax at him, and would slay him, and spake hard words at him, and called him a peace-dastard and a lord-betrayer. Kalf gave no heed thereto, but let bear Finn away from the slain and Thorberg in like wise. Then their wounds were searched, and they had no hurt deadly-looking; they had fallen overborne by weapons and weariness. Then Kalf busied him to bring his brothers down aboard ship, and went with them himself. But so soon as he turned away, then fared away also all the host of the bonders which had their homes anigh there, out-taken such men as were busy there about their kinsmen or friends who were wounded, or about the bodies of them who had fallen. Wounded men were carried to the homestead, so that every house was full of them, and over some tents were pitched outside.

Now as wonderful as it had been, how many people had been gathered together in the host of the bonders, yet men thought this no less far away from likelihood, how swiftly the gathering cleared off, when it came to that; but this had much to do with it, that the greatest part of the multitude had been gathered together from neighbouring country-sides, and they were all very home-sick.

CHAPTER CCXLIV.   OF THE VERDA-LERS.

THOSE bonders who had dwelling in Verdale went to meet the captains, Harek and Thorir, and made plaint to them of their troubles, and said thus: " The fleers who have got away hence, will fare up along Verdale, and will gear our homesteads in un-profitable wise; and for us is no going home so long as they be here in the dale. Now do ye so

well as to fare after them with a company, and
let no child of them get away; for that is the fate
they were minded for us if they had got the best
of our meeting; and the very same will they yet
do to us, if hereafter we shall meet in such wise,
that the odds be against us on their side. Like
enough, they will tarry about the dale if they deem
they have nought to fear; and they will now
straightway be faring with riot about our dwelling."

The bonders spoke hereof with many words,
and urged with mickle eagerness that the captains
should fare and slay the folk that had got away.
And when the captains talked hereover between
them, they deemed the bonders had said many
things true in their talk; so they took that rede,
that Thorir Hound with six hundreds of men, his
own company, to wit, turned him to faring with
them of Verdale. And they went, whenas night
fell in; and Thorir letted not his journey till he
came a-night-time up to Sula, where he heard
the tidings that Day, the son of Ring, and many
other flocks of Olaf's men, had come thither in the
evening, and tarried there but for night-meal, and
had sithence fared up on the fell. Then said Thorir
that he would not drift after them over the fells,
and therewith he turned down into the vale again,
and but few men they got slain. Thereupon the
bonders fared to their homes, but Thorir and his
host went the next day down to their ships. But
the king's men, they who were way-worthy, saved
themselves, hiding in woods, and some got help
from folk about.

CHAPTER CCXLV. OF HARALD SIGURDSON.

HARALD SIGURDSON was sorely wounded, but Rognvald, son of Brusi, brought him to a certain bonder the night after the battle ; and the bonder took Harald in and healed him in hiding, and then gave him his son to guide him away. They went with a hidden head through mountains and wildernesses, and came out into Iamtland; and they fared both together east into Garthrealm to King Jarisleif, even as is told in the story of Harald Sigurdson.

CHAPTER CCXLVI. OF THORMOD COAL-BROW-SKALD.

THORMOD COALBROW-SKALD was in the battle under the banner of the king. And when the king was fallen, and the onset was at its fiercest, then fell the king's company each by the other, but most of them were wounded who stood up. Thormod was sore hurt, and he did then as other men, who all drew aback from there where they deemed was most risk of life, but some ran. Then arose the fight which is called Day's Brunt, wherein there joined all the host of the king that was still fightworthy. But Thormod came not into that battle, for that he was unmeet for fighting, both through wounds and weariness ; but he stood there beside his fellows, though he might do nothing else. Then was he smitten by an arrow in the left side.

Then he broke the arrow-shaft from off him, and went away from the battle home to the houses, and came to a certain barn which was a mickle house. Thormod had a naked sword in his hand; and as he went in, there came a man out against him, and said: "Herewithin they go on wondrous ill, with whining and howling; and a great shame it is that valiant men should not thole their wounds. Maybe the king's men have gone forth on right well, but all unmanly they bear their wounds." Thormod answered: "What is thy name?" He named himself Kimbi. Answered Thormod: "Wert thou in the battle?" "I was," says he, "with the bonders; the better side, to wit." "Art thou hurt at all?" says Thormod. "Little," says Kimbi, "or wert thou in the battle?" Thormod answers: "I was, and with them who had the better."

Kimbi saw that Thormod had a golden ring on his arm, and he said: "Thou must be of the king's men; so hand me the gold ring, and I shall hide thee; for the bonders will slay thee, if thou come in their way." Thormod says: "Take the ring, if thou mayst reach it; now have I lost more." Kimbi reached forth his hand, and would take the ring. Thormod swept his sword, and sheared the hand from off him. And so is it said, that Kimbi bore his wound nowise better than the others whom he had been wyting before; and therewith Kimbi went away.

But Thormod sat him down in the barn, and sat there a while, and hearkened to the talk of men. This was most spoken there, that each man sayeth that which he deemed he had seen in the battle, and the talk was of onsets of men; and some praised most the valour of King Olaf, and some named no less other men.   Then sang Thormod:

> Bold was the heart of Olaf,
> Through blood the king forth waded;
> At Sticklestead the wrought steel
> Bit, and the host craved battle.
> All pines of the gale of Jalfad,
> Save the very king, there saw I
> To spare themselves; yet most men
> In the fast spear-drift did prove them.

CHAPTER CCXLVII. THE DEATH OF THORMOD COALBROW-SKALD.

THORMOD walked away thereafter to a certain outhouse and went thereinto, and within there were already many men sore wounded. A certain woman was tending there, and binding up the wounds of men. On the floor there was a fire, and she was warming water for the cleansing of the wounds. But Thormod sat down out by the door. There one man went out as another came in of them who were busy about the wounded. Then one turned to Thormod, and looked on him and said: "Why art thou so pale? Art thou wounded? or why biddest thou not leechdom for thee?" Then Thormod sang this stave:

> Nay, nowise am I ruddy,
> But the slim white hawk-perch' Skogul,
> She hath a ruddy husband;
> Of me, sore hurt, few mind them.

Thou, wont unto the murder
Of Fenja's meal! that maketh,
That with the deep spoor smart I
Of Day's brunt and Dane-weapons.

Sithence Thormod stood up, and walked up to the fire, and stood there for a while. Then spake the leech to him: "Thou, man, go out and fetch me the billets which lie outside the door." He went out and bore in an armful of billets, and threw them down on the floor. Then the leech looked into the face of him, and said: "Wondrously pale is this man, why art thou so?" Then sang Thormod:

The oak of the hawk-lands wondereth
Why we be pale: O woman!
The arrow drift I found me:
'Tis few grow fair by wounding.
It was the darksome metal,
Driven by main, flew through me;
The perilous sharp iron
Bit nigh the heart, so ween I.

Then said the leech: "Let me see thy wounds, that I may bind them up." Then Thormod sat down and cast the clothes from him. And when the leech saw his wounds, she searched about the wound he had in his side, and she found that iron stood therein, though she knew not for sure whither the iron had turned. She had made there in a stone kettle a mess of leeks and other herbs, and sodden that together, and she gave it to the wounded to eat, and tried in that manner whether they had hollow wounds; whereas she kenned it from the leek smelling out through the wound which was in the hollow body. She bore this to Thormod and bade him eat. He answered: "Take it away; I am not sick for grout." Then she took a gripping tongs, and would draw out the iron; but it was fast, and stirred nowhither; and it stood out but little because the wound was swollen. Then said Thormod: "Shear thou up to the iron, so that it may be well caught by the tongs, and then give them to me, and let me pull at it."

She did as he bade. Then Thormod took a gold ring off his arm, and gave it to the leech, and bade her do with it what she would: "The giver is good," says he.; "King Olaf gave me the ring this morning."

Then Thormod took the tongs, and pulled out the arrow; and on the barbs of it lay sinews from the heart, some red, some white. And when he saw that, he said: "Well hath the king fed us; fat am I yet at the heart-roots." Then he sank aback and was dead. And there is an end to the tale of Thormod.

CHAPTER CCXLVIII. OF THE HAPS OF THE BATTLE.

KING OLAF fell on Wednesday, the iiiith of the calends of August. It was near noon, when they met, and before midday the battle began; but before nones the king fell, and the darkness lasted from midday to nones. Sigvat the Skald tells thus of the end of the fight:

> Hard lack of the foe of the English,
> Since the men of war the king made
> Life-sick: the unsoft war-shield
> There for the king was riven.
> Folk-ruler, forth he wended
> Into the point-mote, whereat
> The host clave shields: the wild host
> Changed Olaf's life.   But Day fled.

And further he sang this:

> The people wrought the king's death;
> Fight-skerry-stems nought wotted
> Of such a strength, so many
> Of bonder-men and hersirs,
> That there the stems of wound-flame
> Such king should fell in onset
> As deemed was Olaf.   Many
> Was the host that lay in blood there.

The bonders did not plunder the fallen host;
and straightway after the fight it was rather so, that
dread smote a many of them who had been against
the king.   Yet they held their illwill, and doomed
between them, that all those men who had fallen
with the king should get no such lyke-help or
burial as beseemed good men; and they called
them all robbers and outlaws.   But those men who
were rich, and had kinsmen there among the fallen
host, gave no heed to this, but brought their kinsmen to churches and laid their bodies out.

CHAPTER CCXLIX.   TOKENS ON A
BLIND MAN.

THORGILS, son of Halma, and Grim, his
son, fared to the fallen host in the evening,
when mirk was.   They took up the body
of King Olaf and bore it away to a place, where
there was a house-cot, little and waste, out away
from the stead.   They had light with them and
water.   So then they did the clothes off the
body, and washed it, and sithence swaddled it in
linen weed, and laid it down there within the
house, and covered it up with wood, so that no one
might see it, though men should come into the
house.   Then they went away and home to the
stead.   Many staff-carles had followed either army,
and poor people who begged their meat.   And the
evening after the battle a many of that folk had
tarried there, and when night fell, they sought
harbour for themselves throughout all the houses,
great and small.   There was a certain blind man,
of whom a tale is told ; he was a poor man, and
his lad went about with him, and led him.   They
walked out a-doors about the stead seeking harbour,
and came to that same void house, the door whereof
was so low that one had nearly to creep in through
it.   And when the blind man came inside the
house, he groped about on the floor, to find whether
he might lay him down.   He had a hat on his
head, and the hat fell forward over his face, when
he bent down.   He found that before his hand
there was a pool on the floor, and therewith he
lifted the wet hand and set the hat right again,

and therewith the wet fingers came up against his eyes. And forthwith fell so great itching on his eyelids, that he stroked the wet fingers across his very eyes. Then he betook himself out of the house again, saying there was no lying therein, for it was all wet. And when he came out of the house, he saw forthwith, first his two hands one from the other, and then all such things as were near enough for him to see in spite of night-mirk. He went home forthwith to the stead and into the guest-chamber, and there told all folk that he had got his sight, and that now he was a seeing man. But that wotted many men, that he had been long blind, for he had been there before, going about from house to house. He said that he had got his sight first when he came out of a certain house, little and wretched, " and all was wet therewithin," says he, " and I groped thereinto with my hands, and I rubbed my eyes with my wet hands." He told also where the house stood.

But the men within there, when they heard these tidings, wondered greatly at this hap, and spoke between themselves what there could be within that house. But goodman Thorgils and his son Grim deemed they knew whence this hap would have come, and were in great dread lest the un-friends of the king should go and ransack the house. Then they stole away, and went to the house and took the body, and flitted it away and into the meadow, and hid it there, and then fared back to the stead and slept through that night.

CHAPTER CCL. OF THORIR HOUND.

THORIR HOUND came on the Thursday down from Verdale out to Sticklestead, and a much host followed him, and much was there still before him of the bonder-host. Now the fallen host was still being broken up, and men bore off the bodies of their friends or kinsmen, and gave help to such wounded men, as men would heal ; but by that time many men had died since the battle was done.

Thorir Hound went thereto whereas the king had fallen, and searched for the body, and when he found it not, he speered thereof, whether any man could to tell him where the body might be. But no one knew how to tell that. Then he asked goodman Thorgils if he knew aught as to where was the body of the king. Thorgils answers: " I was not in the battle ; I know few tidings to tell thereof; many tales fare thereof now ; yea, it is now said, that King Olaf has been met last night up by Staff, and a company of men with him ; but if he has fallen, then will thy men have hidden his body up in holts or warrens."

Now although Thorir deemed he knew for truth that the king was fallen, yet many joined in the murmur that the king must have gotten out of the battle, and that they would have but a little while to wait till he should get together an host and come on their hands.

Then fared Thorir to his ships, and sithence down the firth. Then fell all the bonder-host to drift away, and they brought away all the wounded men that could be moved.

CHAPTER CCLI. OF THE CORPSEFARE OF KING OLAF.

THORGILS HALMASON and Grim, the father and son, had in their keeping the body of King Olaf, and were much mind-sick herein, to wit, how they might so heed it, that the unfriends of the king should not get to mishandle the body; for they heard the bonders say as much as that the thing to be done, if the body of the king should be found, would be, to burn it or to take it out to sea and sink it in the deep.

That father and son had seen in the night as it were a candle-light burning over the spot where the body of King Olaf lay amidst of the fallen host, and also thereafter, wheresoever they had hidden the body, they saw ever at night a light, looking thither whereas the king was resting. They dreaded lest the unfriends of the king should seek for the body even where it was, if they saw these tokens; so therefore Thorgils and his son were wistful to bring the body away to some such place that it should be safe there. They made a chest, and wrought it in the best way they could, and laid therein the body of the king; sithence they made another lyke-chest and put into it straw and stones, so that it should be the weight of a man, and locked that chest heedfully.

Now, when the whole host of the bonders was gone away from Sticklestead, Thorgils and Grim

arrayed their journey. Thorgils got a certain
rowing-ferry; they were seven or eight together,
and all of them kinsmen or friends of Thorgils.
They brought the body of the king on board ship
stealthily, and put the chest under deck. That
chest they also had with them, wherein were the
stones, and set that on board ship, so that all men
might see it; and after that they fare out along the
firth, with a fair wind, and came in the evening, as
mirk set in, down to Nidoyce, and lay-to by the
king's pier. Then Thorgils sent men up into
the town, and let tell to Bishop Sigurd that they
fared there with the body of King Olaf. And
when the bishop heard these tidings, he sent forthwith his men down to the bridges, where they took
a rowing cutter and boarded the ship of Thorgils,
and bade him hand over to them the body of the
king. Then Thorgils and his men took the chest
which stood upon the deck, and bore it into the
cutter; whereupon these men rowed out into the
firth, and there sunk down the chest.

By this time it was the mirk of night. Thorgils
and his men then rowed up the river, until the town
was cleared, and laid to shore where it was called
Saurlithe, which was above the town; and then they
bore the body up and into a certain waste outhouse
which stood there, up away from other houses, and
there they waked over the body the night through.
But Thorgils went down into the town, and met
there men to talk to, such as had been most friends
of King Olaf, and asked them if they would take
over the body of the king; but no man durst to
do it. Then Thorgils and Grim brought the body

up along the river, and buried it in a certain sand-hill which there is, and sithence dight the place, so that no new work might be seen thereon. All this they had done before the dawn of day; and then went back to their ship and put out of the river at once, and went on their way until they came home to Sticklestead.

CHAPTER CCLII. THE BEGINNINGS OF SVEIN, SON OF ALFIVA.

SVEIN, the son of King Knut and Alfiva, the daughter of Earl Alfrun, had been set up in Jomsburg to rule over Wendland. But then had come to him a message from his father Knut, that he should go to Denmark, and furthermore that he should fare to Norway sithence, and there take over that realm to rule over which was in Norway, and therewith have the king's name over Norway. Thereupon Svein went to Denmark, and had away with him thence a great host, and with him went Earl Harald and many other men of might. Of this Thorarin Praisetongue maketh mention in that lay which is called "Sea-calm's-lay":

No doubt there is,
How Danes did make
A faithful faring
With a famed lord.
There was the earl,
The first to upheave,
And each man was,
Of them that followed,
Each fellow better,
Than was the other.

Sithence fared Svein to Norway, and with him Alfiva his mother; and there he was taken for king at every Law-Thing. He was come from the east into the Wick at the very time, when the fight of Sticklestead was fought and King Olaf fell. Svein made no halt in his journey until he came in the autumn north to Thrandheim; and there, as in other places, he was taken for king.

CHAPTER CCLIII.   OF THE LAWS OF KING SVEIN.

KING SVEIN brought new laws into the land for many matters, which were framed after the manner of the laws of Denmark, but some mickle harder.   No man was to fare out of the land but by the leave of the king; but should he go without, his goods were forfeited to the king.   Whoso should slay a man should forfeit both lands and chattels.   If a man were in out-lawry, and inheritance should fall to him, then gat the king that inheritance.   At Yule every man was to bring the king a measure of malt for every hearth, and a thigh of a three-winter ox, that was called pasture-tod, and a keg of butter withal; and every housewife was to give housewife's-tow, that is to say, so much of undressed flax as might be spanned by the biggest finger and the longest. The bonders were bound to build all such houses as the king would have at his manors. . Every seven men older than five years old should make one man war-fit, and therewith have thole-thong. Every one who rowed out for deep-sea fishing should pay the king land-toll, whencesoever he rowed, five fishes to wit. Every ship sailing away from the land should keep for the king one room right athwart the ship. Every man who should go to Iceland should pay land-tax, were he inlander or outlander. That followed this, that Danes should have such mickle account in Norway, that the witness of one of them should undo the witness of ten Norwegians. But when these laws were laid bare before all folk, men began forthwith to raise their minds against them, and murmured among themselves ; and those who had taken no part in withstanding King Olaf would say: "Take ye now, Up-Thrandheimers, the friendship and reward at the hands of the Knytlings for fighting King Olaf and cutting him off from his land ; ye were promised peace and bettered laws, and now ye get bondage and thraldom, and thereto huge misdeeds and nithing." And it was not easy to speak against this ; for all men saw that matters had gone unhappily. But men had no trust to make uprising against King Svein, for this sake mostly, that men had given their sons or close kinsmen as hostages to King Knut ; and this withal, that there was no one to be leader to the uprising. Soon people had many plaints to make against King Svein, yet men laid most blame on Alfiva for all that went against the people's mind. And then the true tale about King Olaf could be got from many a man.

CHAPTER CCLIV. NOW COMES UP THE HOLINESS OF KING OLAF.

THAT winter uphove the word of many men there in Thrandheim, that King Olaf was a truly holy man, and that many tokens befell at his holy relic. And then many began to make vows to King Olaf about those matters whereon they had set their hearts. From such vows many folk got bettering; some the bettering of their health, some good speed for journeys, or other such things as were looked upon as needful.

CHAPTER CCLV. OF EINAR THAM-BARSKELFIR.

EINAR THAMBARSKELFIR was by now come back west away from England to his lands, and had on hand such grants as King Knut had gotten to him, when they met in Thrandheim, and all that came nigh to an earl's dominion. Einar Thambarskelfir had not been in the withstanding of King Olaf, and of this he boasted himself. Einar bore in mind, how Knut had promised him earldom over Norway, and saw that the king did not keep his behests. Einar was the first among the mighty men to uphold the holiness of King Olaf.

CHAPTER CCLVI. OF THE SONS OF ARNI.

FINN, the son of Arni, tarried but a short time at Eggja with Kalf his brother, for he took it most sorely to heart, that Kalf had been in the battle against King Olaf ; and for that sake Finn would ever be laying heavy words on Kalf. Thorberg, son of Arni, was much more ruled of his speech than Finn, yet desired he also to fare away to his own house. So Kalf gave to the brothers a good longship, with all rigging and other gear, and a good company, and they fared back to their homesteads. Arni Arnison lay long sick of his wounds, yet grew he whole thereof and was unmaimed ; and afterwards he went that winter south to his home. All these brethren took truce for themselves from King Svein, and settled down in quiet at their homes.

CHAPTER CCLVII. THE FLIGHT OF BISHOP SIGURD OUT OF THE LAND.

NEXT summer there grew up mickle talk about the holiness of King Olaf, and all word-rumour about the king was changed. There were many now, who took it for sooth, that the king would be a holy man, even among them who had erst gone against him with full hatred and would not in any way own the truth about him. Now folk began to turn to wyting them who had most egged on to the withstanding of the king ; and much of that wyte was laid at the door of

Bishop Sigurd. And men became there so much his unfriends, that he saw that his best choice was to fare away and west to England to see King Knut. Then the men of Thrandheim made men and word-sending to the Uplands, that Bishop Grimkel should come north to Thrandheim. King Olaf had sent Bishop Grimkel back to Norway, when the king went east to Garthrealm, and sithence had Bishop Grimkel been in the Uplands. And when this message came to the bishop, he arrayed himself to go forthwith on that journey. And this urged him much, that the bishop trowed that it was true what was said about King Olaf's working of miracles, and of his holiness.

CHAPTER CCLVIII. THE HOLY RELICS OF KING OLAF TAKEN UP.

BISHOP GRIMKEL went to see Einar Thambarskelfir, and Einar gave the bishop a hearty welcome, and they spoke about many matters, and this withal, of the great tidings which had befallen in the land. And in all their talk they were of one accord together. Sithence fared the bishop up to Chippingham, and there all the folk gave him a good welcome. He speered heedfully at all the wonders that were told of King Olaf, and heard tell well thereof. Then the bishop sent word up to Sticklestead to Thorgils, and Grim, his son, and summoned them down to the town to meet him there. The father and son laid not that journey under their head, but fared down to the town to meet the bishop. And they told him all those tokens, whereof they had knowledge, and this withal, where they had bestowed the body of the king. Then the bishop sent for Einar Thambarskelfir, and he also came to the town ; and he and Einar spake with the king and with Alfiva, praying that the king would give leave to take King Olaf's body out of the earth. The king gave leave thereto, and bade the bishop go about that matter as he would. There was then mickle throng of folk in the town. So the bishop and Einar and other men with them fared thereto, whereas the body of the king was buried, and let digging be done there, and the chest was then come up wellnigh out of the earth. Many men urged that the bishop should let the chest be buried in earth at Clement's Church, and so it was done. And when twelve months and five nights were worn from the death of King Olaf, his holy relic was taken up, and again the chest was wellnigh come up out of the earth, and then the chest of King Olaf was as span-new as if it had been newly shaven.

Then Grimkel the bishop came up to where the chest of King Olaf was opened, and was there glorious fragrance. Then the bishop bared the face of the king, and in no wise had his visage turned, and was as ruddy in the cheeks as they would be, if he were just gone to sleep. But herein men found mickle change, even they who had seen King Olaf when he fell, that sithence had waxed his hair and his nails wellnigh as much as they would, if he had been alive here in the world all the while sithence he fell.

Then came forth to seè the body of King Olaf King Svein, and all the chieftains who there were. Then spake Alfiva : " Wondrous slow do men rot in sand ; this would not have been so if he had lain in mould."

Then the bishop took a pair of scissors and sheared off the hair of the king, and took somewhat off of his beard ; for he had had a long beard, as was then the wont of men. And the bishop spoke to the king and to Alfiva : " Now are the hair and the beard of the king as long as they were when he died, and they have waxen by so much as ye now see has been cut off."

Then answereth Alfiva : " I shall deem this hair a holy relic, if it burn not in fire ; but we have often seen the hair whole and unspoilt of men such as have lain longer in earth than this man has."

Then the bishop let take fire in a censer, and blessed it and laid incense thereon, and sithence laid on the fire the hair of King Olaf ; and when all the incense was burnt out, the bishop took the hair out of the fire, and then was the hair unburnt. And the bishop let the king see that, and the other chieftains withal. But then Alfiva bade the hair be put in unhallowed fire ; but Einar Thambarskelfir answered, and bade her hold her peace, and chose for her many hard words. And so the bishop declared, and the king assented thereto, and all the folk judged, that King Olaf was verily a holy man.

Then was the body of the king borne into Clement's Church, and laid out over the high altar. The chest was wrapt in pall, and hangings of goodly web done around. And straightway many marvels befell at the holy relic of King Olaf.

CHAPTER CCLIX. OF THE MIRACLES OF KING OLAF.

THERE, in the sand-heap, where King Olaf had lain in earth, there came up a fair well, and many folk gat healing of their ills of that water. The well was built over, and that water hath ever since been heedfully guarded. First there was made a chapel there, and the altar was reared where had been the tomb of the king; but now stands on that stead Christ Church; and Archbishop Eystein had the high altar set up on that same stead, where the king's tomb had been, when he reared the great minster which now standeth, and on that same stead had also stood the altar in the ancient Christ Church. So it is said, that Olaf's church now stands, where that waste outhouse stood, where the body of King Olaf was set nightlong. That is now called Olaf's-lithe where the holy relic of the king was borne aland up from the ship, and is now in the midst of the town. The bishop guarded the holy relic of the king, cut his hair and nails, because either grew even as if he were a living man here in the world. So saith Sigvat the Skald:

> I lie if Olaf own not,
> Like quick men, scratching servants;
> But the waxing of the king's hair,
> That praise I most in singing.
> Yet unto him hair holdeth,
> Who left his son, still growing,

In Garthrealm : Waldemar gat him
Woe's loosing from the bright head.

Thorarin Praisetongue wrought on Svein Alfiva-
son `that lay which is called "Seacalm's-lay," and
wherein are found these staves :

> Now for himself
> Hath a seat made handy
> The king of folk
> In Thrandheim country ;
> There will ever
> All his lifetime
> That ring-breaker
> Rule his dwelling.

> There where Olaf
> Dwelt aforetime,
> Or ever he hied
> To heaven's kingdom ;
> And there became,
> As all men wot it,
> A hallow quick
> From a man of king-folk.

> Harald's son
> Had hard areded
> Himself to be
> Of heaven's kingdom,
> Ere the gold-breaker
> Became peace-prayèr,
> The noblest king
> Of Christ belovèd.

> There so clean
> With a whole body
> Lieth in peace
> The king praise-blessèd.
> So that there now,
> Like unto live men,
> Do hair and nail
> Wax upon him.

There round his bed
Of boards arrayèd,
Of their own selves
Are the bells a-ringing,
And every day
The folk may hear
The sound of bells
Around the king.

But up above there
Over the altar,
Candles burn
To Christ well-pleasing.
So hath Olaf,
Or ever he dièd,
Sinless all,
His own soul savèd.

There hosts are coming
Where holy is
The king himself,
And kneel for helping.
Blind men, and they
That pray for speech-words,
Thither seek,
And thence go healèd.

Bid thou to Olaf,
That man of God,
To win thee brooking
Of his land here :
For he doth get
From God himself
The year and the peace
For all men ever.

When word thou openest
Unto the main-bolt
Of the holy book-speech,
Thy very prayers . . . .

Thorarin Praisetongue was with King Svein,
and heard these wondrous tokens of the holiness

of King Olaf, that men might hear over his holy relic, sounds made by heavenly powers; in that bells rang themselves, also that candles would light of themselves over the altar by a heavenly fire. Now, even as Thorarin says that to the holy Olaf came an host of folk, halt and blind, or in other ways held of sickness, and went thence healed; but he tells of nought else, nor setteth forth aught than that there must have been a multitude of men not to be counted, who got healing then forthwith in the beginning of the miracle-working of the holy King Olaf. But of the miracles of King Olaf only the greatest have been most written about, and set forth, and such as did befall later than this.

CHAPTER CCLX. OF THE AGE AND REIGN OF KING OLAF.

SO say men who count with care, that Olaf the Holy was king over Norway for fifteen winters from the time that Earl Svein went out of the land, but the winter before he took the king's name of the Uplanders. So says Sigvat the Skald:

> O'er the land was Olaf ruling
> For winters fully fifteen,
> Ere fell his head the gracious,
> As his life-grant came to ending.
> What land-ruler more glorious
> Hath ever claimed him kingship
> In the northmost world's-end? Shorter
> He held him than he should have.

King Olaf the Holy was forty and five years old

whenas he fell, according to what the priest Ari the Learned says. He had had twenty folk-battles. So says Sigvat the Skald :

> Some men in God they trowèd ;
> Diversely were folk minded.
> The king bold-redy fought him
> A twenty of folk-battles.
> The famed one bade folk christened
> On his right hand be standing :
> The Lord God pray I welcome
> The flight-shy Magnus' father.

Now is written some part of the story of King Olaf, concerning certain of such tidings as befell while he ruled over Norway, also concerning the fall of him, and the coming up of his holiness. But now shall that not lie alow which is of the greatest glory to him, to wit, the story of his doing of tokens, though that be written later in this book.

CHAPTER CCLXI. OF THE THRAND-HEIM FOLK.

KING SVEIN, the son of Knut, ruled over Norway certain winters. He was but a child of age and counsel. Alfiva, his mother, had most to say in the rule of the land, and the folk of the land were mickle unfriends of her, both then and always sithence. Danish men had then in Norway mickle mastery, and the folk of the land were right ill content thereat. When such talk was had up, the other men of the land wyted the Thrandheim folk that they had most wrought it King Olaf the Holy was cut off from his land, and that the Norway men had laid them

under this evil rule, whereby bondage and thraldom had stridden over all folk there, rich men and
unrich, and all the Folk ; and they claimed that the
Thrandheim men were in duty bound to aid an uprising, "to this end, to thrust off from us this over-
mastery." Moreover, the people of the land would
have it that the Thrandheim folk had the most
strength in Norway then, both by reason of their
chieftains and of the multitude of folk that was there.

But when the Thrandheimers wist that the folk
of the land was thus wyting them, they owned to
it that it was sooth speech, and that a great folly
had overtaken them, whereas they had cut King
Olaf from both life and land, and that therewithal
their ill-hap was with great evil yolden.

So the chiefs had meetings and took counsel
together, and Einar Thambarskelfir was at the
head of these redes. So withal was it with Kalf
Arnison, that he found now into what a snare he
had gone by the egging of King Knut, for the
behests he had given to Kalf were all broken ;
for King Knut had promised to Kalf earldom
and rule over all Norway, and Kalf had been the
head-man in holding battle with King Olaf, and in
cutting him off from his land ; but Kalf had no
higher titles now than erst, and deemed he had
been betrayed. Hence words passed between the
brethren, Kalf and Finn, Thorberg and Arni, and
their brotherhood shaped itself again.

CHAPTER CCLXII. THE OUTBIDDING OF KING SVEIN.

WHEN Svein had been three winters in Norway, tidings were heard in Norway, that west over sea a flock was gathering, and over it was a lord who is named Tryggvi, and called himself son of Olaf Tryggvison and of Gyda the English. And when King Svein heard, that an outland host would be coming to the land, he called out a muster from the north of the land, and most of the landed-men fared with him out of Thrandheim. But Einar Thambarskelfir sat at home, and would not fare with King Svein. And when the word-sending of King Svein came to Kalf up to Eggja, that he should row to the war with the king, then took Kalf a craft of twenty benches which he owned, and went aboard it with his house-carles, and arrayed him in hot haste, and then made down the firth, and abode not King Svein. Sithence Kalf went on south to Mere, nor stayed his journey till he came south to Gizki to Thorberg his brother. Then all the brethren, the sons of Arni, had a meeting together, and took counsel between them ; whereupon Kalf went north again. But when he came into Frekislesound, there lay before him in the sound King Svein with his host. So when Kalf rowed from the south into the sound, they called out to each other, and the king's men bade Kalf fall in, and follow the king and ward his land.

Kalf answered : " Fully have I done it, if I have not overdone it, to fight with the folk of

our own land in aid of the rule of the Knytlings."

And so Kalf and his rowed north on their way,
and he went on until he came home to Eggja.

None of the sons of Arni rowed this muster
with the king.

Now King Svein held with his host south into
the land; and when he got no news of the host
having come from the west, he held on even unto
Rogaland and all the way to Agdir; for men were
minded to think that Tryggvi would first want to
make his way east into the Wick, for there his forefathers had been and had most avail at their back,
and there he had great strength in his kindred.

CHAPTER CCLXIII. THE FALL OF KING TRYGGVI OLAFSON.

KING TRYGGVI, when he came up
from the west, hove in with his host to
Hordland. Then he heard that King
Svein had sailed south. Then held King Tryggvi
south to Rogaland. But when King Svein got
the news of the journey of Tryggvi, whenas he
was come from the west, he turned back northward
with his war-host, and the meeting of him and
Tryggvi was inside of Bokn in Sokensound, near
to the place, where Erling Skialgson had fallen.
There befell a mickle battle and hard. So men
tell thereof, that Tryggvi shot barbed shafts with
both hands at once, saying: "So learned me mass
my father!" For his unfriends had said as much
as that he would be the son of a certain priest, but

he boasted hereof that now he was more like to
King Olaf Tryggvison; and indeed Tryggvi was
a man of the doughtiest.

In this battle fell King Tryggvi, together with
many of his folk, but some fled away, and some
came in under truce. So it is said in the " Tryggvi-
flock ":

> Fared Tryggvi, keen of honour,
> From the northward unto battle;
> But King Svein took his faring
> From the south. There fell the slaughter.
> Nigh to their fray then was I;
> 'Twas brought about right swiftly.
> A host there lost their life-days;
> There was the sword a-yelling.

This battle is told of in that " flock " which was
wrought about King Svein :

> Woman! 'twas not last Sunday
> As when a maid is bearing
> The leek or the ale to man-folk.
> There many a clean edge louted,
> When Svein the king his lads bade
> To lash the bows of the war-ships
> Together there; to the raven
> Raw flesh to tear was given.

After this battle King Svein then ruled still the
land, and then good peace prevailed. The winter
following King Svein sat behind south in the land.

CHAPTER CCLXIV. KALF ARNISON AND EINAR THAMBARSKELFIR TAKE COUNSEL TOGETHER.

THAT winter Einar Thambarskelfir and Kalf, the son of Arni, had meetings between them, and contriving of redes, and were meeting in Chippingham. Then there came to Kalf Arnison a messenger from King Knut, and bore him the message of King Knut, to wit, that Kalf should send him three twelves of axes, and let them be much heedfully done. Kalf answers: "Nought will I send axes to King Knut; tell him that I shall fetch axes to Svein, his son, so that he shall not deem that he is short thereof."

CHAPTER CCLXV. THE JOURNEY OF EINAR THAMBARSKELFIR AND KALF ARNISON OUT OF THE LAND.

EARLY in the spring they, Einar Thambarskelfir and Kalf, son of Arni, arrayed their journey, and had with them a mickle following of men, and that the best of all that was in the Thrander-lag. They fared in the spring east over the Keel to Iamtland, then to Helsingland, and next came down into Sweden, and there got a-shipboard, and in the summer fared east into Garthrealm, and in the harvest came to Aldeigiaburg. Then they sent messengers up to Holmgarth, to see King Jarisleif, with this errand, to wit, that they bade to Magnus, the son of King Olaf the Holy, that they would take him up and follow him to Norway, and give him strength hereto, that he come by his father's heritage, and that they uphold him for king over the land.

But when this message came to King Jarisleif, then took he counsel with the queen and other of his chieftains; and they were of one mind to send word to the Northmen, and to summon them thither to a meeting with King Jarisleif and Magnus; and for that journey a safe-conduct was given to them. But when they came to Holmgarth, it was made fast between them, that the Northmen that there were should go under the hand of Magnus, and become his men; and they bound this with oaths from Kalf and those other men who had been at Sticklestead against King Olaf. So Magnus gave them pledges and full peace, and bound it by oath that he should be to all of them trusty and true, though he gat dominion and kingdom over Norway; he should be made foster-son of Kalf Arnison, and Kalf should be in duty bound to do all such works, whereby Magnus might deem that his dominion should be greater and freer than afore.

EXPLANATIONS OF THE METAPHORS IN THE VERSES.

EXPLANATIONS

Of the less obvious "kenningar" (periphrases). For abbreviated references see vol. i., p. 381.

Page 5.

STEED of the blood of meadows: "blakkr dreyra vengis"=ship; blood of meadows=water, the steed thereof, ship.

Page 6. 1. The sea-caster: "unn-varpaðr," an epithet to the rudder.

2. Feeder of swans of fight-ale: "dólg-linns svan-bræðir"=bræðir svans dólg-linns: dólg=fight; linn= lið (cf. iðþri=innri, meþr=menn, saðr=sannr, etc.)= ale; fight-ale=blood, the swan thereof=raven, carrion bird, its feeder=warrior, here King Olaf.

3. The long sea-log: "langr sjá-meiðr"=longship.

King's read kings'; kings' kindred: "jofra kundr," King Olaf.

Page 7. Wolf's foot reddened: "rauð úlfs fót"=shed blood in battle.

Page 9. 1. Warrior-wager: "gildir flotna"=mercedem solvens classiariis.

Isle-syslings' war-host: "Eysýslu lið," the folk of the Isle-sysla or island of Œsel.

Page 10. Steel-wreath: "stáls hrið"=steel tempest, battle.

Page 11. 1. Surf-skate: "brim-skíð"=ship.

2. Gunn's song: "Gunnar galdr"=battle. Gunn, one of the "valkyrjur" (S. E. i. 120).

Peace unlittle was cleft betwixt the kings' host: "ólítill friðr gekk sundr á miðli jofra liðs." The reading of A. M. 61, fol. ólítit, adv., not little = greatly, *i.e.* peace was sundered wide apart, a great battle was fought, seems preferable.

Page 15. 1. The cunning of Ygg's storm : "kennir Yggs éla " : Yggr = Odin, his él, squall, storm = battle, the cunning one thereof, a warrior, King Olaf.—Land of snakes : "linns land " = gold.

3. Ygg's brunt = Ygg's storm.

Page 16. 1. The ward of Harald's heirship : "arf-vörðr Haralds," King Olaf.

Page 20. Where slain was very fleeing : where fleeing was brought to a deadlock, rendered impossible.

Page 21. 1. Peita, Poitou ; Tuskaland, Touraine.

2. Warrand = Guarande, a landscape of Britany.

Page 23. Life-luck unto Wolf's father, *i.e.* to Rogn-vald Wolfson, Earl of West-Gautland, whose sons were Wolf and Eilif. Fs. iv. 198.

Page 26. 1. Praise have I, read : heave I, *i.e.* begin I. The lord be-praisèd. = Knut the Rich ; lord the helm-wont = Earl Eric ; lords be-landed = landed men.

2. The well-praised Thund (not "grove ") of the sea-horse : " leyfðr þundr græðis hests ;" sea-horse = ship, its Thund = Odin, god, here Earl Eric.—Shield-rain, "rönn (*i.e.* rönd) regn " = drift of shot weapons against shields, a battle.

Page 29. 1. Bounteous of the tempest of corpse-fire : "veðr-örr val-fasta " = " örr veðrs val-fasta " : valr, coll. the bodies of those slain in battle = Odin's chosen host, the fire thereof = sword, its tempest = battle ; the boun-teous one thereof, he who frequently gives battle, here King Olaf.—Kings' thoft-mate *:* " Skjöldunga þópti " = a compeer of kings, King Olaf.

2. Ægir, the god of the sea (S. E. i. 206).

Page 31. Feeder of blood-seas' blue choughs : " bræðir ben-gjálfrs blá-gjóða " = feeder of ravens, carrion birds.—Feeder of mew of Thrott's Thing : " þróttar þings má-grennir " = "grennir más þróttar þings " ; Thrott = Odin, his Thing = battle, the mew thereof = raven.

Page 32. Dane-tongue, a geographical expression for those lands of the north within which was spoken the tongue of the Trans-Baltic Germans, the ancient name for which was "dönsk tunga."

Page 51-52. 1. Scather of mirk-blue steed of the tilt: "meiðir myrk-blás drasils tjalda" = vanquisher of warships: tjald = tilt, awning, its drasill = horse, a ship.— Might of singing: "hróðrs hlít" = that support, furtherance, that the celebration in song of worthy deeds may afford.

Page 52. 2. Battle Niord: "sóknar Njörðr," god of fight, warrior, here King Olaf.—Stem of the lair of the brother of the serpent: "þollr látrs linns blóða": blóði = brother, linnr = serpent, the serpent's brother = serpent, its látr = lair = gold, its stem = man, here King Olaf.

3. Gladdeners of fight vulture: "gunnar gammteitendr = teitendr gunnar gamms" = warriors, men; the king's body-guard being probably alluded to.—Sea's fire: "ægis eldr" = gold, i.e. the "golden ring which weighed half a mark."—Waster of lair of mead-fish (not "worm"): "engi-lúru látr-þverrandi = þverrandi látrs engi-lúru," mead-fish = serpent, its lair = gold, its waster, one who freely makes gifts of it to his men, here King Olaf.

Page 57. Rodi's deer: "Róða reinn" (= hreinn = reindeer) = ship. Rodi, a sea-king of fame (S. E. i. 548).

Page 58. 1. Craftsmaster of point-frost: "kennir odda-frosts"; frost, quality of weather, hence weather, hence storm, point-frost therefore = brunt of battle, battle. —Carl's head, name of King Olaf's ship, cf. ch. xlv.

2. Breeze of the moon of battle: "sig-mána gjóð"; sig = battle, its moon = shield, the breeze, wind, storm thereof = brunt of fight.

Page 59. 1. The sark-din of Gondul: "Gondlar serks gnýr": Gondul, a Valkyrja (S. E. i. 557), her sark = a byrny, coat of mail, the din thereof = battle.—Steed of tackle: "strengjar jór" = ship.

Page 60. Ygg's black chough : "Yggs svartr gjóðr" = Odin's black raven.

Page 61. 1. Fight's swift driver: "gunnar snar-rækir" = King Olaf.—Bidder of fire of the ship's out-land : "boði elda knarrar út-hauðrs"; the ship's out-land, the vast main, sea, the fire thereof = gold, the bidder thereof = the bestower, giver of gold, a bounteous man, here King Olaf.—Bole of byrny : "viðr brynju" = King Olaf. The commas after hindrance and outland should be removed, and bidder = to bidder. What the verse expresses is this : "Thou (king) badest me (the poet) farewell; I returned the same answer to you. I, having no time to stop, '*sold*' (= returned) to the 'bidder, etc.' (*i.e.* King Olaf) the very 'word of the high-born' one (*i.e.* King Olaf) that I had '*bought*' (taken, heard, perceived) of him (King Olaf, the bole of byrny)."

2. Bidder of the tempest of the wave-elk : "hríð-boði hranna-elgs" : hranna elgr = waves' elk = ship, its tempest = ships' fight, naval battle, the bidder thereof, a commander at sea, here Earl Svein.

3. Wound-serpent : "sára linnr" = sword, its swayer, a warrior, here King Olaf.—Ati's skate no little : "Ata andurr ólítill" = the big ship, King Olaf's longship (on board which the bracketed lines, compared with this page (61), line 7, seem to indicate that the poet sat long "in fetters ").

Page 63. 1. Sound-sun's spender : "sunda-sunnu verr" : sund = sound = sea, its sun = beam = fire, gold, its spender = man.—Splice - knot's steed : "sam - knúta blakkr" = ship (a doubtful kenning, though what is meant, is certain).

2. Who beardling went in onset: "er fram sótti skeggi" : whose beard was more conspicuous in the onset than the plying of their weapons? or as Lex. Poet. has it : "sækja fram skeggi," ad verbum, barba obversa progredi, ironice, pronum in faciem collabi. Possibly the reading of Olafs saga ens helga, Christiania, 1853, p. 42 : "er fram sottit [= sótti at] skeggi,

qui (exercitus) barba obversa (in prœlium) non progre-
diebatur," really expresses what Sigvat meant to convey
by these studiously-doubtful words.

3. Sender-forth of deck-steed : "sendir þil-blakks " :
deck-steed = ship, its sender-forth = King Olaf (as ruler
over the sea-force of his realm).

Page 64. Fight-up-stirrer : "fólk-rekr " = King Olaf.—
Corpse-worms : " hræ-linnr," spears, arrows. The flight
of corpse-worms had they = they had a hard onset.

Page 68. Dweller in loft of yoke-beast of the wave :
" Loft-byggvir unnar eykja " ; wave's yoke-beast = ship,
its loft = poop, the dweller thereof, the commander,
here King Olaf.

Page 93. 1. Fight-ice reddener : "íss gunn-rjóðr," *i.e.*
" rjóðr gunnar íss " ; íss = icicle, styria, icicle of fight, the
gleaming weapon tapering to a point, like an icicle, its
reddener, a warrior, here Biorn the Marshal.

2. Lace of Listi : "men Lista " = the girth, circle of
Listi, a landscape of Norway, here = earth (pars pro toto),
monile terræ = sea, ocean.

3. When the horses of Ekkil spurn the thorn's moor :
" þar es hestar Ekkils sporna á hag-þorns mó " ; Ekkil, a
sea-king of fame (S. E. i. 547), his horse = ship ; hawthorn's
moor, the shore where rollers of hawthorn are laid down
whereon the ship is hauled up to its shed. We have
preferred the reading Ekkils of some MSS. to the text's
" ekkjum," widows or women : " ték ekkjum ýmsar fðir"
= I tell women of (my) various deeds, which makes the
sense both questionable and meagre.

Page 108. Spoiler of brand of hawk's field : "Lýtandi
branda ifla folda " : hawk's field = the hand on which the
hawk sits, the brand thereof = gleaming gold, its spoiler,
scatterer, a bounteous man, here King Olaf.

Page 109. 2. Word reed : "orð-reyr" = tongue.

3. Kin-lands : " ætt-lond " = lands belonging to the
family (of King Olaf Haraldson).—Gondul's fires' be-
thronger : "Gòndlar elda þrongvir " = strenuous fighter.
Gondul, a "Valkyrja," her fire = sword.

Page 145. 1. The stem of the drift of war-helm : "hjálm-drífu viðr "=warrior, here King Olaf ; "hjálm-drífa"=drift against the helm, weapons brought to bear upon the helm.

3. Howes'-host : "hauga herr "=ghosts, fiends.—Sea-ram : "hafs hrútr "=boat, tub.

Page 146. 3. Fir-trees of the hone-bed : "þollar hein-flets "=men ; "hein-flet," the bed on which the hone, whetstone, stretches itself as it were, a sword, the fir-tree, stem, up-bearing it = man.—Loader of the sea-skate : "hlæðir haf-skíðs "=man ; sea-skate=ship.

Page 147. 1. Breaker of waves'-glitter : "brjótr báru bliks "=man ; waves'-glitter=gold.

2. The son of mighty Saxi Nought found I : meaning : to come to these men was a very different thing from coming to Earl Rognvald, whose father Wolf therefore must have borne the by-name of Saxi.

3. Chieftain of the Sogn-folk : " Sygna gramr "=King Olaf.

4. Thruster down of king-folk : Earl Rognvald, whose defiant attitude towards King Olaf of Sweden " thruster down" seems to be meant to reflect.

Page 148. 1. Groves of the fire-flame of the field of the deer of rollers : " runnar hlunns dýr-loga bekkjar "= " runnar hlunn-dýrs bekkjar loga "=men ; "hlunn-dýr," rollers' deer=ship, its "bekkr," bank, hill-rise, tract of hill-rises (waves), field=sea, its "logi," fire-flame, " low " =gold, the "runnr," grove, thereof=man. The *kenning* refers to Earl Rognvald's inhospitable subjects.

2. Mead-Nanna : "mjöð-Nanna"=woman cupbearer ; Nanna, a goddess, the wife of Baldr (S. E. i. 102).

Page 149. 2. Skates of swan-mead : "andrar (dat. ondrum) svan vangs"=ships ; swan-mead=sea.

3. The gold-ward in Garthrealm : "málma vörðr í Gorðum "=King Jarisleif (p. 148).—Never courtman heard I, etc., must refer to the spokes-man of those " messengers from King Jarisleif," who are mentioned on p. 148.

Page 150. 1. Drowner of the Rhine-sun: "sökkvir Rínar sólar" = Earl Rognvald. Rhine sun = gold (cf. S. E. i. 364 : "þá fálu þeir gullit Fafnis-arf í Rín ": then hid they the gold, Fafnir's heritage, in the Rhine) ; the drowner of gold = largitor auri.—Listi's lord : "Lista þengill " = King Olaf; Listi, a district of Norway.

2. Eric's kin : King Olaf Ericson of Sweden.—Wolf's kin : Earl Rognvald Wolfson.

3. Dele " " and comma after Wolf. The sense is : Wise Wolf (Earl Rognvald's father) let take (= took, accepted, approved of) peace being made between you and King Olaf of Sweden.

Page 151. Thing's (read Things') crafts-master: " þinga kennir," King Olaf. The word ' Thing,' assembly, here probably refers especially to the king in his capacity of commander of armed hosts.

Page 170. Cloud-hall : " ský-rann " = sky, heaven.

Page 200. Jalk-board's waster : " Jalks brík-töpuðr = töpuðr Jalks bríkar " = warrior, man, here Gudbrand a Dales. Jalk, one of Odin's names, his board (brík) = shield.

Page 310. Ling-fish : " Lyngs fiskr " = serpent, here the Long-Worm, Olaf Tryggvison's great war-galley.— Dele the commas after " bore " and " reddened."

Page 313. 1. The refrain fragment of one line with which the verse begins is completed by the last line of the verses on p. 320. So the complete refrain reads :

> Knut was 'neath heaven
> King far foremost.

This is the second case, in Heimskringla, of a "klofa-stef," or split-up refrain ; cf. Eyolf Dadaskald's fragment of Bandadrapa, Heimskringla, i. 346-48.

2. King of the wealth-year: "ársæll jofurr," king blessed with seasons of plenty.—Fish-path : " lýr-gata " = sea.

Page 314. 3. If he get him clear, 'twere better Than a mote on furthest fell-side: "dæla er fyrst (= first) á fjalli fundi, ef hann sjálfr kemsk undan." The idea is : It would be for us a more delightful thing than would be a meeting with a human being for him who finds himself lost in a howling wilderness, if he (King Olaf) should get off clear.— Egilsson, in Scripta historica Islandorum, iv. 324, sees here a proverb: "dæll er fundr first á fjalli": sweet to meet a man in furthest mountains (in the depth of wildernesses).

Page 315. 1. The drift of this verse is: Was it likely, that Earl Hakon's business would be to bring about peace between Olaf and those of his subjects who would have nothing to do with peace with him? Why, they had already made up their mind to shift their allegiance (cheapened chieftains) from Olaf to Knut, before Hakon took in hand the furtherance of that business.—Eric's kindred: "kyn Eiríks" = Earl Hakon.

2. The wood from the west glode: "viðr skreið vestan" = wooden ships sailed from the west (from England).

Page 323. 1. Fight-stall, read fight-staff: "ógnar-stafr" = warrior, here King Knut.

2. The cleaver of the gold rings = he who divides gold rings among his men, a bounteous lord, here King Knut. —The king of the folk of Skanings = King Knut = Svein's son in the next line.

Page 331. Ground of the Rhine's flame: "láð (= land) Rín-leygs" = woman (apostrophe).—Long mare of the din-road: "langr leiðar dyn-marr = langr marr dyn-leiðar" = longship.

Page 332. The isle of heaven's shift-ring: "eyja læ-baugs" = Weather isle: læ = lá = sea, baugr = ring; sea-ring = horizon, weather-region, weather.—Land of falcon's longship: "jörð ifla flausts" = woman (apostrophe); ifill or ifli = falcon, its flaust, the ship carrying it = hand; the land of the falcon-bearing hand, a high-born lady, partaker in lordly sports.—Scantling's falcon: "valr krapta" = ship.—Level ways of Frodi: "flatslóðir Fróða" = sea; Fróði, a sea-king of fame (S. E. i. 546).

Page 334. Wealth-stems: "seims þollar" = men.

Page 337. The wound-sound's oar: "sárs-sunda

árar " = sword(s) ; wound-sound = sea of wounds = blood.—Sender-forth of wick's flame : " sendir víka elds" = man, bounteous of gold, here King Olaf ; "vík"=wick, bight, bay ; hence sea, deep, the flame thereof = gold.

Page 350. The ward of Greece : "gætir Grikklands " = Christ.

Page 351. 1. Of the refrain of Thorarin Praisetongue's poem Togdrapa only the first line is preserved : " Knut's neath the sun's . . ." : Knútr er und sólar. Egilsson (ShI. v. 7) conjectured that the second line must probably have run : setri hveim betri =

> Knut 's neath the sun's
> Seat better than any (lord) ;

sun's-seat = heaven : Under heaven's wide expanse there is none to be matched with Knut.

2. Craver of heaps of the fight-swan : " ör-beiðir svans sigr-lana = ör-beiðir lana sigr-svans " = warrior, here King Knut ; sigr = fight, its swan = raven, its lanir (lön-lanar) heaps = corpse heaps.

3. Surf-boar's sea-skate : " brim-galtar sæ-skíð," boarding of vessels that shows above water, hull. If "brim-galtar" be joined to "sund," the rendering would be : All the surf-boar's = ship's sound, navigable channel, of Eikund was filled with sea-skates = ships.

4. House-fast peace-men : " grið-fastir frið-menn " = inmates of the king's hall, household, body-guard.— Shaft-bidder : " ör-beiðir = örva-beiðir," arrow-bidder = warrior, here King Knut.—Stemcliff's stud : " stafn-klifs stóð " = fleet ; klif = cliff, hill-rise, the hill-rise of the stem = wave, hence sea, the stud, horses thereof = ships.

5. Wind-strong surf-deer : " byr-römm brim-dýr " = ships driven along by a stiff gale.

Page 352. 1. Cold-home's falcons : "sval-heims valar" = ships.

2. Denmark of the swan-dale's dim-hall : "Danmörk svana-dals dökk-salar." Egilsson (ShI. v. 10) translates :

"Daniam, umbrosum illum lucum, mari adjacentem,"
adding, in a foot-note, "versionem celeb. Raskio debeo,
hæc annotanti : dökksalr, ædes obscura, *i.e.* umbrosus et
sylvosus locus, svana-dalr, mare ; h. (= hinc) svana-dals
dökk-salr, lucus maris, aut insulæ sylvosæ, aut ipsa
Selandia (sælundr lucus maris) ; ita *sv. d. dökks.* Danmörk est Dania, multis sylvosis insulis constans, vel
Dania, cujus pars principalis est Selandia, sedi regiæ,
quæ ibidem est, subjacens." The somewhat obscure
figure therefore is taken to mean : the thick-wooded sea-
Denmark = island Denmark. By the only other possible
connection of the words, namely, Svana-dals dokk-salar-
mörk Dana = Swan-dale's (*i.e.* the sea's) dim-hall-mark
(*i.e.* densely-wooded mark or land) of the Danes = the
sea-girt thickly-wooded land of the Danes, a pretty satis-
factory *kenning* comes out, and wide enough to cover all
that is meant, the whole of Denmark, Jutland included.

Page 353. Reddener of the bark of boon-ship : "bænar-
nökkva bark-rjóðr = rjóðr barkar bænar-nökkva" =
warrior, here, as it seems, an apostrophe to the listener.
Nökkvi = ship, bæn = prayer, the prayer's ship =
breast, as the seat of emotions, the bark, covering,
thereof = byrny, coat of mail.—The Frey of the din of
troll-wife of points : "Odda-leiknar jálm-Freyr = Freyr
odda-leiknar jálms" = warrior, here King Knut. Leikn,
the name of a troll-wife maimed by Thor (S. E. i. 258),
hence a general appellation for troll-fays ; "odda-Leikn,"
therefore, a fay of points, battle-fay, Valkyrja ; her
"jalmr," din, roar = battle, the Freyr, god, of which =
warrior.

Page 357. 1. Board-acre : "borð-völlr" = sea (board's
= ship's-field).

2. The youthful Shielding, King Olaf Haraldson, still
young for a king, thirty-four years of age (born 995, this
encounter taking place Thomas-mass, December 21st,
1029).

Page 358. 1. Showers of the axes' skerries : "skúrir
gýgjar-skers" = brunts of battle, fight ; gýgr = axe (S. E.

i. 569), its sker, skerry, (sea-) rock (object against which it is driven)=shield, the showers of (=on, against) which = flights of weapons, battle.—Wide-bottomed guardian cask of the winds: "víð-botn varð-kers glyggs" = earth; glygg = wind, its warð-ker, guardian cask = air, in the sense of the vision's vaulted cupola, the víð-botn, wide bottom of which = the horizon-bounded earth.

Page 359. 1. But that all-rich one with might and main wrought it: "en all-ríkr olli með gagni skipan slíkri": the all-rich (all-mighty) one, which here really means the all-ruthless one, was Aslak Pate o' Fitjar (p. 358), who struck Erling dead.

2. Kin-guilt: "frænd-sekja" = the guilt of having killed a relative, committed "frændvíg," or "ættvíg."—Nought may he gainsay it, kin-slaying: "ættvígi má hann eigi níta" = he cannot deny that he has taken a kinsman's life. Aslak and Erling were great-grandsons of Horda-kari, cf. vol. i. 303.

3. The white good-man: "halr hinn hvíti" = Erling Skialgson.—The clash of Gunn: "Gunnar gnýr" = battle; Gunnr, a Valkyrja (Völuspá, 30, Bugge).

Page 361. 1. 'Tis the land that makes men's murder: "jorð veldr manna morði," *i.e.* it is King Knut's avarice for rule in Norway that is bringing about civil bloodshed.

2. Steed of troll-wife: "gríðar sóti," cf. i. 261, 1, and note, p. 405.

Page 371. 1. The hair of the men bade he shear with the sword: "Skör bað hann fírum efsa með hjörvi" = he bade men's heads be cut off.

Page 373. 1. Bow's reindeer: "hlýr-vangs hreinn," read bow's-field's r. (For storm 'gainst the how's-field's reindeer): bow's-field = sea, sea-surface, the reindeer thereof = ship.—Hill-sides of the flame of bow's-stand: "kleifar funa ý-stéttar" = women (apostrophe); ýr = bow (arcus), its stand = hand; the hand's flame = gold, the cliffs or hill-rises thereof = women, up-bearing it.

Page 376. "London's king let find thee land," *i.e.* promised thee an earl's rule over the land of Norway.

"Yet herein was there dallying" = yet he was slow to fulfil his promise, referring to King Knut's faithless treatment of Kalf as told in chapter cclxi.

Page 402. The yew's grief : "ýs angr " = fire.

Page 405. 1. Thing of war-board : "borða-þing" = battle; war-board = shield.—Wife of Héðin = Hild, the Valkyrja, hence appellatively = battle.—Gale of Ali : "Ala él" = battle, cf. i. 206, 3, and note, p. 398.

2. Thund's storm : "þundar hregg" = battle. þundr, one of Odin's names.

3. Gale of Ali : "Ala él" (see p. 405, 1).

Page 426. Battles' urger : "hildar hvotuðr" = captain, commander of war-hosts, here King Olaf.

Page 429. 2. Throwers of flame of spear-pond : "Geirs log-hreytendr lóns" = "hreytendr logs geirs lóns" = warriors. Spear-pond = blood, its flame (coming from a *thrower*) = cast weapon.

Page 430. 1. The meadow of the hair-path : "tún reikar" = head ; reik = the parting (line) of the hair.

2. The ash-tree of the battle : "askr gunnar" = warrior, here Gizur Goldbrow.—The flame of the High one : "bál Hárs" = sword : bál (cf. bale-fire, A.S. bǽl-fyr), flame ; Hár, the High one, Odin, whose hall was lighted up by the gleam of swords, cf. S. E. i. 208 : "þá lét Oðinn bera inn í höllina sverð, ok voru svá björt at þar af lýsti, ok var ekki haft ljós annat meðan við drykkju var setit" : then let Odin bear into the hall swords, and were (they) so bright that thereof lighted, and was not had light (any) other while at drinking (there) was sat.—The plunger of bow's river : "Dal steypir ár-strauma = steypir dals ár-strauma," a warrior, here Gizur Goldbrow again. Dalr (deal-wood), bow, its river (stream), the flight of arrows from it, the plunger = hurler-onwards thereof, a warrior.—Frey of the dew of Draupnir : "draupnis dögg-freyr = Freyr daggar (gen. of dögg) Draupnis" = a gold possessor, man. Cf. S. E. i. 170 : "Oðinn lagði á bálit gullring þann er Draupnir heitir ; honum fylgði síðan sú náttúra, at hina níundu hverja nótt drupu af honum viij

gullringar jafnhöfgir": Odin laid on the bale-fire that gold-ring hight Dripper; with it followed sithence that (such) nature, that every ninth night (day) dripped from it eight gold-rings equally heavy.

Page 431. Niordings of the shroud- (rather: stays'-) horse: "skæ-njörðungar skorðu = Njörðungar skorðu skæs," sea-fighters, men; skorða, a stay, skær, a horse; stays' horse = ship, its Niordungs (dim.), little Niords, gods, = men.

Page 432. 1. Scatterer of the fire of the mast-knop: "hyrsendir húna = sendir hyrs húna" = a bounteous man, a man, here King Olaf. The fire of the mast-knop = gold.—The Thrott of the storm of fight-shed of the thwart-garth: "þróttr glyggs gunn-ranns þver-garða" = warrior, here Thorir Hound; gunn-rann = fight-shed = shield, the thwart-garths thereof = shield-burg, the storm thereof = battle, the Thrott—Odin—god whereof, warrior.

Page 440. 1. Pines of the gale of Jalfad: "él-þollar Jálfaðs = þollar éls Jálfaðs" = warriors. Jalfad = Odin, his gale = battle.

2. Hawk-perch' Skogul: "Skögul hauka-setrs" = woman; hawk-perch = hand, on which falcon sits; the Skogul or "Valkyrja," who so carries falcons = a woman of high degree.

Page 441. 1. Wont to the murder of Fenja's meal: "morð-venjandi Fenju meldrar" = bounteous man, a man (apostrophe). For Fenja's meal, cf. i. 199, 2, and note, p. 396-7.

2. Oak of the hawk-lands: "eik oglis landa" = woman, cf. note to p. 440, 2.

Page 443. 2. Fight-skerry stems: "ógnar-skers meiðar" = warriors, men; fight-skerry (against which weapons strike) = shield. Cf. note to p. 358, 1.

Page 457. Scratching servants: "ýfs árar" = nails.

Page 459. 5. Main-bolt of (holy) book-speech: "regin-nagli bóka-máls," supposed to mean: "sacer clavus librarii sermonis, vir doctus, clericus, sacer minister ecclesiæ" (Egilsson).[1] Others, bearing in mind "regin-nagli" in the description of the temple in the Ere-dwellers' Saga, translate it "adytum templi," connecting "bóka-máls" with "bænir," preces libro præscriptæ. The broken state of the verse makes a sure interpretation difficult, even impossible. "Bóka-mál" must evidently mean the same as "bók-mál," the language of written books = Latin, in contrast to the rune-written vernacular = donsk tunga. Now, as dönsk tunga, at this time, did not only mean Danish tongue, *i.e.* the language of the Scandinavian Germans, but also, collectively, the nations speaking it, and even the territory occupied by them, so, we suggest, "bók-mál" = Latin here not only means the language of written books, but also of the community that produced books, *i.e.* the church, hence the Christian Church itself. Looked at from this point of view "regin-nagli bóka-máls" would form a "kenning" meaning : God's nail, or main-bolt rivetting the church together, clavus dei vel cardinalis ecclesiam configens = King Olaf the Holy. By this interpretation the sense of this half-verse is, at any rate, rendered quite clear.

---

[1] This interpretation seems clearly out of question ; for the church has never enjoined praying to her priests.

END OF VOL. II.

Lightning Source UK Ltd.
Milton Keynes UK
UKHW02f1206270718
326381UK00011B/614/P